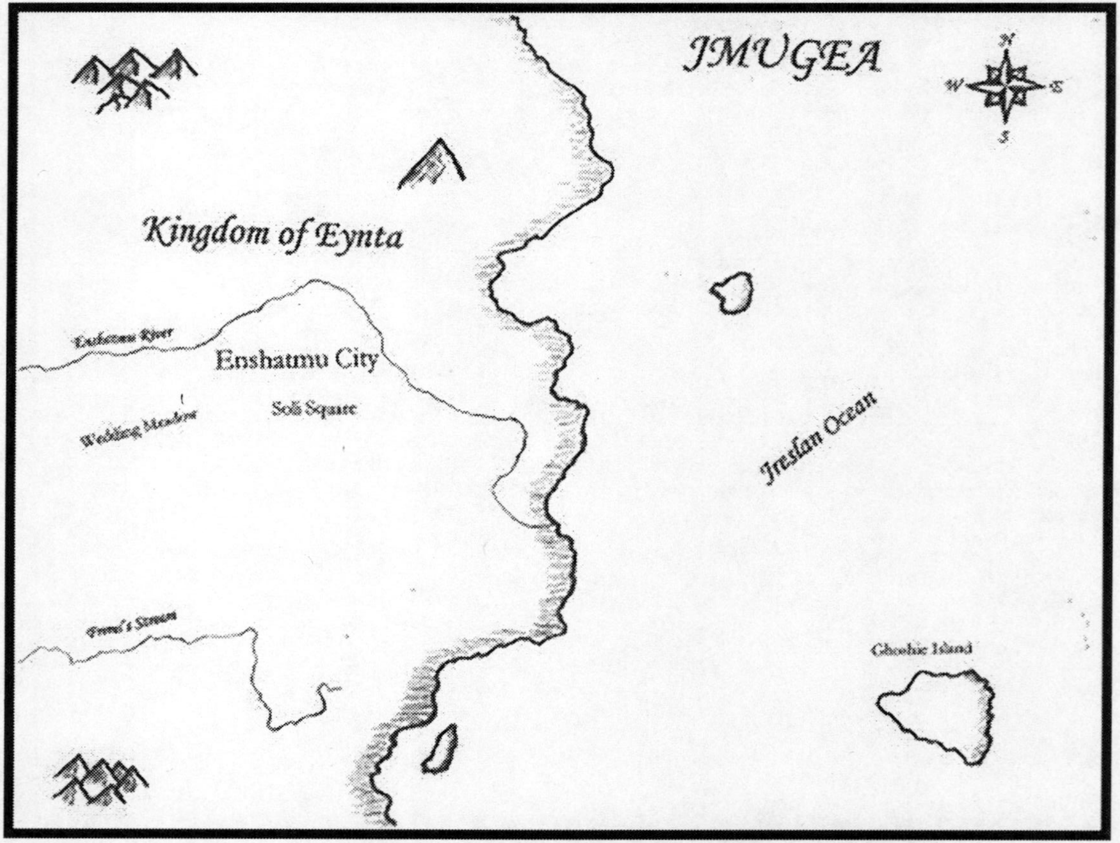
IMUGEA
N
W
E
S
Kingdom of Eynta
Enshatmu City
Soli Square
Wedding Meadow
Ireslan Ocean

RISE OF JMUGEA

Book Two of the Omordion Trilogy

For Helen,
I hope you enjoy the second installment of the Omordion Trilogy as much as I enjoyed writing it! :) Best Wishes,
Nande Orcel
December 2016

NANDE ORCEL
Author of 'Secret of Omordion'

abbott press

Copyright © 2016 Nande Orcel.

All rights reserved. No part of this book may be used or reproduced by any means, graphic, electronic, or mechanical, including photocopying, recording, taping or by any information storage retrieval system without the written permission of the author except in the case of brief quotations embodied in critical articles and reviews.

Abbott Press books may be ordered through booksellers or by contacting:

Abbott Press
1663 Liberty Drive
Bloomington, IN 47403
www.abbottpress.com
Phone: 1 (866) 697-5310

Because of the dynamic nature of the Internet, any web addresses or links contained in this book may have changed since publication and may no longer be valid. The views expressed in this work are solely those of the author and do not necessarily reflect the views of the publisher, and the publisher hereby disclaims any responsibility for them.

Any people depicted in stock imagery provided by Thinkstock are models, and such images are being used for illustrative purposes only. Certain stock imagery © Thinkstock.

ISBN: 978-1-4582-2030-1 (sc)
ISBN: 978-1-4582-2031-8 (hc)
ISBN: 978-1-4582-2032-5 (e)

Library of Congress Control Number: 2016910959

Print information available on the last page.

Abbott Press rev. date: 08/25/2016

OMORDION
N
W
E
S
Laspitu
Sheidem
Sheidem City
Saimino Ocean
Hejdian Sea
Pamoonu
Lavune Island
Saimino Island
Saimino Ocean
Srepas
Srepan Ocean
Hebi River
Saiyut
Hejdi Island
Penshi Islands
Mituwa
Hejdian Pass
Rostumik Ocean
Nikul Island
Stream of Acmit
Nikul Pass
Nikul River
Pontotoma
Penshi River
Dead Forest
Udnaruk
Effit
Feim
Chrulm Village
Rostihme Village
Rostumik Pass

*To my husband, Dwan, and my son, Jaden,
whose imaginations are just as wild and spontaneous as mine.*

ACKNOWLEDGEMENTS

I would like to express my gratitude to my husband, Dwan Irby, and my son, Jaden, for their continued support. Thank you for believing in me and all the love and motivation you have given to me, while I worked diligently to finish this book.

I would also like to thank my family, friends, and especially my awesome readers for all of their kind words and amazing reviews. Because of all of you, the joy you have shown for my debut novel, *Secret of Omordion*, and the excitement for its successor, *Rise of Jmugea*, I have never been so delighted. It makes all the hard work and obsessing over each and every detail so worth it. I cannot thank everyone enough for your continued support and patience. This is for you!

PROLOGUE

The Ardomion Caves.

A dark and foreboding place, deeply shrouded in mystery.

The inhabitants of the volcanic island, Paimonu, never ventured anywhere near it. They perceived it as a haunted place, filled with evil spirits, waiting to unleash their anger on any unsuspecting poor soul who wandered too close. No one dared. For *centuries*.

Until that day.

The day when five strangers arrived, traveling up the road towards the caves, apprehensive–yet determined–to find them. The people of Paimonu were fearful when they saw them descend into the jungle and down the side of their revered Sremati Volcano. They were shocked when they saw them steadily approach the ancient caves and actually enter them.

However, they could not stop them.

When they heard the explosions coming from inside the caves, they could not save them. They hoped and prayed the strangers would survive, yet they knew it was not possible. Even if they did survive, what kind of evil would they have unleashed? What kind of evil would escape with them?

What the people of Paimonu did not know was the five strangers, fifteen-year-olds Atakos Croit, Cristaden Feriau, Fajha Bayaht, and twins Zimi and Zadeia Emyu, did encounter pure evil. Evil of the worst kind. Evil in the form of their missing teacher, whom they had set out on a journey to rescue.

Hamilda Shing.

After barely surviving their ordeal and exorcising the demons that plagued Hamilda, the five teenagers found themselves lost, while attempting to leave the ancient caves. It was there the true secret of the caves was revealed to them—a secret laid hidden for three hundred years.

Their ancestors, the first members of the Dokami Clan to land on Omordion three hundred years prior, had caused the Sremati Volcano to erupt, covering their spaceship and creating the caves the teens found themselves lost in. At first, it seemed like sheer luck had led them to the spaceship. Even an odd coincidence.

They were about to find out it might not have been luck or a mere coincidence at all.

It was there, inside the ancient spaceship, the five members of Omordion's Hope learned their true history. It was there that their ancestor, Tre-akelomin Gre-ashyu, revealed a secret, which had been torturing him for many years. He needed to talk about it. He needed to come out with it even if no one was going to hear him speak. He needed to tell the tragic story from the beginning.

As the teens journeyed into the past with him, one among them—one who could dive deeper into the past than anyone else—was thrown into the depths of the tragic Dokami history.

Back to where it all began.

PART ONE
JMUGEA AND THE DOKAMI CLAN

CHAPTER 1

The warning should have come sooner.
Omerik was in his home, having dinner with his family, when it happened.

"Can you pass the bread dear?" said his wife, who sat directly across from him. She was the most beautiful woman he had ever seen. He loved the way her thickened eyebrows turned up at the ends, grazing her perfect, leathered, and tall forehead. The way her nose pointed downwards, almost touching her wrinkled, dark lips. Her eyes were small, but not too far apart. The closer the eyes were, they said, the better looking the person. That was the Shaergan philosophy.

"Sure, honey," Omerik said. As he passed her the bread, a piece of raw vegetable (he wasn't sure which kind) sailed over his arm and hit his six-year-old son square in his face. The boy, who was taken by complete surprise, started wailing, tears immediately erupting from his eyes as if a dam had given away and released a raging river. Omerik turned to his nine-year-old daughter and scowled at her. "Stop it! Apologize to your brother."

"Sorry..." his daughter said sadly and looked down at her plate.

Suddenly, a loud noise caused the entire family to jump in their seats. A broom had fallen over and hit the wooden floor, creating the unexpected sound. Omerik's son immediately stopped crying as fast as he started and stared at the broom, wide-eyed. Before they could question why it fell over, the whole house shook violently, as if there had been an explosion somewhere nearby. For a brief moment, Omerik contemplated bringing his family down to the cellar to seek shelter. He hesitated when the sirens outside started blaring.

"What—?" Omerik said. Those sirens were meant for emergencies only. *Real* emergencies. They had never been used before. The only emergency that came to mind was…*no*. It was not possible.

"Honey?" his wife said, her eyes searching his, as if he knew why the sirens were going off.

When another explosion rocked their house, Omerik ran to the front door and yanked it open.

He could not believe his eyes.

Spaceships, from the planet Dre-Ahd, loomed overhead in the darkened sky. There were hundreds of them, dotting the horizon, bent on destroying Shaerga once and for all. The Shaergan army was attempting to fight back, but their weapons were meager compared to the weapons of the Dre-Ahd army.

Omerik had never seen the type of weapons they were using to destroy Shaerga. Weapons that plummeted from their spaceships and, upon hitting the ground, exploded into great fireballs, killing anyone and destroying anything in their paths. So *many* of them were falling from the sky.

"Run for your lives!" Omerik's neighbor shouted as he ran by, waking Omerik up from his shocked, frozen state. "Save yourselves!"

"We have to go," Omerik said, looking fearfully back at his family. "Now!"

They did not grab anything. They ran out of the house without looking back. As another explosion rocked the ground nearby, Omerik's distressed family joined the hundreds of people, trying desperately to escape from their city. They ran to the first place they could think of: the home of a high official who had the only working spaceship in their immediate area. The official was nowhere to be seen, but Omerik's neighbors slowly began the boarding process despite his absence.

Too slowly.

"Hurry up!" Omerik shouted. With the training he had in the Shaergan army before he retired, he was prepared to fly the spaceship himself to save his family and as many people as possible. As soon as he had his family on board, Omerik was already in the captain's chair and starting up the engines. He then tried to wait patiently for the rest of his neighbors to board. When a Dre-Ahd weapon of destruction hit the ground up the road, practically knocking everyone over with its force, Omerik knew he could not wait any longer. Closing the door on the screaming masses still outside, he regrettably lifted the spaceship off the ground and away from harm.

What Omerik and his family saw that day would be the worst sight they would ever witness.

Rivers of lava spewed out of the ever-expanding cracks in the shaking ground. The smell of ash, sulfur, and burnt flesh enveloped the atmosphere and the horrid sounds of the Dre-Ahd weapons pierced through the darkened sky. Great mountains were falling and the people who lived on them had no chance to escape before the crumbling rock crushed their diminutive homes. Babies and small children were screaming hysterically as the frightened people carrying them held on to them tightly as they ran. Shaergan spaceships riskily waited for the inhabitants to board them all over the planet. Unfortunately, many of the spaceships were destroyed while they were still on the ground. The remaining spaceships began to shut their doors and leave when staying on the ground became too risky.

Tearstained, Shaergan faces pressed against the windows of the spaceships as the only surviving inhabitants of Shaerga left their beloved planet, knowing they would not have a planet to return to. They then flew to the one planet they hoped would take them in and give them shelter.

Jmugea.

"They wish to land, sir," the young messenger boy said bravely in front of the Jmugean Council, located within the country of Eynta, Jmugea. He was out of breath, having just run from the Airspace Control Tower straight into the Grand Meeting Hall, ringing bells along his way to gather the members of the council together. Shaergan spaceships loomed overhead, beckoning for a place to land. The boy was speaking to Ghosh Hres, the head of the council.

Hres was a short and slightly balding man who was relatively calm but could, at times, be threatening and cruel if things were not going his way. He intimidated the other seven members of the council. They found it difficult to get their points across even when he was in a passive mood. Although he was strict, the people of Jmugea owed their freedom to him, for he was the only one who could dissuade armies, especially the Dre-Ahd army, from trying to take over their world. The Jmugeans did not know how he did it, but they trusted him to keep them safe.

"Why have they left Shaerga?" Hres said to the determined messenger boy.

"Shaerga has been destroyed, sir," the boy said with a shaky voice.

A wave of shocked exclamations erupted among the other members of the council. "Silence!" Hres shouted. He stood up with fire in his eyes. "What do you mean Shaerga has been *destroyed*? Did they not sign the peace treaty with the other planets?"

"Well–sir–they did. They say the peace treaty had some unfair rules, which granted one planet more control over Shaerga than what had been originally agreed upon. The Shaergans refused to abide by some of those rules and refused to surrender their planet. Therefore, an order was carried out to destroy Shaerga."

"By *whom*?"

"The Dre-Ahds, sir."

Hres immediately sat back down. The Dre-Ahds were their most powerful ally. To go against them would harm the alliances he formed many years ago. He would have to come up with a significant excuse as to why he would harbor fugitives. He knew all too well the unjustified rules of the peace treaties and he respectfully obeyed them to keep his planet off the list of annihilation. At the same time, he had so many lives from Shaerga on his hands hovering over Jmugea, begging to be rescued. If he turned them away, he would lose the respect of his people and riots would threaten to arise once again, as they did before the peace treaties were signed.

"Were they followed?"

"They traveled a great distance before they came our way, sir. They are absolutely positive they were not followed."

Hres rubbed his chin while he remained deep in thought. He then glanced at the other members of the council as if looking for their approval, knowing full well the decision was his to make. "How many spaceships are there?" he asked the messenger boy.

"There are around three hundred and forty, sir."

"And how many people?"

"They claim to have over one hundred thousand, sir."

Shaking his head, Hres' shoulders dropped. Those people had nowhere else to go and they were asking for his help. He had to make a decision and fast. "I would like to speak to their leader or whoever they have placed in charge." He stood up, along with the other members of the council.

"Yes, sir!" said the messenger boy as he turned to run.

"Oh, and tell them they have my permission to land."

The boy gleefully ran back towards the Airspace Control Tower with the exciting news.

CHAPTER 2

"It's a... girl," the Jmugean midwife said as she carefully swaddled the newborn baby in a small gray, woolen blanket. "She's—" The old woman's thick eyebrows drew together into a frown and her mouth froze in mid-sentence, as if her breath had been stolen from her.

The young Jmugean mother, whose name was Jreslan, sucked in her breath and held it when she saw the old woman's reaction to her baby. "What's wrong?" she said, panicking. "What's wrong with my baby? Is she okay?" She had recently lost her Shaergan husband to an infection he had succumbed to while working in the mines. The anticipated birth of their only child was the only thing keeping her going after his death. The baby had to be okay, she could not possibly suffer another heartache.

The midwife blinked, as if she had just woken from a strange slumber by the sound of the new mother's voice. "Oh, I am so sorry, dear," she said, taking deep breaths. She walked around the bed and carefully handed Jreslan the wrapped baby. Clearing her throat, she took a few steps back, her face looking incredibly pale.

Jreslan tore her eyes away from the strange reaction of the midwife and brought them down to her newborn daughter. She slowly unfolded the blanket and gasped. She was unlike any baby she had ever seen in all her life. So unlike the facial features of the Shaergans and the rough, leathery exterior of the Jmugeans. She had soft skin, brown curls, and her eyes—her eyes were the color of bright green emeralds. Tears rolled down Jreslan's cheeks as she embraced her new baby. "Oh, my darling, you *are* different. To me, it does not matter. You are our daughter and I will love you always. Your father would have adored you just as much as I do now." She wiped her eyes and ignored the midwife, who had quickly stormed out of the room.

"I shall call you Soli," Jreslan said. "Beautiful as the morning sun."

"Soli!" Jreslan cried out for her two-year-old daughter. She had run away from her again and bolted up the cobblestone hill outside their home in Enshatmu City. The little girl stopped short at a small, rickety, old house on top of the hill. She stood just outside the front door, listening, as if waiting for something to happen.

"Soli, what are you *doing?*" Jreslan breathlessly asked her daughter once she reached her. "Don't run away from me ever a—" She was interrupted by a loud, crashing sound of dishes breaking, followed by a woman screaming, coming from inside the house. After quickly picking up Soli, Jreslan ran in.

At first, all Jreslan could see were pieces of broken dishes all over the wooden floor of the tiny kitchen. The bathroom door stood ajar and she saw her good friend, Fremi, hugging her knees on the floor and whimpering, her tearstained face wrought with pain.

"Oh!" Jreslan said, gasping. "I will get the midwife!" She put Soli down and told her to stay as she bolted out of the house. Soli slowly walked into the bathroom, approached the distressed woman, and gently patted her on her head.

"It's okay," Soli said, in a tiny, but confident voice. "Baby boy. He's okay."

Fremi looked up at her and smiled, although she did not believe the little girl could know the gender of her determined, unborn baby. Another wave of contractions came and she screamed in pain. Jreslan came back with the midwife and picked Soli up to move her out of the way. For several hours, Soli refused to leave until the baby was born. When the midwife held up Fremi's son, who was equally as different looking as she was, Soli squealed with joy. She had found a new friend and she was never going to leave his side.

"Wow, what beautiful children you have!" a passerby gushed over five-year-old Soli and three-year-old Rueslon.

"Thank you!" Jreslan and Fremi said in unison.

The best friends giggled with each other, ecstatic about how much the people of Enshatmu City were enthralled with their children. Both of their husbands were from Shaerga. After the Shaergans sought refuge on Jmugea, the Jmugeans did their best to stay away from them. Some Jmugeans, including Jreslan and Fremi, had taken pity on the Shaergans and offered them their friendship. They eventually fell head over heels in love with the Shaergan culture and married two members of their clan.

Because of Soli's need to be with Rueslon at all times, the two friends became inseparable. Fremi was constantly comparing Rueslon to Soli—how fast they grew, how intelligent they were, how they got along so well, and how exceptionally different, unlike any other children, they were. They believed the accelerated rate in which their children were developing was because their fathers were of Shaergan descent. Also, they both looked very similar to each other. Soli had brown, curly hair, beautiful green eyes, and soft skin and Rueslon was much like her but had black, curly hair, and bright gray eyes.

Compared to the other children in their town, who were quite average, Soli and Rueslon were tall for their age and their teachers could not understand how they came to know so much, so early. They knew things about other planets and constellations that would not be taught to them until they were in their teenaged years. They knew so much, it shocked the people around them. They were also tremendously polite and liked to help everyone, to the best of their ability, no matter what their tasks entailed.

The townsfolk were so fond of Soli and Rueslon, some Jmugeans warmed up to the Shaergans *because* of them. Marriages between the two races became more and more common and the consummations of those marriages were made solely because of the anticipated births of their future Jmugean-Shaergan offspring. Of course, Jreslan and Fremi thought they were being absolutely ridiculous, but a baby boom was in full effect as some of the inhabitants of Jmugea sought to create what they referred to as 'wonder babies'.

Life on Jmugea as everyone knew it was changing drastically and it was becoming more and more evident with each passing year.

"Mother?"

"Yes, darling?"

Seven-year-old Soli twiddled her fingers together in the middle of the kitchen and looked down at the floor. "I have to tell you something."

"What is it?" Jreslan said from the kitchen sink.

"Is uncle here?" Soli asked, referring to Jreslan's brother, who had come from the outskirts of the city to live with them for the past year. He wanted to be closer to the only family he had and to work in the mines to help support them. Soli really enjoyed having him around and regarded him as if he was the father she never had.

"No, dear. He went to the mines. What do you want to tell me?"

"Well…" Soli looked up, her face full of worry. "Rueslon and I have been having these…dreams."

Jreslan stopped washing the dishes and turned to her daughter with curiosity. It was the way she said it that made her turn. "What kind of dreams?"

"They are the same dreams, mother. Strange. Very *strange* dreams."

"Do you mind describing them to me?"

Soli dragged a chair over from the kitchen table and sat down. Jreslan thought it best to do the same and followed suit. When she was sitting down, she urged Soli to continue.

"In the dreams, we are on a different planet—not Jmugea. We know because it looks…different. Even the trees are different. When I spoke to Rue about my dreams, he described the same trees. The same rivers. Unlike anything we have ever seen here in Enshatmu City. Rue and I, we are much older in the dreams. Even older than you. We have dozens of children."

"That's preposterous," Jreslan said laughing. "The dreams must have come from the make-believe stories the two of you have been coming up with since you could run around together."

"They weren't make-believe stories, mother," Soli said in a small voice. "Something terrible always happens in the dreams. We have to separate and leave the planet before it is destroyed. Our people die out. Many die because an awful sadness took hold of them after we were driven apart. Including us—Rue and I."

Jreslan's eyes widened. She was shocked her daughter would talk about death so carelessly. "Soli, that's enough talk for now. We have a lot of cleaning to do." She stood up and walked back to the sink, picking up a plate to wash, hoping her daughter wasn't feeding the same stories to Rueslon and trying to scare the poor boy.

Soli stood up to stand next to Jreslan. "Mother, these dreams are memories. Memories of a *past life*. The people, on the planet we moved to, gave us a name because we were so different. They called us the

Dokami. It meant 'the peaceful'. Dokami was not our name before, mother. We were called…something else…but I can't remember what it was."

Jreslan stopped what she was doing, turned to her daughter, and frowned. She *was* serious. "What?"

"We have lived before, mother. All of us. And now we have come back."

"Soli, you have got to be joking," Jreslan said halfheartedly to her anxious eight-year-old daughter. "Where do you think you're going?"

"Mother, I must go," Soli said. "She needs me!" Her teary green eyes searched Jreslan's 'have you lost your mind?' expression on her face.

Jreslan grabbed her daughter's arms when she realized Soli was edging closer to the front door. "Who? Who could possibly need you right now? At this time of night?"

"*Reyshi*. Mother I must go." Soli tried hard to pull her arms free, intent on running out of the house as soon as her mother released her.

Jreslan sighed deeply with frustration. "Reyshi doesn't need you, honey. It's the middle of the night!"

"Mother…"

"You can wait to see her tomorrow."

Tears filled Soli's eyes. "I can't expect you to understand—"

"Soli. Everyone is *sleeping*."

"Please, mother. Please let me go!"

Jreslan observed her daughter's distressed face. The sheer intensity of her determination made her stomach turn. She knew Soli had an uncanny awareness when something was wrong, but this was ridiculous. Jreslan just wanted to go back to bed. She also knew her daughter would not give up. She suddenly wished her brother was there to talk to Soli. He had passed away the previous year in a mine explosion. Soli had a tough time with his death. To her, he was the only father figure she had ever known. Since the tragedy, she had been acting more and more difficult. Jreslan could not help but feel sorry for her.

Jreslan sighed again. "Okay, I'll come with you. But if there are no lights on, we are coming *straight* home and going back to bed."

Soli nodded solemnly and wiped her eyes. "We must hurry," she said.

Before Jreslan could grab a lantern and her shawl, Soli had run out into the street.

"Wait! Soli, slow down!"

The girl was already at the bottom of the hill when Jreslan stepped outside, making her way to Reyshi Maephit's dwelling, about two hundred paces from their own. Jreslan did not know the family well because they had recently moved to the south end of Enshatmu City a few months prior, but she knew Reyshi was only two years old, born of Jmugean and Shaergan parents.

Upon reaching the small, one-room cottage at the bottom of the hill, Jreslan stopped to catch her breath. "No!" she whispered frantically when she realized Soli was about to knock on the wooden door. "They're sleep—" She paused when she heard what sounded like someone–a woman–crying. A man was trying to calm her down with soothing words.

"The doctor will be back in a few days," the man said calmly. "She will be all right."

"She's dying," the woman said between her fits of crying. "She won't make it through the night."

Hearing the sense of urgency in the woman's voice, Jreslan unintentionally hesitated before attempting to stop her daughter from ignorantly barging in, catching the couple off guard.

She was too late.

"What is the meaning of this?" the Jmugean man, who must have been Reyshi's father, said to them. He and his Shaergan wife were sitting at the edge of Reyshi's tiny bed, bent over her while she slept.

"Soli?" Reyshi's mother said, wiping her tearful eyes so her daughter's friend would not see her cry. "What are you doing here?" She looked up and searched Jreslan's eyes as if she was looking for an answer to her question.

"I–I'm sorry to barge in on you like this," Jreslan said. "It's just…" She let her voice trail off when she realized she did not have any real explanation to give. She had not expected to walk into their home and she certainly did not expect something to be wrong with Reyshi, as her daughter had insisted.

Soli ignored Reyshi's baffled parents. She slowly walked over to the two-year-old's bed and gazed down at the sleeping child. After a few moments of silence, she softly called her name.

Reyshi's father reached out and touched Soli's shoulder with a shaky hand. "Reyshi isn't feeling well right now," he said. "Why don't you come back tomorrow?"

Soli looked up at him, blinked, and then frowned. "She will not be here tomorrow," she said bluntly.

Reyshi's mother burst into tears once again. Her father's face turned red with anger. Nevertheless, he kept his mouth shut. He knew the truth. He knew his daughter was going to breathe her last breath during the night. He did not want to admit it to himself or to his wife. It was his fault it happened. He was trying not to blame himself, but he knew, if he had only been there at the right time, he could have prevented it.

"It is not your fault," Soli quickly said, interrupting his thoughts. "Reyshi told me. It is *not* your fault. The poisonous spider would have bitten her even if you were with her. You cannot blame yourself. The infection has spread to her heart. She is dying, but it is not your fault."

Reyshi's mother fought to keep her voice steady through her tears. "She—told you?" she said. She seemed very confused, but her confusion turned to fear when a thought dawned on her. "That's impossible. She hasn't left the house since it happened. No one knows besides my husband and I."

Jreslan cleared her throat. "Soli, I think it's time to go back home now." Her daughter's chosen words appalled her. It was apparent the couple was already grieving their daughter's impending death and she did not want to watch Soli make it worse for them.

Soli ignored her mother's plea and put her hand on the little girl's perspiring forehead. "Reyshi asked for my help, mother." She pulled the white bed sheet off the small child, revealing her badly infected leg. The bitten foot was dark purple and appeared lifeless.

Reyshi's mother stood up in an attempt to pull Soli away from her daughter, but her husband put his hand out to stop her. He was confused about the whole situation, but he thought it would be okay if Reyshi's good friend said goodbye to her before she expired. He urged his wife to sit back down with him and wait.

"Soli," Jreslan said. She silently pleaded with her daughter to go before she made things worse.

Ignoring her mother once again, Soli covered Reyshi with the sheet and closed her eyes before bending low to kiss her friend's head. She then stroked her bright, red hair and gently called her name again.

Still, no response from the unconscious child.

"Soli…" Reyshi's mother said.

"Reyshi?" Soli said again.

Reyshi's parents stood up in shock when the little girl's green eyes slowly opened. Her eyes rolled around and she squinted, trying to see what was going on around her. When her vision came into focus, she noticed Soli standing by her bed. In a tiny voice, she said, "Dodee?"

"Yes, Reyshi," Soli said, smiling. "Go back to sleep. You will be okay now."

"Da-too," Reyshi said, thanking Soli before closing her eyes again.

Soli lifted the bed sheet to inspect Reyshi's leg.

Reyshi's mother gasped and covered her mouth with her hands after dropping to her knees. Her father simply stared, shocked beyond belief. Heat rose to Jreslan's face and her heart began to hammer hard against her chest. *This is bad*, Jreslan thought. *Really, really bad.*

There was no visible sign of infection.

Reyshi's skin was a perfect shade of pale pink, as if it had never been infected in the first place. Her badly infected foot was soft and perfect as it was before the spider bit her.

With a big smile, Soli covered the little girl and bent down to kiss her forehead again. She was so happy to have been able to save her friend's life.

Reyshi's parents looked at each other in shock. Both of them turned to look at Jreslan. This was nothing like a strange miracle, this was an *impossibility*. They had heard tales about evil witches doing magic spells, but this was an innocent eight-year-old girl, who had just saved their only child's life. Who could chastise her?

Silence filled the room as Jreslan quickly grabbed Soli's hand and pulled her towards the front door. She mumbled her apologies for disturbing the bewildered parents in the middle of the night and left the house, her shaky hand gripping her daughter's hand, refusing to let go. Terrified, to the point of shaking in fear, Jreslan considered asking Soli how Reyshi healed so quickly, but decided against it. She was too stunned to talk about it. Too worried that Reyshi's parents would tell everyone that Soli was a witch.

Holding on to Jreslan's hand, Soli joyfully skipped up the hill, humming an upbeat melody. She was so happy—beyond ecstatic—to have saved her friend from imminent death. Before they reached their house, however, Soli yawned, loudly indicating how tired she truly was.

"Fremi, I want to ask you something."

"What is it, Jreslan?"

Jreslan watched as her daughter and Rueslon ran around the courtyard behind their house with six other neighborhood Jmugean-Shaergan born children, including Rueslon's two-year-old brother, Drae. They looked so happy and never displayed any hostility towards each other, as if they understood one another's feelings and boundaries.

"Well...how do I put this?" Jreslan twiddled her thumbs together. "Have you ever noticed anything...unusual? I mean—with Rueslon and Drae? Like strange things they do? Things you can't explain?"

Fremi frowned at her and looked down at the ground to think before looking back at her. "No," she said quickly. "They never give me any trouble."

"That's not what I mean." Jreslan thought long and hard before continuing. How could she explain what happened with Reyshi the previous night? How could she explain all of the strange things Soli had told her or shown her over the years?

Fremi touched her friend's shoulder and offered a smile. "I know you are concerned. They are *special* children. Do not worry about them. They will be just fine."

Jreslan continued to watch the laughing children. Try as she might, she could not figure out a way to explain the events of the previous night to her friend. Reluctantly, she decided to keep it to herself and prayed Reyshi Maephit's parents did the same.

CHAPTER 3

An old beggar walked the cobblestone streets of Enshatmu City, seven years later, asking the local residents for food, money, or clothing. Shunned over twenty times already since the sun had risen, he was not having much luck. He glared at the happy children running around and sneered at the noises he heard all around him as the people of Enshatmu City drifted about their lives without a care in the world. The bright sun was burning high above his head and there were no clouds in sight to give him relief from the heat. Deciding to take a small break, the old beggar found the usual side alley he liked to use for rest throughout the day. He was especially annoyed to see that his private little space was already occupied.

A young boy stood at the end of the alleyway, playing with several intricately crafted metal blocks. The boy had not noticed the old beggar. He just continued to play, uncaring that he was inhabiting space that *wasn't* his to occupy. The old beggar was so angry that the boy would be there, without regard for anyone other than himself–just like everyone else in Enshatmu City. He grunted and was about to scare the trespasser away, but stopped when he noticed something abnormal about the boy's blocks.

They were floating in front of the boy, moving in a slow, circular motion. At first, the beggar thought there might have been strings on the blocks, but he was startled when one of the blocks shot high up into the air and back down, without the boy ever putting his hands on it to toss it up. That was when he noticed something else.

All the blocks *had no strings.*

"Witch!" the old beggar shouted, pointing at the boy. All of the floating blocks dropped simultaneously when the boy jumped back. He was frightened and his blue eyes widened in fear.

"Witch!" The old man screamed again. He backed out of the alleyway and grabbed people walking by him. "Don't you see?" He yelled into their faces. The putrid smell of his crusty, yellow teeth and his dirty clothing made them pull away from him and quickly walk away. "Those children." He grabbed a passing woman. "They're evil. They are all evil. They do tricks—horrible tricks."

"What kind of tricks?" the curious woman asked him.

"*Evil* ones. Look, I will show you what I mean." The beggar pointed down the alleyway and froze when he saw nothing there. The boy and his blocks were nowhere in sight. How did he get past him? There were no other exits. A high, brick wall blocked the other end of the alleyway.

"Let go of me, you crazy lunatic!" The woman snatched her arm from the beggar's grip and stormed away, muttering curses under her breath.

"He was right there," he muttered to himself, pointing to where the boy once stood. He was *sure* of it. "Perhaps the sun is affecting me…." he said, looking up at the sky. It was a hot day. Shrugging, the beggar leaned back against the wall and sunk down to the cobblestoned ground. After rubbing his eyes, he covered his face with his hands. "He was there. I *know* he was." In no time, he had drifted off into a deep sleep filled with floating objects without strings.

A slow, steady feeling of dread overcame her, causing her to double over her kitchen table. Her heart skipped a beat. She suddenly felt as if the air was absent in the room, although a gentle breeze flowed in from an open window by the door. Her hands felt clammy and wet and she almost lost her footing as her legs buckled beneath her. After taking deep breaths to bring air back into her lungs, she began to panic. She had experienced this feeling before. It was a feeling she was all too familiar with.

Something terrible was about to happen.

Wiping her hands on a small, yellow towel, Soli decided the remaining dirty dishes would have to wait. "I'll be right back, mother," she said, pulling her long, brown, curly hair together into a ponytail.

"Is everything okay?" Jreslan said as she came out of her bedroom. She was used to her fifteen-year-old daughter unexpectedly running out of the house to attend to 'important' matters she rarely discussed anymore. It was something she stopped fighting against years ago.

"I hope so," Soli said. She ran out of the house and into the hot summer day. A small breeze enveloped itself around her and birds flew by her house, chirping loudly, in search of their next meal.

After taking just a few steps onto the cobblestoned road in front of her house, Soli knew the general direction to go. Her pace steadily increased as she climbed the hill towards Enshatmu Square.

Determined to get to where she was going fast, Soli hardly noticed someone calling her name the first time. The second time her name was called, she quickly turned around and groaned when she realized who was approaching her. She wished she had ignored the call.

"Hello, Fhoten," Soli said through her teeth.

Fhoten was a fifteen-year-old Shaergan boy who was desperately head-over-heels in love with Soli. He sometimes followed her around, asking her ridiculous questions just to make conversation with her. She wouldn't be surprised if he had been hiding in the bushes, waiting for her to leave her house so he could have an opportunity to talk to her. She was sure he lived on the *other* side of town.

"Where are you off to in such a hurry?" Fhoten said, looking undeniably concerned. He tried to reach out for her hand, which she easily avoided by taking a step back. He frowned, his thick uni-brow almost covering his small, beady, brown eyes. "What's wrong?" he asked her. As if he didn't know how creepy he was.

"I–I have to get something for my mother," Soli said. "I have no time to talk, Fhoten, it's an emergency."

"Let me go with you." He took a few steps in the direction she was going so he could walk with her. "I'm going that way anyways."

If Soli had said she was going the other way, Fhoten would have said he was headed that way too. "No!" Soli threw her hands up as a means to stop him from going any further. "I mean–it's okay. I will be faster if I go *alone*. Goodbye, Fhoten." She spun on her heels and ran away from him, looking back only once to make sure he was not following her. Fhoten was still standing at the top of the hill, looking lost and confused. Turning back around, Soli ran faster towards the square.

As Soli approached the heart of Enshatmu City, another feeling of dread came over her, but she could not pinpoint what was giving her the awful feeling. As she walked through the busy square, a few Dokami children almost ran into her as they sprinted past, shouting her name. She smiled awkwardly at them, attempting to hide her anxiety. Tearing her eyes away from them, Soli steadily looked around her. A nauseating feeling exploded in the pit of her stomach. She strained her neck and listened for anything out of the ordinary. Hearing nothing strange, she concentrated on why she was getting the sick feeling.

Nothing.

Whatever is about to happen, she thought, *I have to put a stop to it, but I don't know where to go!*

A hand touched Soli's shoulder. She yelped, quickly turned around, and breathed a sigh of relief. "Rueslon," she said, happy to see her best friend standing behind her and not Fhoten. Nothing much had changed about Rueslon over the years. He still had a thick head of black hair and his gray eyes were just as bright as ever. At thirteen years old, two years younger than Soli, he was slightly taller and appeared to be her age instead of merely thirteen.

"Do you feel that?" Rueslon whispered, his eyes shifting from left to right.

"Well, yes…but I don't understand—"

"*Witch!*"

The pair turned their heads towards the sound of a man's desperate cry coming from somewhere close by.

"Let's go," Rueslon said. He immediately grabbed Soli's hand and they ran in the direction of the shouting.

Right away, they spotted the old beggar man backing out of an alleyway, up ahead to their right. "Witch!" he said again, waving his arms, reaching out for anyone who would stop and listen.

Soli and Rueslon wasted no time and ran past him, catching a glimpse of the scared boy in the alleyway. They only had seconds to act. Running to the end of the block and making a sharp right turn down a side street, they cut around the back of a merchant building, stopping just behind the tall brick wall blocking their view of the alleyway. After glancing around to make sure no one would bear witness to his power, Rueslon levitated off the ground and peered over the tall, brick wall.

They could hear the eccentric old man telling someone about the 'tricks' the children were playing.

"Hurry, Rue," Soli fearfully whispered. In seconds, the little boy in the alleyway was in Rueslon's arms and he was slowly bringing him down, his metal blocks trailing behind him over the wall as if attracted to the boy like magnets. The three of them huddled against the wall, listening to the activity transpiring behind it.

"Let go of me, you crazy lunatic!" they heard a woman yell.

The frightened, nine-year-old boy looked up at Soli with big blue eyes filling with tears. Drae was the spitting image of his older brother, Rueslon, down to his thick, black hair and flushed cheeks. Soli patted his head to comfort him and the three slowly crawled away. When they were a safe distance away, they ran down the street, and away from the square, as fast as they could.

Soli listened as Drae described his encounter with the old beggar. She had called a Dokami meeting when they returned to their village. A devastated Drae cried all the way to her house. He was horrified. Disappointed in how careless he had been. At the age of nine, Drae had grown exceptionally powerful, especially with his ability to attract metal and move it around without touching it. He described how he had been petrified when it happened, unable to move or make a clear decision on what to do next. He was scared the people of Enshatmu City now knew about their powers. And it would have been his fault they did. Rueslon tried his best to reassure his brother, telling him everything would be okay, but the little boy was inconsolable. After Drae explained what happened, he broke down into fits of crying once again.

Soli looked at Rueslon for his advice, but he simply shrugged his shoulders. He didn't know what to say either. They were all devastated that it happened, but they could not reverse time. Soli took a quick glance around at the crowd of children in the basement of her house. There had to be over one hundred Jmugean-Shaergan born children now—and counting—although she had lost count long ago. Their ages ranged from two to fifteen years old, the oldest being herself.

Soli's only hope of consoling Drae was Reyshi Maephit. Nine-year-old Reyshi stopped playing with the ringlets of her red hair when Soli made eye contact with her. She came forward to stand on the platform next to them.

"Tell me what you see," Soli said to the young girl.

Reyshi cleared her throat and closed her eyes. She concentrated for a moment and even smiled a little bit from time to time. It was not long before she opened her eyes. "The old beggar is confused...he has not eaten in a few days...his perception of all things is a little abnormal than most...no one believes him...he thinks it was all...a hallucination." Elated, Reyshi smiled and stepped off the platform.

Drae released the breath he had been holding and murmurs erupted throughout the basement as everyone felt immediate relief from what Reyshi had seen.

"Thank you, Reyshi," Soli said and looked back at the members of the Dokami clan. She seemed content, but her green eyes portrayed a sadness she could not hide. "This is not the time to celebrate. Drae was lucky this time. It could have been a lot worse. I have told you, time and time again, the people of Jmugea will not be able to accept who or what we are. We cannot expect them to understand. For most of them, only malice fills their heart." She looked at Reyshi for confirmation. Reyshi nodded in agreement for she had heard their evil thoughts as well. "We cannot allow ourselves to get carried away with our gifts. It could mean the difference between life and death." Turning to Drae, she added, "For all of us."

Drae's head dropped in shame.

"Does anyone have anything to say about this matter?"

"May I say one thing?"

Everyone turned to see who had spoken. It was a twelve-year-old girl, named Nariele, one of the first Dokami born during the sudden baby boom after Rueslon's birth. Her hair was so light in color, it was almost white, and her eyes, an extraordinary shade of light blue. Along with her wispy voice, she walked as if she was floating in air.

"You may," Soli said and nodded.

Nariele stepped up on the platform to stand next to Soli and Rueslon. Clearing her throat, she spoke to the crowd of Dokami children. "In addition to the way we look," she said with her wispy voice, "the people of this planet can sense something *different* about us. We know this. Since we were born. They know we are not like them. And they are constantly looking for reasons to fear us. Even now, rumors about us are forming in their circles and, I can only say, nothing good is being said. We must listen to Soli. We must restrain our abilities. Keep them hidden—no matter what happens. And we must protect each other at all times."

Silence filled the room. Because they were a peaceful clan, the Dokami had always hoped to be accepted. With each passing year, the chance for acceptance was dwindling fast. Their only plan was to keep their abilities hidden, and hope the people of Jmugea would eventually learn to accept them as one of their own.

CHAPTER 4

"Let me just point them out on the map," the tall, lanky teacher said. She walked over to a map of the solar system, hung up on the wall by her desk. She hesitated before gesturing towards a small cluster of rocks, as if she wanted to be sure she was pointing out the right ones before speaking. "Do you see these circle of rocks, floating in space? This was where the planet Shaerga once orbited…"

Soli glanced out of the window of her classroom, bored with her teacher's lesson—information they already learned when they were small. Now, at seventeen, and about to graduate, Soli did not feel the need to relearn their entire solar system. She knew more about it than any of her teachers could teach.

Soli's school was situated a mile away from her home, in the outskirts of Enshatmu City. It was a cluster of one level rooms—one room for each grade. She walked there and back every day, with Rueslon, his brother, Drae, and all the Dokami children who attended the school as well. Since she was the oldest, none of her Dokami friends were in her class. It was just her. Along with two dozen Jmugean-born and Shaergan-born teenagers her age. Some of them were nice to her, especially the Shaergans, but others—some Jmugeans—were not as friendly. A few of them even called her a 'freak of nature—not normal in any *real* sense'. She ignored them, of course, and focused on her studies. It was the sole reason she tolerated going there several days a week.

Soli sighed and glanced around the left side of the room. The only side of the room she allowed her eyes to observe. One Jmugean boy had his head tilted back, his eyes closed, and his mouth hanging open. He was sleeping, of course, having the greatest nap of his life. Another student had her head down on her desk and would lift it up at times, groaning under her breath every time the teacher increased the pitch in her voice. It was as if she was upset the teacher was disrupting her marvelous sleep session. Shaking her head, Soli looked back at the teacher. She never dared to turn and glance at the students to her right. And for good reason. Too many times in the past, she had learned what a mistake it was to do so. Even now, she could feel his eyes boring into her, unwavering. Determined to catch her eyes and smile at her. Determined to speak to her.

"...Omordion. The farthest, most mysterious planet," the teacher was saying. "No one knows much about it. All we know is the planet remains unscathed by the interplanetary wars. Many people view it as a cursed planet, where only the rejects of the solar system venture to, never to be heard from again." She cleared her throat and smiled, proud of herself for teaching the most important lesson of the year. "This concludes our lesson for today, children. Class is dismissed."

Okay. Now is my chance. It has to be today.

Soli's shoulders dropped. At times, the power to read minds was a blessing, but most of the time, it was a curse. She quickly gathered her books together and stood up, intent on reaching the door before everyone else. Especially *him*. However, it was too late. He was already next to her.

"Fhoten," Soli said, looking the seventeen-year-old Shaergan boy right in the eyes. She smiled politely. "I can't stay and talk. I have to go."

"I–I know," Fhoten said. "I just have something to ask you."

Soli's eyes shifted to the door and back at Fhoten. She knew what he was going to ask, but dreaded the moment when she had to turn him down. So, instead, she tried her best to avoid him at all costs. Marriage was a big deal. Definitely not something she was willing to endure with someone she had no connection with at all. A lifetime. With creepy Fhoten? She shuddered at the thought. "I have to go Fhoten...you know I have small children under my care. I must ensure they reach home safely."

Hear me out! Fhoten angrily said in his mind before smiling at Soli and nodding. "I understand." Fhoten's angry, mental outburst caused Soli's eyes to–unconsciously–open wide and she took a small step back.

When Fhoten saw her reaction, his eyes narrowed and his thick unibrow crumpled together into a frown.

Did she just read my thoughts? he thought.

Soli smiled and hugged her books closer to her chest. "Thank you for understanding," she said. "See you tomorrow." Turning on her heels, she hurried out of the room and into the bright sunshine.

Soli knew Fhoten was staring after her, puzzled more than ever about what had transpired. She groaned in frustration. Ever since her ability to read minds grew stronger, she had been working on her facial expressions and her reaction to what people said about her, or any other member of the Dokami clan, in their heads. It was not an easy task and it was obvious she had a lot to work on. If anyone truly suspected she was a mind reader, she wasn't sure what they would do to her.

In the schoolyard, located in the middle of the small, one level schoolrooms, fifteen-year-old Rueslon stood with several Dokami children, including his eleven-year-old brother, Drae, and eleven-year-old Reyshi Maephit, looking around for more Dokamis to take home. When he spotted Soli, his eyes lit up, as they did every day when she stepped out into the schoolyard, and he waved.

Soli had never been so happy to see him.

"Are you okay?" Rueslon said.

Soli could tell he was sensing something was wrong. "I'm fine," she said, making the decision to tell him about Fhoten later, when the other children were not in earshot. She did not want them to worry. Besides. Fhoten? She could handle him. A panicked group of one hundred and forty-five Dokami children? Not so easy.

Soli quickly stepped out into the darkness of her porch in the middle of the night. She slowly shut her front door behind her so as not to awaken her mother. She wiped tears from her eyes with a quivering hand and shivered slightly from the chill, attempting to take in several breaths of fresh air. Her dreams were getting worse. Dreams of a past life...death, destruction, anger...it was always the same. This time, along with all of the death, she felt lost. Abandoned. As if she was supposed to be somewhere, but was left behind or thrown away. Like garbage. It was an awful feeling, a heavy, depressed feeling. When she awoke, she had burst into tears and could not stop crying, until she got out of bed and walked out of the house. She knew she was not the only one who had experienced the dream. Since Soli was small, whenever she dreamt of a past life, Rueslon experienced the same dream, at the exact same time. Therefore, she wasn't surprised to see him walking towards her house in the moonlight and approaching her porch with the same troubled, worrisome expression.

"What do you suppose this one meant?" Rueslon said as he came closer. He sat down on Soli's front steps as he so often did and waited until she sat next to him before turning to her. She could see his eyes were puffy and red. Evidently, the emotion she felt when she woke up was mutual.

Soli shook her head. "I don't know," she said. "We're pretty sure these dreams are of a past life, but what do they mean? Why are they getting worse?"

"Maybe it's not the past. Maybe it's a vision of the future."

Soli looked down at her hands. "Yes, you've mentioned this before. But we can't ignore the dreams we had when this whole thing started. Remember?"

"Yes, I remember. The dreams about us, the Dokamis, dying out hundreds of years ago. Returning to this world, as we are now. Now the dreams seem so much more extreme. So much more *crazy*."

"Imagine if we could tap into our dreams. Find out what they are about? If you knew where Dokamis actually came from—the place in our dreams—would you want to go there?"

Rueslon looked Soli straight in the eyes. "No."

"Neither would I. But I always wondered what it would be like."

"After tonight's dream, I'd rather not go there at all."

"True." Soli sighed and looked up at the moon. She wished the dreams would stop. The nights they did not experience them were glorious. Sometimes it would be several months before the dreams came back. Any amount of time, not spent diving into the past, was an absolute blessing.

"So what happened at school today?" Rueslon said, interrupting her thoughts. "Do you want to talk about it?"

"Oh," Soli said and sighed again. "I almost forgot."

Rueslon looked at her expectantly, waiting for her to continue.

"Fhoten tried to talk to me again. I heard his thoughts. I knew what he wanted to ask me. You want to know the worst part about it? He realized I could read his mind."

"How?"

"My reaction when he became angry in his mind. He showed the complete opposite on the outside. It was...scary."

Rueslon frowned, but tried his best to reassure her. "I'm sure it's nothing to worry about. The folks around here know there is something different about us. There will always be rumors. We know this. Unless Freaky Fhoten knows for sure, he will always wonder about it. In the meantime, if he told anyone else, he will look just as crazy as the notion that you can read minds."

"Do you really think it will be okay?"

"Of course. Fhoten's harmless. You've said so yourself."

"Sure." Soli looked down at her hands and wrung them together in a nervous gesture. "I suppose you're right. I just won't let it happen again."

"He still wants your hand in marriage?"

"Yes. He is getting serious now. School is almost over for us, you know?"

"Do you think...I mean—would you say yes? One day—I mean?"

Soli turned to look at Rueslon so fast, she felt as though her neck could have snapped if she turned any faster. "Rue, don't be *foolish*. There are people on this forsaken planet who are the nicest, kindest people I have ever met. Fhoten is not one of them. And besides, I will only marry someone I love. I don't *love* him."

Rueslon looked at her with sadness in his eyes. Soli wished she could read his mind, but she had never been able to. The day she realized she had the ability to read minds, they discovered one of his Dokami powers was to keep his mind blocked. No matter how hard they tried, she could never read his mind. Yet their minds were connected in some strange way since his birth.

"What's wrong?" Soli asked.

Rueslon tore his eyes away from hers to study the cobblestoned street. After a few moments, he spoke. "Soli," he said. "I know I'm two years younger...than you." He nervously looked back at her and spoke quickly. "If—when we're older...do you think maybe—there's a possibility...?"

Soli did not need the power to read his mind to know what he was trying to ask. "Of course," she said. "There's no question about it, Rue."

Rueslon's face lit up and he smiled. "Promise?"

"Yes. I love you, Rue. I always have."

"I love you, too, Soli."

CHAPTER 5

"Congratulations!" the midwife shouted. "She's a beautiful baby girl!" She wrapped the wailing baby in a blanket and lovingly handed her to her mother.

Soli thanked the midwife, who was a member of the Dokami clan and a few years younger than she. She wiped her tearful eyes, and looked down into her daughter's brown eyes and beamed. "She has your smile, Rue."

Affectionately, Rueslon caressed his daughter's forehead and then ran his finders down to her cheek. She immediately stopped crying, finding some satisfaction studying his face instead. "She is beautiful," he said.

Taking a moment to kiss and embrace his wife, Rueslon gazed into her eyes. In them, he could see all he cherished and adored. It was so easy to reflect on the journey of their life, as he so often did when gazing at her.

Soli had been his best friend for twenty-one years, since the day he was born. Being the first Dokami born on Jmugea, they had endured so much together. Routinely referred to as the leaders of the Dokami clan, they were appointed their unofficial king and queen when they married just one year ago.

Rueslon's stomach flip-flopped when he remembered the unspeakable events of their wedding day. The ceremony was beautiful, set in a beautiful, vacant meadow near Enshatmu City. It was a gloriously warm day. Not a cloud in the sky. Every member of the Dokami clan was there to witness their marriage, along with their parents and the Shaergans they had befriended over the years. Rueslon and Soli had said their vows to each other under a willow tree and accepted their new roles as king and queen of the Dokami clan.

They were elated.

Everyone was so happy.

Until they left that beautiful meadow and were walking back to the city.

"Coo," the baby said, interrupting Rueslon's thoughts.

Rueslon smiled when he looked down at her face. She was beginning to fall asleep in her mother's arms, so comfortable and warm. "What are we going to name her?"

Soli closed her eyes. "Well…it seems to me…we will name her… Me-Meela."

"Meela. What a wonderful name. I bet I was the one who came up with it."

"In truth, you were…actually."

Rueslon smiled again. Soli's gift of selected vision had grown stronger over the years. She could now see certain things that have yet to occur. Things such as events, places, and names. She could not predict major catastrophes, but could still sense when someone was going to be in danger. Rueslon had the same gift, but he could not see specific things like Soli could.

Soli looked up at him. "Should you take Meela out to meet her family?"

"Oh, I think so. They have only been waiting for two days. I don't think they could wait any longer." He laughed and reached down, carefully taking Meela from Soli.

"I miss her already," Soli sadly said.

"Don't worry. I'll bring her right back."

"I know…I love you."

"Always and forever, my darling. Be right back."

Rueslon walked towards the door, proudly holding his newborn in his arms. She felt so light, only weighing about six pounds, and she looked so peaceful.

Peace.

All the Dokamis ever wanted was peace.

All they ever dreamt of was peace.

All they got in return was *hate*.

A feeling of dread overtook Rueslon, as it so often did, before he opened the front door of the one room house he shared with his wife. Stepping out into the porch always took him back to that tragic day.

The day of their wedding.

Soli was proclaimed queen of the Dokami clan, and Rueslon, their king. Everyone was rejoicing as the procession headed back to Enshatmu City, intent on celebrating throughout the night.

The highly anticipated celebration never began.

Instead, an angry mob halted their march before they reached the city. The mob carried torches, stakes, and bats, determined to use them against the peaceful and joyous procession.

The Dokami could not understand why the Jmugeans were so angry. They had no idea what started the rage. Regardless, the Dokami clan, their families, and friends were under attack. Pure hatred enveloped the entire mob like a thick cloud. They shouted obscene things at them—cruel things—things young children should not have heard.

Soli, Rueslon, and other members of their clan tried to explain how peaceful they were. They would never hurt anyone. The people of Jmugea had *nothing* to fear.

Their frantic pleas went unheard.

The crowd was out for blood.

"Burn them!" someone shouted.

A torch flew into the wedding procession from within the angry crowd. Horrifically, a young female member of the Dokami clan caught on fire and started screaming, attempting to run away as others struggled to put out the flames that engulfed her body.

The angry mob took it as their opportunity to begin their relentless attack.

The Dokami, determined not to use their powers in front of the Jmugeans, fought back using their strength alone. The mob was merciless, beating down any Dokami they could get their hands on with bats and torches, regardless of their age. Carnage and screaming permeated the field around them. Rueslon tried his best to save his people but he saw many of them go down, one by one. He wanted to crush the Jmugeans with his mind, but everything he learned growing up, rules of restraint and hidden secrets, held him back. The fight did not cease, until the Jmugean Army conveniently showed up.

Too late.

Forty-two Dokami clan members between the ages of five and twenty either perished or ran away, never to be heard from or seen again. Twenty-six Shaergans and Jmugeans were also killed, trying to save their children and their friends. His parents and Soli's mother were among the twenty-six. He never bothered to find out how many out of the angry Jmugean mob were killed, because he was sure the answer would have been zero.

Rueslon was devastated. Soli was inconsolable. Along with the horrific loss of her beloved mother, Soli also felt as if she had lost her children. In a way, she was like their mother, having cared for them all their lives. She felt like it was all her fault. That she should have taken them away long ago to protect them. To protect their families. Deep down inside, she knew the fight with the Jmugeans was only the beginning.

It was not long before the Jmugean Army, under the direction of the leader of the Jmugean Council, Ghosh Hres, built a reservation in the middle of the city, equipped with high fences and locks, for the Dokamis' 'protection'. The Dokamis were forced to live within the enclosure under lock and key. They were free to walk around the city during a specific two-hour timeframe during the day, typically in mid-afternoon. They shamefully used the time given to them to get food from the marketplace, subjecting themselves to ridicule by the people outside of the reservation. It did not help that they had to pay with ration tickets given to them by the army because they could no longer work. It was a degrading and horrible way to live, but they were given no other choices.

Rueslon shook his head slightly to take the images of that fateful day out of his mind. He stepped out into the reservation, and held up his newborn baby so the eager, yet patient, members of the Dokami clan could meet her. His people shouted for joy when they saw her. She was the first Dokami born between two Dokami parents. An extraordinary miracle, Meela was meant to rule the long line of Dokami-born offspring to follow her.

"This is Meela," Rueslon said.

"Welcome Princess Meela," the crowd greeted. Some bowed to her, while others got down on one knee, offering their respect and loyalty to her.

Rueslon's heart dropped, as it did every day, when he looked around the reservation. The rest of their homes were built in the same fashion as his: a one-room house per family. Again, it was degrading. Highly unnecessary. He felt the Jmugeans were the ones who needed to be locked up and punished. Not *them*. Every day, Rueslon tried to think of a way to help his people escape to a better life, but they had nowhere else to go.

CHAPTER 6

"Meela. Say carrot. *Car-rot.*"

Soli held up a carrot in front of her one-year-old daughter's round face. She was out shopping with Meela in the Enshatmu City marketplace, just outside the reservation. Meela stared back at her with big, brown eyes and smiled, unsure of what to think of the command given to her. Her thick, curly, black hair had grown long over the past year and fell just below her waist. Enchanted by her beauty, a few Shaergans stopped to stare at her before walking away, shaking their heads with sadness.

"Figures," Soli said to Meela. "You only talk when you want to." She put the carrot back down on the vegetable cart and shrugged at the Shaergan merchant. He laughed and shook his head before picking up his cart and rolling it down the street.

Soli sighed. Her people had half of an hour left until the alarm sounded and they were forced to retreat to the reservation. The gates would then be slammed shut behind them with a powerful bang, locked again for another twenty-two hours. Looking around the marketplace, Soli watched as her fellow Dokami engaged in sales transactions with the merchants, paying them with the shameful ration tickets they were provided. She glanced at the soldiers, spread all around to keep the peace for the two hours the Dokami were allowed to come out. Most of them watched their every move, as if *they* were the dangerous ones and not the Jmugeans.

Soli's heart always sank when she saw the Jmugeans treating the Dokamis with cruelty. She could hear what they were saying in their minds and wished she could tune them out, like Reyshi could, but she could not. Unwillingly, she listened, her heart wrenching with every cruel thought and every malicious gesture.

Despite what they endured with the Jmugeans, the Shaergans were always nice to them. They knew how it felt to be outcasts so they sympathized with them. Most Jmugeans became just as cruel to the Shaergans as they were with the Dokamis after they built the reservation. The leader of the Jmugean Council, Ghosh Hres, passed a law, forbidding the mating between Jmugeans and Shaergans and the reproduction of their so-called 'demon' children. He threatened that they would be thrown in jail, or worse, killed for disobedience and the offspring would be sent to the reservation upon birth. Soli knew there were many Jmugeans and Shaergans who still loved each other. She knew they had to move far away from the watchful eyes of the council and the radical Jmugeans, to live their lives in peace with their Dokami children. She also knew, since the reservation was built, there had been twenty-seven undocumented births of Dokami children from those families. They could never return to their homes for as long as they lived. And their Dokami offspring? Well...for now they were on their own.

Soli shook her head in disgust. How easy things could change in just two short years. She hugged her daughter tighter and approached a Jmugean merchant. The woman glared at her and said some nasty things about her in her mind. Soli ignored her, as she always did. She was used to the stares, the bad comments, and the anger. It would never change or get better. She had to learn to accept it in order to keep from going insane day after day.

Soli gave a courteous smile, to show her gratitude to the Jmugean merchant, and thanked her for the fruit. The woman only grunted and turned to attend to something–*anything*–to keep her from associating with another member of the Dokami clan.

Soli frowned and glanced at the sundial over the main merchant building. It was time to head back, before the gates were closed and she would be arrested for non-compliance. She started walking back towards the reservation, trying hard to tune out the ecstatic voices singing with jubilation whenever it came time for the 'demon children' to return to their prison.

Time is ticking for the Shaergans. Their days are numbered.

Soli stopped dead in her tracks and quickly glanced around. *Who said that?* she thought.

Soon we will be rid of them and their demon offspring, once and for all.

Soli was used to hearing horrible things about the Shaergans and her people, but this was different. The man sounded so *sure* of himself, as if what he was implying was *definite*. But who could it be? Looking around, Soli could not pinpoint who it was. She knew it was a male voice…

The moment she figured out who it was, Soli's heart flew up to her throat. He smiled at her when she made eye contact with him.

The *mayor*.

The jolly, old mayor of Enshatmu City.

Mayor Jubi.

Soli had never seen him in the square before. He was a man people said was *against* the ousting of the Dokami clan. He only did as he was told, they explained. There was nothing he could do to help the council, even when he wanted so much to do so.

All *lies*.

Mayor Jubi shifted his eyes to a young Shaergan man walking by him. *As soon as Hres carries out his plan to kill them all,* he thought, rather too excitedly.

Fear gripped Soli's heart, which began to beat rapidly, and her stomach turned.

Mayor Jubi continued his silent statements of euphoria. *It won't be long now. The time has come to reclaim Jmugea for purebred Jmugeans again. The time has come to reverse the damage Hres created when he allowed those dirty Shaergans to make Jmugea their home.* Mayor Jubi looked crazily around him, his eyes shifting from left to right. *To eliminate a whole race of people will not be an easy task. It will be better to execute them in their sleep. Maybe relocate them slowly and kill them elsewhere until they are all dead.* He gave a hearty laugh, pretending he was laughing at a little Dokami child, running towards the reservation gates with his kite trailing behind him. He then glared at Soli when he caught her still staring at him.

Soli turned, dropping a couple of her fruits and vegetables, causing Mayor Jubi to stare at her even harder. "Let's go, Meela," she said, after picking up the food. She quickly walked to the reservation, trying hard not to look back at the evil man she once had so much respect for. She knew he was still watching her as she walked away, sending chills up and down her spine.

"Yes, this is what I heard," Soli said.

The head of every Dokami household sat around Soli and Rueslon's one-room house, listening as Soli explained to them everything Mayor Jubi had said in his thoughts. They were shocked, but not at all surprised. The Jmugeans hated them. They knew that already. Eventually the time would come when the Jmugeans would try to reclaim their planet. Unfortunately, they never dreamt it would happen so soon.

"What are we going to do?" Drae said, shifting uncomfortably in his chair. He was just recently married, and his new wife, Reyshi, was sitting next to him, appearing thoughtful. They had both grown into a handsome couple. Drae still looked like a younger version of Rueslon and Reyshi was known for her beautifully long, curly mass of red hair and her sparkling green eyes. On their seventeenth birthday, which happened to fall on the same day, they said their vows in the middle of the reservation, with the entire Dokami clan looking on. Reyshi moved into Drae's one-room house, right next door to their king and queen.

"There's nothing we can do," Twenty-one-year-old Nariele said, her soft voice breaking through the dozens of voices murmuring around the room. "How would we be able to stop them from behind these fences?"

A tall, slim, nineteen-year old man, by the name of Amzin, spoke up. His usual straight blonde hair was disheveled, appearing as if he had just woken up from a nap when the meeting was called. "We cannot," he said. "We are already as good as dead here—"

"I disagree," another young man, an eighteen-year-old by the name of Ollige, interjected. His skin tone was a shade of mocha and he never liked to wear his brown hair long but kept it short, almost bald. He looked around the room, his brown eyes narrowing into slits. "I say we are as good as dead if we don't do anything about it. We have to fight for our lives. We have to escape. Run away!"

A chorus of exclamations erupted around the room as everyone attempted to get their point across all at once.

"Well," Soli said, "there is one thing we *have* to do."

Everyone stopped talking and looked at Soli, interested in what their queen had to say.

"We are not the only ones marked for death. The Shaergans are too. We have to warn them."

"How can we do that?" Reyshi said. "We are stuck here in this reservation and, when we have our two hours of freedom, those Jmugean soldiers are watching our every move."

"I will go," Soli said. "When they least expect it. I will sneak back into the reservation before anyone realizes I left."

"No," Rueslon firmly said.

Soli looked into his eyes and frowned. "What? But we have to—"

"Absolutely *not*."

"But we can't sit around here and do *nothing*. We can't just let the Shaergans die. We have no choice. We have to help them."

"Yes, we do have a choice. At night, we can sneak out of here. *Quietly*. We can take one of those Shaergan spaceships. One of the spaceships they used to come here thirty years ago. We can escape."

"Exactly what I was trying to say," Ollige said.

"And go *where*?" Soli said to Ollige. She turned back to Rueslon. "We have nowhere to go, Rue. Enshatmu City is our home. *Jmugea* is our home. Who would be willing to take us in? We don't know what's out there. We have to stay and fight for what is right."

"What if something bad happens to you?" Rueslon said. "What about Meela?"

He hit a nerve. Soli looked down at her hands resting on her lap. "I will be just fine."

"But what if your plan to warn the Shaergans backfires? Meela will lose her mother. Just like we lost ours—"

Soli's head snapped up. Rueslon was being selfish. If she did not warn the Shaergans, hundreds of thousands of people would die. It was a risk she was willing to take to save many more lives than their own. She could not live with herself if another innocent life was lost. "I trust, if anything were to happen to me, you will give Meela the care she needs. As if I was still here."

Rueslon stood up. "What are you *saying*, Soli? I reject your proposal. No."

"But Rue, you're not being reasonable—"

"Enough!" he cried out, his face turning bright red in anger, shocking everyone in the room. "We will find a way out of this mess without killing ourselves in the process. And I don't want to hear any more ridiculous notions about risking your life to warn the Shaergans."

Soli did not say anything. Rueslon had never undermined her position before. Especially in front of the entire Dokami Council. Being the oldest, she had always been the decision maker, with no questions asked. She knew Rueslon was worried and afraid to lose her. Nevertheless, she still felt like she should do something. She could not wait until something tragic happened again. It was a risk she was willing to take with or without the Dokami Council—or her husband's—approval.

CHAPTER 7

Chirp, chirp.

Rueslon opened his eyes. The steady stream of light from the bright sun blinded him for a moment and he tried to gain some focus. A happy bird was perched on the ledge of their only window, chirping loudly. It suddenly flew away when he moved. Peering over the side of the bed, Rueslon watched his little princess for a few moments, as she slept soundly in her tiny bed. She always liked to sleep with her mass of black, curly hair over her eyes, shielding them from the rising sun.

Rueslon smiled and sighed. Stretching, he turned around to plant a kiss on his wife's cheek as he did every morning.

He kissed the pillow. She was not there.

"Soli?" he whispered, careful not to awaken Meela.

No answer.

He looked around the one-room house. She was not there. Panic stricken, he jumped out of bed and rushed out of the house, carefully closing the door behind him. The reservation was just beginning to wake up. People were walking around outside, carrying out their usual, early morning duties.

"Soli?" Rueslon said, calling out her name in a feverishly loud whisper. Everyone outside stopped to look at him. He was glancing back and forth and appeared disheveled, unlike his usual calm self. "Has anyone seen Soli?"

Dokamis nearby shook their heads in response.

Reyshi stepped out of the house next door, followed by Drae. "What is it, Rue?" she said.

"It's Soli. She's not here. I–I don't know where she is."

"Calm down, brother," Drae said, trying to reassure him. "She has to be here. The reservation isn't big—"

"It's not like her to leave the house without saying anything." Rueslon stepped away from their house. "I wonder where she—" He froze after a mysterious nagging feeling tugged at the strings of his heart. Rueslon took a step back towards the house. The feeling was gone. He took a deep breath and stepped forward again.

There it was again.

The nagging feeling in his heart steadily turned into a dull ache. Rueslon glanced at Reyshi, who was standing on her porch. She had a blank look in her green eyes and she was staring off in the distance, in the direction of the reservation gates.

"Reyshi?" Drae said and touched her shoulder. She neither spoke nor reacted to his touch, but her eyes watered and a small tear rolled down her cheek.

Rueslon's pulse quickened. Reyshi was having another one of her visions. Something was wrong. He could feel it now. Something was dreadfully wrong.

"Eh hem."

Soli removed the hood of her black cloak from her brown, curly hair and looked around at the immense crowd gathering before her in the basement of a Shaergan merchant store. She had no time to wait for the remaining Shaergans to arrive. "Can I have your attention please?"

All eyes were focused on her, the crowd eager to hear why she called them in for a meeting.

"I don't have much time. What I have to say must be quick and direct. I have to get back to the reservation as soon as possible." Soli hesitated for a moment, unsure of the reaction she would receive from the Shaergans when she gave them the warning she came to deliver. She took a deep breath before continuing. "I overheard a–a conversation yesterday. The mayor of this city was discussing something, which should not be taken lightly." Soli took another deep breath and realized her hands were shaking with nervousness, her heart pounding in her chest. "We are all in grave danger. Dokamis and Shaergans alike. Ghosh

Hres, leader of the Jmugean Council, plans to kill us all in our sleep or take us away to execute us far from here. Some of us at a time—maybe by poisoning us slowly—so that the rest of us won't notice they're doing it until it is too late. Until all of us are dead."

Angry voices rose all around the basement. A few Shaergans began to cry.

"How do you know this is true?" a burly man asked. "Where did you overhear—?"

"But there's so *many* of us," a woman said, interrupting him. "They couldn't *possibly* kill all of us. I don't believe it."

Soli put her hands up in defense. "I know it sounds ludicrous, but I am only here to *warn* you. I am only here to tell you to *be careful*. Watch your backs and keep one eye open at all times. We all have known for some time—most of our lives even—that we are unwanted. 'Their days are numbered.' Those are the exact words I heard from our mayor. Mayor Jubi."

"What are we going to do?" another man said.

"Just be careful. Spread the word to Shaergans everywhere. Watch what you eat—what you drink. Lock your doors and gather anything you can use as a weapon. Keep a lookout on duty *every* night. For goodness sakes, fight against being relocated! Do what you can to protect yourselves and your families."

Soli's audience nodded grimly. For the Shaergans, it seemed like life would never be peaceful for them. Only thirty years prior, they had escaped certain death from their planet, Shaerga. The majority of them still remembered the destruction of their home planet, along with most of their population. It was as if they were reliving the nightmarish day all over again.

"And furthermore, you must keep what I said today a secret. You must not tell *anyone* outside of your Shaergan circles. Do not even discuss this among yourselves after you've passed the warning along." Soli placed her hood back over her hair. "I have to go." She stepped off the chair she was standing on, pushed her way through the crowd of Shaergans to climb the stairs, and left the merchant store.

What Soli failed to realize was the hidden enemy among the Shaergan people. This was someone who avoided her so she would not read his mind ever since he had suspected her of being able to do so many years ago. The same person who instigated the brutal attack on her wedding day. He was listening. His moment of revenge had finally come.

Rueslon was standing by the gates of the Dokami reservation, biting his lip, and looking around for a glimpse of Soli. He had searched the entire reservation and came to a horrific realization. She had escaped somehow, either over the gate, when no one was looking, or underground. He still had the unwavering feeling something bad was going to happen. Reyshi had confirmed his fears, but did not go into any details of what she saw in her vision. She only said she was sure the events could be *stopped*. He knew she did not want to worry him, but it still frustrated him that she kept what she saw to herself.

Everything outside the reservation seemed normal and quiet. The townsfolk walked back and forth, some selling merchandise, others buying or trading them. Nothing seemed amiss. It seemed like just another day. Except for the feeling Rueslon had, as if something horrible was about to happen.

Rueslon had informed the members of the Dokami clan to be on high alert. Soli was missing, but he needed them to go about their daily activities as if nothing was wrong. There was no need to bring unnecessary attention to the reservation. Unless, of course, he called for action. He silently prayed he would not have to make that call.

Rueslon wrung his fingers together and shifted his weight from one foot to the other. His breath came out rapid and shallow as he began pacing back and forth in front of the gate.

"Relax, Rue," Reyshi said from behind him. She was standing in the shade of the first house closest to the gates, bouncing Meela up and down as the toddler tugged on her fiery red hair.

Drae was standing apart from them, near the other side of the front gate, staring into the city streets with a determined look on his face. His nostrils flared a little as he watched a soldier walk by, patrolling the city. He quickly looked around the square again. No sign of his sister-in-law—anywhere.

Rueslon balled his hands into fists. "What if something happened to her?" he said. He did not like the feeling of not being able to do anything. All he could do was pray for her safe return. *If* she returned. "Reyshi, what if it's already too late. What if she's—"

"Soli," Drae whispered.

Rueslon quickly approached the gate and searched the crowd. He spotted her.

Soli was wearing her black cloak, the hood pulled over her head, blending in with most of the people in the square who were wearing their cloaks due to the unwelcomed chill in the air. She was slowly making her way back to the reservation, careful not to draw any attention to herself.

Rueslon was full of elation when he saw her. His heart leapt with joy. She was okay! A broad smile lit up his face. "Yes," he said.

"Hey. *You!*"

Soli stopped dead in her tracks. Two army soldiers pushed their way through the crowd, staring hard at her as they moved forward. Some Jmugeans and Shaergans turned to watch what was happening.

"No…no…no…" Rueslon moaned. Soli made eye contact with him. He could see she was frightened.

A trembling hand gripped Rueslon's shoulder. "Rue," Reyshi said in a frantic whisper. She was holding on tightly to Meela, who had begun to cry. "Rue, you must go get her. Please. Rue get her—now!"

"I can't!"

"You *have* to."

Rueslon shook his head, hoping beyond all hope Soli was not who they were after. "You know we can't show them what we can do. It would mean death for all of us."

"You've got to Rue. Please. Before it is too late. You have to *try*."

Much to their dismay, the two soldiers grabbed Soli. Several more soldiers were steadily entering the city square.

"Let go of me," Soli said. She screamed when she saw the stream of soldiers headed towards her. "What is this about?"

The soldiers yanked off her hood.

"What are you doing outside the reservation, little bird?" one soldier sneered. He cruelly spat in her face. "How did you wander so far from your *nest?*"

"I think we have a criminal on our hands," the other soldier said to him. "What do you think?"

"No–I–I," Soli stammered, wiping the disgusting spit from her face. She made eye contact with Rueslon again, pleading with him to help her with her eyes. Being caught outside the reservation meant certain death.

"Let her go!" Rueslon bellowed from behind the gate. "She's not a criminal!"

"We have reason to believe otherwise," the soldier bluntly said. He turned to Soli. "You are under arrest, little *spy*."

They knew.

When her arms were forced behind her back, Soli screamed again. This time, her terrified, high-pitched scream bounced off the walls of the town square, shattered some store windows, and rattled the reservation's fence. If she did not have everyone's attention before, she had it now.

The soldiers were shocked for a moment, but recovered when a cry of 'Witch!' was heard from somewhere in the crowd. They yanked Soli by her hair and began to drag her away. The crowd in the square became increasingly rowdy.

"Let her go!" Rueslon shouted, along with the rest of the Dokami clan who ran to meet him at the gates. There were about fifteen soldiers now in the square. Some of them began walking towards the reservation gates, intent on silencing the desperate voices echoing beyond them.

"Rue," Reyshi said, pleading. "You have to stop this. This can be *stopped*."

Rueslon remembered Reyshi's terrible vision. She said he could stop the events from happening. He had hesitated too long to act. He looked over at Drae, who gave a slight nod. He glanced at Meela, who was gripping onto Reyshi with tears in her eyes as she watched her mother being dragged away. He looked back at the growing crowd of Dokamis who were ready to take action on his word. Then he looked at the soldiers dragging his wife away. Her desperate screams could be heard over the shouts of the angry crowd. "No," he said through his teeth.

The reservation gates began to bend with Drae's help. They slowly ripped apart, screeching and grinding with every pull. The soldiers approaching the gates stopped their advance. It took them a moment to realize what was happening. They were too stunned to move as the gates tore apart and opened.

"How is this possible?" a voice cried out in the crowd outside the gates.

Everyone in the square turned back around when the two determined soldiers, whose hands were forced to release Soli's hair, lifted a hundred feet into the air before slamming into each other. They fell all the way back to the ground with a sickening crack, dying on impact.

Screams erupted all around and Jmugeans began to run away, while Soli stood between the two dead soldiers in utter shock. This was not supposed to happen. It was not her intention when she went to warn the Shaergans. The events she tried desperately hard to prevent had been triggered. Two army soldiers lay dead, right at her feet. It was what she feared the most. The members of the Dokami clan, her family, were all marked for death.

"Arrest them all!" a horrified soldier cried. "And anyone who tries to fight back, kill them!" The other soldiers snapped out of their trance and made an advance towards Soli and the destroyed reservation gates.

Rueslon knew the entire Jmugean Army was going to be upon them soon. He knew he had only moments to act. The tips of his fingers sparked with electricity. "Is everyone here?" he called out. He did not have to look back to know the entire Dokami clan, along with their children, were behind him.

"Yes!" A female voice rang out from the crowd.

"Let's move out!"

"Freedom!" someone shouted.

As Rueslon electrified the closest soldiers, several Dokami jumped over the crowd from behind him and reigned fireballs at most of the bewildered soldiers before touching the ground of the square. Some soldiers, engulfed in flames, ran around screaming, attempting to put out the fires, but to no avail.

"Go!" Rueslon shouted.

Following their king, the Dokamis ran out of the reservation, intent on destroying anything and anyone who got in their way. Drae hurled anything metal he could find at the soldiers and angry Jmugeans alike. Amzin hurled energy balls at them and watched as they flew back, hitting buildings and the ground with deafening noises sounding like thunder, resonating in the square. They were dead before they knew what hit them. The Jmugean and Shaergan crowd was scared and continued their retreat. Even the soldiers were terrified. They had never witnessed the powers displayed before them. Even though they thought the Dokami clan might have possessed some strange abilities, they did not actually believe the rumors to be true.

A soldier brought his hands to his throat as if someone was strangling him. His screams came out as a gurgling sound when blood poured from between his trembling lips. He frantically looked around to see what was causing his pain. As his body crumpled to the bloody ground, he saw Reyshi, holding the youngest member of the Dokami clan in her arms, smile and lower her free hand. *How could she be so cruel?* he thought before his eyes rolled back in his head and he died.

"Go back to the depths from which you came from!" a rough male voice cried out. Rueslon turned his head quickly in time to see a Jmugean civilian grab a sword from a dead soldier and swing it right at his head. Before he could react, the man's body bent at an odd angle, his bones snapping as his body broke in half. He was dead before he hit the ground. Turning back around, Rueslon saw it was Soli who had helped him. She had tears in her eyes and looked completely devastated.

"Soli..." he whispered. He longed to be reunited with his wife. While pushing through the chaotic crowd to get to her, he had visions of leaving the planet with the entire Dokami clan. If they could only find a new place to live, they would finally be free. Free to live and be who they wanted to be, without restraint. They would go in search of an isolated place, no matter how long it would take, and they would be happy, finally at peace.

A piercing scream erupted over the noise and the chaos around them. Rueslon suddenly felt a stabbing pain in his heart. He gripped his chest and quickly looked down, expecting to see blood.

Nothing.

Confused, Rueslon looked back up at Soli and saw something he never expected to see.

Blood was spreading across Soli's chest as she crumpled to the ground. Rueslon was not the one who had been stabbed. He had felt *her* pain. "Soli," he cried and ran to her, pushing everyone out of his way with his mind.

The entire Dokami clan turned to see what happened. Some began to scream in anger. A teenaged girl got to Soli first. She placed her hand on her chest and closed her eyes. When Rueslon reached her, the girl abruptly opened her eyes and angrily pointed through the crowd.

"He did it!" she cried out.

As if someone had parted the crowd by force, everyone stepped aside, revealing the person who had stabbed Soli. Rueslon froze when he saw who it was.

He was attempting to run away, his hands shaking as he let the knife fall to the ground. He was Shaergan born. He was not supposed to be their enemy. When Rueslon realized who he was, he understood why he had stabbed Soli. It occurred to him what sparked the riot on their wedding day. The reason Soli was caught on her way back to the reservation. Rueslon knew why he would do it and could not believe he had been overlooked for so long. He was in love with her. He had always been. Out of all the people Rueslon knew, Fhoten was the most likely person to want Soli's wedding day destroyed. He *would* want to see her dead. Because he knew he could never have her as long as she lived.

Drae immediately turned Fhoten into a raging fireball and Rueslon did not hesitate to electrocute him. Fhoten let out a horrifying, piercing scream and fell to the ground, violently shaking as his body surrendered to a swift death.

Without any remorse, Rueslon turned his attention to Soli, who Reyshi was desperately trying to heal along with the teenaged girl, named Faslin, another Dokami healer.

"Soli," Rueslon whispered, his eyes filling with tears. She was unresponsive, her slightly opened eyes seemed void of color as if she was already… "Please don't die." He quickly took her hand in his, intent on helping Reyshi and Faslin with the healing process even though he had never been able to administer it.

Reyshi shakily let Soli go and put her hands down by her side.

Rueslon looked up at her in shock. "What are you *doing*? Keep trying!" He was even more disturbed when Faslin did the same. "Faslin! Please? Keep trying."

"Rue," Reyshi said, tears filling up her eyes.

"No. Keep trying." Rueslon gripped Soli's hand and attempted to transfer his energy to her. His transfer was blocked.

"She died instantly when the blade pierced through her heart, Rue. We can't heal this type of wound and we definitely can't heal someone who has already *passed*." Recalling the well-known story of how Soli had saved her life when she was a toddler, Reyshi burst into tears. She would never be able to return the favor. Faslin looked away and started crying as well, rocking back and forth on her heels.

Rueslon stared at his wife's unmoving body and his vision became cloudy. She was only trying to save everyone. She was only doing what she thought was right.

"Ma-ma?"

Rueslon head snapped up when he realized Meela had been standing next to Reyshi, looking down at her mother the whole time. Reyshi must have set her down next to her before she attempted to heal Soli. He could not believe he was so blind as to not see her standing there the whole time. His daughter looked terrified and grief stricken, as if she knew her mother was never going to wake up.

"We have to get out of here," Rueslon said, swiftly picking up Meela. He needed to get his daughter and the Dokami clan to safety as quickly as possible. The entire Jmugean Army was headed their way, intent on killing them all. Before anyone else lost their life, he had to get them all far, far away.

After ordering Drae and Ollige to pick up Soli's body, Rueslon signaled for his clan to move out. They grabbed their children and retreated, quickly running away from the horrifying scene of destruction, and headed to the Shaergan section of Enshatmu City. Rueslon had befriended an old Shaergan man by the name of Omerik, who still owned a spaceship from when he and his family landed on Jmugea, with thousands of Shaergans, thirty years prior. Once they received the go ahead from Omerik and given the key, Rueslon directed everyone to the outskirts of the city, where the Shaergan spaceships were being held. He made sure everyone climbed aboard Omerik's ship. When the ship was ready to leave, Rueslon bid farewell to Soli, handed Meela to Reyshi, and disembarked.

"What are you doing?" Drae asked him from the captain's chair. "Let's go!"

"Take care of Meela for me," Rueslon solemnly said.

"What are you talking about?" Reyshi said. "Don't try to be a hero, Rue."

"I will not be going with you. Please have a proper burial for my best friend. My wife. I have to finish what she started. The Shaergan people are in danger and you cannot ask me to forget about the Dokamis who have been living their lives in peace away from Enshatmu City. As long as the Jmugean government still exists, they will never forget what we did today. They will come after us and them." Rueslon quickly looked around when he heard angry shouts coming from the direction of the city. "Go! Quickly, before they burn the ship down and everyone inside. You have an important job. To get our people to safety. As the guardians of the new queen of the Dokami clan, this responsibility is in your hands until she is of age to rule on her own."

Drae reached out for him with tears welling up in his eyes. "Brother, no!"

"Just go. Now. Before it is too late. Give Meela my love and take care of her. One day she will come to understand I had to do what was right. Goodbye, my brother." Rueslon did not hesitate and took off running back towards the city to take on the army on his own. He only looked back once to make sure his people had escaped Jmugean airspace.

He was never heard from again.

CHAPTER 8

The Plight of the Dokami Clan

"They drove us out. We had nowhere to go."

"Who drove you out?"

"The Dokami."

"What are you *talking* about? We are the Dokami."

"*Your* people. They drove us out of our homes on Jmugea. A terrible plague— it took the lives of our women and children. Our race, the Jmugean race, was dying."

"So you came here to destroy us."

"Our leader thought we could overpower you. We had no *idea* you were so...many."

"How did you know where to find us?"

"We've known about your existence on this planet for nearly one hundred and fifty years. *They* knew..."

"Tell me about the Dokami on Jmugea. Quickly and I might let you live."

"When your clan left Jmugea, our government was destroyed. All the members of our council–killed. Ghosh Hres was brutally murdered. We had no law. No direction. No leaders. The prohibition set in place to prevent mating between Jmugeans and Shaergans, became nonexistent. Your abandoned Dokami came out of hiding and appointed a Dokami king—"

"A *king*?"

"Yes. Shaergans wanted only to mate with Jmugeans to produce Dokami children because they *worshipped* them for saving their lives. Some Jmugeans obliged. The ones who did not, were forced to live on an island, isolated from all of Jmugea. We were the last of the Jmugean race. The Shaergan race on the planet died out, leaving only the Dokami to rule."

"And then this plague, you say?"

"Yes. They cursed us. The plague hit us and killed most of our men. It killed all of our women. Our *children*. It did not affect the Dokamis at all. We had no hope left. We were *dying*."

"And now you're dead."

A sword was plunged into the heart of the dying Jmugean soldier. He screamed and tried to speak, attempting to ask for forgiveness and understanding. It was too late. Before the sword was wrenched from his chest, he was already dead.

After killing the last purebred Jmugean alive, the current king of the Dokami clan, Braechal Yu-omi, looked around at the carnage around him. There were perhaps ten thousand Jmugean soldiers, who had descended on their peaceful planet, Dokar, intent on controlling or destroying them, whichever they could accomplish first. Unbeknownst to them, the few hundred Dokami, who had left Jmugea one hundred and fifty years prior, had increased their small population to over two hundred thousand. The Jmugeans were hardly prepared for what was waiting for them once they touched Dokar soil. Shamefully annihilated within a two-hour time span, the Jmugeans had no chance.

Braechal rubbed his chin. *An entire planet full of Dokami?* he wondered. *They have known where we were all this time, but have never sought to contact us? They named someone else king over the Dokami clan when the true, royal bloodline resides here? On Dokar? Why would they do that?*

Braechal looked around him. Dokamis were rejoicing in the streets. The brief battle against the wretched Jmugeans was over. After all this time, they finally had their revenge for what happened to their ancestors and their Queen Mother, Soli, so long ago. However, Braechal was worried. What if more came, seeking to control them as the Jmugeans had? He could not bear the pain of killing so many more, misguided people. It was not in their nature to do so.

We will have to move the planet and hide it, Braechal thought. *It will take some time, but it can be done.* For a brief moment, he considered making contact with the Dokamis on Jmugea, but he thought otherwise. He would tell the Dokami Council about this new revelation, but he knew not to tell his people. He did not know what the Jmugean Dokamis were like. It was best the two planets continued to lead separate lives as they had done for over a century. The fact remained; the Dokami on Jmugea had always known where their people were and never once sought to make contact with them. To bring them back home. No, he would not disappoint his people with the sad news.

We *don't need their help*, Braechal thought, *and we never will.*

"Shhhh."

"I'm scared."

"Just be quiet," another frightened voice whispered from the anxious, imprisoned crowd within an enormous makeshift tent. "They won't hear us if we're quiet."

"What if they come in—what if we're discovered?"

"I don't want to die!"

"Shhhh!"

"Be quiet!"

A panel on the ground shifted by itself and made a slight grinding sound. The frightened faces in the crowd of about one hundred Dokami turned towards the sealed door, expecting to see malicious soldiers come bursting in with their weapons drawn. After a couple of fearful minutes, when they heard nothing, they turned back to the heavy panel and watched as it rose ten feet above the ground, as if on invisible strings. Beneath the panel was a tunnel, dug into the ground two hundred years ago, before the Dre-Ahd war began.

"Quickly. Everyone!"

One by one, the Dokamis jumped into the unlit tunnel. After the last person touched the dirt ground, the panel slowly moved back into place, blanketing everyone in darkness. Small fires sprang up on shaky, sweaty palms as the crowd ran away from their makeshift prison. Other tunnels opened up into theirs from escape routes created underneath their city long ago. Groups of people came out of hiding from those tunnels when the larger group ran past them. Tearful words were exchanged as a mother, who had lost her husband and two of her sons in the Dre-Ahd war, was reunited with her youngest son. The element of fear was extremely high as they ran towards their destination.

All of a sudden, angry shouts erupted from the ground directly above their heads and everyone stopped to listen, their hearts pounding with fear. Beads of sweat poured down their faces and they silently prayed they had not been discovered. A small child was heard sobbing from within the crowd. The angry shouts continued for what seemed like an hour to the people underground, until they heard a loud scuffle, followed by an eruption of laughter. Breathing sighs of relief, the immense crowd once again took off running towards the end of the tunnel.

When they reached their destination, a giant spaceship loomed before them, hidden in a cave, situated beneath their tallest mountain. It was the same spaceship used to help the Dokami make their escape from Jmugea some two hundred years prior. It was painted black the previous night so it could blend in with the darkness and it was large enough to accommodate thousands of people. Sadly, they had no need for the space it held because less than one thousand Dokami remained alive on Dokar.

"Hurry before they realize we are gone!"

"There's not much time!"

Cries of anticipation erupted as they boarded the ship as quickly as possible. Several minutes later, the last five remaining members of the Dokami Council, and the current king of the Dokami clan, boarded the ship.

"Do we have everyone?" King Tre-akelomin Gre-ashyu asked as he climbed aboard.

"Are we the only ones left?" a member of the Dokami Council asked.

"I'm afraid so..." someone within the crowd answered.

"I can't get a read on anyone else on the entire planet!" another person cried.

"This is dreadful," Tre-akelomin said sadly.

"What will become of the Dokami race?" another person asked.

"All those people...all those *children*!" someone cried.

Sobs erupted all over. They had made a grave mistake when they decided to stand and fight, instead of escaping, assuming they could win the war, just like they had when they were attacked by the Jmugeans fifty years beforehand.

"We have no time to panic," a council member said. "We must leave Dokar."

"All together now!" Tre-akelomin said.

Silence permeated the air inside the spaceship, and, without the engine starting or the lights turning on, it began to rise. The spaceship exited through a large hole in the cave ceiling and out of the mountain. Through the windows, the last remaining members of the Dokami clan could see hundreds of blazing fires lit around the prisons they were once held in. It angered them to see their enemies enjoying their last night on Dokar, looking forward to taking them, their prisoners, back to their dreadful Dre-Ahd planet early the following morning.

Several decades earlier, the Dokami moved Dokar behind a partially destroyed, uninhabited planet named Rute, to avoid another war. They lived in absolute peace for fifty years. Unbeknownst to Dokar's inhabitants, their planet was discovered by two Dre-Ahd scientists. After making their unprecedented discovery, the scientists immediately returned to their planet, eager to share the news of what they found. After what became of their ally on Jmugea, all of their plans to destroy Jmugea were always thwarted by the power of the Dokami clan there. They were now given the opportunity to capture the Dokami on Dokar and utilize them to enter Jmugean airspace, under the false pretense that their lost tribe was returning home.

For several years, the Dre-Ahds trained hundreds of thousands of fighters to attack the unsuspecting Dokami clan on Dokar. They developed weapons never before heard of in history. Weapons, which shot pieces of metal at the Dokami, leaving them and their powers virtually defenseless against the Dre-Ahds.

The soulless Dre-Ahds were trained to kill any moving or breathing target, including children. When the Dokami realized they were being massacred and gradually losing the fight, their queen, Gemnon Greashyu did something her predecessors would have been ashamed of.

She desperately sent a distress call to the Dokami on Jmugea.

And received a response.

No.

Shocked and disappointed beyond belief, Gemnon lost her courage during the battle and was mercilessly killed by a ruthless Dre-Ahd soldier. Her leadership was passed down to her eldest child, Tre-akelomin Greashyu, who was next in line to inherit the Dokami throne. Tre-akelomin tried his best to save the remaining Dokami but was devastated when so many more were killed. The killing did not stop until he ultimately surrendered and he and his people were taken into captivity before escaping via the underground tunnels.

Hovering above the only planet they had ever considered home, the Dokami clan watched as the ground began to shake. Lava erupted from every crevice of the earth beneath them. Thousands of Dre-Ahd soldiers on the shaking ground were in a state of panic and rushed into the makeshift prisons, only to discover they were empty. They tried to run to their spaceships but frightfully watched as they exploded before they could reach them.

The engine of the hovering spaceship turned on, its lights shining brightly on the terrified soldiers. Those lights were the last things the Dre-Ahd soldiers saw before the ship flew away and the entire planet exploded—with them on it.

The surviving members of Dokar's Dokami clan were devastated and heartbroken. For weeks, they traveled past immense planets, destroyed long ago during the interplanetary wars. Those planets laid in ruins, just pieces of rocks, floating in space.

They even flew past Jmugea.

They did not stop.

The Dokami clan finally decided to land when they fell upon the one planet they could possibly call their new home.

A planet shrouded in superstition, yet thankfully unscathed by the interplanetary wars.

A planet where they could be safe and live forever in peace.

Omordion.

PART TWO
OMORDION
PRESENT DAY

CHAPTER 9

Tre-akelomin Gre-ashyu had tears in his eyes when he described the horror of that fateful day, when the Dre-Ahds attacked Dokar. He was there. He had witnessed all of the devastation and the mass murder of his people. The fact that an entire planet, full of powerful Dokami, declined their plea for help, destroyed every last ounce of hope he had left. That, more than anything, broke his heart.

"They refused to help us," Tre-akelomin said. "They stood by and allowed thousands of their own brothers and sisters to perish against the deadly weapons of the monstrous Dre-Ahd army. They stood by and let us *die*. I have vowed never to allow this to happen again. We have landed on Omordion, hoping for infinite peace. We will spread out among the people of Western Omordion, blend in with the general population, and obey their leaders. I am the last king of the Dokami clan. Only the Dokami Council will remain and a Wise Man will be appointed every fifty years to watch over our people and make sure our secret remains just that. A *secret*. The monarchy is dead. We will never speak their names again, those wretched Dokami on Jmugea. We will never seek their help as long as we live. As far as they know, we are dead! And this is the way it shall remain." Tre-akelomin pressed a button in front of him and the hologram blinked and then shut off.

Atakos Croit let out the breath he was holding. His heart was wrenching for the hundreds of thousands Dokamis who were murdered on Dokar. Hamilda Shing, their teacher at Lochenby boarding school, was wrong about a few things during her history lessons. "This is unbelievable," Atakos said, folding his arms across his chest. After everything they had been through, after everything they had witnessed, this new revelation was probably the most atrocious.

Over the past few weeks, Atakos and his four friends had been on a mission to rescue their kidnapped teacher, Hamilda. Their journey had led them to discover secrets of Omordion—much bigger and more deadly than the Dokami's own secret existence. They were shocked to learn of the magical creatures who resided on Omordion, long before the Dokami and the humans migrated there. From what they discovered, fairies resided in the forest near Lochenby, the last of their kind on Omordion. Queen Lhainna, ruler of the Sheidem Forest fairies, told them of *ceanaves*, magical creatures of the sea, *flitnies*, small magical beings who lived on land, and *chlysems*, big, colorful birds who aided the flitnies by getting them from one place to another. She explained how the ceanaves left the protection of her forest long ago, how the flitnies died out due to their sadness, and how the chlysems mysteriously disappeared.

The inhabitants of Omordion did not know of the Dokami or of the magical creatures. They only knew of a threat from the East, led by King Tholenod, to take over the entire planet. Secretly, the Western Army recruited five Dokami children ten years prior, to be taught by Hamilda to deal with the menace. According to Lhainna, the Western Army, led by General Komuh, were out to use their powers to take over the world as well. The corrupt General Komuh and his soldiers followed the teens to the Suthack Desert and tried to take them prisoner. Their hope of escaping him appeared slim, until a mythical chlysem came out of nowhere, reigning fire on the unsuspecting soldiers. It disappeared as fast as it came, allowing the teens to continue their journey to find Hamilda in peace.

All they had experienced along their journey did little to prepare them for the shock they experienced once they reached their destination. Hamilda herself was the one who lured them to the Ardomion Caves on Paimonu Island. She was never kidnapped in the first place, but had every intention to kill them when they finally found her. After an arduous battle, Hamilda was overcome by Cristaden Feriau, who helped heal her from the demons that plagued her.

With a newly discovered gift, Cristaden brought Hamilda into the past, reliving all of the happy moments of her life. She even took her to the spirit realm, where she was reunited with her lost loved ones. There, Hamilda discovered she was carrying the child of her late husband, Jogesh Shing. While aiding Hamilda, Cristaden discovered a personal secret of her own. Her real father, Kheiron, who was of Dokami blood, was romantically involved with Queen Lhainna for many years. Together they had twin girls. Cristaden, who's true, birth name was Kira, and her sister Keirak, who inherited all things fairy, unlike her more human-like twin. In an attempt to save Kira's life, Kheiron was killed by deadly creatures—minions of an evil man named Brulok—and Kira was adopted by Kheiron's sister and brother-in-law. They were the ones who gave Cristaden her name and she became the only known Dokami-fairy half-breed, making her a much sought after target by Brulok's minions throughout the teen's journey to find Hamilda.

After a disheartened Hamilda ran away, the five teenagers were attempting to find a way out of the caves when they stumbled upon an entrance to the same spaceship, which carried the Shaergans to Jmugea, the Dokami to Dokar, and the Dokami to Omordion. They entered the 'Memory Room', which held holograms of their ancestors' previous life on Dokar. They explored the development of the system of restraint for all Dokamis and the election of the first Wise Man. Atakos pressed a black button, heavily sealed over with tape, and Tre-akelomin Gre-ashyu appeared on a hologram to address the reality of what happened all those years ago. He revealed the biggest secret of all.

An entire planet full of Dokami.

For all they knew, the Dokami on Jmugea still existed to this day. With *no* restraints.

"Can you imagine?" Zadeia Emyu said. In a nervous gesture, she brushed the short tuft of black hair off her forehead and ran her hand down the longer strands clinging to her face in the heat of the cave. Her brown eyes were wet, as if on the verge of tears, and her hands were shaking.

"An entire planet full of Dokami," Zadeia's twin brother, Zimi Emyu said. He was almost an exact replica of his twin sister, Zadeia, down to his tan complexion and black hair. The only difference was his hair, which was steadily growing out of the military-styled haircut he was forced to receive whenever they returned to Udnaruk for the summer, while Zadeia was always permitted to grow her hair long.

"And they allowed their own people to die," Fajha Bayaht said. "This is *insane*." He pushed his glasses back up his nose and adjusted the frame in front of his almond shaped, brown eyes. With shaky hands, much like Zadeia's, he pushed his shoulder length, straight black hair away from his face and wiped at the sweat building on his forehead. He looked sick. His usual cream-colored complexion turned a shade of green and it looked like he was about to vomit all over the Memory Room floor. After everything they had been through, this was not what he wanted to hear.

"Cristaden?" Atakos said. "What's wrong?"

Everyone turned to look at Cristaden, who was standing completely still and staring blankly at seemingly nothing at all. Her pale blue eyes appeared lifeless. The way she stood there—perfectly still without moving—it was difficult to tell if she was even breathing.

"Cristaden," Zadeia said.

No response.

"What?" Zimi said, frowning. "Cristaden. Are you okay?"

Cristaden neither moved, spoke, nor appeared to draw in a single *breath*.

Atakos, fearing something terrible was happening to his friend, reached out and touched her, placing a steady hand on her shoulder.

As if awaken by Atakos' touch, Cristaden started shaking violently, her long, white-blonde hair thrashing about as she tried to draw in one shallow breath after another. It seemed like she could not get air into her lungs as hard as she tried. Her naturally pale complexion became even paler, right before the eyes of her terrified friends.

Fajha and Atakos simultaneously grabbed Cristaden, attempting to stop her from convulsing, but she began fighting both her friends, punching and kicking them. Atakos' heart wrenched, seeing Cristaden so completely removed from reality. He was in shock, unable to speak. Like Atakos, Zadeia was too shocked to say anything. Her hand was over her mouth and tears were filling her eyes once again. *This is too much*, she thought. *How can this day get any worse?*

"No!" Cristaden suddenly shouted. "We have to fight! We have to fight to save them! They are all *doomed*. Noooo…"

"Cristaden!" Fajha said. "Calm down, it's us! Your friends!"

"Cristaden, wake up!" Zimi said.

Cristaden continued to scream and fight as if she was fighting for her life, forcing Fajha and Atakos to release her and reluctantly take a step back. Abruptly, just as fast as her violent episode began, she stopped thrashing about. Her unfocused eyes seemed to recognize where she was as she slowly sunk to the ground and started sobbing uncontrollably.

Atakos bent down and grabbed Cristaden's hands. She looked up at him with tears in her red, stricken eyes. "It was awful, Atakos," she said. "Just *awful*."

"Tell me what you saw," Atakos said.

Between sniffles and deep, shallow breaths, Cristaden managed to get out several sentences. She was unable to stop crying. "I–I was there. I saw everything. I was there, in the outskirts of Enshatmu City when Soli was born. I was there when they got married. Soli and Rueslon. I felt Rueslon's pain. I experienced the birth of their daughter. Meela. Princess Meela. I witnessed the death of…oh…so much *death*."

"How were you able to see all of that?" Zimi said.

Cristaden took some deep breaths in and let them out slowly before continuing. "I don't know. It's like–what happened with Hamilda. Except this time, was different. Tre-akelomin–he started talking. This room–it disappeared. Everything was pitch-black. I tried to call out–but my voice was stuck in my throat. My body felt frozen–frozen solid. Only my eyes could move. Then I was transported through time and space. I saw the destruction on Shaerga," she cringed when she said it, "I followed a man–his name was Omerik–to Jmugea…" Cristaden recollected every detail of her experience to her bewildered friends. When she finished, they seemed more confused than ever.

"You saw everything Tre-akelomin described," Atakos said. "And you saw things he didn't even mention."

Cristaden looked up at him. "What sort of things?"

"For one, he never mentioned that Soli and Rueslon had a daughter named Meela. Drae and Reyshi? Nariele? The names of Soli and Rueslon's mothers? All the other ones you mentioned? He never talked about any of them."

"He never said how Soli was killed," Fajha said. "Hamilda told us a girl was killed for knowing too much, but we never knew what the girl knew."

"And also," Zimi said, "according to Tre-akelomin, Rueslon was on the spaceship when the Dokami clan left Jmugea. Technically, he should have died on Dokar."

"Right," Zadeia said. "He said all of the ones living on the reservation left Jmugea together."

Still a little shaky, Cristaden steadily rose to her feet. It was starting to make sense. She was transported back in time and was shown only specific images. The most important ones, she assumed. However, one thing did not make much sense to her. "I wonder what happened to Rueslon? He must have taken down the entire Jmugean Empire. That would explain the sudden collapse of their government."

"He was killed," Zimi said, shrugging his shoulders. "I mean one man...against an entire empire? Dokami or not, that seems impossible."

"Why was I not shown what happened to him? I would think it would be important for us to know."

Atakos placed his hand on his chin to think. It did not make any sense to him either. "Maybe—" Sounds coming from the tunnel outside the opened Memory Room door interrupted his thoughts. It wasn't hard to determine what it was.

Footsteps.

The five teenagers held their breath. Who could it possibly be? Hamilda was long gone, having fled the island moments after her recovery, and the inhabitants of Paimonu could care less about them or the caves. Maybe General Komuh found a way to the island after all. On the other hand, perhaps an animal, which made the caves its home, was coming to defend its territory.

Nevertheless, the five teens braced themselves, gearing up to fight, even though they were still exhausted from the battle they fought against Evil Hamilda.

Nothing could have prepared them for the shocking blow they received when a figure stepped through the doorway and into the room.

It was the last person they had ever expected to see.

CHAPTER 10

Zadeia's jaw dropped.

Colnaha.

The reddish-brown haired teenager they met in a hidden village in Osmatu. The one Zadeia had unintentionally fallen in love with because of his charming demeanor. Colnaha spied on them when they were there, figured out they were of Dokami origin, and admitted that he, too, was of Dokami blood. He was the only one who could have given away their position to General Komuh when he found them in the Suthack Desert. They were *sure* of it.

Atakos lost his nerve. Colnaha deserved to feel *pain* for what he did.

"Atakos, no!" Cristaden said, picking up on what he intended to do with her mind.

It was too late.

Colnaha's body violently jerked up into the air. With a scream, he was thrown back. His body slammed into a young man who had stepped into the room behind him. They hadn't even notice him before. The man looked to be in his early twenties and had wavy, black hair and dark, blue eyes. After catching Colnaha in mid-air, he glared back at the five teenagers with eyes full of rage.

Prince Aillios' temper flared when Colnaha was thrown against him. He did not know what to expect from the five teenagers he was sent to warn. Brulok, an old wizard, demanded his father, the tyrannical King Tholenod, to go to Paimonu and eliminate the teens. If the old wizard was as powerful as Menyilh, Tholenod's assistant, said he was, he must view the five teenagers as a serious threat. *They must be dangerously powerful*, Aillios thought, *or have the potential to be.*

After setting Colnaha back on his feet, Aillios placed his hand on the hilt of his sword, looking back and forth at the five teenagers inside the strange room. They were dirty and wearing mostly green cloaks—the blonde girl was wearing a white one—and the same uniforms, a white shirt with an emblem on the right breast pocket, and black pants with green lining. Although they were dressed the same, it was obvious they were from different countries, except for the two who seemed like they could be brother and sister. How in the world did they get together and end up on Paimonu, an island in the middle of nowhere?

The teens were staring back at Aillios now, looking as though they needed some quick answers before launching an all-out attack on him as well. One of the girls, the one with dark hair, addressed Colnaha with hatred in her eyes. "How could you do this?" she said. "You betrayed us. We thought you were our *friend*."

"And who is *this*?" her brother said, pointing at Aillios.

Colnaha put his hands up in defense. "Let me explain," he said.

The boy with the caramel complexion and hazel eyes sneered at him. "You have *one* minute," he said.

Colnaha touched Aillios' hand. "Relax, my friend. They have every reason to despise me. I cannot blame them."

Aillios released the hilt of his sword and slowly lowered his hand. He gave Colnaha a sideways look and wondered if he should be attacking *him* instead of the others. The way Colnaha described their friendship, Aillios would have never expected them to be so upset at him, almost, it seemed, ready to kill him.

Colnaha cleared his throat, appearing distraught before he began his explanation. "I did not intend for this to happen—," he started.

"We want the truth," the boy with the hazel eyes said. "No more lies."

The girl with the blonde hair turned to her friend. "Atakos, let's just hear what he has to say," she said.

Prince Aillios was curious as well and turned to glare at Colnaha. *What did he do?* he wondered. *He seemed genuine enough. What makes them hate him so much?*

"Like I said, it was not my intention," Colnaha said and sighed. "My father. Maldaha. He would not listen. I told him not to do it, but he refused to listen to me."

"Now you're going to blame this on your father," Atakos said.

"No—I mean—yes. My father asked me to spy on you. When I found out you were of Dokami blood, I told him what he wanted to know. I had *no idea* what he was planning to do. I only did what I was told. He was the one who contacted General Komuh and told him where to find you. I tried to stop him! In the end, it was my fault. I should not have told him the truth he was seeking."

"So," Atakos said, "knowing how much he hated the Dokami Council, how much he yearned to get back at them, how could you expect us to believe you didn't know what you were doing when you told him about us?"

"No, I did not know it then. I told him what I saw in the mountains before we spoke at the festival. I did not know you had ties with the Dokami Council. I was concerned you were exercising your powers too close to our village. The Council would have been alerted to your position and sent people to look for you. Therefore, they would have found *us*. When I discovered the truth, when I earned your trust, I realized what my father was doing. I tried to stop him—"

"You never had our *trust*. And now you've brought someone with you to finish us off?"

Prince Aillios took a step forward and stopped when the teens simultaneously took a step back. "On the contrary, I am not here to kill you," he said. "I only just met Colnaha a short while ago. I have been sent here to give you a warning. My father and his soldiers are on their way here to kill you."

The blonde girl stepped forward. "Your father?" she asked. Her eyes were searching his, desperate to find answers. She took another step towards him and her mouth opened in shock.

"Cristaden," Atakos said. "What is it?"

"I know what's going on here," Colnaha said. "Aillios, Cristaden is reading your mind. Whatever you're thinking, she can pick up on it."

"Reading my...?" Prince Aillios started to say, but then understood. She was displaying a Dokami ability to read minds. He wondered then what she was seeing.

"The devastation," Cristaden said, as if answering his thoughts. Tears escaped her eyes, ran down her cheeks, and onto her white cloak. "You saw it all happen. You couldn't stop it. Your father is evil. He is the epitome of *all* evil."

Prince Aillios sighed and allowed his shoulders to drop in defeat. "Yes, he is," he said. Looking at each of the teens standing across from him, he did not know how he was going to explain himself after the rest of them found out who his father was. They already had immense distrust in regards to Colnaha. Aillios cleared his throat, knowing it would be better if he explained himself, rather than wait until Cristaden or Colnaha did it for him. "My father is King Tholenod," he said and waited until the startled gasps and exclamations subsided before continuing. He could not ignore the fear in their eyes. Cristaden stared back at him, patiently waiting for him to continue. He knew, by now, she would have figured out his character and not see him as a threat anymore. He would not blame her, though, if she still did.

"Our monarchy was dying," Prince Aillios said. "At least that's what my father told me. He said we had little resources and the common folk only wished to benefit themselves. He vowed to get everything back to the way things were before his father, my grandfather, destroyed the monarchy by allowing the commoners to live freely. Since I was young, he trained me to be the best fighter in Mituwa. I surpassed even his expertise. I helped him halt many rebellions before they even got started. Before I turned eighteen, I had killed *many* innocent men. I am not proud of this. They were simply fighting for what they yearned for the most. Their freedom.

I can relate to Colnaha's story because I, too, could not grasp what my father was capable of doing, even though it was *right* in front of my eyes. I only needed to open them to see his true intentions. I could have stopped it. All of it. Unfortunately, my vision was clouded by the hate my father, the great king of Mituwa, felt for our commoners, the ones who killed my mother. In fact, I hated them, too." Aillios paused and balled his hands into fists. "Tholenod turned all of them into slaves, persecuting anyone who defied him. I have seen men, women, and children begging for their lives before his soldiers mercilessly cut them down. I have seen the dead, dragged around by the very chains holding the slaves together, for *days* before they were thrown into the marshes with hundreds of thousands of other bodies, left to rot without a proper burial. When my eyes opened, when I saw what was happening, I vowed to save them. My people. My father threatened to kill me if I did. I was no good to them dead, so I pretended to obey him, trying to come up with ways to help them without his knowledge. However, without an army, without the manpower to overthrow him, I could do nothing." Aillios sighed in frustration and waited for the teens to respond.

The boy with the black hair and glasses was the first to speak. "You said your father is on his way here. To kill us. How did he…?"

Prince Aillios nodded. "That is a good question. Several days ago, my father ventured out on a quest. I followed him and joined his soldiers in disguise. We traveled for miles to the northern country of Effit to—and I am sure you are not going to believe this when I tell you—to visit an old wizard who lives in a mountain, in the middle of a dead forest." He watched as a few pairs of eyebrows lifted and others came down in a frown. "This wizard told my father about you. All of you. He pointed to where this island was on an ancient map and told Tholenod you needed to be killed without hesitation. When he was finished with his request, he removed my disguise. Just by looking at me. My death was ordered by my own *father*." Aillios shuddered. It still hurt him to think about it. "I fought for my life and managed to get away. When I was free of them, a curious thing happened. You will not believe this—I am sure you won't—but a fairy came to me."

Cristaden's eyes were wide. "Kapimia," she said, reading her name from his mind.

"What?" her friends said in unison. They looked back and forth between Aillios and Cristaden. Kapimia was Queen Lhainna's eldest daughter, who lived within her mother's protected forest on Sheidem Island. How was she able to get all the way to the eastern country of *Effit*?

"You *know* her?" Prince Aillios said in astonishment.

"She is my…sister," Cristaden said before correcting herself. "My half-sister."

"Your—"

"Please continue. What did Kapimia say?"

Frowning, Aillios thought for a moment about what Cristaden said. About a fairy being her half-sister. He supposed, if it was true, his company would have no difficulty believing anything he said. Shaking his head, he decided to continue. He had much to learn about them—and

Omordion. "Kapimia brought me here, along with my horse, Thashmar. She said she was under some kind of...magical cloak. So the old wizard would not sense her and send his monsters to kill her. What did she say the old wizard's name was?" Aillios thought for a moment and found his answer. "Oh, yes. It was—"

Cristaden's mouth opened again in shocked disbelief. "Brulok."

CHAPTER 11

Zimi, Zadeia, Atakos, and Fajha were just as stunned as Cristaden was. It could not be possible. Prince Aillios actually *met* Brulok? The same monster, who instructed his minions to kill all the magical creatures of Omordion? The same monster, who sent them to kill Cristaden?

Prince Aillios confirmed it to be true. "Yes. It was Brulok. How do you know him? Kapimia seemed frightened when I mentioned him, but she would not tell me why. She only said we had to hurry."

Fajha stepped forward. He took a moment to introduce himself and his friends to the wayward prince. Aillios acknowledged each teenager and folded his arms, waiting patiently for Fajha to answer his question.

"Kapimia and Cristaden's mother, the fairy queen, Lhainna, told us about him. She said that five hundred years ago, Brulok came to Omordion and nearly destroyed every population of magical creatures living on this planet using fierce creatures to assist him. He hated them all and wanted to see them suffer before he killed them. When he grew tired, Brulok left his minions in hiding all around Omordion, waiting for the magical creatures to come out of their hiding places to attack them. His goal is to kill all of them."

"Magical creatures?" Prince Aillios said. "All the tales…they are true? The old wizard–Brulok–has *minions*?"

"Yes," Atakos said. "There may be thousands of them around the world. These beasts are incredibly strong. The humans do not know they exist. They only have revealed themselves to magical creatures as far as we know."

"But you are magical. Have you seen these beasts?"

Zimi laughed. "We are not magical creatures. You might as well call us aliens if it would better describe us. Our ancestors came from a different planet three hundred years ago. But, don't get me wrong, we have fought Brulok's minions. We were attacked a few times before we discovered Cristaden was half-fairy and they were really after *her*." He continued on to describe the oblots and the desert karsas that tried to kill them during their journey.

"This is all extraordinary," Prince Aillios said. "I cannot believe you all exist. Including the magical creatures of Omordion. Right under our noses this whole time. It's unbelievable what the rest of the world doesn't know and probably will never know."

"Yes," Zadeia said. "This world holds many secrets."

During the exchange between Prince Aillios and the five teens, Colnaha kept quiet. He was devastated the only people he called friends considered him a fraud. How could he convince them otherwise? He kept attempting to make eye contact with Cristaden, so she would know how he was feeling, but she was too caught up with what Prince Aillios and the others were saying. Even Zadeia, the one who seemed the friendliest to him before, would not even look at him. He tried desperately to think of something to say. Something to get them back on his side.

Colnaha cleared his throat.

Everyone stopped talking and looked at him.

Just stared at him as if they had forgotten he was there.

Colnaha felt shy all of a sudden. He was almost positive his face had turned an embarrassing shade of bright red. He definitely had everyone's attention now. "Well–since–Brulok is–on his way here–perhaps we should–leave, you know? I have an airship–on the volcano. Just up the road…"

No response.

Atakos blinked. It was as if he was trying hard to understand why Colnaha was talking. At least, that was how Colnaha interpreted the look. Nonetheless, he looked down, embarrassed he even opened his mouth in the first place.

"You have an airship?" Cristaden said.

When Colnaha looked back up, she was smiling at him.

"Best news I've heard all day," Fajha said, much to Colnaha's astonishment. "Otherwise, we would be stuck here for a long time."

"Yes," Prince Aillios said. "The sooner we get out of here, the better."

"He's right," Zimi said.

Colnaha felt instant relief. He still did not make eye contact with Atakos, knowing it was probably not a face he wanted to see. Zadeia quickly looked away when he made eye contact with her. He sighed. Slow steps. He would gain back her confidence in him even if he died trying. Colnaha yearned so much to see her pretty smile again.

"Before we go," Cristaden said, looking back and forth between Prince Aillios and Colnaha. "I think there is something you both should know. This information might be useful if we're going to take down King Tholenod and, hopefully, Brulok." In detail, she described what she witnessed when she was taken back in time to when the Dokami on Jmugea history began. The two listened intently to her story. When she finished, they were just as surprised as her friends had been.

An entire planet full of Dokami. Without restraints.

Colnaha was wide-eyed, unable to form words. It was shocking. Unimaginable. Wouldn't his father be surprised to learn this little secret? He would be so *enraged*. Colnaha found himself a little amused thinking about what his father's reaction would be when he found out the Dokamis living on Omordion were not alone in the universe. That there were beings more powerful than them out there. Much more powerful.

Prince Aillios frowned. He walked over to the black button and grazed his fingers over it. He decided not to press it though, allowing his hand to linger there. It just did not make any sense to him. Why here? Why now? So many questions flooded his mind. He thought about their stories, how they all ended up in the caves. Together. "This is fate," he said.

"What is?" Atakos said.

"Why we have all been brought here. To this place."

"What do you mean?"

Prince Aillios tried to put together his jumbled thoughts. So much had happened to all of them in the past month. A possessed teacher. An old, powerful wizard. A malicious king who ordered the deaths of many, including his own son. *Fairies...* It was all for this. *This* place. "We need their help."

Cristaden knew what he was suggesting. The thought of it brought her back to the moment when she personally witnessed the deaths of so many on Dokar because the Dokamis on Jmugea refused to come to their aid. "No," she said. "We can't *possibly* ask for their help."

"Never," Atakos said in a practical growl. "Not them. Our ancestors vowed to never seek their help ever again. We are obliged to follow their lead."

"Why should you?" Prince Aillios said, pounding his fist on the panel next to him, startling everyone in the room. "That was over *three hundred years ago*. Times have changed here and times have most likely changed there. I am telling you, we are all here for a *reason*. I am sure *this is it*."

The five teens thought about Aillios' suggestion for a moment. What he said did make sense. Paimonu, in connection to the Dokami clan, was a place Hamilda did not know much about. It was a place she never mentioned during her history lessons. For Evil Hamilda to lure them to the first island ever inhabited by the Dokami clan—and to those very caves—was beyond all reasoning. Aillios, the son of the malevolent King Tholenod, was brought to Paimonu to find them by Kapimia, a fairy who seemed to be stuck to a certain area of Sheidem Forest for centuries, but managed to find her way all the way to Effit without being attacked by Brulok's minions. If Aillios had not been against his father, he would not have left Mituwa to follow him, would not be in the caves in which they stood, and would not be able to warn them about Brulok.

"It has to be fate," Fajha said.

Atakos turned to look at Colnaha. "Then why is *he* here?"

Colnaha was already ahead of him. "I think I can answer your question," he said. "The airship. My father showed me how to operate everything on it. He showed me how to use the airship's communicator. Our ship is an old model and is one of the few remaining ships that still have one."

"What…kind of communicator?" Prince Aillios said.

"It's a device, which indicates all the key points of our solar system. You only have to pinpoint which planet you would like to contact and the communicator would then send a signal to their highest radio tower, which is usually the one their king or leader uses. A distress signal. Once the signal is received, they can choose to respond. They can also track the communicator wherever it goes. They can find us. Engineers stopped placing them on airships long ago, because the need to contact other planets became unnecessary."

Fajha's mouth dropped.

Atakos was dumbfounded. He had studied a similar type of communicator in his technology class back at Lochenby, but he never knew there were any others left out there that worked.

"It can be taken off the ship?" Zimi said.

"Yes. The difficult thing is it is not like a two-way radio. You have to send a signal to the planet in code. A code comes back to the communicator with their response. *If* we get a response."

"How do you know they received it if a response is not returned?" Zadeia said.

"My father said if you have the coordinates exact, the signal is received immediately once it is sent. If you do not receive a message within a few minutes, no message will be coming."

"Then it is settled," Prince Aillios said. He was beginning to lose his patience. Every moment they stood around, discussing their next move, could mean many more deaths on Omordion. If only the Dokami on Jmugea *could* help them. They could finally put an end to the war. "We all know why we have been brought together. Let us go to the airship and commence communication with the Dokami on Jmugea."

Atakos glanced at his friends. Cristaden appeared glum and Zadeia had fear in her eyes. Fajha and Zimi seemed worried. They kept shifting their weight from one foot to the other, appearing dreadfully uneasy. He knew what they were thinking. The Dokami on Jmugea had no restraint system like the secret clan of Dokami on Omordion. From the time the first Dokamis left Jmugea, the Jmugean Dokamis had been able to maximize their abilities from birth and for generations afterwards. They *had* to be exceptionally powerful. Three hundred times more powerful than even Hamilda herself. Contacting them was going against what the Dokami Wise Men taught them about restraint and secrecy. They would be revealing their existence to an entire planet. They were not even sure the Dokami on Jmugea were still there. By accident, they could make contact with beings far more dangerous. Perhaps the Dre-Ahds, if they still existed.

"We will not contact them," Atakos said finally. "At least not right now. We will seek the advice of the Dokami Council before we do anything irrational."

Prince Aillios sighed. He was trying to save his people and this was the only way he thought possible. This was why he was sent to Paimonu. Unfortunately, he knew the truth. It was their secret. It was not up to him to reveal it. He nodded and decided to take a step back. Although he was royalty, Aillios knew he was not their leader. It would be wrong of him to act as if he was.

"Okay," Colnaha said. "That seems reasonable." He always wanted to come face-to-face with the Dokami Council. See what they are all about.

Atakos looked to his friends for their approval and was not surprised when they agreed. They always seemed to look to him to make the decisions. It was as if he was their unofficial leader. "We must hurry," he said.

When the group of seven finally found an exit to the musty caves, they met the warm sunshine with welcoming arms. Dew still rested on the leaves from the freshly fallen rain, the sun had started a swift descent in the orange sky, and the air was moist and smelled of the beautiful, tropical forest surrounding them.

"I landed my ship on the road," Colnaha said, gesturing to the black volcano they were steadily approaching. "Near the homes of the people who live there." He chuckled as they made their way up the path to the village. "We might as well call them family. They are of Dokami blood, are they not?" He was trying to liven up the mood, but no one said anything. He glanced at Zadeia and caught her smiling at him. Her cheeks reddened before she quickly looked away. Colnaha smiled back even though she was no longer smiling at him. *Slow steps*, he thought.

After climbing up the side of the volcano to the road, the group of seven stopped and took in their surroundings. The inhabitants of Paimonu were in their colorful cement houses, most likely getting ready for dinner and sleep after a long day. There were puddles all along the ground, reflecting the descending sun's rays on the road, which was clear, except for Colnaha's airship and Aillios' horse, Thashmar. The horse whinnied and shook his head when they started walking towards him and the ship.

Cristaden could feel the decision to visit the Dokami Council was causing Atakos extreme doubt and worry. She tried to think of a way to help him feel better. Putting her arm around his shoulders, Cristaden offered him a warm smile. "Don't worry," she said. "I think you've made the right decision."

Atakos seemed startled when Cristaden put her arm around him. His reaction caused her to feel as if she had done something wrong. After a moment, he smiled back. "Thanks," he said.

Cristaden nodded with a shy grin. She could not understand why she was nervous. Offering support to her friend was a natural thing for her to do. Something she had always done over the years. Now, after everything they had been through, and the way she had begun to feel about him, she felt so awkward. Being this close to him was so foreign to her...so different.

In a move to break the uncomfortable moment between them, Cristaden decided to drop her arm, but was stunned when Atakos caught her hand on its way down. Much to her surprise, he slowly entwined his fingers with hers. She noticed that Atakos was trying hard not to look at her out of sheer nervousness, just like she was. *What was happening?* she thought. Did he feel the same way about her? Did he feel the way she was beginning to feel about him? Cristaden tried hard not to think about it. It was not possible. They were just friends.

Atakos' hand felt warm to the touch, though. Soothing. The warmth of his hand slowly began to climb up Cristaden's arm, as if he was expelling some kind of intoxicating energy through it. The exchange of energy made her knees weak. Confused, she looked down at her arm and was about to say something to him. That was when she felt an abrupt, unpleasant change in the air. Cristaden gasped loudly, released Atakos' hand, and looked around in fear. Her sudden outburst caused everyone to stop as well.

"What is it?" Zadeia said. She looked back and saw Cristaden looking around fearfully. Before she could ask Cristaden what she was feeling, she felt it too.

Something was terribly wrong.

The hair stood up on the back of Cristaden's neck. She slowly turned around to look out over the mountainside, at the tropical forest they had just come from. "Something's out there," she said, keeping her trembling voice as low as possible. "I think we're in *serious* trouble."

CHAPTER 12

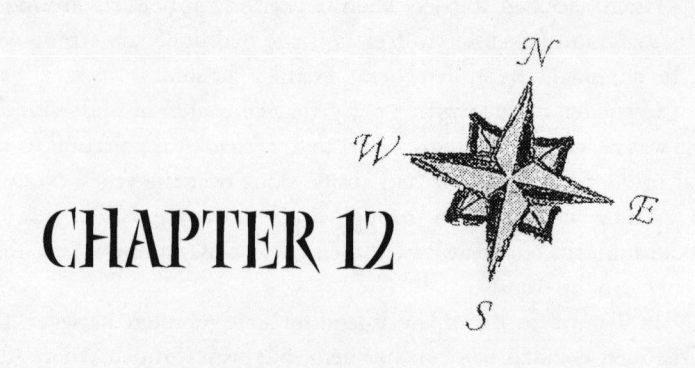

Cristaden wasn't the only one who felt like something was amiss. A few seconds later, the rest of them felt it too. Even Colnaha, whose extrasensory powers were minuscule compared to those of his fellow Dokami peers, felt the hairs on his arms stand on end. Prince Aillios was confused, but placed his hand on the hilt of his sword to prepare for anything.

"What do you think it could be?" Zadeia whispered.

"I'm not sure," Cristaden said, her voice barely audible as the wind rustled the leaves in the nearby trees. "Whatever it is, this is not a good time."

"Yeah," Atakos said. "I agree." After the fight they had with Evil Hamilda mere hours beforehand, the members of Omordion's Hope were exhausted and hungry. Getting into any sort of altercation at this point could be disastrous.

"I say we make a run for it," Zimi said, pointing up the road. "Colnaha's ship is *right* there."

"And leave whatever it is out there to attack the innocent people of Paimonu?"

"I'm pretty sure whatever it is, is after us, Atakos."

"We can't be so sure—" Atakos was interrupted by a shriek, resonating from the forest beyond the volcano. It was a steady sound, lasting a total of about five seconds, but growing with strength, sending chills down everyone's spine. When it abruptly ceased, it left a silence so deafening, the group of seven could almost hear their own hearts beating loud and hard against their chests. They had never heard such a sound before. It was *horrifying*.

"What was that?" Colnaha said under his breath, his chest heaving up and down. He was trying to keep himself from hyperventilating.

"I don't know," Fajha said. "But I have a good idea of what it might be."

"Prince Aillios did say Brulok would be coming here to destroy us," Atakos said.

"But how could he get here so fast?" Zadeia said.

"He can't," Cristaden said, "but his minions can."

Another sound erupted in the forest from a distance, but it wasn't a horrific shriek like before, it was more like a loud rustling sound. As the sound grew louder, they could see branches from some of the trees dipping and snapping back up, as if invisible forces were landing on them and jumping right off, coming closer and closer to the volcano.

"We should run," Colnaha said, backing up in absolute terror.

"Stand your ground," Atakos said. "It's too late to run. If we turn our backs on whatever it is now, we will die. We need to fight to survive."

"And the people of Paimonu need us," Zadeia said, turning to look at Colnaha. "We *cannot* abandon them."

"I am no fighter," Colnaha said through his teeth. Without hesitation, he turned to run up the road, towards his ship, intent on abandoning everyone if they didn't come with him. But froze in mid-step. Quivering like a leaf, he slowly turned around with fear in his eyes.

The five other teens turned just as Colnaha did to stare at the edge of the volcano. Prince Aillios could only respond to their reaction, gripping tighter to the hilt of his sword as he turned around as well.

At first, they did not see anything. Then suddenly, a hand reached up and grabbed the edge of the cliff. This was no human hand. The fingers were long and scaly, covered in some sort of slimy wetness, as if it had just come out of the filthiest swamp. The group of seven horrifyingly watched as another hand came up and grabbed the edge. A face then appeared when the creature slowly pulled itself up onto the road.

"Oh!" Zadeia gasped.

Everyone else stood frozen, staring in absolute terror.

Covered from head to toe in green-brown scales, the creature had long arms and legs, similar to a human being, but much longer, disproportionate to the rest of its body. Its head was the most frightening of all. Scales covered it completely and its mouth was opened in a sneer, baring frightening rows of sharp looking teeth, while its eyes stared back at them, red and lifeless, as if it had been dead a long time. The creature crawled forward on its knuckles and the balls of its feet, baring its teeth and growling at them as an animal would do when it wants to protect its territory from other creatures.

"What—" Prince Aillios said as he drew his sword. He was interrupted by a loud whimper from Colnaha who was still contemplating running but was frozen in fear.

"This is nothing like the monsters we've seen," Fajha said, recalling their run-ins with the oblots and the desert karsas' in the Suthack Desert. They seemed like they could have been some sort of animal. *This* creature was too human for comfort.

A shriek erupted from the creature, similar to the one they had heard in the forest, forcing everyone to take a step back in surprise. Almost immediately, more creatures pulled themselves up over the side of the volcano. Some had the same features as the first one, while others had a hint of red or black within their scales, giving an entirely different, nightmarish look to them. A few of them actually stood up to clumsily shuffle towards the frightened group, as if it was their first time walking on two legs. Their overextended, long arms dangled at their sides and the teens and Aillios were astonished to see sharp, black claws growing out of the ends of their fingers as they walked, until they were about two or three inches long.

"Oh my…" Cristaden said. She and her friends were slowly backing up as the creatures advanced closer and closer to them.

Prince Aillios was stunned. When the teenagers described Brulok's minions, he never imagined they would be even close to what he was witnessing. He still did not want to believe this unknown side of Omordion truly existed. Yet there he was, witnessing it firsthand. Even though Aillios had won battles in his lifetime, nothing could have prepared him for what he was seeing. It was something out of a nightmare he wished he could wake up from.

"Steady," Atakos said. Right now, they had no strategy to kill the creatures. He needed to think this one through, considering how worn out they were. Nevertheless, time was not on their side as the creatures closed in on them. Any moment now, they would attack. Atakos said the first thing that came to mind. "We're going to have to start with the crawlers. Seems like the walkers have a much harder time moving around."

Everyone nodded in agreement and prepared themselves to fight. Before they could launch an all-out attack though, the strangest thing happened.

The ghastly, human-like creatures stopped moving.

Just froze.

Their contorted faces were twisted, but not moving.

Their dead eyes staring, but not blinking.

Even the wind seemed to have stopped blowing.

Everything around them became dead silent.

The five teens looked at each other for answers, but could not find any. They turned to Colnaha, who was standing there, trembling, with fear in his eyes. He shook his head. He was not responsible for what was happening. They regarded the prince and noticed, in utter shocked disbelief, he stood frozen too.

"Cristaden," Zimi said. "Do you know what's happening here?"

Cristaden shook her head. "I can't even get a read on the prince's mind. It's as if it is frozen too."

"Do you think Brulok has something to do with this?" Zadeia said.

"I'm not sure."

Crack.

All six teens turned to the sound of a twig snapping nearby.

And their eyes opened wide with surprise.

A boy, about the age of ten, had climbed up the path from the tropical forest and onto the road. He had wet, dark-brown hair and wore only a pair of brown shorts with brown sandals. He must have been caught in the rain, which hit the island recently, most likely because of Zadeia's sadness in the caves. His chest was heaving up and down, his bottom lip was trembling, and tears fell from his eyes. Before the teens could stop him, he bolted towards the motionless creatures and weaved his way through them, all the while jumping in fear and giving small yelps whenever he looked up at their faces. When the boy finally ran past the creatures, he seemed to be even more bewildered that the startled teens were staring at him in shocked disbelief, so unlike everything else frozen around them. Without any further hesitation, he ran past them with full speed and did not stop until he reached a bright green, cement house, a few houses down the road. The boy fiercely pounded on the door and, when someone in the house opened it and grabbed his arm to drag him in, he gave one last look of troubled confusion at the befuddled teens before the door slammed shut and bolted right behind him.

Before the teens could say anything about the boy, Prince Aillios began to move again.

And so did everything else.

CHAPTER 13

With horrific shrieks sounding like metal scraping against metal, the hideous creatures simultaneously pitched forward, intent on ripping every single one of them apart.

A burst of energy surrounded the stunned group and powerfully fanned out, causing the closest creature to fly back, shrieking in the most vilest and stomach-turning way. The creature slammed into the ones coming up behind it, who shoved it aside with enraged shrieks and growls. Atakos had sped around his friends, using his powers to put some much-needed distance between them and their attackers, giving them the opportunity to launch a defense strategy.

While Colnaha stood in shock, eyes bulging in horror, the rest of the group got in front of him in a semicircle, facing the vicious creatures. It shamed Colnaha to think he was their weakest link, having had no experience in fighting whatsoever. Although he could not help, he felt comforted they were willing to protect him, despite how they felt about him, and despite the fact that he almost abandoned them.

Before the creatures could get close to them again, Prince Aillios was surprised to see Atakos, Cristaden, and Fajha throw their arms out, severely wounding three of them with their powers. He was shocked to see Zadeia form raging balls of fire in her hands, setting two of them on fire, and Zimi freeze two others, which had gotten too close for comfort.

Amazing, Prince Aillios thought, watching the teens in action. *Brulok has a right to fear them.*

The unharmed creatures climbed over the wounded ones and, with loud shrieks of anger, barreled towards the group all at once. Some of them were bleeding when they were hit with an unseen force. Others were frozen or set ablaze. Prince Aillios managed to plunge his sword into the heart of one attempting to jump on top of him. With a screech, the creature swiped at his shoulder, its long, razor-sharp claws tearing into his flesh. Aillios twisted his sword, plunging it deeper into the creature's chest and swiftly yanked it back out with an angry cry. The creature fell dead at his feet with dark, red blood oozing out of its gaping wound.

"Arg," Prince Aillios said, trying to ignore the ache in his shoulder. Without looking at his torn flesh, the excruciating pain was enough to tell him the bone was exposed. He could feel the blood dripping down his arm like a slow, steady river. He knew, without the proper care, he could rapidly bleed to death. Unfortunately, nursing a wound was not an option with so many creatures attacking them.

"Look out!" someone shouted.

Prince Aillios quickly looked around and saw another creature take one giant leap towards him. The angry determination in its eyes locked with Aillios' head, ready to bite it off with its jagged, razor-sharp teeth. Aillios tried his best to swing his sword at it but the creature reached out with its long arms and took it from him so easily, it briefly stunned him. The creature cast the sword aside, grabbed Aillios' neck with its other hand, and lifted him off the ground. It snarled at him, snapping its jaws in anticipation, threatening to devour him. Aillios kicked the creature as hard as he could, but it seemed like he was kicking solid rock. The creature was so strong, he felt at any moment it would crush the bones in his neck and end his life.

Unexpectedly, fire blasted in the creature's face, forcing it to release Aillios as it flailed its arms around, trying to put out the fire. By the time he landed on his feet, Atakos was in front of Prince Aillios with his arms raised. Instantly, the creature's head exploded into a few dozen chunks of flesh and bone. And, as if it were just a momentary glitch in his defense, in the blink of an eye, Atakos was on the other side of the semicircle and continuing his attack on some perplexed creatures.

Prince Aillios shook his head to clear it. He was not sure if it was the extreme loss of blood or if the determined teenager was exceptionally fast. A hand touched Aillios' wounded shoulder, waking him up from his temporary frozen state of disbelief. Pain shot through his arm like an electrical current. He wanted to scream, to tell the person touching his shoulder to stop. When he looked up to see who it was, Cristaden released her hold on his shoulder. Without a moment's hesitation, she sprinted back to her place within the semicircle and reigned terror on an irate creature who was about to attack Zadeia.

Confused, Prince Aillios lifted his arm.

No pain.

No deep wounds or exposed bones.

If it were not for his ripped tunic and the blood all over it–his own blood–Aillios would have thought he had never been hurt in the first place. Cristaden actually *healed* him.

"Incoming!" Zimi shouted.

Prince Aillios immediately lunged for his sword. He was not expecting the creatures to be as strong as they were. Now that he knew, he was ready to do his all to defeat them.

Creatures, more hideous and faster than the last bunch, climbed over the side of the volcano as the remaining few attacking them were killed. Six of those creatures leapt over the carnage of fallen beasts all at once with loud shrieks, stopping so close to the semicircle, the group barely had enough time to react.

Colnaha was scared. Being of Dokami decent, he was ashamed he could not defend himself like his fellow comrades. Sure he knew a few 'tricks', like making a light-weight object move without touching it, but his tricks were of no use to him there. Even Prince Aillios, the warrior son of the evil King Tholenod, almost lost his life. With the creatures as close as they were to their semicircle, he could be at risk if one were to bypass just one of his friends.

Growling fiercely, the creatures charged. Energy and wind pushed them high into the air, away from the group. While the five teenagers froze, burned, and hit them with powerful bursts of energy to blow them up in midair, several creatures on the ground, who had just climbed over the side of the mountain, barreled towards them with full speed.

"Push them back!" Atakos shouted.

A synchronized, powerful, burst of energy and wind pushed both sets of creatures high into the air, buying the teens a few more seconds to strategize. There were about fifteen of them in the air now, shrieking in anger, while more creatures stumbled forward to attack them on the ground.

"Fajha! Cristaden!" Atakos said. "Air!" He pointed to the creatures steadily falling from the sky. "The rest of us will take the ones on land. Do not lose focus! Do not let the ones in the air touch the ground!"

To Prince Aillios and Colnaha's amazement, Cristaden's white cloak and school uniform was replaced by a long, white dress, cinched around her small waist with a white rope. The dress reminded Prince Aillios of the dress Kapimia was wearing when she grew to human size. Beautiful white wings spread out behind Cristaden when the dress appeared and a faint glow radiated from her. She looked like an *angel*: so similar to Kapimia, but so unlike her at the same time, with the different type of wings she possessed. Cristaden soared into the air and Fajha surprisingly levitated off the ground to fight alongside her.

In the air, the creatures were being obliterated, while the ones on land were blown up, torched, frozen, and sliced or decapitated by Prince Aillios. A small hill of sour smelling carcasses steadily grew around the remaining semicircle of friends.

Cristaden and Fajha could see the entire tropical forest over the side of the volcano from their viewpoint. To their unfortunate surprise, there were so many more creatures, impatiently waiting for an opportunity to climb up the volcano and attack them, pushing and viciously gnawing at each other to get their chance.

"Oh, my…" Cristaden said under her breath. Fajha's eyes were wide as he observed the severity of their situation. In addition, Cristaden could feel the energy draining from her friends down below at a much faster rate than the approaching creatures. They would not last much longer.

"We have to get back down," Cristaden said to Fajha when the last creature in the air was killed. Before touching the ground, they were already helping their friends fight. "Listen," Cristaden said, as she critically wounded an approaching creature. "There's so many of them waiting to climb up. *Too* many. There doesn't seem to be an end to this fight, guys."

"You can't be serious!" Atakos shouted.

"It's true," Fajha said.

"What do we do?" Zadeia said, suddenly realizing her energy was draining from her and her fireballs were beginning to get smaller.

Like Zadeia, Atakos felt his reflexes slowing with each administered explosion. He was determined to regain some strength even though he knew it was next to impossible after their fight with Evil Hamilda. If one creature was allowed to penetrate their line of defense, a member of their group would be at risk of being seriously injured or killed instantly, beyond Cristaden's repair. It was something they did not want to consider. One slip up. That's all it would take. One of them could be lost forever.

"I don't know how long I can take this," Zadeia said. She was exhausted. As soon as she spoke though, she felt the last bit of her energy drain from her hands. Her once powerful fireballs had become flickers of flames in her open palms. Scarcely bigger than a candle's flame, the fires flickered and died. "What?!" Zadeia cried out. "No!" Unable to ignite another fire, she felt vulnerable and lost her concentration, completely forgetting her ability to manipulate wind.

The events that followed happened so fast, it took everyone by surprise.

"Zadeia!" Zimi screamed. The instant he realized what happened to his twin sister, he knew it was too late. He could not help her in time. A ferocious creature leapt over the small heap of burned carcasses and headed straight for her. Fear gripped his heart. Distracted, Zimi had ceased his defense strategy. One green and red creature ran towards him and, before Zimi could react, pushed him to the ground. Zimi flung his arms out in an attempt to freeze it. The creature was too strong for him and avoided his weak attack. It bit into one of his outstretched arms with its sharp teeth, cutting deep into his flesh. Zimi didn't even have a chance to scream because Zadeia's loud piercing scream freaked him out even more than the severe pain he was feeling. With a quick glance her way, Zimi saw someone position himself directly in front of Zadeia, right before she was attacked.

Colnaha.

Standing up on its long legs, the monster grabbed Colnaha's head, pushed him down on top of Zadeia, and tilted its distorted head to the side. After opening its mouth, it clamped its jaw down hard at the base of Colnaha's neck and shoulder, piercing it with its rows of sharp teeth, threatening to rip a part of his neck clean off. Colnaha fainted from the shock of being bitten and his eyes rolled back into his head. Zadeia was screaming hysterically, unable to do anything to help Colnaha because of her drained energy and the weight of his body on top of hers.

With the loss of the twin's help, the situation became much worse. More creatures climbed over the mountainside and crawled or staggered towards the group with greater speed. Growling and shrieking, they headed straight for the ones left standing. Two of them came at Atakos and, with his hands up, he hit the creatures repeatedly with his explosion power, but only managed to create deep gashes across their bodies. The bloodied creatures came closer, forcing him to push them back and try again to blow them up. He knew if he did not kill them quickly, whatever strength he had left would dissipate and he would be defenseless.

Cristaden and Fajha found themselves in the same predicament as Atakos with their failing strength. Unable to assist their fallen friends, they could only watch in horror as the creatures swiftly advanced towards them.

They were losing the fight.

Only one person among them still had a considerable amount of strength. After cutting down three creatures one by one, Prince Aillios plunged his sword through the head of the creature attacking Zimi, leapt over the teenager, while yanking his sword out of the creature's head, and killed another creature on his way to rescue Colnaha. With an angry war cry, he drove his sword into the back of the creature biting down on the teen's shoulder and watched as it released him with an angry screech. Aillios kicked it away after pulling his sword out of its back, killing it, and turned to assist Fajha and Cristaden by killing two creatures about to attack them. Atakos was struggling to keep two of the monsters from getting too close to him, so the prince leapt over a few dead carcasses to help him. After decapitating one, he turned to the other and drove his sword through its chest.

"Thanks," Atakos said, trying to catch his breath. He felt so *weak*. How could they go on? Some of them were critically injured. The ones left standing had almost no energy left.

They were done for.

Prince Aillios reached out and grabbed Atakos' arm. When Atakos looked up at him, he could see the fear in his eyes. "We need to go," he said. "*Now.*"

Atakos turned back to look at his friends and the creatures coming towards them and he saw what was frightening Prince Aillios—a man who had seemed unfazed by the battle with the nightmarish creatures. The steady stream of monsters climbing over the side of the mountain seemed to double, almost triple, in numbers. They were rushing to climb over, at times pushing each other out of the way to get ahead. This next wave of creatures seemed more determined than ever to put an end to the battle.

Fajha and Cristaden were trying to keep the creatures from attacking their injured friends. It was obvious to Atakos they were not aware of the deadly attack headed their way. Zimi was attempting to stand up, but the pain in his arm was preventing him from moving without screaming in pain. Colnaha's limp and bloodied body was still lying on top of Zadeia, who seemed to have no strength left to push him off. There were tears in her eyes and she appeared to be in complete shock.

"Help me get him off of her!" Atakos shouted. Prince Aillios put his sword in his belt and helped Atakos pick up Colnaha by his arms and feet as Zadeia rolled out from under him.

"Is he dead?" Zadeia asked. In her attempt to wipe the fallen tears from her eyes, she had inadvertently placed Colnaha's blood all over her face. When she felt the wetness on her face, she brought her shaking hand down to look at it.

And saw red.

So much *red*.

Zadeia lost the last shred of sanity she had left and started screaming.

Atakos looked up at the sky and noticed dark clouds rolling in. "Zadeia," he said. "You have to remain calm!" Zadeia didn't hear him and continued to scream, while looking at her bloodied hands. He glanced at his other friends and tried to show them the urgency of the situation with his eyes. Trying to keep his voice steady, he said, "We have to get to the ship."

"But—" Cristaden started to say, but was interrupted by Fajha. He was alerting her to the creatures who were about to attack them. Both of them pushed back a few of them simultaneously, giving themselves an opportunity to kill them. That was when they noticed the large wave of creatures headed their way.

"R-Run!" Fajha shouted. He ran to Zimi and grabbed his uninjured arm, pulling him to his feet.

Cristaden's breath caught in her throat as she grabbed a shocked Zadeia's hand and pulled her along as she ran. Atakos and Prince Aillios were trying to run with Colnaha's body and she could tell it was slowing them down. By the look of it, it did not seem like Colnaha was still alive, but she understood why they would risk taking his body. If there was a small possibility to heal him, they were taking that chance. Even if it meant they would be placing themselves in even greater danger than they were already in.

The creatures were getting close as the exhausted group of six ran towards the ship with Colnaha in tow. To get on the ship before the creatures reached them was not something they had thought through. Firstly, they did not even know if the door was locked or if there was a special way to open it. The only person who knew the fastest way to get on board was unconscious and possibly dead. Secondly, what exactly would they do when they got on the ship? If they could not take off with it easily, it would be a death trap for them. Clearly, the number of creatures behind them would overtake the airship in an instant and find a way to get inside, even if they could get the door opened and locked before they reached them. Things did not look promising for them *at all*.

"My horse," Prince Aillios suddenly said as a rumble of thunder rolled in the distance. He was struggling to hold on to Colnaha's arms as he ran and almost dropped him when he remembered Thashmar, whom he had left tied to a tree before descending to the caves. The horse was not where he left him. In fact, he was nowhere to be seen. *He must have broken free and ran away when the attack began*, Aillios thought. Thashmar had become his only friend during his journey. He felt an attachment to him and was sure no one would understand his need to make sure he was okay.

"He'll be fine!" Cristaden said, sensing his fear. As long as the horse was far away from them, he was better off than they were. "We need to get on the ship!" She was not sure everyone realized just how close the creatures were. The screeching sounds they made when they bumped into each other was horrendous. Some were growling fiercely. Others whimpered when they were shoved aside or stomped on if they were moving too slow.

When the group reached the airship, Fajha pulled on the door handle.

Nothing happened.

He yanked it again.

The airship door was locked.

CHAPTER 14

"No!" Fajha shouted and then banged his fists on the airship door. He turned to his friends with fear in his eyes. They did not have enough time to figure out how to unlock the door. In a few short moments, the nightmarish creatures pursuing them would be upon them.

Atakos and Prince Aillios placed Colnaha gently on the ground. The prince yanked out his sword again and prepared to fight, while Atakos, Cristaden, and Fajha, summoned up any remaining energy they had left to fight as well.

Zimi reached out and put his good arm around his sister, who had stopped screaming. She seemed to be in absolute shock and trying hard not to look down at Colnaha. He didn't think she realized the degree of what was happening. The creatures outnumbered them at least fifteen to one. The odds of winning this fight were definitely not in their favor.

"Love you, sis," Zimi whispered in Zadeia's ear. He wanted it to be the last thing she heard before they were ripped apart. Zadeia abruptly looked up at Zimi with reddened, tearstained eyes. Something about the way she looked at him reminded him of the times they would leave home after summer vacation to attend Lochenby. Zadeia would break out into crying fits over the thought of not seeing their parents for ten long months again.

Zimi knew instantly what would happen next.

The sudden downpour of rain came from the sky without warning. It hit the Sremati Volcano with such a powerful force; it was a struggle to remain standing. The creatures immediately stopped their relentless advance towards the teens and Prince Aillios. Those who stood up were knocked off their feet and thrown to the ground by the force of the storm. It was obvious they did not have an appreciation for heavy rainfall as they screeched and hollered, trying hard to cover their heads with their long, gangly arms.

As a lightning bolt lit up the darkened sky, Cristaden took the opportunity to reach out to Zimi and place her hand on his wounded arm. Under her touch, his wound came together and healed, leaving behind a glowing handprint for a few moments. Zimi gave Cristaden a quick smile and, after releasing Zadeia, brought his hands up to the sky. He had done this once before, in the Suthack Desert, when dozens of Valdeec birds attacked them. He knew exactly what he had to do.

Counting the seconds between lightning strikes, Zimi was able to grab a hold of one, freezing it in mid-strike. "Get down!" he shouted to his friends before he pulled the lightning bolt towards the crowd of creatures, cowering from the onslaught of rain. The lightning hit several of them, who flew back due to the sheer force of it, slamming into creatures behind them, electrocuting them as well. The transfer of electricity continued as the creatures made contact with each other. The remaining dozens of unaffected creatures saw what was happening, ran away, and quickly climbed back down the side of the mountain in sheer panic, trying hard to escape being electrocuted as well. There were others who, ignoring the rain, lashed out at the teens and Aillios, determined to kill them despite what was happening. Those creatures were blown up and frozen before they had a chance to get too close. It was not long before the masses of ravenous creatures were either dead or gone, leaving the road empty once again.

Breathing hard, Cristaden bent down to examine Colnaha. She felt awful that she could not concentrate on healing his wound beforehand. His skin was pale and he was not breathing as Cristaden thought he had been. It was evident he had lost a significant amount of blood.

Worst of all, she was pretty sure he was dead.

"No," Cristaden whispered.

Zadeia bent down next to her, sobbing with tears in her eyes. "I–I don't know," she said. "He may still be alive. He saved my life. Cris– please let him be alive, please…let him…" She choked on her words and tried to reach out to touch Colnaha, but her hands were shaking uncontrollably. She realized his chest was not moving up and down at all. "This can't be happening."

Cristaden did not even feel Colnaha's *presence*. She was certain he was too far gone. If so, she knew he could not be brought back. The lack of blood flow and oxygen to his brain made the situation even worse. It was not in her ability to raise the dead. Nevertheless, she would try her best. Glancing up at Zimi, Cristaden gestured with her eyes for him to move Zadeia out of the way. Zimi immediately grabbed his sister's shoulders to pull her away from Colnaha's body. Zadeia did not put up a struggle and allowed him to pull her back.

Cristaden placed her hands on Colnaha's neck and shoulder. For a moment, as she transferred her energy to her hands to bring the wound back together, she did not think it would work. When the wounds started to heal, a glimmer of hope surfaced. Was it possible to heal a wound of someone who had already passed away? Whatever the case, Cristaden was about to find out.

Before long, during the intensive healing process, Cristaden felt a slight blinking of Colnaha's presence. It was faint, but steadily gaining strength. "Colnaha, hang on!" she cried. Pulling from all, if any, of the remaining energy she had left, Cristaden put all she could into his wounds and watched as they closed up faster. She placed her hands on his head to repair the brain, if possible. Color steadily returned to Colnaha's face as blood flowed through his body once again. Instantly, a thought came to Cristaden's mind. Colnaha's thought. It was his fear of losing Zadeia.

Colnaha took one horrid sounding, deep breath in and then another, as if he had been holding his breath for far too long. When he opened his eyes and saw the airship in front of him, all of the events of the day came flooding back to him. "No," he said and sat up with fear in his eyes. The steady rain ceased and the sky began to clear just as fast as the storm had begun. Colnaha looked around at everyone and saw the face he was searching for. Zadeia. Smiling back at him. She was *okay*. The last thing he remembered was her being attacked by–Colnaha quickly glanced around. "Where are the...?" He could not believe what he was seeing.

Prince Aillios and the others glanced around them as well and paused. Not only were the creatures *completely* gone, but their dead carcasses were gone as well. As if the creatures had never been there in the first place.

"What the...?" Prince Aillios said, his eyes darting to and fro. "How could this be?"

"They were just here a second ag—" Fajha said, but was interrupted by a distant screech coming from over the side of the volcano.

"No way," Zimi said.

"They're still here," Atakos said.

"Colnaha," Cristaden said with a shaky voice. "We don't know how to get on board the ship."

Colnaha nodded and searched for a set of keys inside one of his pockets. "Here it is," he said, closing his hand around it.

"Great," Zadeia said. Turning back to look at Fajha, she gasped. The rest of them turned to see what had startled her.

One of the creatures was standing directly behind them.

It opened its mouth, revealing rows of sharp teeth, frightening even the strongest among them. Then it screamed. An incredibly loud, piercing scream. The terrified group took a couple of startled steps back and held their breath.

The sound coming out of the creature's mouth. It sounded like a *man's* voice.

Screaming.

To everyone's horror, the creature spoke.

"You think you have won," it said in a deep voice. "You can run. Wherever you go, I will find you. Now I know your strengths. Your *weaknesses*. I *will* kill you."

In the blink of an eye, the creature suddenly vanished, leaving the stunned group staring, with mouths opened, at nothing at all.

CHAPTER 15

"Get inside!" Atakos shouted.

"Quickly!" Fajha shouted.

Trying to catch their breaths, the bewildered teens boarded Colnaha's airship with great speed. They needed to leave. They needed to get as far away from Paimonu as possible.

"Where's Aillios?" Atakos asked. The prince had not boarded the airship with them and he was not outside.

"I believe he's out looking for his horse," Cristaden said.

"What?" Zimi said. "Is he crazy??"

"He'll find him. He's not far."

"What are we going to do?" Fajha said, bringing them back to their situation. He pushed his glasses up his nose with a shaky hand.

"I don't know," Atakos said.

"We have to think of something!"

"Don't you think we know that already?" Zimi said. He was just as frightened by what they witnessed as everyone else. What Prince Aillios told them was true. Brulok's minions were no longer just after magical creatures, they were targeting them directly. And Brulok was watching them fight through their eyes.

"How was that even possible?" Colnaha asked. "How could he speak through that thing? How could he see what was happening?"

"Brulok is a powerful man," Cristaden said. "Who knows what else he's capable of doing."

"We have to get out of here," Zadeia said. She appeared as if she was about to start hyperventilating. "*Where* is Aillios?"

"Wait," Atakos said. He was thinking hard about everything they had been through. How they had come too close to perishing during the fights with Brulok's minions way too many times. Brulok's last words also rang in his head. They needed help. Now more than ever. "I think Aillios had a point."

"About what?" Colnaha said.

Prince Aillios appeared at the doorway of the airship with his horse, Thashmar, in tow. His eyebrows were raised at the mention of his name. "What point?" he said.

"In the caves," Atakos said. "You said we should contact Jmugea as soon as possible. We need help. We *can't* wait to speak to the Dokami Council. They probably don't even know of the Dokami on Jmugea. For all we know, this knowledge was lost when our ancestors landed on Omordion and they never spoke of them again. When we tell the council what we learned, it might take them a long time to discuss what the next steps will be. They may even tell us not to contact them. We need help *now*." He glanced at everyone around him. They knew he spoke the truth. They had to act fast, sooner, rather than later.

"Why not?" Zimi said.

"Definitely," Fajha said. He shuddered at the thought of their recent attack and how close they had come to being shredded meat.

"Cristaden?" Atakos said. "Zadeia? What do you think? This has to be a unanimous decision."

Cristaden cleared her throat. "What if the Dokami on Jmugea *had* been wiped out? What if we send a signal to a dangerous enemy?"

"What if the Dokami on Jmugea *are* our biggest enemy?" Zadeia said.

Atakos considered what they were saying. It was something he himself had pointed out previously. "We don't know. That's the thing. We don't *know*. But we can't say we didn't *try*. Fate brought us all together. The West is losing. Brulok is only getting stronger and, with the help of the Eastern Army, he will be unstoppable. The Dokami Council was wrong. We can't save Omordion by ourselves."

Cristaden nodded. "I guess it's worth a shot," she said.

"Okay," Zadeia said, still looking worried.

"Great," Atakos said. "We all agree."

Colnaha nodded and removed a small, silver device from the airship's control panel. The device was rusty, as if it was very old—ancient even. Atakos had studied communicators before at school, but the one Colnaha pulled out was nothing like he had ever seen before. Just by looking at it, he was positive he would not know how to use it, even if he tried.

Before utilizing the device, Colnaha pulled a lever on the control panel, opening the back of the ship so Aillios could bring Thashmar inside. Turning around to face the others, Colnaha cradled the small device in his hands and switched it on. Blue light erupted from the screen on its surface and words flashed across it as it started up. The blue light faded, replaced by a black screen with tiny white dots displayed across it.

"This represents space and beyond," Colnaha said. "We just need to find the right coordinates and send a signal to Jmugea. It's a little tricky so this may take some time."

Atakos looked the old communicator over and sighed. "We don't have much time," he said.

Fajha patted Colnaha on the back. "Excuse me," he said. "I think I can help. I have taken a science class on the coordinates of our solar system. We studied all the positions of our planets. I can find it for you before you even take your next breath."

"Okay," Colnaha said with a shrug and handed the device to Fajha. "Go for it."

Fajha took the device, slid his index finger across it, and tapped the screen several times, punching in a series of numbers. One of the tiny white dots blinked a bright red. "There you go," he said, pushing his glasses back up his nose and handing the device back to Colnaha.

Surprised, Colnaha's eyes opened wide and his jaw dropped. "Wow. That's great. Now all we have to do is send a signal." He looked up at the five teens and Prince Aillios, who had Thashmar settled in and cozy at the back of the ship. "Are you sure you want to proceed? Once we do this, there is no turning back."

Atakos glanced at his friends. They seemed apprehensive but they nodded. "Yes," he said. "Do it."

"Okay." Colnaha pressed three different places on the screen and sent the signal, a series of taps and finger sliding the teens could not understand. The red blinking light representing Jmugea blinked twice, indicating the signal had been sent. "It's done."

"Just like that?" Fajha said, fascinated.

"Yes. I sent them one word. 'Help'. Now we wait."

The group became quiet and crowded around Colnaha. This was what they feared. The response—if any. They held their breath as they waited for any sign of life on Jmugea. Anything at all. Each second felt like hours as they waited. Their eyes never left the screen. Colnaha's hands were shaking so much, Zadeia had to place her hand over his to keep the device steady.

"How long should we wait?" Cristaden said.

"Up to five minutes," Colnaha said.

"Is that a rule? Do they have to give a response within five minutes?"

"If they are to give a response, it has to be given within the first five minutes or all communication could be lost. If they did not care for the connection, they will not respond."

"I hope you're right," Atakos said.

"How long has it been?" Fajha said.

"About two minutes," Cristaden said.

Zimi shifted his weight. "This has been the longest two minutes of my life."

"Shhh," Fajha said. "We don't want to miss the signal. We need to know what their response is going to be."

The group became quiet once again. The minutes ticked by slowly. *Too* slowly.

When four minutes had passed, the anticipation among the group increased. This was it. They would find out if a response would be given or not within seconds.

"Come on," Atakos said under his breath.

Nothing.

"I can't take this anymore," Zadeia said.

As if to respond to Zadeia's frustration, a sound erupted from the device.

Beep, beep-beep beeeep.

"Oh!" Zadeia shouted in surprise.

"What was that?" Fajha said.

"Their response," Colnaha said, his voice shaking.

"What did they say?"

Colnaha shook his head. "I'm pretty sure they sent the code for... 'who'?"

"Who?" Atakos said. "Are they asking who we are?"

"I don't know."

"What do we say?" Cristaden said. "Do we tell them who we are?"

"Isn't that why we contacted them?"

"Well, yes…but what do we say?"

"We tell them who we are," Atakos said. "One word. Dokami. They should know what it means. If they don't, we turn off the device and end the connection with them."

"Sounds like a good plan," Colnaha said. He tapped the screen and slid his index finger across it. Hesitantly, he looked around at the group of people standing around him before submitting their response. Apart from Prince Aillios, they all looked deathly afraid. Colnaha looked questioningly at Atakos, who nodded his head slowly. "Okay. Here goes nothing."

He submitted their response.

The five members of Omordion's Hope held their breath again.

And waited.

And waited some more.

Beeep beeep.

"What did they say?" all six said in unison.

Colnaha's shoulders fell. Bad news. "They said 'no'."

Silence.

Zadeia's eyes searched Colnaha's. "Are you sure they said no?" she asked.

"I am positive."

Atakos slammed his fist on the pilot's chair. "If they said no, it only means one thing. They know who we are and they do not want to help us."

"I am so sorry," Colnaha said.

"Well—let's keep hope alive," Cristaden said. "Sometimes a negative answer could turn into a positive one later on. Who knows?"

Prince Aillios sighed. "She's right. We might not have given them enough time to discuss it among themselves. I say we leave the communicator on and with us at all times in case they choose to reach out to us at a later time."

"I don't think so," Colnaha said. "Once a response is given, it is final."

"But what if *they* just found out we exist," Fajha said. "What if they are scared, just like we are? They may change their mind."

Atakos thought about it. He put himself in the position of the Jmugean Dokami. They would be apprehensive. Of course, they would. *He* would. "Colnaha. You said they can pinpoint our location if we kept the communicator on and with us, right?"

"Yes…" Colnaha said. He seemed worried about where Atakos was going with his question.

"Let's do that then. We'll keep it on. Take it with us. If they send another response, great. If not, so be it. We can't say we didn't try."

Colnaha nodded, although he thought it was a bad idea. "Okay."

Prince Aillios sat down on the closest seat and strapped himself in. "Let us not waste any more time then. To the Dokami Council it is."

CHAPTER 16

"Going to Paimonu now would be futile. They will not be there for much longer."

King Tholenod blinked and looked up at Brulok. He was riding some sort of demon horse, one Tholenod regarded as truly terrifying and nightmarish. It was shiny and black–bigger than any normal horse, with muscles rippling throughout its entire physique. Its eyes seemed to be red in color and, if Tholenod was not mistaken, he was certain he could see smoke billowing from its nose and mouth. Brulok himself was wearing a long black cloak, which covered his body all the way down to his feet, with a large hood hiding his face from view. He had cut his long, gray beard and hair, leaving them short enough not to get in his way and finally descended from his mountain dwelling, within the dead forest in Effit, for the first time in almost five hundred years. King Tholenod was certain Brulok could not possibly know what was happening on an island thousands of miles away. "How could you know that?" he said.

"I have my ways," Brulok said, sneering.

When Brulok, King Tholenod, his assistant Menyilh, and the remaining Mituwan soldiers left the dead forest, Tholenod had noticed something incredible but frightening at the same time. The lifeless forest behind them began to come to life. The ground started to turn green with blades of grass and leaf sprouts erupting from the previously dead trees. It was a terrifying, but an amazing thing to see. The evil wizard had immense power, more than Tholenod could have ever imagined. When they left the now budding forest, the live trees around them began to die, renewing life only after Brulok rode past them. Tholenod glanced at his assistant, Menyilh, to see what the little man thought about the events displayed before them. He stared straight ahead, as if what he was seeing was a normal occurrence. Furthermore, he looked *proud*. Tholenod frowned. What had he gotten himself into?

"We will make camp here," Brulok said, practically leaping off his evil horse without much effort.

King Tholenod glanced around them. "There are more trees here than the rest of the forest. How can we rest *here*?" He watched as the trees around them lost their color and began to die.

Brulok mumbled something under his breath and waved his hand around.

The trees disappeared.

Disappeared.

"Are you satisfied now?" he said, glaring at the king.

"Fine," Tholenod said with a grumble. He contemplated calling off the whole alliance. Telling Brulok he no longer required his help. He could handle the destruction of the West all on his own. Just as he had been doing before. Sadly, he shook his head. Unfortunately, he knew he needed the old wizard's help more than anything. It was not as if he was any closer to winning against Western Omordion before he sought Brulok. He would just have to find a way to get rid of him after their victory.

After dismounting his horse, King Tholenod glanced at Brulok again and shuddered. Even though his black hood covered his face, he was almost positive he was staring right *at* him. *I will not let him intimidate me*, he thought. *If he did not need me, he would have taken over Omordion years ago.* Tholenod removed the blanket under his horse's saddle and placed it on the dried up ground. He laid to rest on it and, even though he wasn't even tired, closed his eyes, shutting out everything going on around him. He needed to clear his mind and not let anything affect him or deter him from his ultimate goal. No, he would not be intimidated by the old wizard. Not now. Not ever. He was King Tholenod and he was meant to rule the *world*.

King Tholenod awoke with a start. When exactly had he fallen asleep? Darkness had fallen and a dying fire crackled in the middle of their camp. All of his soldiers were sleeping. Even Menyilh was curled up in a ball under his blanket with an idiotic smile on his face.

He must be having a good dream, Tholenod thought, and then grunted. *What a fool.* He turned around to look for Brulok and tried unsuccessfully to stifle a loud gasp. The old wizard was levitating in the air, his hood down over his shoulders, no longer covering his face.

His gray eyes were fixated on King Tholenod with an unwavering, steady gaze.

"Wha—?" Horrified, Tholenod tried to stand up but was frozen in place. Fear gripped him when he realized he could no longer speak. Only his eyes were able to move. He helplessly watched as a dark shadow poured out of Brulok's dark eyes, slowly slid down his face, and crawled down the entire length of his body to the ground. The shadow then glided towards him at a rapid pace, gripping the forest floor with spider-like arms, enabling it to move with incredible speed.

Tholenod wanted to scream.

He wanted to run away.

The horrifying shadow grabbed him with its many arms and slowly crept up his body. When it painfully entered his eyes, Tholenod saw the dead forest surrounding him begin to fade away and then—

Nothing.

Only darkness.

And a laugh.

A laugh so eerily frightening filled Tholenod's ears, becoming more and more intense until he thought his ears would bleed from the sound. It felt like death. *But surely death would be better than this*, he thought. He would welcome it. If it meant the pain would end.

At the last moment, Tholenod indeed called out for death–to end his suffering–but his call remained on his lips and was left unanswered. It was his last attempt before his mind seemed to be set on *fire*. Deep down inside, he was screaming. He screamed and screamed and screamed. Nobody helped him. No one came to his aid. He was finished, this great King of Mituwa. Done for good this time.

And he was never, ever coming back.

CHAPTER 17

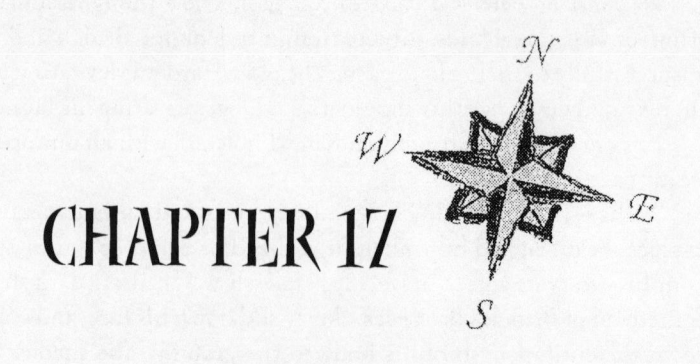

She was not afraid.
This was not the first time she was hunting a dangerous creature and she was certain it was not going to be her last. Steadily releasing the breath she was holding through her slightly parted lips, she crouched low and advanced across the muddy ground, careful not to make a sound as she moved. Her lightweight, knee-high, brown, leather boots provided her the protection she needed in case she stepped on anything potentially harmful. It was difficult to see around the leaves of the exotic plants surrounding her, but it was even more difficult because the fallen rain had left behind an impenetrable fog, coating the forest floor in a thick, white haze. It was bad enough she was so high up the mountainside that the air gradually thinned out as she climbed.

Even though she was not afraid, she was still on high alert, her heart hammering hard in her chest with anticipation. Despite the unpleasant air she was breathing, her goal was to find the creature before it spotted her. Before it could unleash its fury on her, as it had done to so many others. One false move could mean certain death so she needed to be extremely careful.

"Come on," she whispered under her breath, scanning the foggy forest with her dark eyes. "Where are you?"

As if to answer her question, a twig snapped behind her, causing her to quickly turn her head. Her long, black, wet hair clung to her face so she had to brush it away from her eyes in order to see. She balled her hands into fists and steadied her breathing. Whatever it was, she was ready for it.

Taking her time to scan the area ahead of her, she did not see anything out of the ordinary. She was about to turn around again when a bright, blue bird suddenly flew out of the nearest tree and disappeared into the fog with a loud shrill.

What scared you little bird? she wondered. Sweeping her eyes back and forth, she did not see anything. *What was it?*

She froze, the hairs on her neck standing up on end.

It was there.

Camouflaging with the forest trees, its scaly, green, and brown flesh was so well hidden, she almost missed it.

It had been watching her the whole time.

When the creature realized she had spotted it, a low, guttural growl escaped its throat. Its mouth turned up into a horrific grin, revealing rows of jagged teeth. Without any warning, the creature lunged at her, its massive body slithering across the muddy forest floor like a large snake, except it had short legs—six to be exact— which propelled it to move quicker than any creature she had ever seen. She hardly had time to react. Rolling out of the way to avoid being ripped apart by its teeth, she was careful to stay clear of its long tail, complete with dozens of spikes so long and sharp, one would not survive if impaled by any one of them.

The creature whipped its tail too close to her back for comfort, almost tearing into the tight, brown, leather bodysuit she wore to protect herself. With a grunt, she stood up, quickly facing the creature as it advanced towards her again. This time, her hands flew out, sending shockwaves at the creature to prevent it from getting any closer. Recalling all the villagers killed over the past few weeks by the deadly creature, she did not hesitate to seek justice for them. She slowly closed her fists and the creature started flailing its massive body, screeching as its bones began cracking one by one, its body bending in angles it could not possibly bend. She smiled to herself as she watched the spectacle before her. This was the end of the foul creature, who thought it could make her its next victim. This was the revenge she sought after, for the villagers who died when the beast descended from the mountain and attacked, killing and eating its fill before ascending back up the mountainside until it was time to feast again.

Satisfied, she regarded the ball of scaly flesh she had created of the beast with an air of triumph. The villagers living nearby need not be afraid any longer.

Rising off the forest floor, she ascended into the sky until she was no longer enveloped in the dense fog. For a few, precious moments, she hovered in the air, allowing the rays of the bright sunshine to cascade over her, warming her tensed muscles, and she finally breathed a sigh of relief. All she wanted to do now was fly as she so often did. She flew back down into the mountain fog and descended over the trees until she reached ground level and kept going, gliding this way and that to avoid hitting any trees. She travelled this way for miles, heading south towards the Kingdom of Eynta, far away from the mountain where the dangerous creature had once called home. She flew past village after village, not having a particular destination in mind, just enjoying the feeling of the wind whipping through her hair and taking in the beautiful sights.

Moments later, she knew just where she wanted to go and veered left. The trees whizzed past her as she flew so fast, she had come to a grinding halt when she reached her destination. As her feet touched the ground, she heard the distinct sound of laughter and walked towards the sound, a smile playing on her lips as she entered a small clearing, surrounded by trees in the forest. A small pond, filled with lily pads, rested in the middle of the clearing, bordered by rocks.

She laughed. "I knew I'd find you here," she said.

"Amilana!"

Three villagers ran up to Amilana, surprised she had come to see them again. She knew the oldest, named Lenasi, to be thirteen years old. The other two were twelve-year-old Jadien and eight-year-old Ayairi. They were not siblings but cousins, all three having beautiful brown complexions and curly dark-brown hair. Lenasi and Ayairi wore their curly hair in braids, while Jadien's hair, cut short on the sides, was left curly on top. The girls were wearing long, flowing, pastel-colored dresses, cinched tight around their waists and Jadien wore a dark black robe tied around his waist with loose fitting pants of the same color, tucked into his favorite pair of rugged black boots.

The three children bowed to Amilana when they approached her to show their respect. She cringed and blushed with embarrassment. It took her a couple of years to get them to stop referring to her as

'Princess Amilana' or 'Your Majesty'. Unfortunately, the bowing thing was something that would never go away.

"What are you three up to?" Amilana said.

The youngest one, Ayairi, responded by waving her small hands around. She brought dead leaves up from the forest floor and caused them to swirl all around them like a small tornado. Ayairi put her hand down and the leaves simultaneously dropped to the ground. Lenasi took it as her cue to reach out with both hands to the small pond nearby, causing the water to ripple and churn until a huge wave splashed against the shore and immediately turned in on itself. Jadien opened his hand and a ball of green energy formed in his opened palm, the energy whirling and swirling around like small waves. When he felt it was ready, he hurled it into the pond and the four of them had to cover their heads as the energy ball exploded, creating a brief shower of water, raining down on them.

They fell to the ground, the four of them, laughing hysterically.

When they finally settled down, Amilana sighed. "You are all so amazing," she said.

"Thank you, Amilana," Lenasi said, the dimple on her cheek deepening as she smiled.

"We learn something new every day," Jadien said. "You should see us—"

Ayairi interrupted him by throwing a tight fist into the air. "Soon, we will be strong enough to join the Jmugean Army," she said.

Amilana laughed. "Of course," she said. "If only I had more time to train you..." Her voice trailed off as she turned her head towards the direction of Eynta. It was the strangest thing. A nagging feeling was tugging at her heart like strings on a kite. Something of importance was happening at the castle. She could feel it. This feeling was nothing she had felt before.

This was serious.

Turning back to her company, Amilana was about to politely excuse herself but realized that all three children were now standing together, several feet away from her when, mere seconds before, they had been seated next to her on the leaf-ridden ground. Their eyes disturbed her the most. They were staring off in the direction of the kingdom of Eynta. A moment later, their eyes slowly shifted to stare at her.

They had felt it too.

Amilana quickly stood up. "I–I have to go," she said, stammering. The children did not respond but continued to stare back at her with sadness in their eyes. The haunting way they watched her was frightening.

As Amilana pushed off the ground and flew up to the sky again, she could not help but feel like something was wrong.

Very wrong.

PART THREE
SAIYUT

CHAPTER 18

Past the Hejdian Sea, and the vast Saimino Ocean, lay Saiyut, two thousand miles south of Sheidem Island. As the sun began to set, its largest snow-capped mountain came into view from miles away, resembling a soldier guarding its kingdom. Luscious green hills, forests, and lakes were a sight to see when Colnaha's airship flew over the countryside. Most intriguing were the large palaces and mansions dotting the landscape, providing a scene of grandeur and style. The estates varied, some resembling castles, while others seemed more like resorts rather than homes. Fajha explained that some of them were deserted, being used only as vacation homes in the summertime by royalty from all over Western Omordion. Abundant wealth, beautiful beaches, and a lineage wrought with prestige and influence was the core of Saiyut. Even the common folk owned large homes, making Colnaha's beautiful blue mansion appear as if it could have been their guesthouse.

Colnaha focused all he could on the scenery as he piloted the airship. He had provided his six companions with nourishment, while showing them everything the ship held and all of its uses.

Everything.

Except one thing.

The *orb*.

The orb that could make all Dokamis in its immediate area virtually powerless and undetectable. The last remaining orb of its kind, developed three hundred years prior, to aid the Dokami by preventing the accidental use of their abilities. All but one had been destroyed and

Colnaha's grandfather, the Dokami Wise Man before Bontihm, whose name was Olshem, had acquired it.

Colnaha had stolen the orb, along with the airship, when he ran away from his hometown, Osmatu. He kept the thought of it out of his mind so Cristaden could not read it off him. He did not know why he felt the need to conceal it. Perhaps he was worried the Dokami Council would have it destroyed. Perhaps he thought he had done something terribly wrong by removing it from Osmatu. Perhaps he might even return it if he goes back home. Nevertheless, he made sure he kept it out of his thoughts and out of Cristaden's head.

As they flew towards the center of Saiyut, the passengers on board Colnaha's airship could see majestic, golden shrines resting on top of hills. The prestigious performed their weekly, religious rituals there, while elaborate red temples had been erected for the common folk to worship in daily.

The Dokami Council's headquarters was located within the Saiyutan Museum of Cultural History, in the city of Isre. Fajha knew exactly where it was and pointed them in the right direction. He had only visited the museum once before he found out the Dokami Council resided there. Since he was told, he was no longer allowed to go back there with that knowledge. Even Hamilda had told them they were forbidden to visit the Council unless requested to do so.

Sometimes, rules were meant to be broken.

In Isre Square, the shops seemed to have been built hundreds of years prior because of their magnificent, ancient design. There were no tall buildings; all were mostly one story with an occasional two-story department store resting among them. As the sun descended, the shopkeepers could be seen closing their doors and locking up for the night when they flew past. Some stopped to stare at Colnaha's airship, most likely wondering what important person might be in it and where it was headed.

"Just over that hill," Fajha said, pointing to an intricately decorated golden shrine resting on top of a small hill, away from the bustle of the square.

They did not expect to see anything as glorious as the museum. Built like a castle, it was majestic and its grounds—extensive. Statues of ancient war heroes bordered the entrance of the grand building and a large fountain glowed brightly, with different colored lights exploding from its base, turning the water into a rainbow of colors. The museum seemed larger than Lochenby itself, which housed hundreds of students and faculty throughout the school year. They could see people leaving the museum from the front of the building as it was closing for the day.

"It's amazing," Zadeia breathed. All of them were leaned over the control panel as Colnaha guided his airship to a grassy field towards the back of the museum.

"I know," Fajha said sadly. "Even though I came here one time, this place became my favorite. I was heartbroken when I was told I could never return."

"Tragic," Cristaden said, sympathizing with Fajha. "I have heard that the Dokami Council neither have family nor friends. It is rumored that they were plucked from Dokami orphanages at a young age and forced to live their life in seclusion until they died and new members were chosen."

Prince Aillios frowned. "I do not understand. These are your leaders, the ones who made you a part of this mission. They should be available to guide you at any time."

"Hamilda was the only true guidance given to us," Atakos said. "And if she was no longer available, Bontihm, our Wise Man, was to be our guide as his predecessors have been for three hundred years. The Dokami Council is only here to help the Wise Man when he needs help making big decisions regarding the Dokami clan. No one but the Wise Man knows who they are or has ever seen them. Unfortunately, Bontihm died, so we are without a Wise Man."

"That is impossible. No one but the Wise Man has ever seen them? I don't believe this."

"Believe it," Colnaha said. "Even my father told me only the Wise Man meets with them. All other important decisions are carried out by letter, left outside their quarters for a messenger to pick up and hand deliver. I don't know what the big deal is."

"It's as if they are scared for their lives."

"Or rather," Zimi said, "they don't want outside influences to affect their decisions so they can stick to our ancient traditions. Sort of like religious people who remain chaste and live only to serve one purpose in life—"

"But much more extreme," Zadeia said.

"Do you think they will meet with us?" Prince Aillios asked.

"We don't have a Wise Man," Atakos said. "The Dokami clan of Omordion is in danger. *We* are in danger. They would *have* to see us. If they don't…well…we're on our own."

Silence fell among the group as Colnaha cut the engine of the ship. Under the blanket of night, the group disembarked and headed to the back of the museum, being sure to take the communicator with them. After a short, brisk walk, they approached the museum. There were lights on in some rooms at the back of the building and the apprehensive group could see more lights flickering on as they approached the gates.

"They're expecting us," Cristaden said.

"You can *hear* them?" Prince Aillios said with a bewildered look on his face. *This Cristaden*, he thought, *is simply* incredible.

"No. Look." Cristaden pointed to an open door, which most likely had served as a servant's entrance years before the building was converted into a museum. A heavyset, older man stood beside it, a small candle flickering in his hand. He was patiently waiting for them to approach.

"Oh."

When they approached the man, who was dressed in a long, yellow nightgown, he quickly ushered them in. "They have been expecting you," he said. "Come in. Quickly." He firmly closed the door behind them as they stepped into a long hallway. Red and gold carpet covered the floor and the only things providing any light were the drippy candles mounted on the walls. There seemed to be no overhead lights and no electrical wires whatsoever, as if the owners of the museum had neglected to update them for decades.

The man neither introduced himself nor asked them for their names as he guided them up two flights of stairs to the third floor. As they walked down the dark, third floor hallway, he shocked them when, with just a wave of his hands, he lit every candle all the way to the end of the hallway. Unexpectedly, he stopped short. "Please proceed to the end and turn right," he said, as if what he had done was perfectly normal. "When you reach the end of the hall, open the last door on your left. From there, I cannot tell you where to go. You will be on your own." When no one responded, he sighed. "Let your senses guide you. You will find your way." Without hesitation, he turned around and scurried back down the stairs.

The teens and Prince Aillios looked questionably at each other. No one dared say a word. Colnaha seemed even more apprehensive and hung back as they made their way down the magnificent hallway, decorated with paintings of Saiyutan landscape and statues of nymphs and angels. He kept his eyes on the carpet mostly, as they continued to go the direction the man told them. A hand gently patted Colnaha's shoulder. Startled, Colnaha looked up into Zadeia's reassuring eyes and his heart practically leapt out of his chest with happiness. She must have sensed how he was feeling. Because of his family history, he was the one person who had no right to be there. Even Prince Aillios, a non-member of the Dokami clan, the son of the evil King Tholenod, had more of a right to be there than he had. If his father, Maldaha, ever found out where Colnaha was, he would be deeply troubled. Slowly but surely, the next time he saw him, he would make him suffer unspeakable horrors, worse than the punishment he would have received for simply running away with the ship. Worse than the *closet*. Zadeia squeezed his shoulder and smiled at him. Colnaha smiled back. Somehow, she made him feel like everything would turn out okay.

When the group reached the end of the second hallway, they turned to the last door on their left. A lonely table stood next to the door, most likely where the letters were placed when a decision had to be made. It was amazing to think a secret society occupied a part of the museum the public was not allowed access to. No one, except for the man who let them in, knew of them. Not even the restrained members of the Dokami clan who visited the museum on a regular basis.

"Here goes nothing," Atakos said, turning the doorknob.

Everyone held their breath but, much to their disappointment, they entered yet another dark hallway. Zadeia groaned as she lit a fireball in one hand, providing them with light to see. They had no idea where to go next as they continued to walk forward.

"The man said to let our senses guide us," Zimi said. "Fajha and Cristaden. Think you could sense where to go?"

"I can't locate people I've never met," Fajha said flatly.

"I'm trying to sense anyone's presence but I can't feel a thing," Cristaden said.

"Then we'll just have to keep walking," Atakos said. "Whichever direction we decide to go would have to be the right way. Remember how we found the Dokami spaceship in the caves? Our senses should guide us the right way, like the man said."

"Okay, concentrate everyone," Zimi said. "We can do this."

The teens nodded and focused on their senses as they walked. For a few minutes, as they walked past door after door, they could not feel anything worth paying attention to. All of a sudden, simultaneously, all except Prince Aillios, turned around.

"Whoa," Zimi said. "You guys felt that too?"

"Yeah," Fajha said.

Surprisingly, Colnaha agreed. "Yeah, I felt it too."

"We passed the door we needed to take," Zadeia said.

"I don't think I can get used to this," Prince Aillios said, turning around with a sigh.

After opening the door, going down yet another hallway, and up a flight of stairs, the group of seven entered a large, well-lit hall. It looked as if it was a ballroom at some point in the past. It was apparent the museum must have been a real castle before it was converted into a museum and the Dokami Council began to occupy it. The royal families of Saiyut, maybe even Fajha's ancestors, might have resided there before the conversion.

"Hello?" Atakos said, taking the lead once again. "Anyone here?"

At first, they did not receive a response. All they could hear was the echo of Atakos' voice.

"Do you think we should keep moving?" Zadeia said.

"Come in," a female voice called from behind a door across the room, making them all jump slightly.

Taking a deep breath, Atakos led the others to the door and hesitated before opening it. Why did it feel like he was walking into the private lair of living *gods*? They were just members of the Dokami clan. Just like him and his friends. Nevertheless, it still felt so...*wrong*. They were not supposed to be there.

Unfortunately, they needed the Dokami Council's help. The Dokami clan's secret way of life was compromised. Every precaution enforced by their ancestors was crumbling.

They had no choice.

Colnaha took a step back as Atakos slowly turned the doorknob. His eyes fell to the ground and he seemed to shrink three inches in height as a feeling of inherent discomfort settled in his stomach. Without thinking of whether Cristaden was reading his mind or not, Colnaha contemplated leaving them there, running back to his airship, and returning to Osmatu. He would gladly beg for his father's forgiveness with his tail between his legs. Colnaha took a few quick breaths and let them out slowly. He shook his head to clear it. Despite how he felt, he knew he was not a coward. He had to live up to his father's expectations, even if it meant going against his wishes. He had to be strong. However, he knew it was not going to be easy.

Atakos sucked in a lung full of air and opened the door.

CHAPTER 19

The Kingdom of Eynta was a gorgeous landscape of ancient ruins, centuries-old homes, and modern ones, nestled in the heart of Jmugea. Previously called Eynta Province, it was taken over by the Dokami clan four hundred years prior when the pureblooded, uncompromising Jmugeans were driven out, ordered to live the rest of their days in solitude on a desolate island far away.

Within the Kingdom of Eynta was a city, called Enshatmu, as it had been for centuries before. Enshatmu City was a beacon of success for traders and merchants selling their goods and a place of rest for the weary traveler or explorer. Members of the Dokami clan, who fell ill, would often come from miles away to visit Tasonar, the Dokami clan's Master Healer, and his exceptional cast of talented apprentices. They lived in a luxurious house in the middle of Soli Square—renamed after the Queen Mother when the Dokamis took over Enshatmu City—and were the ones who kept the Dokami clan healthy and free of ailments. Just outside the city, the main branch of the Jmugean Army trained endlessly to defend the planet in case of a hostile invasion, while scientists studied the stars and the interplanetary systems surrounding them in the observatory nearby, keeping an eye out for any threats from outer space. Fortunately, the Dokamis had been safe for centuries and avoided any such attacks with the peace treaties, set in place long before they took over the planet.

Princess Amilana descended from the sky and quickly walked through Soli Square, towards the castle, nestled in the north end of Eynta. She always liked to walk the cobblestoned streets of the city before going home, no matter how exhausted she was from the day's travels. The streets were bustling with merchants and traders who bowed to her as she walked past. They were used to seeing her on a daily basis, walking among the common folk as if her royal status did not mean anything to her. Their kingdom was so peaceful, even the castle gates were left open and unattended. They had absolutely no need for security against one another.

Amilana was unable to shake the feeling that something was horribly wrong. It had tormented her all the way from the forest where she first felt it. Because of her ability to sense when something dreadful was happening from a great distance, she was elected as the Ambassador of Jmugea on her 21st birthday. A year had passed since she had taken over her new role but, in all of that time, she had never felt the way she felt at that moment.

Beyond a beautiful meadow, where the infamous Wedding Day Massacre occurred against the first members of the Dokami clan, lay the castle. The castle grounds were vast, rivaling in size against that of Enshatmu City. The castle itself was made of gray stones and held hundreds of beautifully designed rooms within its massive interior. The entire royal family, including Amilana's aunts, uncles, and cousins, made the castle their home, while dozens of brick homes were built on the grounds to house the Jmugean Army branch in Eynta, members of the Jmugean Council, and the servants as well.

As she approached the castle gates, Amilana stopped and turned around when she heard someone shout her name. It was her sixteen-year-old sister, Drissana, who most likely had been trailing her from the city, running to catch up with her. She was a stark contrast to Amilana with her bright red, unruly hair and golden eyes compared to her sister's jet-black hair and dark eyes. She had her hair tied up in a knot and wore a boy's style, light-blue tunic with brown pants and brown boots. As usual, she was covered in dirt and mud, as if she had been rolling around on the ground. Amilana shook her head. If she knew her better, she would say Drissana was wrestling with boys from the city again to prove who was strongest without the use of their Dokami abilities.

When her sister caught up to her, Amilana sneered at her. "I see you've been fighting again," she said.

"Someone has to teach those boys a lesson," Drissana said with an air of authority. "They think they can beat me. They lose every time."

Amilana turned back towards the castle, inviting Drissana to walk with her. "Mother is not going to like this. You know she hates it when you grovel on the ground."

Drissana laughed. "I'm not groveling, sister. I'm having fun. I mean, what else is there to do in that boring, old castle?"

"You haven't been doing well with your studies. It would do you some good to open more books."

"And learn what?" Drissana rolled her eyes. "The history of our people? The rise and fall of the Jmugean Empire? Microscopic organisms, living deep within the soil beneath our feet? Ugh. I just want to use my gifts to help people. I want to be able to see outer space and travel to other planets. Like you do."

"It's my *job*."

"Yes and the *best* job ever."

"I didn't get to where I am without excelling in my lessons."

"Your gifts got you the position as Ambassador and you know it."

"But my studies have kept me here."

"That's what you think."

Amilana groaned angrily. "You are so…insufferable."

Drissana grinned as they passed through the castle gates and walked the length of the long path to the front doors. She knew exactly what to say to get on her sister's nerves. Two soldiers, who were walking by, rushed to open the doors for them as they came closer. Amilana thanked them for their kindness and ushered her sister through the massive and heavy, wooden doors before they were closed behind them.

"Now," Amilana said, turning her sister around by the shoulders so she could look her straight in the eyes. "I suggest you get cleaned up and changed before you are spotted looking like," she gestured to her clothes, "this."

Drissana rolled her eyes. "Ami, by now you should know I don't care about what people *think*."

"Well, I do. It is my duty to care. It should be yours too. You are a direct descendant of the royal bloodline—"

"Sure—where are *you* going?"

"I have some business to attend to," Amilana said, annoyed the topic of discussion had been deliberately changed. As if being a princess of Jmugea was the worst thing ever handed to Drissana at birth.

Drissana gave Amilana an inquisitive look. It was the same look she always gave her when she wanted to come with her and join in whatever she was about to do. Ever since Drissana was little, she had always followed her around. It did not help that they were six years apart. When Amilana wanted to do something bold and daring, her little sister would be right there, preventing her from following through with it. Amilana loved her though, as annoying as she was. They shared so much over the years. Especially being the heirs to the throne of Jmugea. Even though she was a pain in her backside, Drissana was the only other person who knew what life was like in Amilana's world. She leaned on her little sister many times when her responsibilities grew too great and vice versa. She did not know what she would do without her.

Amilana smiled. "No."

"Oh, come on!"

"You have to go wash yourself and change. Mother would kill you and I will be the only one left in line for the throne."

Drissana huffed and muttered the word 'fine' under her breath as she turned on her heels, heading for the stairway leading to their chambers. Amilana could only shake her head and sigh. She then made her way down the hall to the throne room. Before she approached the doorway to the throne room, she could hear a rather heated discussion, taking place between some members of the Jmugean Council and the king and queen.

The Council? If the council members were there, having an impromptu meeting, it could only mean the bad feeling Amilana was experiencing was, in fact, genuine. After opening the doors to the throne room, Amilana was taken by surprise when the heated discussion ended abruptly when they heard her enter the room. *All* eight members of the Jmugean Council were there in the beautifully designed throne room, standing before her parents, who sat on their thrones. Her mother, Queen Serai, was a vision of young beauty even though her jet-black hair, which was identical to Amilana's, was graying at the edges. Although her father, King Azahr, was the same age as her mother, his hair had already grayed completely and he seemed much older than she was, at least by several years.

"Why was I not invited to this meeting?" Amilana said as she approached the throne. She found it extremely odd that the council members, four men and four women, watched her approach as if they were shocked she was there. Their eyes looked shifty, looking at her but not actually making eye contact with her at all. Some kept glancing back and forth between her and her parents. "What has happened?"

King Azahr cleared his throat. "My daughter. I was not expecting you to be back so soon. Were you able to take care of the little problem in the mountains?"

"Yes, father."

"Good. The villagers can rest peacefully now."

"Do you mind explaining to me what's going on?"

It was her mother's turn to speak. "We gathered the members of the Jmugean Council to discuss the shortage in food supplies in the cold north. We will need to send an envoy to bring them relief." She nodded to the council members and waved her hands, indicating their dismissal.

As the council members quietly took their leave, Amilana could not help but feel even more disturbed by the actions of everyone in the room. "Mother," she said. "We had discussed the need to bring food to the north yesterday. I believe the wagons are being prepared already."

"Yes," King Azahr said. "But the situation has become more complicated than we feared."

"Has it?" Amilana raised her eyebrows. "I would have sensed their urgency." The King and Queen glanced at each other in confusion, but did not respond. Was her power to sense when something bad was happening a little off? On the other hand, was it possible that her parents were keeping something important from her?

"I sensed something bad was happening," Amilana said. "*Here*."

"I'm not sure what you are talking about," Queen Serai said. "Darling, everything is fine here."

"Are you sure you are feeling well today, daughter?" King Azahr said.

"Yes, I am feeling *well*. I was miles away. I got a horrible feeling coming from Eynta. *Our* kingdom."

"You must have sensed the urgency we felt here about the people in the north."

"My power doesn't work that way, father. In fact, I still have the bad feeling *as we speak*. Tell me what is going on!"

Queen Serai stood up and took a few steps forward. She carefully took a hold of Amilana's hand and looked deep into her eyes. "Ami, perhaps you need some rest. Why don't you sleep it off?"

"I need to know...I am the Ambassador..." Amilana blinked a few times and yawned. "I–I need to lie down."

"Yes, dear. Please. Get some rest."

When Amilana awoke from a deep slumber, she turned to the nearest window and practically fell out of bed. A fierce storm was raging outside. She did not even remember when it had begun. How long had she been out for? And when exactly did she come to her room and lie down to sleep?

Shaking her head, Amilana sat up in bed and squeezed her eyes shut. She gradually came to the realization that the horrible feeling she was experiencing earlier was gone. However, she didn't quite remember the outcome of the conversation she was having with her parents in the throne room. It was as if, at that moment in time, she had completely *blacked out*.

Taking a few deep breaths, Amilana opened her eyes and looked around her room. Because of her status as the Ambassador to Jmugea, she knew she could not tell anyone what happened. They would think she was unfit to do her job.

No, I mustn't say anything, she thought and then stood up to stretch. Despite the odd lapse in time though, everything else seemed strangely... Normal.

CHAPTER 20

Stepping into the Dokami Council's meeting room was like stepping into a different world. The high ceiling, intricately painted to resemble a bright, morning sky, with little cherubs playing on one of the many clouds, was a beautiful sight to see. One cherub had a small bow in his pudgy fingers, which had expelled an arrow, leaving a trail across the sky and down the side of the right wall, exploding into an array of fireworks and hearts. Under the exploding hearts was a small town, which resembled Isre Square, but with a beach next to it. A giant tsunami was headed towards the town with so much force, one could almost hear the rage of the impending destruction. The ocean water continued onto the wall beside it, which resembled a huge undersea aquarium with many sea creatures in it. On the ocean floor, the ground had risen and was still shaking due to a powerful earthquake, which had displaced the ocean water, causing the tsunami. On the next wall, a volcano had erupted on the opposite shore and lava rolled down its side, cooling when it touched the ocean. An animated cloud from the sky was attempting to blow the volcano out as if it were a candle with a powerful windstorm. The mural looked so brilliant; they could have been in the museum instead of there, in a part of the building where no one would ever see it. It was so magnificently done that, for a moment, the group of seven stood enchanted by it, as if under a strange spell.

"Welcome," a voice said, interrupting their thoughts.

Abruptly coming out of their intoxicating trance, the group finally noticed the rest of the room. They were shocked to see five people, sitting behind five tables, strategically placed against each section of the painted mural. Why hadn't they notice them before?

Cristaden frowned. Something seemed so familiar about the five people in the room—yet so *unfamiliar*. She knew she had never met them before so she didn't know why she was feeling that way.

Dressed in long, ivory robes, the five members of the Dokami Council stood up to greet their visitors, who stood frozen by the entryway. One woman, who had long, fiery-red hair and green eyes, spread out her arms, welcoming them once again. She stepped around her table, which was the last one on the right, and came towards them before stopping several feet away.

"Please, do come in," she said. Her accent was thick, an accent Fajha was sure he had never heard before in all his studies of distant languages. "We have been expecting you. My name is Lady Feir." She bowed and turned to the first table on the left, gesturing at a man with long blonde hair and dark, blue eyes. "This is Lord Lovanthe." The man at the table next to his, who had short black hair and blue eyes, she introduced as Lord Watten. The man next to him, who had a skin tone the color of mocha and brown eyes, was introduced as Lord Eavthon. The table between Lord Eavthon's table and her own was Lady Arren who, despite her long, silky, white hair and light blue eyes, seemed young, perhaps in her twenties. They were beautiful and had a vibrant youth about them, yet they seemed wise beyond their years. It was hard to place what made them appear so abnormal. They were just people after all—not gods. Weren't they?

"Please, do have a seat," Lady Feir said. She waved her arms and a secret door opened in the volcano behind her desk. Seven, plain, folding chairs flew out, startling their guests. The chairs glided, one by one, across the floor and unfolded in the middle of the room.

Atakos cleared his throat. They were being rude! While Lady Feir introduced all of the council members, they did not even do as much as bow to them. They were too mesmerized by them all to respond. Instead, they stood at the door like frightened little children going to their first day of school, scared stiff about their new teachers and meeting other children. They have battled wild creatures and monstrous beasts for goodness sakes! "On behalf of my friends," Atakos said, feeling a drop of sweat roll down the side of his face, "we are pleased you have allowed us to meet with you. We seek your advice."

"Our advice we shall give," Lord Eavthon said, his accent just as thick as Lady Feir's. He gestured for them to sit down.

Atakos straightened himself and pushed his shoulders back. He proceeded to take the first seat with his friends following his lead. Cristaden sat next to him, followed by Fajha, Zimi, Zadeia, Colnaha, and Prince Aillios.

Lady Feir glided back to her table and the five members of the Dokami Council sat down at the same time with remarkable poise and elegance.

"Let me start by introducing myself and my friends," Atakos said.

"We know you," Lord Watten said with a smile. "The five of you. Samatakos Croit. Cristaden Feriau. Fajhalti Bayaht. Zimildan and Zadeia Emyu. We chose you for this mission, of course. Although we have never met you personally, we would recognize you from anywhere."

Atakos' eyebrows rose at the mention of his full name and the full names of his friends. He hadn't been called 'Samatakos' since he was a small boy. "How would you recognize us if you never met us?" he said.

"We recognize your spirit," Lord Lovanthe said. "The powers you possess. We can sense you from miles away when you use them."

The five friends looked at each other. Colnaha was right about one thing. The Dokami Council *could* sense them. However, if so, why didn't they come to their aid when they were in trouble?

"If we could have helped you," Lady Feir said, reading their thoughts, "we would have. As you know, we are unable to leave the museum. I hope you understand."

Lady Arren, with the white hair, spoke, her voice wispy like the wind. "What we do not understand is why you have brought those two here," she said. "Especially the boy. He has no place here with us."

Colnaha's face grew red and he looked down at the floor. He tried to stand up, with the intent to run away, but was held down by Zadeia's hand on his and a strong hand on his shoulder, from Prince Aillios.

Aillios stood up. "If anyone has no right to be here, it is I, Prince Aillios of Mituwa, King Tholenod's son. The evil tyrant who brought us all together. I am not of Dokami blood." He pointed at Colnaha. "He is."

"Of course you have a right to be here, Son of Tholenod," Lady Feir said, silencing him. "Your heart is as theirs. Kind. Loving. You share the same mission, the same objective. The love you have for your people is overwhelming. It eliminates the wrong you have done in your life."

"I have killed...many innocent people." Prince Aillios looked down at his hands and then back up at the Council. "With these hands. That is nothing to be proud of."

"You were misled."

"As was Colnaha."

"His destiny is different than yours," Lord Eavthon simply stated. "Do sit down, Prince Aillios of Mituwa, you have chosen one path, he will ultimately choose another."

Colnaha frowned. How dare Lord Eavthon imply anything about where his life was headed? They did not know him. They did not know what he endured his entire life. Living in Osmatu, isolated from the entire world, given only one opportunity to escape its clutches by attending Lochenby, only to be sucked right back in when he was tricked to return. He had no friends. The neighborhood children regarded him as their leader, not their friend, not someone they could count on to keep their secrets. The Dokami Council had no idea what he had been through. No one ever would. As Prince Aillios sat down, Colnaha stood up, shaking Zadeia's hand away. He heard a gasped from her, but he did not care. He had no choice but to defend himself.

"All my life," Colnaha said, "I have lived under my father rules. He dictated my life from the moment I took my first breath as a baby. His way was all I was taught—all I knew. He told me the reasons why he wanted to stay hidden from everyone. He made me despise you because I was ignorant to the truth. When he drove me to put my friends in danger, my eyes were opened to the truth. I denounced my father and his ways and I will *never* return. I have a new mission now." Colnaha bowed his head. "I want to learn to advance my abilities. To aid my friends in their fight."

The members of the Dokami Council were quiet. They had allowed Colnaha to speak and waited for him to continue. When they felt he was finished, Lord Eavthon spoke up again.

"Colnaha, Son of Maldaha, please step forward."

Colnaha's heart swelled as he took a few steps towards the Dokami Council. Maybe they finally saw the truth. He was there to help. He would never stray as his father had.

"Your father, Maldaha, had given the *same* speech."

Colnaha's eyes flew up in surprise. He looked at each of the faces of the solemn Dokami Council. He turned to look back at his friends. Their eyes were wide with surprise as well.

"Yes," Lord Lovanthe said, his blue eyes reduced to slits. "It is true. He blamed his father for his actions. Olshem was the last Wise Man before Bontihm. He was also a seer. He saw the future. He predicted what Maldaha would do, what *you* would do. After trying his best to change things, he realized he had to just let things be. The future could not be altered. Olshem would never drive Maldaha to do what he did."

Atakos was curious. "What...did he do?" he asked.

Colnaha put his head down in shame. He knew the truth. He always had. He knew what they were about to say. He took one glance back at his friends and his heart sank when he saw the looks on their faces. Turning back to the Dokami Council, he waited for them to respond.

Lady Arren was the one to speak. "When Maldaha heard our decision to choose Bontihm's apprentice as the next Wise Man, he flew into a rage. He believed he would be the next Wise Man because he was Olshem's son. As if it was an honor he was to inherit. In his fury, he brutally killed the messenger and three others who attempted to stop him. His hands are tainted with their blood. Maldaha needs to be brought to justice for those *heinous* crimes."

Colnaha looked back at his friends again in shame. He saw something different about the way they looked at him now. It was not just disappointment. No. It was more like...*disgust*.

"Why didn't you *tell* us?" Zadeia said in a whisper. Tears glistened in her brown eyes.

"I–I'm sorry," Colnaha said. However, he knew it would not be enough. He had kept the truth from them. They had already begun to judge him. Colnaha's shoulders dropped. He felt defeated and humiliated at the same time.

"That was not all he did," Lord Eavthon said, but Colnaha already knew what he was going to say. "He defied our laws by not turning himself in for the brutal murders. He took his family, including his sick father and ran away. Not only did he run away, he stole something from us. An orb. One of the last remaining Orbs of Restraint. The orb kept his whereabouts hidden from us so we could never find him."

Colnaha's eyes shifted from left to right at the mention of the orb. He tried hard to keep the location of the orb from his thoughts and to think of something else, fast. "I told you where he is," he quickly said. "He deserves to be punished for his crimes. You can find him now. The orb has been destroyed." His eyes widened as the blatant lie rolled off his tongue.

"Has it?" Lady Feir raised an eyebrow.

"It has." Colnaha's breath caught in his throat. He was too upset to tell the truth. And the lie—it came to him much too easily. He could not tell the truth now. Ever. If his friends found out, it would only prove that the Council members were right about him. "I am not a liar. Check your 'radars' yourself. Osmatu is no longer hidden. The orb is gone."

"Son of—" Lord Watten started.

"Don't call me that!" Colnaha shouted, putting his hands over his ears in a spasm of insanity. "I am not *like* him!" He looked back at his friends' astonished faces and cringed. Turning back to the Dokami Council, he knew what they were all thinking. He *was* like his father. He was no different. Nevertheless, they did not know him. They did not! Suddenly, he wanted so much to leave and never return. "I don't have to take any more of this...*ridicule*. I am leaving."

"You will desert us here?" Prince Aillios said.

Colnaha lowered his eyes. No, he was not like his father. "I will not leave you. I will prove to you I am not like *him*. Nevertheless, I will not stay in this room and be humiliated any longer. Please excuse me," he said under his breath and practically ran out of the room.

The silence, which permeated the air when Colnaha walked out, was thick. The people he had left behind were dumbstruck. Even Prince Aillios wasn't so sure Colnaha was exactly who he said he was.

Cristaden was the first to speak. "I read his mind, my lords and ladies. What he said was the truth. He is not like his father. In fact, he hates him." Her friends backed her up by nodding in agreement. They wanted so much to believe Colnaha that Cristaden's statement cleared any doubts they had.

"Cristaden," Lady Feir said. "Your gifts are extraordinary. However, you can only see what the mind is *allowing* you to see. Search deeper and you will find that sometimes, when a leaf falls from a tree, it just might provide the very moisture and protection needed to help the tree grow. Don't set your sights so low, my dear."

Lady Feir smiled, but Cristaden could not return the smile. Instead, she lowered her eyes. Lady Feir was right. She could only hear what someone wanted her to hear, if they knew of her powers—which Colnaha did. He could easily say one thing to avoid thinking something else. She turned to Zadeia and instantly felt sorry for her. She knew her friend had strong feelings for Colnaha. Even now, tears of sadness were rolling down Zadeia's cheeks, which she desperately tried to wipe away. Turning back to Lady Feir, Cristaden caught Atakos staring intently at her. He was visibly worried for all of them. *What have we gotten ourselves into by trusting Colnaha?* she thought.

Lady Feir interrupted Cristaden's thoughts by clearing her throat. "Please tell us," she said, changing the topic. "What became of your teacher, Hamilda Shing?"

It was as if the dark cloud, forming over the group with the talk of Colnaha and his father, descended even further. The five teens took turns recounting their journey to find Hamilda and what they discovered along their way. They told them about Queen Lhainna and the fairies, including the story she told them about Brulok and his minions. They told them how they were attacked and how they learned to fight and survive. They spoke of what happened when they reached the caves in Paimonu with heavy hearts. It pained them to go into detail of how their beloved teacher had lured them there to kill them and how they almost killed her. Cristaden explained how she brought Hamilda back from her despair and when she discovered she was Queen Lhainna's daughter, half-Dokami and half-fairy. At the end, she explained why Hamilda felt the need to run away.

"So you do not know where she is now?" Lord Watten said.

"No, sir," Fajha said. "She was gone before we even knew she left the caves. I couldn't even pinpoint her location right afterwards."

Lord Watten made eye contact with Lady Feir. Cristaden knew what they were thinking. Bontihm was dead. His only replacement was gone. It could take a long time to find the next Dokami Wise Man.

"But there's something else," Zimi said. "After Hamilda left, we were trying to find our way out of the caves and fell upon a spaceship."

Surprisingly, Lord Eavthon nodded. "Yes," he said. The other council members nodded as well, as if they knew of the spaceship and what Zimi was about to say.

Zimi frowned but continued. "On the spaceship, we found out there are Dokamis still living on Jmugea. In fact, there might be an entire planet *full* of them." The Council's reaction to his statement was not what he and his friends had expected. They just simply nodded and waited for him to continue.

"Wait," Fajha said. "You know?"

The council members glanced at each other before saying anything. "Yes," Lady Feir finally said.

"It is not in our, or your, best interest to discuss the Jmugeans," Lord Watten said. "To them, we no longer exist. And we would like to keep it that way."

The five teens looked at each other in astonishment. This was not what they expected to hear.

Atakos quickly stood up. "And…also…" he said. "There's something we haven't mentioned…"

"What is it young man?" Lord Watten said.

"We were attacked by Brulok's minions after we left the caves. It was the worst attack we had ever experienced. I'm pretty sure we would have died if it wasn't for Zadeia and Zimi and their abilities." Atakos pulled an object from his pocket. The object was silver in color and rusted along the edges. "Colnaha's airship had a communicator. It's used to make contact with other planets and to send them distress signals if necessary."

All five members of the Dokami Council sat up in attention.

"A communicator?" Lord Watten's eyebrows came together into a deep frown. "To contact other *planets*?"

"Y-Yes," Atakos said, knowing what he was about to say was probably not going to go over well with them.

"Could it be the same one?" Lady Feir said.

"Couldn't be," Lord Lovanthe said.

"Maybe it was acquired through the Western Army," Lord Eavthon said.

"It *can't* be," Lady Arren said. She appeared to be in shock.

"What do you mean?" Fajha said. "This one was attached to Colnaha's airship. We've used it—"

"What?" Lady Feir said, while the others gasped, interrupting Fajha's explanation.

Lady Arren stood up and glided to Atakos faster than a blink of an eye. The wind carrying her swept around him and took the silver device from his hands, placing it into hers. She slowly sank to the ground as she examined it.

"What's wrong?" Zimi said.

"What did you *do*?" Lady Arren said, looking up at Fajha. Her eyes were almost stark white. Her face was full of fear as she held the device in her hands.

Fajha sank deep into his chair. He glanced at his friends but did not know what to say. It was obvious they had done something horribly wrong.

"Do not blame them," Prince Aillios said. "It was my fault. I convinced them to do it."

"No," Atakos said. "It was my fault. I wanted to wait for your permission but, after we were attacked, I made the decision to send out the signal."

"*Where?*" Lord Eavthon asked.

Atakos lowered his eyes. "To Jmugea."

Gasps were heard around the room from the members of the Dokami Council. They said nothing, just stared at the group of six in astonishment, so Atakos continued. "We made the distress call to the Dokami on Jmugea, thinking they could help us. That they were our last hope."

"Did you get a response back?" Lord Watten curiously asked.

"We did," Zimi said. "They said 'no'."

Lady Arren stood up and cradled the device in her hands. "To think…after all these years," she said in her air-like whisper. "Generation after generation had come and gone and they still refuse to help us." She chuckled softly under her breath. "Those—"

"Arren!" Lady Feir said, interrupting her. "Mind your tongue." To the group of six, she sighed. "This exact device was stolen from us. Years ago. Before we ventured away from Paimonu."

"How do you know it wasn't just hidden?" Fajha said. "Like the spaceship?"

"No, it was stolen from *us*, the Dokami Council." Lady Feir waved her hand around the room at her fellow council members. "We were there when it disappeared."

"That's impossible," Prince Aillios stated. "That would make you… three hundred years old."

"Try a little older," Cristaden said as a thought dawned on her. She knew the truth, although she had forced herself to believe it could not possibly be true. The reason they seemed so familiar to her. As if she had seen them before. Cristaden stood up and took a step towards Lady Feir. "I know you," she said. "I knew I have seen you before but I just could not place it. I thought it was impossible."

Lady Feir raised her eyebrows but allowed her to continue.

"You–you're Reyshi. Reyshi Maephit. Aren't you?"

She smiled.

"What?" the others said in unison.

"I knew it," Cristaden said. She turned to Lord Watten, the one with the short black hair and blue eyes. "And Drae! Rueslon's brother, Drae!"

Lord Watten nodded. "How did you know?"

"My vision. I saw the events of the past unfold before my eyes. I saw what happened. The combining of the two races to create Dokami children. The hate. The segregation. That's why you seemed familiar to me. But how? How is it possible? How can you have lived so long?"

"It is difficult to explain," Drae said. "At first, we did not understand it either. We are *not* immortal. We never were. I am sure we will die one day and I know we can be killed. We discovered it after we left Jmugea. When we reached a certain age, the growing process essentially *slowed*. The power within us was so great, it would not allow us to grow old at a normal rate. To be more specific, over the past five hundred years, we believe we have only aged five or so years."

"Unbelievable," Prince Aillios said in a whisper.

"Incredible," Zadeia said, all thoughts of Colnaha slipping out of her mind.

"Is it the same for all the Dokami of your time?" Atakos asked.

"Unfortunately, we had to learn the truth the hard way. It only happened to some of those directly born from Shaergan and Jmugean parents. At the instant of their special union, an immense surge of power recreated us, the Dokami. Therefore, the strength of it gave us extreme abilities. To live a long time is a rare Dokami *ability*. When our children began to surpass us, we understood. It was sad to see our children growing old and dying. Because of this, we stopped having children and chose, rather, to stay in seclusion here. We do not allow anyone to see us because they will not understand. The owners and the workers of this museum is of Dokami blood, which makes it easier for us to reside here without being questioned. We also did not wish to attach ourselves to the generations who came after us. It hurt too much to watch them die."

"So it isn't true that the Dokami Council chooses orphaned children as their successors," Zimi said, more like a statement than a question.

Lord Lovanthe shook his head. "No. Someday we will, if and when we begin to expire."

"I see," Atakos said. "How did you come up with your names?"

Lady Arren took it upon herself to explain. "Our names are from the ancient language of Omordion. My real name is Nariele. Lovanthe, whose real name is Amzin, uses the ancient Omordion word for love. Watten is the word for water. Ollige uses the name Eavthon, which is the ancient word for earth. Feir—"

"Fire," Zadeia said, guessing the obvious.

"And Arren is air, right?" Fajha said.

"Precisely," Nariele said.

At that moment, the six friends realized the meaning behind the murals, positioned directly behind the tables of each member of the Dokami Council. The erupting volcano stood for fire, the cloud blowing the fire stood for air, the earthquake under the ocean was obviously for earth, the tsunami, heading towards the shore of Isre Square, stood for water, and the exploding hearts from the cherub's arrow over the sleeping town stood for love. They could now see the explosions were meant to warn the town of the tsunami headed their way. The entire mural was good versus evil. Each destructive force was met with a solution to solve the cataclysmic event and prevent certain death.

"Wow," Zimi said.

Reyshi stood up and walked around her desk to Cristaden. "You said you had a vision of the past," she said. "How much did you see?"

Cristaden explained her entire vision to Reyshi. All the while, Reyshi kept glancing back and forth between her and Drae, tears filling her eyes at the mention of Soli's name. When Cristaden was finished, she wiped her eyes and took a few steps back. She looked as if she was about to sink to the floor and cry, but Nariele glided forward and grabbed a hold of her shoulders to keep her standing.

Reyshi looked down at Cristaden and her tearful eyes implored her. "By any chance…?" she asked, seeming as though she could not bring herself to say one more word, as if she did not want to know the answer to her question, but had to ask.

Drae finished her question for her. "Did your vision show you what happened to my brother? To Rueslon?"

Cristaden sadly shook her head. "No. I know he was the reason the Jmugean Council and their armies were destroyed but I wasn't shown what happened to him. When the Jmugeans attacked Dokar, a dying soldier told the king what happened to their planet. That was all."

"Do you think…by any chance…?" Reyshi asked, but hesitated again.

Cristaden sighed. "I do not know. Nothing I was shown suggests he might still be alive."

Reyshi made eye contact with Drae and he shook his head. He then stood up to address the teens and Prince Aillios. "I know you must be famished and tired," he said. "Our meeting is adjourned for today. We will discuss what your next steps will be. You are free to return when you have had plenty of rest. Lord Lovanthe will walk you out."

Prince Aillios looked at Atakos and the teenager shrugged. To be dismissed so suddenly was strange. Despite their confusion, they knew they would need to save their many questions for the morning and respect the Council's wish for them to leave.

Fajha smiled broadly and invited his friends to join him at one of his grandfather's estates, located not too far from Isre Square. The estate had many rooms and they could stay there as long as they wanted, while they were in Saiyut.

Prince Aillios was hesitant. Considering the fact that he was the son of King Tholenod, he did not feel it was right for him to reside in the home of a Western Omordion emperor. Amzin, sensing his hesitation, offered him to stay in one of the rooms in the museum and he graciously accepted. He did not wish to separate from the ones he was sent to fight alongside with, but he felt he had no choice. And besides, it would give him the opportunity to learn more about the Dokami clan directly from the ones who started it all. "I just need my horse," Aillios said to Fajha. "Do you mind removing him from the airship?"

"Of course," Fajha said.

As Amzin led their visitors out, Reyshi stepped away from Nariele. "Why didn't we tell him?" she said, looking back and forth at Drae, Nariele, and Ollige. "How long do we have to keep this secret?"

"He is not ready," Drae said. "He will not understand the *importance*."

Nariele looked down at the silver communicator in her hand, sighed, and looked up at Reyshi's imploring eyes. "When the time is right," she said in her thin, wispy voice. "We *will* tell him. When the time is *right*."

CHAPTER 21

Fajha decided to bring his friends to the summer estate belonging to his grandfather, Emperor Vermu, because he knew his family would not be there. They would be free to stay as long as necessary without having to answer any questions or risk being returned to Lochenby. He was sure his parents probably thought he was still being held 'for his protection' at the Sheidem City Army Base by the corrupt General Komuh. No need to worry them any further.

During the whole ride east of Isre, Colnaha had not uttered a word. He kept his eyes focused straight ahead, following the directions given to him by Fajha, it seemed, without even blinking. The tension in the air made the others nervous because, essentially, their lives were in his hands. Finally, when Fajha pointed out that they were approaching the grand estate, they began to breathe a little easier.

Emperor Vermu's summer home was comparable to the sheer size of the entire Saiyutan Museum. Nestled on top of a cliff and overlooking the Saimino Ocean, it was hidden away, far from civilization, but close to the Pensiki Islands, which the teens could see miles away from shore. The estate was gorgeous. The red brick, main living area had about fifty or so rooms. Nestled a little ways away from the main building, was the guesthouse, which was much smaller but still expansive in its own right. Fajha told Colnaha to land the airship in the grass closest to the guesthouse and indicated it would be where they would be staying.

"Wow," Cristaden breathed when they disembarked. "This is amazing."

Fajha smiled and looked around. "I love it here," he said. "This is where we usually stay when I am away from Lochenby for the summer. I like to climb down the cliff over there and spend hours by the ocean. It is peaceful here and one could feel as free—"

"As a bird," Zimi said, cutting him off with a smirk.

"At any given time," Atakos said, laughing. "We know."

"Come on guys, cut it out," Zadeia said, reaching out to touch his arm. "It's lovely Fajha. Say whatever you want about it. It is something to be proud of."

Fajha smiled at Zadeia for being supportive, but his smile faded when he felt a pair of unwavering eyes boring into him like steel daggers. It was obvious Colnaha was still upset about what the Dokami Council had said about him and his father, but it did not explain why he was staring at *him* in that way.

"Fajha," Atakos said, interrupting his thoughts. "I think we have company."

Fajha turned away from Colnaha and spotted the head butler and two security guards briskly walking in their direction from the main house. "I'll handle this," he said. He marched towards the three men to meet them halfway. The other teens could see a change in their demeanor the closer they got to Fajha. At first, they seemed full of rage, intent on throwing out some highly unwanted guests as quickly as possible, but their rapid footsteps began to slow. Eventually, the two security officers stopped their advance and allowed the hesitant butler to approach Fajha on his own. It wasn't surprising when he and the two security guards bowed to their friend as if he was a king who had just returned home.

Colnaha muttered something incoherent under his breath while the others looked on in silent amusement. So this was what it was like to live a day in the life of Fajha Bayaht outside of Lochenby. It was a miracle he never once displayed signs of being a spoiled child.

After a brief conversation with the butler, Fajha walked back to his friends. "We're good. I told the head butler we will be staying here for a short time and we were on a top-secret mission. He will not be disclosing our whereabouts to anyone. I also asked him to have food prepared for us within the hour. Let me show you around."

Fajha gestured for them to follow him across the lawn and into the three-story brick house. When he flung opened the white, double front doors, the teens were in even more shock as they stepped onto the foyer.

The floors were a shiny gray and black marble and the walls were all white with white statues of angels and cherubs carved into them along with beautifully painted portraits of Fajha's ancestors along the walls. Two white, grand staircases were on either side of the foyer, leading up to the second floor.

"How many bedrooms are in this house?" Cristaden asked.

"There are seven," Fajha said. "Four on the second floor and three on the third. Two of the bedrooms on the third floor are mine. I use one to sleep in and the other to do my studies. We will go upstairs after we've eaten. First though, I would like to show you something." He led the five teens through the foyer and out the back door. Spreading his arms out, he sighed deeply. "This is our garden. One of my favorite places to get lost in."

It was unlike any garden they had ever seen. Even Lochenby's garden, full of flowers and trees, could not compare to Fajha's garden. There had to be hundreds of flowering trees of every shade and color, every single species of plant life from roses to creeping vines, and, what was more incredible, right smack in the middle of it all was an impressive maze of tall hedges.

"Remember how I would walk through a maze when I was meditating?" Fajha said. "This is it."

"Wow, Fajha," Atakos said. "It's amazing."

"Thank you. Want to do something fun? Let's see who can make it to the end of the maze first."

"Obviously, you're going to win," Zadeia said.

"No way. I always get lost."

Giggling like little school children, Atakos, Cristaden, Zimi and Fajha ran towards the maze. Colnaha seized the opportunity to grab Zadeia's arm, stopping her from running off with them.

"I–I need to talk to you, Zadeia," Colnaha said with a look of desperation in his eyes.

Zadeia cringed and gently pulled her arm out of his grasp. She glanced in the direction her friends had run off to, wondering why they would leave her alone with someone so deceitful. She had once stood up for Colnaha, defending him because she believed he was a good person. Now, even Cristaden doubted her power to read minds because of his apparent deception. Zadeia was not sure who he was anymore.

Colnaha tried to ignore Zadeia's uneasiness and how frightened she seemed when he grabbed her arm. He just wanted her to hear his side of the story. He wanted her to have faith in him again. "What the Council said about me—it wasn't true. I'm not like my—"

"Everything okay here?"

Atakos, who was standing close to them all of a sudden, as if he had magically appeared out of thin air, interrupted Colnaha's explanation. Colnaha's jaw tightened when he saw the others exiting the maze as well, heading back towards them with fear in their eyes.

Seriously? he thought.

"Everything is *fine*," Colnaha said, sneering at Atakos, who kept glancing back and forth between him and Zadeia, as if he was waiting to hear the actual truth. When Fajha reached them, Colnaha said he was not hungry and demanded to know where he was sleeping. Fajha gave him directions to a room at the end of the second floor hall and he turned, walking away from them—jaws clenched—seething with anger. He turned back only once when he heard Zadeia's *friends* asking her if she was okay. They were gathered around her as if she had been hurt in a horrific fight and Atakos was staring after him with a look he was sure was close to absolute resentment. Colnaha practically growled as he turned away. No one would ever understand him. At this point, he was on his own again.

Atakos, Cristaden, Fajha, Zimi, and Zadeia ate their dinner in silence. The past few weeks had been an emotional and physical roller coaster ride for the five members of Omordion's Hope. Their training was supposed to end when they were eighteen, when they had been trained enough to help win the war brought upon the world by King Tholenod. They were supposed to have three more years to complete their training. However, just in the past few weeks, as they searched for Hamilda, they had learned more than they could have ever imagined. In the end, they were exhausted and weary of what the future would bring.

"Can someone pass the bread?" Zimi said groggily after he shoveled down his third plate of food. He and his friends were having dinner on the first floor veranda, overlooking the garden.

"Where do you find the room in there?" Atakos said, picking up the glass bowl of rolls and handing it to Zadeia so she can pass it to her brother.

"I'm just so—hungry," Zimi said, attempting to stifle a giant burp but not succeeding in the slightest. Zadeia made a disgusted face as she handed him the bread.

"Well," Fajha said. "There's plenty more where this came from so take it easy." He placed his own fork down on his empty plate and sat back. "So. Where do we go from here?"

"We will meet with the Dokami Council tomorrow, I guess," Atakos said. "See what else they have to say."

"With Colnaha?" Zimi said. "He's our only form of transportation right now. I don't think the Council will be happy to see *him* again. And besides, they told us to come back when we've had plenty of rest. That could take *weeks*."

"We don't have *weeks*."

Fajha rolled his eyes. "I don't even know why you bother to argue with him, Atakos."

Cristaden laughed. "But he does have a point about Colnaha. What the Council said about his father...who Colnaha really is...? I was beginning to think my power to read minds and 'feel out' people had gotten stronger. They made me feel like my power is just a cheap parlor trick. A power anyone could figure out and easily manipulate."

"I don't think that's it, Cristaden," Zadeia said. "I think Colnaha actually believes he's not like his father. He believes he is a good person. Your power will allow you to pick up on what he thinks, but nothing more." She looked down and stared at her hands as tears filled her eyes. "I miss home at times like this."

Zimi rolled his eyes and quickly glanced at the evening sky. When he didn't see any impending storms coming their way, he sighed. "Well, don't miss home too much, Zadeia. I wouldn't want to be on a military base right now. *This* is living."

Atakos' shoulders dropped at the mention of home. The last thing he heard, when he had contacted his parents, was how sick his mother still was. She had been sick all throughout the summer months and did not seem to be getting any better. His father tried not to worry him but he had heard the fear in his voice. He did not know what he would do if his mother succumbed to her illness. A world without her in it would be a sad, sad place to live.

Cristaden reached across the table and squeezed Atakos' hand. He was suddenly aware that everyone had been staring at him and, when Cristaden touched him, she confirmed something was wrong.

"Atakos," Fajha said. "What is it?"

Atakos looked around at his friends and glanced at Cristaden, who had released his hand and nodded with a grim smile, as if to tell him it was okay to share his fears with his closest friends. "It's my mother," he said. "She's sick. I'm worried about her. I have tried to push it out of my mind but lately I can't help feeling like I need to be there. With her."

"It's been a while since you contacted them," Zimi said.

"Maybe she's doing better," Zadeia said, trying to go in the direction Zimi was headed.

"Yes," Fajha said. "Who knows what might have happened in the past few weeks."

"The problem is," Atakos said. "I don't know. That's what scares me."

"If it were possible, I would try to heal her," Cristaden said. "But so far I've only been able to heal wounds. I have no idea if I would be able to cure illnesses or even how to begin."

Atakos' shoulders seemed to drop even further. "And the thing is, even if you wanted to give it a try, Cristaden, we can't go all the way to Pontotoma. With Colnaha the way he is right now, it's impossible."

"Maybe the Dokami Council will have a way of getting in touch with them," Zimi said.

"Did you see how old-*fashioned* everything was over there?" Fajha said. "I doubt they even know what a line communicator looks like."

This made Atakos crack a smile. The Dokami Council members seemed to have been living in the ancestral ages for so long. He wondered if they even remembered what an airship or spaceship looked like. Three hundred years living in a building they can't leave, hidden from the entire world? What a life. He knew, for sure, he would never accept *that* job even if they begged him to take it.

"Don't worry, Atakos," Zadeia said. "I'm sure your mother will be okay. She is of Dokami blood, isn't she? She'll pull through."

"Thanks, Zadeia," Atakos said. "That's what I want so much to believe."

CHAPTER 22

Colnaha folded his arms behind his head and stared up at the white ceiling of the large bedroom Fajha had assigned to him. He had blown out the candles on the dresser near the bed so the only light in the room was the moonlight, streaming in from a pair of large windows across from his bed. The bed was comfortable, with soft white pillows and a warm blue blanket, matching the blue furniture in the room. It was all warm and cozy…if he cared about how comfortable the room was.

Colnaha was furious.

The Dokami Council had looked down on him and his family as if they were the lowest scum on Omordion. How dare they humiliate him in front of everyone like that! And the looks on their faces…the look on Zadeia's—

Colnaha closed his eyes, attempting to block out the image, but he still saw her, the look of disappointment written all over her face. How could she ever learn to trust him after all of those lies?

It's so terrible…It's enough to make me cry…

A strange voice came into Colnaha's head but, oddly enough, he did not consider for one second it was not his own. "Yes," he said aloud, his eyes welling up with tears. "So terrible…"

They will always look at me as if I was a treacherous snake…hissssss.

He nodded. "Yes."

They don't like me…and they never will…

"I know." Tears fell from Colnaha's eyes and rolled down the sides of his face, stopping only when caught by his reddish-brown hairline.

Those people were not his friends. No matter what he said, they would always think he was the reason General Komuh came after them in the desert. They would always look at him as if he was a traitor, one who could not be trusted. They would always look at him as a murderer's son, capable of carrying out the same vicious acts.

They want so much to watch me die.

Colnaha frowned and shook his head. Where did that thought come from? "That's *not* true," he said. They would never want him dead. It was not in their nature…right?

I can change all that.

Colnaha blinked. Something was not right. Was he going insane?

I can become a hero…save the day.

"How?" Colnaha said mechanically and then frowned. What was happening to him? He felt like he was losing control of his own mind.

Zadeia would want me…she would want to be with me forever…

Colnaha quickly sat up in bed. "What the…?" He was frightened. The thoughts in his head were not his own. "Who are you?"

I am you and you are me. Together we are one and we will make them feel… make them understand.

Colnaha looked around the room. He was still alone. And going crazy. "N–no, I–I…"

Yesss, the snakelike voice said.

"No, I…yes…"

Yes, we will make them see.

"Yes we wi—we? No! What is going *on* here?"

Keep quiet! They will hear you!

Colnaha lowered his voice. "But who *are* you?"

He received no answer.

The frightening voice had vanished from Colnaha's head. In fact, he had not realized there had been so much pressure in his head until it lifted when the voice had gone. Something was wrong. His friends–they were in danger. He must do something! He must warn the others! He must—

A soft noise interrupted his jumbled thoughts.

It sounded like a window sliding open.

He turned towards the large window across the room. A cool wind came into the darkened room with a soft 'sigh' as one of the window panels slid close. A black shadow slowly crept from the window, down the wall, across the floor, and onto his bed. Colnaha tried to get off the bed, to run away, but he was frozen in place, unable to do anything but breathe and shift his eyes. He wanted so badly to scream, but no sound would come out of his frozen throat.

The black shadow crept up to his bed and touched his pajama-clad legs with a deathly cold he had never experienced before in all his life. Sweat poured down his face as he struggled to break free of his paralyzed state but could not.

The shadow slowly crept up his body and rolled over his chest and up his neck. Colnaha watched in complete horror as it forced his mouth open and slid inside, invading his entire being with its icy touch. He immediately felt an explosion from within, the force of it throwing him back down to the bed where his body erupted in severe convulsions.

As the room lurched into darkness, Colnaha suddenly wished for death. Death's swift hand would have been *mercy* compared to the pain and suffering he was experiencing. Even absolute torture was far better. However, he did not meet death. All he was given, instead, was torture and pure *agony*.

CHAPTER 23

"Hello?" Atakos called out into the dark of night. "Is anyone there?" He did not expect to get a response and wasn't at all surprised when he didn't receive one. Just silence—apart from the occasional echo of his shaky voice.

Atakos looked around him. *Why does this place look so familiar?* he asked himself.

Yes.

He was standing in the middle of Isre Square.

The square was void of human life with only a few softly lit lanterns, hanging from the signs of the old shops, lining the empty street around him. One particular store, he noted, was titled *Mystics*, its windows draped in black curtains with a crystal ball sitting in one, overlooking the cobblestoned street. Atakos shuddered when he saw the store and looked away. It gave him a dreadful feeling, as if pure evil lurked inside.

Atakos then blinked and shook his head. He could not remember how he had managed to get there. The last thing he remembered was saying goodnight to his friends and crashing on the soft, warm bed, in the room given to him by Fajha. He was so tired, he barely remembered closing his eyes. Yet, when he opened them, he was in the square. But how? It all did not make sense to him. Looking up at the hill leading up to the museum, Atakos ran several yards towards it, determined to get to the Dokami Council as fast as possible.

However, something made him come to an abrupt halt.

A small figure slowly stepped out of the shadows of a shop called *Medicinal Goods*. It was a boy, most likely around the age of six or seven. He had dark, wavy hair and, despite the darkness enveloping them in the square, Atakos could see that his eyes were bright blue in the moonlight. The boy walked towards him, taking slow but careful steps. He was wearing a long, white nightgown and his feet were bare on the cobblestoned street. He seemed determined, but frightened at the same time, as if he was scared of Atakos, but needed to say something important to him as soon as possible.

"What are you doing out here by yourself?" Atakos asked.

The boy shuffled closer still, but did not answer Atakos' question.

"Do you need help?"

The boy nodded as he came to a halt. His eyes steadily shifted from Atakos' face to look at something behind him. "Gral. Fi. Hadomna," he said, making eye contact with Atakos again.

"What?" Atakos said.

"Gral. Fi. Hadomna," the boy said again.

"I...don't...understand. What does that mean?"

As if to answer Atakos' question, a low, intense growl echoed in the quiet of the square.

Startled, Atakos turned around, trying to figure out where the sound had come from. His stomach turned when he realized he was the only one out there who could fight if Brulok's minions ambushed him. His friends were not there to help him this time.

The boy! He had to protect the boy. Turning back around, Atakos didn't see him anywhere. It seemed like he had vanished. *He probably ran away when he heard the growl*, he thought. *I hope he finds somewhere safe to hide.*

The growl came again, followed by a high-pitched screech, cutting through the silence of the square like a sharp knife, causing Atakos' heart to pound hard against his chest. The sound steadily grew louder until he had to cover his ears. It reminded him of the shrieks from the creatures they had fought on the Sremati Volcano, which terrified him most of all. How could he fight them on his own?

Just as abruptly as it began, the horrifying screeching stopped, leaving complete silence in the square once again, without as much as an echo to follow.

Atakos lowered his shaking hands and balled them into fists at his side. Whatever evil creature was out there, he was never one to back down from a fight or head for the hills, screaming. He spread his feet a little further apart to steady himself and prepared for a fight.

The empty silence following the screech was deafening. Atakos searched the shadows around him. Looking around and around, he could not see anything out of the ordinary. Frustrated, he stopped looking and stood still. Perhaps he could sense where the creature was. Upon closing his eyes, he realized it was already too late. Putrid, hot air grazed his neck and entered his nostrils. He did not have to turn around to know the obvious. The creature, whatever it was, was behind him. With amazing stealth, it had snuck up to him without his knowledge.

Atakos slowly turned around.

Nothing could have prepared him for what he saw.

The sheer size of the beast surprised him. At first, all he saw were yellow eyes, which were only slightly bigger than Atakos' head—each. Gradually, the rest of its body came into view. Almost as black as the night, Atakos could barely make out the scaly skin covering the body of the dragon-like creature. It was *massive*. Furthermore, it was levitating off the ground, which explained how a monster that size could sneak up on him so quietly.

With one look at the creature, Atakos knew he could not fight it alone. He would surely lose and most likely be eaten alive. One thing was for certain, although the odds were against him, he would not go down without a fight. The little boy, who must have been trying to warn him, would be in danger if he didn't. Without a moment's hesitation, Atakos took a step back and summoned his energy to send a powerful attack towards the beast. Faster than Atakos would have predicted, the creature turned its head to the side and had its mouth around his midsection, its massive head threatening to swallow him whole. The creature's sharp teeth were sinking deeper into his flesh as he hollered in pain. Atakos tried desperately to push the creature away, but the more he pushed, the tighter the monster's jaw became. Tears sprung up in his eyes when he realized the lower half of his body was slowly being *ripped* apart.

"H-Help! Help me!" Atakos screamed, knowing that no one could hear him. He tried desperately to blow up the creature but only some scales flew off its enormous head without as much as a scratch on its thick skin. Atakos wailed when he realized how weak his powers were and how strong Brulok's minions were becoming.

The excruciating pain was unbearable and Atakos could feel his blood soaking his clothes and dripping down his legs. Lots of it. He was *dying*. Better yet, he was already dead. How could he recover from the amount of blood seeping from his wounds? No blood transfusion could save him if he was saved in time. As his vision started to dissipate, due to the severe loss of blood, he glimpsed something moving at the other end of the square, behind the vile creature.

A figure in white was coming towards them.

At first Atakos thought it was a vision, the result of his impending death, but, as he squinted his eyes to gain a few moments of clarity back, he could not believe what he saw. Before the figure in white got close to him and the creature, a blinding, white light erupted from it and plowed towards them. The dragon-like monster released its deadly grip on Atakos and whipped its head around, shrieking a most hideous sound, which exploded in Atakos' ears, causing him to cover them as he fell, mortally wounded, to the cobblestoned street. When he realized he was lying in his own pool of blood, he started screaming in absolute horror. This had to be what it felt like to die.

The blinding light, upon touching the beast, seemed to disintegrate it, tail first, right before Atakos' eyes. After disintegrating the entire monster within seconds, the light lashed out at him. He could feel the intense heat of it blinding him with its rays. Covering his face with his arms, a thought dawned on him. He felt no more pain. He felt an overwhelming sensation of…peace. He knew then that he *was* dead. Disintegrated. Just like the creature.

Atakos screamed.

"Atakos!"

"No! I don't want to die! I don't want to *die!*"

"Atakos! Wake up!"

No longer feeling the intense heat of the blinding white light, Atakos' arms flew down from his face and he jumped back in his bed, bringing his legs up to his chest. He was sweating and shaking uncontrollably. His vision still had not cleared and it took him a moment to realize the pain had returned, more excruciating than before. Through his blurred vision, all he saw was red. Red all over his clothes. All over his bed. All over his hands.

Blood.

Tons of blood *everywhere*. The puncture wounds from the creature were still there, but he was still alive.

"Hold still, Atakos. I'm trying to help you..."

As his vision slowly came into focus, Atakos realized he was back in Emperor Vermu's estate, far from the city of Isre. Back in the nice, comfortable room Fajha had given him. The moonlight filtered in from the largest window near his bed, providing the only light in the room. The meager light enabled him to see the blood. So *much* of it.

Cristaden was sitting next to him, her eyes filled with tears, pleading with him to keep still. She had her hands on his abdomen, attempting to heal him.

Atakos coughed several times and tasted blood. He had not been dreaming. It was real. He panicked, trying desperately to escape, as if the creature was still there, right in front of him.

"Please be still, Atakos," Cristaden said. Her plea seemed to work this time when he made eye contact with her and stopped trying to run away.

"How–did I–get back here?" Atakos said, cringing in excruciating pain.

"Atakos," Cristaden said, her hands glowing white on top of his wounds. "You've been here the *whole* time."

"What—?" Atakos almost jumped up but thought better of it when he felt a gush of blood seeping from a hole near his ribcage. Why was it taking so long for Cristaden to heal him? "I was out there–in the square. Isre–Square." He tried to recall the details of what happened, but all he could remember was the attack from the dragon-like creature. He felt there might have been something else of importance but, for some reason, he could not remember. "I saw a bright light...was that *you?*"

Cristaden, frustrated with the healing process, quickly nodded. "You were dreaming."

Atakos frowned. "I couldn't have been. Why am I hurt? How did you—?"

Cristaden shook her head. "I'm not sure. I fell asleep. Next thing I knew, I woke up in the square. Drawn to your screams. When I saw you, I thought I was too late. I called your name but you couldn't hear me. I knew I had entered your nightmare. That I was thrown into it because you were in desperate need of my help. I'm not sure how I killed that monster. I only wished it would go away and a bright light shot out of my hands and—killed it. I grabbed you and we both woke up. I don't remember how I got to your room. Or when."

Atakos began to understand. "He's trying to attack us in our sleep."

"Yes, but now he knows he cannot."

"Do you think the others are okay?"

"I believe so."

Cristaden placed her hands on her lap and examined the closed wounds. She frowned. He still had scars. Was she losing her healing touch? "I don't understand…"

"What is it?" Atakos looked down at his wounds and touched them, feeling the round and jagged scars. They still felt raw, as if they had only been bruised and were never opened in the first place.

"Well. Your body is not completely healing."

"I know. It still hurts. Why do you think that is?"

"I don't know." Cristaden tried to heal his scars again, but they only turned white against his caramel skin and faded to their normal color when she pulled her hands away. The scars were still there. Could Brulok's minions be getting stronger? Or was she losing her touch? Both thoughts terrified her.

"It's okay," Atakos said, sensing Cristaden's fear. He reached out and pulled her into a tight embrace before leaning back to look at her. "At least we're still alive. Whatever is happening, we will figure it out." Cristaden looked up at him and smiled. Atakos offered her a reassuring smile back. A few strands of blonde hair had fallen over one of her eyes, which he gently brushed away from her face with his hand. Before he knew what was happening, his eyes traveled down her face and fell on her mouth. He could not stop himself from what came to mind. The sudden longing to kiss her took over everything he was thinking, everything he was feeling. Looking back up at her eyes, Atakos knew she had read those thoughts from him. He was okay with that. She had to have sensed how he felt about her. It was impossible not to figure it out.

"Cristaden…I…"

Cristaden leaned forward unexpectedly and kissed Atakos. His heart leapt in his chest and a feeling of elation took hold of him, as if he was flying, high in the clouds. Her lips were even softer than he had ever imagined. And warm. So warm. He realized his whole body felt warm, from his head to his toes. *What a feeling*, he thought. Atakos did not want it to end. It was so…*magical*.

Cristaden pulled away unexpectedly, a bewildered look on her face. "What?" she said. "No." Her eyes were searching his in astonishment.

"What is it?" Atakos asked. "What's wrong?" Did she read something from his thoughts she did not like? All he remembered thinking was how nice it was to kiss her, the warmth, the intensity of it all…

Cristaden shied away from Atakos and sat back. She took a few deep breaths and looked like she wanted to say something, but then thought better of it. "Nothing. It was nothing."

"What was it?" Atakos asked. By the way her eyes regarded him, so frightened and confused, he understood then that it wasn't anything she picked up from his thoughts, it was something more. "Did you see something? Tell me what you saw."

Cristaden cringed, but didn't say what she wanted to say to Atakos. He was right, she *did* see something. A vision. Nonetheless, how could she tell Atakos what she saw if she did not understand it herself? "I–I'm sorry. It's gone. I can't even remember what it was." She reviewed it in her mind. The vision had to be nothing less than a glimpse of the future. She was sure of it.

"Will you try to remember?"

Cristaden could not help but feel sorry for lying to Atakos. On the other hand, she needed to verify the vision first before jumping to conclusions. "Yes…I will try."

Atakos smiled at Cristaden, to show her that he wasn't upset. She returned the smile and quickly stood up. "I must be going back to bed. We have a long day ahead of us tomorrow."

"But hold on. You don't have to leave…yet?"

Cristaden gave a half-hearted laugh and took a few steps towards the door. "I have to, Atakos. Take a bath if you can and change your clothes and bed sheets. You don't want to sleep in all of that blood—" She suddenly stepped back and gasped, her hands flying up to her mouth.

A dark figure loomed in the doorway.

"What is it?" Atakos asked, quickly standing up to see what had frightened Cristaden. He ignored the pain in his midsection and frowned. "Colnaha?"

Colnaha sauntered into the room, his eyes sunken in their sockets, as if he hadn't slept in days—weeks even. Even in the moonlight, his eyes seemed to be a dull gray-green color compared to his usually green eyes. He was wearing a black shirt and black pants, it seemed, to blend in with the darkness. Cristaden immediately sensed a significant change in him, but it didn't take a mind reader to figure it out. When he began to speak, Colnaha's voice was deeper than usual and, although it was dark in the room, his lips seemed to be barely moving. "I will be returning to my people now. They will need me when my father is arrested by the *Dokami Council*." He spat their title as if he detested even speaking the words.

Atakos became furious. He ignored the pain he was still feeling and rushed forward. "You can't be *serious*. We have to go back to the Dokami Council tomorrow. How do you suppose we do that?"

Colnaha menacingly looked Atakos square in the eyes as if he was ready to challenge him to an all-out brawl, ignoring the fact that Atakos was shockingly covered in blood, or perhaps not caring at all what might have happened to him. Shockingly, Colnaha backed up into the hall and uttered three words before walking away. "You will *manage*."

CHAPTER 24

The sky had finally cleared after the raging rainstorm and the sun was brightly shining. Princess Amilana was walking among the ruins of an ancient city, on a large, isolated island, far from Eynta Province. It was in the middle of Jreslan Ocean, renamed after the Queen Mother, Soli's mother. Amilana often came to the neglected city to be alone. To find peace. To walk through the tall grasses which overran it, the wooden and brick homes that had collapsed into a fraction of what they once were, and to walk among the remnants of a time, long ago, when people lived there, fighting every day to stay alive. No one ever ventured to the ancient city due to its violent past. The Dokami clan of Jmugea chose to forget, rather than immerse themselves in the choices their ancestors made.

But not Amilana.

Few people knew she visited the island, but she often did. How could they forget what happened? How was it possible to forget the mass murder of hundreds of thousands of Jmugeans, perhaps millions of them, driven to live on the island if they did not conform to mating with the Shaergans to create more Dokami offspring? It was a part of their dark history and should never have been forgotten or tossed aside as if it did not happen.

The island was named after the ruler of Jmugea, at a time when the first Dokamis were forced to live in a reservation and humiliated for all to see. Ghosh Hres, they called the island. *Ghoshie* for short. If you traveled to the mainland and mentioned you were from Ghoshie, your face was spat on, you were shoved, and forced to go back to the island where you came from. The Dokamis at the time had no need to cater to the likes of the purebred Jmugeans. They had taken too many years of hatred and hostility from them. Too many members of the Dokami clan at the time had died at their hands, including their Queen Mother, Soli. A once peaceful clan sought revenge.

And then a fatal decision was made to poison the Jmugeans of Ghoshie. To rid the planet of them. Slowly. Just like the plan their leaders had come up with to rid themselves of the Shaergans and the Dokami clan before the revolt.

Amilana took a few deep breaths in and then out. She looked up at the sky and studied the clouds rolling by. She then squeezed her eyes shut and opened them again, while taking a few more deep breaths. Every time the thought of what she read in their history books came to her mind, she had to breathe deeply to keep from getting sick.

The Jmugeans—they thought it was a plague. It affected mostly the women and children, until there was none of them left to carry on the purebred Jmugean race. The last of their men decided it was time to leave Jmugea, stole several spaceships from the Shaergans and left, never to be seen or heard from again.

Amilana sauntered over to an empty field of tall grass and shook her head to clear it. It was so long ago. Often times, she had to convince herself to live in the present and not in the past. That it was not *her* people, the ones living on Jmugea now, who had made those decisions. They were better than that now. Well—at least she *hoped* they were. Hopefully, they had learned from the past that there were other ways to handle things.

Amilana removed her knee-high, brown leather boots and flexed her bare feet before lying down on the wet grass to look up at the sky. She did not mind the rainwater soaking through her clothes, it made her feel alive in some sort of strange way. She closed her eyes and smiled when she realized she was no longer all alone in the emptiness of the tall, grassy field. Should she address the presence who interrupted her brief moment of sanity? No, her best option would be to wait it out. Eventually—

"AH!"

Yes. He never ceased to amaze her.

Amilana opened one eye and shook her head. "I knew you were there the whole time."

"It's not possible," the young man, named Rehahn, said. He was wearing the classic Jmugean Army uniform: a long white linen shirt with a brown, leather belt tied at his waist and brown, leather pants shoved into a pair of brown, leather boots. "I made sure to block my mind–shielded my presence–anything I could think of. You should find another place to hide though, it's so...depressing here."

Amilana sat up and turned to look up at him. "Shielded your presence?" she said, ignoring his comment about Ghoshie. He knew how important it was for her to visit the island when she needed an escape from life. "Honestly, Rehahn."

Rehahn smiled down at Amilana with his typical, silly grin. He still reminded her of the young boy she met when she was barely six years old. Hair just as golden as ever and eyes, still a creamy, chocolate brown. It seemed like he had recently spent days in the sun because his usual milky skin tone was now a darkened, tan color. At twenty-six years old, he was still her best friend, despite the four-year gap between their ages. He had always been. When she was little, he had taken her under his wing and taught her many things, unbeknownst to the king and queen. There were times she wished she was just as free as him, without any rules, which came with being a member of the royal family, and longed to run away with him to be free. She could never bring herself to do it though. Now, since both of them had important positions, they hardly saw each other the way they were so accustomed to while growing up. Rehahn was now Captain of the Jmugean Army and Amilana had her duties to fulfill as the Ambassador. Once in a great while, whenever they could get away from their duties, they would meet in the grassy field, to catch up with life and reminisce about old times.

On Amilana's twentieth birthday, in a desperate attempt to hold on to their friendship, Rehahn had posed the idea of asking the king and queen for her hand in marriage. Amilana refused, stubbornly declaring she would never get married, much less marry her best friend. It would be too...*weird*. She convinced Rehahn that marriage was not what he wanted either and made him vow never to speak of it again. For a while, Rehahn seemed hurt by her statements but, overtime, fell back into the role of being just her best friend once again. The thought of marriage only came up once after–what she began to refer to it as– 'the incident'. It was Rehahn's way of stabilizing their unbreakable bond once again. He explained that, if Amilana's parents had decided to marry her off–

which was the custom thing to do when a member of the royal family became of age—he would never have been able to see her again. Nothing more, nothing less. Amilana accepted his explanation but always had the feeling there was more to his proposal. Nevertheless, she would never know how he truly felt because the topic of marriage was never going to arise again.

She was never—*ever*—getting married.

"Yes," Rehahn said, sitting down on the ground next to Amilana. "Shield myself. The army has been teaching us this top-secret ability. It is classified. I'm not even supposed to be telling you."

Amilana laughed. "If this is true, you *have* to teach me."

Rehahn flashed her another big, toothy grin. "In due time, princess, I will."

Amilana rolled her eyes. "Don't call me that."

"You are a princess, by the way."

"I know. But, for a few, short moments, I just want to pretend I'm someone like you. Free to make my own choices. Free from any rules and regulations."

"In the army? You don't want my life, Ami. Trust me."

"How are you so sure?"

Rehahn turned away from her, plucked a few blades of grass out of the ground, and twirled them between his fingers. "You would miss living in castles and having your lavish lifestyle in a blink of an eye."

"Is that so?"

"Yes."

Amilana sighed. "I don't think so."

Rehahn looked up at her and smiled. "I hear this every time I come here. When will you ever accept your life the way it is?"

Amilana did not return his smile. "This time I think it's finally taking its toll on me." If one person existed on Jmugea, who she could talk to about the events of the previous day, it was Rehahn.

"Why would you think that?"

"Yesterday. I had a strange feeling something was wrong. That something terrible was happening back at the castle. I remember going to see the king and queen about this feeling I had. I can't recall what happened when I got there. I woke up in my bed. Hours later."

Rehahn frowned. "What do you mean? You forgot what happened? Like you blocked it out or something?"

"Yes. Why do you think that happened?"

Rehahn shook his head. He felt a wave of déjà-vu, as if she had told him a similar story before, but he could not quite remember if she had. "Hasn't this happened to you before?"

"No–I mean–I don't think so."

"Did you tell anyone?"

"No."

"Good. We don't want anyone thinking the heir to the throne of Jmugea has gone completely insane. Can you imagine your sister ruling the planet when your parents are no longer able to? It's probably exhaustion. Stress. You've been doing too much lately, you know?"

"It's my job, Rehahn."

"But you need a break."

"That's why I'm here."

"I know."

The two sat in silence for a few moments, not saying anything. Rehahn wanted to help Amilana feel better, but he was not sure how to anymore. It seemed like every time he saw her, she felt even worse about the direction her life was headed. He sighed. Unfortunately, he could not do anything to help. Furthermore, he knew the little time they had together would not be enough. It was never enough. Soon they would have to go back to their normal lives and say goodbye, not knowing when they would see each other again.

All of a sudden, Amilana groaned and glanced up at the sky.

"What is it?" Rehahn said.

Amilana's sixteen-year-old sister, Drissana, unexpectedly plopped herself down next to them from the air in a reckless, but sure shot landing. She had pulled her bright, red hair back into a bun and was wearing a light blue, formfitting long shirt with tight, dark blue pants, with absolutely nothing on her feet. And, once again, she was dirty. *All* over.

"Can't I just have a moment of peace, Drissi?" Amilana said, frowning at her attire and wrinkling her nose.

Drissana giggled, in the most obnoxious way ever recorded in Drissana-Annoying-Laugh-History, and sighed. "No. Of course not. The magistrate had a question about some boring law and requested your assistance. Therefore, I told him I would find you. I knew you would be here."

"Thanks ever so much, little sister."

"Not a problem. Hello Hahns!"

"Drissi," Rehahn said and nodded with a smile as he stood up with Amilana. He placed a hand on his best friend's shoulder and gave her a gentle squeeze. "Don't worry about a thing, Ami. Remember. Even if we are worlds apart, I will always be there for you. Don't ever forget that."

Amilana returned his smile with a quick nod and sadly watched as he lifted off the ground and glided through the tall grass backwards, waving to the two sisters until he was no longer in view.

"Bye Hahns!" Drissana called out. She turned to Amilana and frowned. "Is everything all right?"

Amilana nodded. She felt it best not to tell Drissana about what was bothering her. Her little sister had the tendency to come up with all kinds of crazy conspiracy theories, so unrelated to what she would be trying to explain to her. "Let's just…stay here a little while longer and then we'll go see the magistrate. Just pretend that you haven't found me yet. Is that okay?"

"Sure." Drissana looked puzzled, but she knew not to press her sister. She would get nowhere fast asking questions until Amilana was ready to tell her what was on her mind. She plopped herself down on the grass to wait. "Whatever you want."

"Thank you, little sister."

"You're welcome."

CHAPTER 25

As the first light of the morning sun rose over the glorious garden Fajha loved, he slowly walked through the tall maze of hedges. It was his objective to walk through the entire maze, while he waited for his friends to awaken. It was the perfect opportunity. Everything was so quiet and peaceful. He could hear the birds singing their sweet melodies along their way to find their morning feasts.

Fajha smiled as he weaved his way through the maze: right, left, and right again. Although he told his friends he did not know his way around the maze, he knew every twist, turn, and dead end like the back of his hand. He always made it to the end in no time. He only wanted to have fun with his friends, but not to win. Winning was never his goal.

After taking another right and a left turn, Fajha was strangely met with a dead end. "Wait," he said. "What?" He was sure he had taken the correct turns. Turning back around, Fajha was immediately met with another dead end. *I just came this way*, he thought. *What is happening here?* Turning back around, Fajha's eyes widened in surprise and he stifled a scream by covering his mouth with his hands. His heart thundered hard in his chest and shivers ran down his back.

Crouched in a corner of one of the hedges was a little boy. His blue eyes, which were red as if he had been crying, were trained on Fajha and unwavering. He had black, wavy hair, and fair skin. Why did he seem so familiar to Fajha? The boy abruptly stood up and pointed a finger at him as he slowly walked towards him.

Fajha took a couple of quick steps back and practically crashed into a six-foot wall of hedges. They were definitely not there before.

He was trapped.

The boy advanced towards him and his lips started moving. He was saying—maybe chanting—something Fajha could not understand. When he came closer, Fajha was able to make out a few words.

Gral. Fi. Hadomna.

The language the boy spoke. Fajha had studied it before. It was definitely not a dialect of Western Omordion. It reminded him of…it was a language of the East. From *Mituwa*. What would a Mituwan be doing in Saiyut?

A thought occurred to him. There *was* a Mituwan in Saiyut.

Prince Aillios.

The boy, with eyes almost identical to those of the prince, stopped when he was just inches away from Fajha and repeated himself once again. This time, as if a dense language barrier had completely lifted, Fajha understood him perfectly.

Gral. Fi. Hadomna.

They. Are. Coming.

Startled, Fajha woke up in his bed and took a few deep breaths. Pink light was pouring into his bedroom, indicating that it was still early morning.

It was just a dream, Fajha thought and shook his head. "But what does it mean?" he said aloud. A knock on his door interrupted his thoughts and he sat up in bed. "You may enter."

Atakos opened the door and Fajha could see that everyone was with him. They had a solemn look in their eyes. He knew right away they came bearing bad news.

"Colnaha left," Atakos said.

"What?" Fajha said, jumping out of bed, the strange dream he just had banished from his thoughts.

"Last night. He came into my room and said he was leaving. That he was going back to Osmatu. And then he left."

"Not only that," Cristaden said, "Atakos was attacked in his sleep." She described his dream and how she was pulled into it to save him. "We're pretty sure it was Brulok who had something to do with it. What worries me is, even when we woke up from the nightmare—when we were fully awake—Atakos still had the wounds he suffered *in* the dream. There was so much blood everywhere. I healed him—but it was difficult. After I stopped the bleeding and put the wounds back together, he still had the scars."

"Sorry about your sheets," Atakos said with a sheepish grin. He then lifted his shirt to show everyone his scars.

"I don't see anything," Zimi said.

"They're gone," Cristaden said, frowning.

Atakos looked down and was shocked. They *were* gone. "That's strange. They were still there when I got up this morning."

Fajha frowned. Colnaha had left, taking their only means of transportation with him. In a way, it was to be expected. They didn't honestly believe he would stick around to be their chauffeur forever, did they? It was inevitable. Now, the question was: How were they going to get to the Dokami Council? Because of Atakos' nightmarish experience, they had to go see them as soon as possible.

Fajha sighed. It was more convenient when they had the airship to get around. "I'll have to get us a driver," he said. "And don't worry about the sheets."

After speaking with the butler in the main house, Fajha brought his friends some fresh clothes. He made sure not to give them anything too big, bright, and colorful, which was the traditional attire for Saiyutan royalty, but opted instead for hues of blue, black, green, and a white fitted sweater and pants for Cristaden.

Cristaden beamed with joy when she saw what he had chosen for her. "My favorite color! Thank you, Fajha."

"Of course," Fajha said. He handed Zadeia a black and white striped shirt and a pair of blue pants and proceeded to give the same colors, a blue and white striped shirt and black pants, to Zimi, who scrunched his face in disgust.

Zadeia frowned as well when Fajha handed the clothes to her brother and blurted out a stern, "No."

"You expect me to wear the same colors as my sister?" Zimi said. "What are we? In preschool?"

"Well, you are twins," Fajha said with a snicker. "I just thought it would be fun if you dressed the same."

"It's bad enough we had to wear the same color uniforms."

"As did all of us."

"I won't do it."

"Neither will I," Zadeia said.

Fajha laughed at his attempt at a bad joke and then handed Zimi a plain green shirt to go with the black pants and gave Atakos a black shirt with tan colored pants. For himself, he kept the blue and white striped shirt, which he matched with another pair of black pants. Zimi burst out laughing when he noticed Fajha and Zadeia were now about to wear matching colors.

Fajha rolled his eyes and ignored him. "Let's just get ready," he said. "Our driver is waiting to take us wherever we need to go."

When everyone climbed the stairs to change in their rooms, Atakos asked Cristaden to hang back and waited until everyone was out of hearing range.

Cristaden's heart fluttered and started beating hard against her chest as they waited. She had not forgotten what happened between them in the middle of the night. Cristaden also had not forgotten the vision she had when they kissed. She was positive it was a vision of the future. And, if it was, she knew it was probably best for them to keep things from escalating again.

After everyone was out of earshot, Atakos cleared his throat. "Cristaden," he nervously said. "About what happened last night—"

"I know," Cristaden quickly said. "I'm not sure what happened either. It must have been one of those things—you know—caught up in the moment of it all. I mean—you almost lost your life."

Atakos frowned when he realized she was referring to their kiss. "Yes, but…" He had meant to talk about her *vision*. Did she feel like their kiss was a mistake? "That's not what I…"

Cristaden chuckled slightly. "I mean, we, all of us, have been best friends all our lives basically. It would be too weird. So, yes, I absolutely understand." She stuck out her hand and smiled. "Friends?"

Atakos could not help but feel like he was hit in the head with an airship. When he finally took her hand, he suddenly felt like he could not breathe. A few months prior, when he was home in Pontotoma, he never imagined he would feel this way about one of his best friends. This was *Cristaden*. He had known her since they were learning how to read. Now, as he shook her hand, he realized for the first time, at some point over the past ten years, he had fallen in love with her. *If* this was how it felt to be in love. He wasn't even sure. But it just had to be. "Oh–okay," was all he could manage to get out.

"Okay," Cristaden said as she let go of his hand. With a quick smile, she climbed the stairs with Atakos following behind her and did not turn around until they reached the second floor landing. "See you in a minute."

"Sure," Atakos said and smiled back, hoping she would not see how hurt he actually was. He took the left at the top of the stairs and headed to his room, careful not to turn around so she would not catch him staring at her as she walked away.

Cristaden did not look back either as she quickly made her way to her room and shut the door behind her. She leaned up against it and looked up at the white ceiling with tears building up in her eyes. She then sunk to the floor and buried her head between her knees. The devastation she was trying not to feel hit her hard and she burst into tears. Why couldn't she be irrational and just let things be? Even though she knew what she said to Atakos was the best thing, it still hurt her to say it. She still felt like the world was closing in around her.

A soft knock came at the door. "Cristaden?" Zadeia said. "Are you ready?"

Cristaden quickly wiped her eyes and opened the door.

Zadeia's eyes flew open at the sight of her tearful friend. Cristaden had always been the strong one between the two of them. It was strange to see her eyes red from crying. "What's wrong?" she asked.

"Come in," Cristaden said, ushering her friend in. If anyone could understand what she was going through, it was Zadeia.

CHAPTER 26

Riding in one of the estate's black and sleek vehicles was an experience Zimi, Zadeia, Atakos, and Cristaden would never forget. Seeing the sights of Saiyut via airship was nothing compared to being on the ground and seeing everything up close. The mansions along the road to Isre were magnificent. Even though they were much smaller than Emperor Vermu's summer estate, they were still amazing in their own way. At times, they drove by miles of rolling hills of grass with occasional mountains in the distance, which was a sight to see. Saiyut was beautiful and seemed like a wonderful place to live.

It was not long before Isre Square came into view and they were driving along the cobblestoned streets, admiring the small shops and watching the people of Saiyut walking around, running their daily errands, and making purchases from the merchants on the street.

Atakos shuddered. Isre Square reminded him of his nightmare. The dragon-like creature…the pain of almost being torn apart in real life… Looking around the square, it appeared the shops were similar to the ones he saw in his dream, which was strange because they had only flown over it the day before, making it hard to tell how the shops looked like from the ground.

"Medicinal Goods," Zimi said, pointing to a small shop they were passing. Atakos' head whipped around to stare at the shop and his eyes opened wide. Why did the name of the shop ring a bell? "Maybe you can get something there to help heal your mother, Atakos."

"She would have to come here so they could figure out what's wrong with her," Fajha said. "Then they could prescribe something."

"Didn't Atakos say they tried everything in Pontotoma but don't know what's wrong with her?" Zadeia said. "I'm assuming that means they have tried everything that store has to offer?"

Atakos did not hear Zimi's suggestion, Fajha's response, or Zadeia's questions because he was too busy staring at the shop until it was no longer in view. He didn't even notice that everyone was staring at him. He was searching his memory, trying to remember where he had seen the name of the shop before. Could it have been from his dream? Not being from Saiyut, he had every reason to believe it was. But what was so significant about it? He wanted to ask Cristaden what she thought about it, since she had been in his dream, but thought better of it. He was trying to get over their earlier conversation. Still, that shop... Why did it seem so important?

"Atakos," Cristaden said. "Is everything okay?"

Atakos blinked and shook his head as if to clear it. "I–I don't know. Fajha. Can we...turn back? Can we go back to the shop?"

Fajha immediately told the driver to turn around. Everyone thought Atakos wanted to go back to seek medication for his mother. But that was not the case at all. He knew no medicine could cure her. They had already tried all of them. His mother had an incurable illness and they did not know what it was. No. He asked Fajha to turn around because they had passed the area of the square where he got attacked in his dream. He also felt the Medicinal Goods shop could provide some answers to his confusion.

"Yes," Fajha told the driver after he asked him where he should stop. "Stop here."

The five teenagers stepped out of the vehicle, made their way through the crowds of people bustling around the square, and approached the shop. Much like the other shops of Isre Square, it was a small, one story building, crammed in between two other shops, with a big display window next to the glass door. The words 'Medicinal Goods' were painted on the window in an arch and the teens could see a display of different styles of glass medicine bottles with different color liquids inside them, placed on various pedestals. It gave the shop a majestic feel, as if it should be the one called 'Mystics' instead of the mystical shop a few shops down. Inside was dark and did not seem inviting at all but rather mysterious. The teens hung back, hesitating to go in.

"This was one of the shops I saw in my dream," Atakos said and then turned around. "I was attacked right over there." He pointed to the

163

middle of the square where the dragon-like creature had attacked him and his friends followed his gaze.

"But this is your first time here, Atakos," Fajha said.

"I know…it just doesn't make sense. Everything looks exactly the same. Everything. Except there was no one here before Cristaden came… no. There was *someone* here—"

Just then, the bell over the Medical Goods shop door jingled, signaling someone's arrival or departure. The five teens turned around and watched as a woman walked out of the store. She wore a long, velvet green cloak with the large hood covering her head. In her hand, she carried a brown, leather pouch she had obtained from the shop. She clutched it tightly in her hand and quickly walked up the road, away from the shop in a quick but steady pace.

Atakos and his friends exchanged glances with each other and frowned. It almost seemed like the woman was trying to get away as fast as she could. The way she kept her head down and veered away from the shop made it seem like she was trying to run away, or did not want be seen by–*them*.

They looked up the road in the direction she went. At first, they did not see her. They thought, perhaps, she had run away so fast, she was already gone. Then, as if to answer their thought, the crowd parted and there she stood. Stock still. Staring right back at them. Her hood was partly shielding her face, but they could see her eyes…and her hair…

"What?" Zimi said.

"It can't be," Cristaden said.

"Hamilda?" Zadeia whispered.

Before the teens could get their feet to move, she was gone.

"No!" Atakos cried, startling the crowd of people around them. He took off running in the direction Hamilda went, his friends following close behind him. "Wait!" he shouted.

"Atakos!" Cristaden cried. "It was her wish to go away. We have to let her heal, Atakos!"

"No," Zadeia said, with tears in her eyes. "She needs us!"

They reached the place they had spotted her and, indeed, she was gone.

"Fajha," Atakos said. "Locate!"

"I'll try," Fajha said and closed his eyes.

"No!" Cristaden said. "She wants to be left alone."

Atakos turned around and stared hard at Cristaden. "Do you honestly believe that? We are all she has left. She lost her parents, her adoptive father, and her *husband*. Our mission was *her* mission. It was all she knew since she left Hortu ten years ago. We were her family. Now she has *no one*. Tell me. Do you honestly think she doesn't want to be around us?"

Cristaden looked down at the ground. "Yes," she said before making eye contact with Atakos again with tears in her eyes. "You are wrong about one thing. We *are* her family. We *are* all she has left. And she almost killed us. She *wanted* to kill us. Don't you get it? She needs time to heal. She doesn't want to put us in that position again. Her fight right now is to find Hamilda again. To care for the child growing inside her before…she hurts him too."

Fajha slowly opened his eyes. "She's gone," he said. "I can't sense her anywhere near here."

A sad silence fell among the teens as they looked around at the busy crowds of people in Isre Square. Either Hamilda was extremely fast or she learned how to block Fajha's location ability. Either way, it made them feel terrible that she really did not wish to be around them. It was heartbreaking and tragic. Hamilda had always been like a second mother to them at Lochenby for ten years. Nothing could replace the love they felt for her as a teacher and as an adoring caregiver. Now, she was gone again. Just like that. Running away from them like before.

"Let's go," Fajha said sadly. He reached out and placed his arm around Zadeia's shoulders when he noticed dark clouds rolling in. "There's nothing we can do. If she needs time to heal, we have to give it to her."

"Okay," Zadeia said. She wiped her tears, took a few, deep breaths, and allowed Fajha to guide her back to their vehicle, waiting for them by the Medicinal Goods shop.

Atakos did not even glance at the shop and decided to put his dream out of his mind for the time being. He knew he had to explain it to the Dokami Council when they saw them, but he did not really care about why the shop was important anymore. Not after what just happened.

When the driver announced their approach to the museum, the teens tried to snap out of their sadness and bring their attention back to their objective. They did not want to keep thinking about Hamilda's reason for running away from them and they were sure she wouldn't want the Dokami Council to know they had spotted her so they decided not to mention it.

Their driver drove over a small hill and the castle-like Saiyutan Museum of Cultural History loomed in front of them once again. Fajha instructed the driver to drop them off at the back entrance and to wait for further instructions. When the five teenagers stepped out of the vehicle, they were surprised to see Prince Aillios waiting for them. He was leaning against the brick building with his arms folded across his chest, wearing a long, ivory robe tied around his waist with a brown leather belt, similar to the robes the Dokami Council wore. His horse, Thashmar was close by him, nibbling on a patch of grass.

When the teens stepped out of the vehicle, Prince Aillios gave them a slight nod. "Had a restful night?" he asked.

"Not exactly," Atakos said. "How was your night here?"

"It was…interesting. I learned a lot about your history, which is quite helpful. I still cannot believe your people have lived among humans here in Western Omordion for centuries. Right under their noses."

"Our ancestors did a wonderful job of keeping our heritage a secret," Fajha said, opening the heavy, wooden back door to let everyone in. "Until now, of course."

They made their way up the three flights of stairs to the third floor and let Prince Aillios lead the way, not to the room they had met the Council in before, but to a different room, in a different part of the building. When Aillios opened one of the many unmarked doors down a long hallway, the teens were surprised to see the members of the Dokami Council in a more relaxed environment. The room was long and narrow, with big windows practically covering the opposite wall, allowing the sunlight to illuminate the entire space. And what a space it was. The walls were painted red and the plush sofas and armchairs, which filled the room, were red as well.

Lady Feir, or Reyshi, was lounging on a red velvet, fainting sofa, engrossed in an old book, while Lady Arren, or Nariele, was seated on a red armchair, leaning over a small table, writing a letter on white parchment paper with a fine tipped, black feather quill pen. Lord Eavthon, or Ollige, and Lord Lovanthe–Amzin, were busy at the far end of the room, painting a mural on a large canvas. The colors were vibrant, but they must have just begun, because their visitors could not comprehend what it was supposed to be yet. Lord Watten, or Drae, was standing by a nearby window and turned to greet them as they walked in.

"It is a pleasure to see you again," Drae said, shaking each of the teens' hands.

"Nice to see you too," Zadeia said with a big grin.

Reyshi sat up on the red fainting sofa and put her book down beside her. She was glancing back and forth between the six of them and appeared confused. "We weren't expecting you back so soon. What became of the Son of Maldaha?"

"During the night," Atakos said. "Colnaha made the decision to leave us. He said he was returning to Osmatu."

"Is that so?" She did not seem the least bit surprised.

"Yes. That is not why we had to come back so quickly though. I had a…dream last night."

Reyshi could tell by his tone that it had not been a good dream. Instead of reading it from his mind, she stood up and took a few strides towards the teenagers and Prince Aillios, to listen to him tell it. The other members of the Council caught the change in his tone as well and stopped what they were doing.

"What was your dream about?" Drae asked as he, and the other members of the council, gathered around them.

Atakos explained his dream with Cristaden's assistance. He even lifted his shirt to show where the marks had been after the dragon-like creature bit him. Prince Aillios' jaw tightened as the story progressed. To think the evil wizard, who had sat on his throne for so many years, had the power to enter their *dreams*. The Dokami Council listened quietly until they were finished and glanced at each other before responding.

"You are in terrible danger," Nariele said finally in her soft, wispy voice. "We must advise you to stay here. To not leave this museum under any circumstances or until further notice."

"Not leave the museum?" Fajha said. His shoulders dropped when he realized they would not be returning to his grandfather's summer estate. Instead, they would have to live in the old, stuffy, museum. Like prisoners once again.

"Yes," Drae said. "Until we can figure out our next move. I am sure Brulok will try to find other ways to kill you. As long as he lives, you are in grave danger."

"He must be terribly afraid of what you could do," Ollige said.

"Do you honestly believe that?" Zimi said. "I mean, a man with his power?"

"We are not confident," Reyshi said. "But he wants to destroy all of you for a reason. It has to be a good one. Why else would he be trying so hard?"

"You will stay here," Nariele said. "There are no other choices. It is for the best."

The five members of Omordion's Hope looked back and forth at each other. What choice did they have? At least they would have the strength of the Council with them at all times. It was a lot better than being out in the world, alone.

"Okay," Atakos said. "We'll stay." His friends nodded in agreement. Even though they would have to stay in the ancient museum, it was a lot better to have help.

"I will let my driver know to return to my grandfather's estate," Fajha said.

"Good," Amzin said. "We will accommodate your stay. There are many rooms to choose from. If you will come with Ollige and I, we will get you settled in."

The teens nodded and waited until Amzin and Ollige left the room to follow them. Before they left though, Reyshi spoke, stopping them in their tracks.

"Please report to the ballroom when you are finished getting settled in, after the museum has closed for the day. You do remember where it is, don't you?"

"I'm sure we'll find it," Atakos said.

"May we ask why?" Zimi said.

"To begin your training, of course," Reyshi said with a smile. "You don't think we would not offer you any training while you are under our care do you?"

The five teens smiled back at her. An invitation to train with the ancient members of the Dokami Council?

This should be interesting.

CHAPTER 27

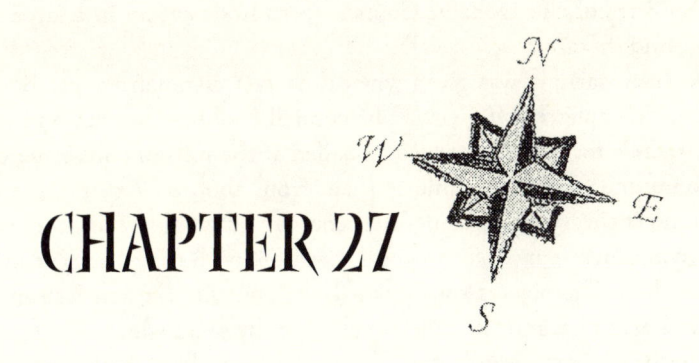

By the time the five teenagers made their way to the ballroom, the council members and Prince Aillios had transformed it into a makeshift training room. There were ropes attached to the ceiling, a pile of rocks on one end, bags of sand on the other, and even a large container of water, along with a pile of wood in the middle of the floor. A panel on one of the walls had been slid back to reveal a small array of weaponry. There were several swords, bows with arrows, and heavy, wooden sticks for practice.

"What the…?" Fajha said under his breath.

"They're really serious about this, aren't they?" Zimi said.

"Why do they have weapons?" Atakos said. "Do they even need to use them?"

"Yes," Ollige said from behind them, startling them all. "We do need them. If you have forgotten, Omordion is in the middle of a war. Saiyut has been and could be attacked again. Of course, we wouldn't want people to know of our powers if the museum is taken over so we've learned to fight the more…*natural* way."

"And it would help you a great deal if you knew how to fight this way as well," Nariele said, coming towards them. "If you lack the stamina to continue using your powers in battle, you must be able to fight a different way." Nariele looked the five teenagers over, as if she was sizing them up. "Before we get started with your training, let's see what you can do. Please come with me." She led them to the middle of the floor, near the barrel of water and wood, and told them to wait as she and the other members of the Dokami Council spread out evenly in a large circle around them.

No warning was given when their test commenced, catching the teens completely off guard. The council members did not even move. Or *blink*, for that matter. Rocks sailed at them from one corner of the room and sand bags came at them from another. At first, the teens flung their arms out, using their energy and wind to push them away, buying them a moment to get in position, with their backs facing one another. The objects they pushed back quickly retracted, prompting Atakos, Fajha, and Cristaden to blow up the rocks while Zimi froze the sandbags. As the sandbags hit the ground with loud crashes, the pile of wood flew up over them and burst into flames. Zimi and Zadeia had to immediately pull water from the large container and douse the flames while the others pushed them away. Some of the water splashed on the teens, which left them momentarily confused. When a few bags of sand flew over them, they were accidentally blown up.

For a moment, the teens, covered in wet sand, were stunned. How could they allow this to happen? And in front of the Dokami Council? They looked around at the council members and they were standing still, as if they were waiting for them to continue.

"What do we do now?" Cristaden whispered.

"I'm not sure," Fajha said.

"We're covered in sand," Atakos said. "This is such a—"

"I have an idea," Zadeia said, interrupting him. "Zimi, we need to create wind. Lots of it."

Zimi understood and summoned the winds along with Zadeia. Within moments, the winds were swirling around them, collecting the sand as it went along, and drying their clothes as well. In a circular motion, resembling a small tornado, the wind moved away from them and dissipated until only a pile of sand remained on the ground. Suddenly, a loud crashing sound caused the group to jump and turn around. The large container was lying on its side. Pouring out of it was a stream of electrically charged water. Blue currents sparked here and there like little determined spider webs, illuminating the water rolling towards them.

Fast.

"Up!" Atakos shouted.

Cristaden's white robe and wings appeared and Fajha levitated off the floor. The others grabbed the ropes closest to them and pulled themselves up off the floor as well. Looking back down, they noticed the water had gathered directly beneath them in a steady pool, threatening to electrocute them if anyone was to lose their grip on the rope they were hanging onto.

Zimi wrapped both legs and one arm around the rope he was holding and shakily reached towards the water with his free hand. Utilizing the technique he used to pull lightning from the sky, he pulled at the electricity in the water and grabbed a hold of it. "Zadeia," he said.

Zadeia understood what he was trying to do and pulled up on her rope so she can wrap it around her legs and one of her arms as well. She used her free hand to reach towards the water. As Zimi pulled the electricity away from the water, she pushed the water back to the container. When the two elements were finally detached, Zimi hurled the electricity at the pile of sand they had formed with their tornado and Zadeia managed to get all of the water back in the container, while Fajha waved his hand to stand it back up.

"Impressive," Reyshi said, when the teens came back down. Cristaden's wings and white robe had disappeared, replaced by the white shirt and pants Fajha had given her.

The Dokami Council approached them and Drae nodded in agreement with Reyshi. "Your skills are extraordinary," he said. "But, I am sorry to say, not good enough."

The five teens glanced at each other. They had come a long way since their last practice with Hamilda, achieved so much more in a short period of time than they did in the ten years Hamilda taught them. It was disappointing to hear their skills were not meeting the standards of the Dokami Council.

"It's okay," Reyshi said. "I understand your disappointment. You had three more years of practice left with Hamilda. Three years you had to shorten in just a few weeks. It was an impossible feat. Nevertheless, you did it. For that, we are especially proud."

Amzin nodded. "We will show you how to use your powers, without the use of your hands. We will show you how to crush the heart of the enemy—without blowing them up. We will show you how to fight without the use of your powers. And how to *win*."

"Are you ready?" Ollige said.

"Yes," Atakos said, speaking for his friends as well. "We are ready."

"Okay," Nariele said. "Let us begin." She gestured for the teens to follow her to the opposite side of the room, where the weapons were held.

Zadeia nudged Cristaden and quickly whispered in her ear. "Are you going to tell Atakos?" Cristaden shook her head and Zadeia rolled her eyes. "Why not?"

"I have to confirm it," Cristaden whispered.

"And how are you going to do that?"

"I have an idea."

Cristaden turned around, away from her friends, and headed towards Reyshi, who seemed to have been waiting for her. "Can I speak with you privately, Reyshi?" she said.

"Yes, of course," Reyshi said and invited her to follow her into the meeting room. After closing the door behind them, she asked Cristaden what was troubling her.

Cristaden described her vision to Reyshi, expecting her to laugh and perhaps tell her how ridiculous she sounded, but Reyshi sighed and looked down at the floor before meeting her gaze again.

"I feared this would happen," Reyshi said finally. "I was scared one of you would foresee what is to come. Due to the recent turn of events, it very well could happen."

Cristaden put her hands over her mouth in shock. Reyshi took her hands into hers, gently pulling them away from her face. "Cristaden. I need you to do me a favor. It will be hard for you...but I ask you to forget this vision. Do not speak of it to anyone—if you have not done so already. In addition, please do not speak a word of it to Atakos. It is not something he would be able to handle right now. We will tell him when the time is right. *If* we need to tell him anything at all."

Cristaden's hope, that her vision was far from the truth, was shattered. "Okay. I won't say anything."

"Good. We have a lot of work to do if you and your friends want to beat the Eastern Army and Brulok."

"Yes, of course."

Reyshi guided Cristaden back to the makeshift training room and noticed how the girl miraculously changed her sad face to reflect someone who was happy, so her friends would not notice how sad she was.

Good girl, Reyshi thought. She looked over at the other trainees and caught Atakos staring at Cristaden, his face full of concern. It was not hard to place the look of utter embarrassment on the fifteen-year-old's face when he noticed Reyshi staring back at him. Atakos looked down sheepishly, his caramel skin flaring up with a touch of red. Reyshi stopped walking with Cristaden and allowed her to join the group on her own. *I understand now,* she thought. *He is in love with her. And given her reaction when I told her the vision she had was true, she is in love with him, too.* Reyshi folded her arms across her chest and sighed. This realization made the situation particularly difficult indeed.

CHAPTER 28

King Tholenod shuffled into the throne room in Mituwa in a somewhat foggy daze. The past few days had been extremely cloudy. He was not sure when he got up in the morning or when he laid down to go to sleep. It was as if the days had melted together into one, long day of wandering around, lost in a hazy dream. Except today was different. Today Brulok requested his presence in the throne room.

His throne room.

"Bring the Alliance together," Brulok said, barking orders at King Tholenod as he sauntered in.

It had been several days since they left the dead forest in Effit. Brulok had completely and entirely taken control of Tholenod's castle in Mituwa, treating even the guards and the king's soldiers as lowly, disgusting creatures he loathed. The throne, he claimed as his own, allowing the king to sit near him at first but ordering him to remain out of his sight as time progressed. For three days, Brulok had sat on the throne, in deep and utter concentration. So deep, Menyilh, his new, and unbelievably eager assistant, forbade anyone to disturb him. Now, after what seemed like an extensive period of time, Tholenod was ordered to sit by Brulok once again.

"The Alliance?" Tholenod said, confused at Brulok's request. It seemed like the fog he was trapped in gradually lifted when he spoke. Suddenly, a thought occurred to him. This was the first time he had spoken in *days*. "All of them?"

"Yes, you dim-witted fool. All of them. King Haudmont of Srepas, Gomu of Effit, and Basanpanul of Feim. They will allow us to take complete control of their armies."

"They would never agree to such a ridiculous request."

"I have ways to make them comply," Brulok said with a sneer. "We will gather our armies in Southern Feim, near the Rostumik Pass bordering Udnaruk. There, we will launch a full attack at the Cliffs of Thegahn and work our way up Western Omordion until we have conquered it all."

Tholenod took all but one second to know what Brulok was planning to do was a bad move. *Very bad.* "We cannot send every soldier there," he said through his teeth. "If we are defeated, there will be no coming back from that."

"The Western Army will be completely caught off guard."

"We *will* lose!"

Brulok stared back at Tholenod with hatred, as if his presence was only being tolerated and not obligatory. Tholenod understood. No matter what he said, Brulok would make him do what he wanted him to do in the end. He defiantly stood up and marched towards Brulok. "Do you need me to repeat myself, *Brulok?* It. Won't. *Work.*"

Brulok stood up, his eyes darkening with every heated breath he took. "You dare challenge *me?*"

After Tholenod's sudden, defiant outburst, cruel images exploded in his mind. Images of Brulok sitting on *his* throne, commanding *his* soldiers, treating him as if he was someone *lower* than he was.

This was a mistake.

All of this.

A big mistake.

He never should have listened to Menyilh. How could he have allowed this to happen?

Tholenod sneered at Brulok, determined to take back his throne from the old wizard. "I order you to leave this place, Brulok. From now on you are banned from my castle." When Brulok did not answer him, he shouted for his guards to come to his aid.

They did not come.

The little imp, Menyilh, was heard atrociously giggling in the corner behind the throne.

"Guards!" Tholenod shouted again.

"They are not under your control," Brulok said with a smile. "Anymore."

"What?"

Strangely, it suddenly appeared as if Brulok was slowly swaying. Just slightly. Rocking from side to side. It was making Tholenod annoyingly dizzy. Was he imagining this? Tholenod quickly shook his head to clear it. "What are you...?" His voice was thick in his throat. Dark shadows moved across the room as his vision steadily became cloudy. The shadows slowly made their way towards him, slithering like snakes. He shivered when he realized how cold the room had gotten. He tried to move but felt completely numb and frozen all over. Before he knew it, he could no longer get a breath of air into his lungs as hard as he tried. Panic rose in his throat. The dark shadows came together and shape-shifted into a fierce looking creature with red eyes and sharp teeth. Growling ferociously, it flew at Tholenod with amazing speed.

Tholenod did not have the opportunity to blink before the room pitched into darkness and he was hit with extreme pain. He wanted to scream, to make it stop, but he felt like he was falling. Down, down, down into a deep, dark abyss, with only the sound of someone laughing hysterically filling his eardrums.

This time, he knew who it was.

It was *Brulok*.

Again, within a dreadfully short timeframe, Tholenod wished for a swift end to his suffering.

Again, he wished for death.

CHAPTER 29

"Frolemin."

Frolemin, King Tholenod's head maid, looked up from the side table she was dusting in the king's chambers. Along with other servants, she had been cleaning most of the castle all day, her tired, over-worked muscles screaming for her to rest. Nonetheless, she knew she could not take a break. King Tholenod would be returning at any moment and would have her flogged if his rooms were not to his liking. She recalled the last time it happened and winced, still feeling the sting of the king's whip on her back even though it had been so long ago.

"Yes, Trisalan," Frolemin said to Prince Aillios' former chambermaid, who had entered the room quickly and quietly closed the door behind her. Frolemin referred to Trisalan as Aillios' former chambermaid because he had not returned with the king after his secret quest. In fact, the king never mentioned him, as if he had never existed. This made her fear the worst for the prince. He must have died, killed by King Tholenod himself. She would not be surprised.

When Frolemin helped Aillios escape the castle, she never thought it would be the last time she would see him. At times, Frolemin could only stare off into the distance, remembering the sweet little boy he used to be and the kind, generous person he had grown into. All hope of Aillios freeing the slaves was now lost and, sadly, she would never see him again.

"What is it?" Frolemin asked Trisalan.

"I am sure you have not heard the news," Trisalan whispered, her brown eyes bulging out of her head and her chest heaving as she tried to catch her breath.

"Heard what?"

"What's happening." Trisalan gestured for Frolemin to sit down on King Tholenod's grand, four-poster bed before continuing.

"What is it?" Frolemin said. She was searching Trisalan's eyes, when the other woman sat down beside her, looking for answers.

Trisalan took one deep breath after another, trying to steady her nerves. "The king," she said breathlessly, "has called every soldier to war with the West."

"Well, yes. We are at war, Trisalan. This is nothing new—"

"You do not understand," the younger chambermaid said. She looked around quickly and lowered her voice even more as if she had not been speaking in a whisper before. "You do not understand, Frolemin. Every. *Single*. Soldier."

"Every one of them?" Frolemin was confused. "Are you sure?"

"Yes. The other kings were here today—"

"What?"

"They were sent away to ready their armies. Our soldiers leave tomorrow! The only ones staying behind are the guards in the castle and the slave overseers."

"But why would the kings agree to do such a thing?"

"The old man. You know, the one who sits on the throne? He seems to have something to do with it. He is so dark and frightening, Frolemin. I have heard rumors he will not even allow the king to speak! He has called *every* soldier from the East to battle. This means every soldier in Srepas, Effit, and Feim, as well as our own!"

"I cannot believe it. The king has never suggested something like this before." Frolemin looked down at the floor, suddenly feeling ill. "This is it then. They mean to end this battle with the West, once and for all. The dream of having our freedom will end. It will never happen. They must think the West is weak enough for this to work, otherwise—"

"Frolemin, there is something else you need to know."

"What?" she said, looking back up at Trisalan.

"Word is going around. About a revolt."

"You cannot be *serious*?"

"Yes."

Frolemin frowned and shook her head. "But this has been tried before, Trisalan. We lost so many lives."

"When the soldiers leave, we will outnumber the guards and the overseers one thousand to one, Frolemin. Maybe more."

"So you are not joking. This is actually happening?"

"The slaves, who came here with the other kings, will be spreading the word when they reach home. This is *happening*, Frolemin."

"When?"

"The morning after the full moon."

Frolemin stood up and started pacing the floor. "How are they sure this will work? What if the slaves in Effit, Srepas, and Feim choose not to join in the revolution?"

"Why, on Omordion, do you think they would not?"

"Out of sheer terror. Fear for their *lives*. There are any number of reasons why they would not."

Trisalan stood up and stopped the aging woman from pacing. "We lost our sense of fear a long time ago. It is time to reclaim what is rightfully ours. Our freedom. Our lands. They will revolt. And if they do not, we will help them once *we* are free. Prepare yourself, Frolemin. We have five days." Trisalan then left the chamber, tiptoeing away so the guards would not know she had been there.

Frolemin sat back down on the four-poster bed and looked down at her calloused hands. *No need to finish my work now*, she thought. *King Tholenod will need me to prepare him for battle.* She sighed and looked up at the ceiling, unconsciously taking the time to study it for a moment.

This is it, Frolemin thought. *We would either be free or die trying.*

CHAPTER 30

Prince Aillios woke up drenched in sweat. He felt as if he had been holding his breath for a long time, so he attempted to force the air back into his lungs as quickly as possible. He had not realized he had fallen asleep, especially during the day, which was unlike him.

When he recalled the dream he was having right before he woke up, Aillios suddenly felt panicked, as if the world was closing in around him, and there was nothing he could do to stop it. He gripped his chest, astonished at how powerful and *real* the dream had seemed. His head spun crazily when he stood up on the blanket he had placed on the ground outside, near Thashmar. He had intended to just lay on it and stare up at the sky, but time slipped by after he fell into the deep sleep.

Aillios adjusted his ivory robe and brushed his wavy, black hair back with his fingers. After taking a deep breath and slowly releasing it, he made the quick decision to meet with the Dokami Council as soon as possible and ran inside. There had to be some meaning behind the dream he just had.

Since the members of Omordion's Hope were required to stay at the museum a couple of weeks prior, the Dokami Council took their time to teach them many valuable lessons. Lessons even the teens' teacher, Hamilda, was incapable of teaching. In regards to Prince Aillios, they introduced him to the notion that he had become more and more psychic through his dreams. That he could connect with spirits while he slept. It was not a Dokami trait but it was a gift nonetheless, a gift he had possessed since he was small. His connection with spirits was fully realized during his experience with the dead witch, Asmis, who had given him his magical disguise, which further accelerated his gift. The Dokami Council also convinced him he was the one who had contacted Asmis through his dream, begging her for help, which she so graciously gave because of her hate for the Mituwan monarchy. Aillios recalled the story of her death before he fell asleep, but did not remember seeking her help. Looking back at the most significant dreams he had experienced in his lifetime, he tried to make sense of them once again with this newfound notion. However, nothing made much sense anymore. Not even who Asmis was and why her powers affected him as they did.

Now Prince Aillios had this new dream to think about. A dream, which seemed so real to him, yet so *unreal*.

Udnaruk.

Evil.

He climbed the three flights of stairs to the Dokami Council's floor and raced down the hall, his heart pounding in his chest. He believed his dream was more important than any other dream he had ever had in his entire life.

It was a warning.

That, he was *sure* of.

"Break. Yield. Fire."

"Concentrate!"

"Break. Yield. Fire."

"That's it."

Prince Aillios ran into the makeshift training room, which had once been a grand ballroom. Even more props had been set up all over the room to aid in the training of the five teenagers. These training sessions were nothing Aillios had ever witnessed back in Mituwa when he was training for battle with his father.

It was incomparable.

Prince Aillios thought the Dokami Council should have been the ones training the teenagers all along; making what Hamilda was forced to do seem highly unnecessary. She had to live her life at a boarding school she hated because of her devastating past. She was not allowed to have any children during the entire mission. With the death of her husband, her dream to have a normal life with him could never be fulfilled. Aillios did not blame her for running away. Still, he knew the

Dokami Council wanted the five teenagers to lead a somewhat normal life. To train them, they would have had to live in the museum, isolated from the entire world.

The sheer strength and abilities the Dokami Council possessed were immeasurable. Their age reflected in their power, a power so intense, it was easy to see why they kept it hidden and restrained all those years. What's more is how swift and clean their attacks were. They did not exert much energy when executing any attacks. If one was not looking directly at the person who performed the attack, he would not know who had done it. They barely flinched.

Furthermore, the members of the Dokami Council were astonished the teenagers had not learned any group attacks or group abilities. They explained how easy it was for members of the Dokami clan to execute such attacks. It explained how the Dokami moved and eventually blew up the entire Planet Dokar after the fatal Dre-Ahd attack. They did it as a group. Not individually. The concept of a group attack seemed, to Aillios, tremendously powerful and potentially dangerous if accomplished by the wrong people. In a way, he was glad Colnaha left when he did. He was unstable, which could never be a good thing combined with so much power.

No one understood why he had left so abruptly that day, in the middle of the night for that matter. The Council was cruel to him but brutally honest. They could not pretend to trust the boy without outright lying about the way they felt, which was not in their nature.

The day after the training began, Nariele had left a letter for the Council's messenger, addressed to the Western Army. She called for the arrest of General Komuh and Maldaha, and the release of R.K. Rohjees, Principal of Lochenby, who had been arrested in suspicion with the kidnapping of Hamilda. She also notated that Hamilda was alive and well and will not be returning to Lochenby and neither would her students for the time being.

Prince Aillios spotted Lord Eavthon, or Ollige, teaching the teens how to execute an attack without the use of their hands. The use of hands, he explained, was more like an unnecessary gesture used to convince oneself that the actual attack would occur, when the attack and every other ability was being performed with their minds alone. For example: the fireballs, which appeared in Zadeia's hands, allowing her to throw them at an enemy, was an unnecessary step when executing her attack. By simply fixating her gaze on one point, she could set anything on fire with the right amount of concentration, and without the need to use her hands. She had managed to set a couple of things on fire with her mind, but she was still working on her new talent. For the others, it was the same. Freezing, controlling wind, causing storms, blowing things up, and levitation were all a state of mind. It was something they were still working on and would take a long time to achieve. Cristaden's healing power was the only exception. Not being a regular Dokami ability, the power to heal was derived from her fairy lineage, so it came directly from her hands.

Aillios made his way to the meeting chamber and found Lady Arren, Lady Feir, Lord Lovanthe, and Lord Watten, strategizing on what their next practice session would be.

"Good morning, Lio," Reyshi said, beaming when she saw him come in. She had given him the nickname when they suggested his identity should be concealed from the public. It was difficult to get used to at first, but he adapted, even calling himself 'Lio' from time to time.

Reyshi noticed he was drenched in sweat and practically shaking with fright. The others had noticed as well and gathered around him. "What has happened?" Reyshi said.

Aillios hesitated a moment to catch his breath. His heart was still pounding incessantly and he willed it to stop. "I had the most disturbing dream."

"Do tell," Ollige said from behind him, with the five teens following close behind him into the room. Cristaden had sensed something was wrong and suggested they find out what was going on. She knew all too well dreams might mean more than what they seem.

"It was the strangest thing. I was a small boy and I was lost in Mituwa. In the castle. Just lost, wandering around. It was as if I had never been there before. Everything looked so different."

"You were little?" Fajha said, looking somewhat bewildered.

"Yes." Aillios took another deep breath to steady his breathing before continuing. "I finally found my way to the throne room and my father was there. He was...kneeling. On the floor. At the foot of someone who was sitting on the throne. As if he was cowering like a servant to this...whoever it was. All I could see was darkness so I could not see this person's face. However, I am *sure* it was Brulok. He told my father to go to Udnaruk."

"Udnaruk?" Zimi said and looked at Zadeia, who looked just as surprised as he did.

"They are coming," Prince Aillios said. "I am pretty sure of it."

Fajha's eyes grew wide. "I had a dream. Back at my grandfather's estate. Two weeks ago. I was walking through the maze on the grounds and I ran into a small boy. This boy—he looked like *you*, Aillios."

Prince Aillios frowned. "What?"

"Yes. He had your eyes and reminded me of you. He approached me and said something in Mituwan. I think it was… *gral fi hadomna*."

"They are coming."

"Yes."

Atakos frowned. "Wait. That sounds so familiar…" He searched his memory, trying to remember why. A small boy…blue eyes… gral…fi… hadomna. The *Medicinal Goods* shop. Yes. "The boy. He was in my dream too. When I was attacked by Brulok in Isre Square. He—or you—came to me as well. He said the same thing. I can't believe I forgot about him…"

Prince Aillios frowned. What was his younger-self doing in their dreams? "I never could recall my childhood," he said slowly. "It always seemed so cloudy, so unreal."

"Perhaps something bad happened when you were young," Reyshi said. "Something terrible, which caused you to block out your memories. I saw this happen with many small Dokami children when we left Jmugea. It was devastating. They never could recall the event that led us to flee Jmugea. Or our life there when they were older."

"Perhaps…" Prince Aillios shook his head to clear it. He was young when his mother died during the slave revolt. All his life, he could not even remember how she looked like. In fact, he could not remember anything about her. Could he have witnessed her death? Perhaps the event traumatized him. Nevertheless, he knew he should not try to delve into the past. He, along with Fajha and Atakos, were given a warning. He was sure of it. "One thing stood out to me the most. Udnaruk. It was as if I needed to be there right now or get there as fast as I can. This will sound strange but I felt extreme evil. As if even the *word* Udnaruk was shrouded in evil." He looked at the ten pairs of eyes staring back at him. "Can any of you make sense of it?"

"Hmm," Drae said. "It's definitely some kind of warning. But we haven't been given much to go by. If they are planning an attack on Udnaruk, all of you need to go there as soon as possible."

"But what if this is one of Brulok's tricks?" Reyshi said. "What if he wants them to go there to throw them off?"

"And attack somewhere else?" Lady Arren said.

"It's a risk we would have to take," Lord Watten said. "If anything happens elsewhere, you would just have to get there as soon as possible."

"But how can we get to Udnaruk?" Atakos said. "It's thousands of miles away. It would be impossible to get there fast, without any means of transportation."

"We have much to discuss about your next course of action," Drae said. "This is to be our last meeting. We will find a way to get you there." To everyone's surprise, he continued to say, "Also...we will give you back the communicator you used to contact Jmugea. It is right, since you were the ones that contacted them, that you should take it with you in case they decide to...contact you again. If they do, we hope it is good news. You—all of you—have to leave. As soon as possible."

Prince Aillios nodded. "Agreed."

CHAPTER 31

"Can you believe it? Did you hear the news?"

"Yes. I heard. A distress signal!"

"From *Omordion* of all places!"

"The nerve of them. To think King Azahr would ever respond to that!"

"Shhh. We don't want anyone to hear us."

"Right. Best keep it quiet."

Princess Amilana stepped out from behind the stairs and watched as the two young soldiers walked away. *A distress signal from Omordion?* Amilana shook her head. The last time Jmugea had received a distress signal three hundred years ago, they made the fatal decision to reject it. She scowled, wondering why she had not been notified. Storming down the hallway towards the throne room, she crashed into Drissana, who had been flying down the stairs in an awful hurry.

"Amilana," Drissana said. "Where are you going?" Glaring at her older sister, she adjusted the diamond tiara resting on her fiery red hair and smoothed out her peach colored dress. She looked so different, dressed more like a princess and…clean. She almost seemed like an entirely different person.

"It is none of your business, little sister," Amilana said. She paused, her eyebrows coming together in a frown. "Aren't you supposed to be with your professor right now?"

Drissana smiled sheepishly. "I–I was just on my way there. I'm late."

"Then I suggest you get going." Amilana quickly dismissed her and began to walk away.

"Ami?"

Amilana stopped and sighed heavily. "What is it?"

"If something was going on, you would tell me, right?"

Amilana turned to Drissana sister. She knew her sister could sense something was wrong. There was little she could hide from her. "I will."

"Okay." Drissana gave her a quick smile before walking away.

Amilana approached the heavy doors to the throne room and flung them open. Her father, King Azahr, and her mother, Queen Serai, were seated at their thrones. She knew they would be discussing matters about the villages with the Jmugean Council and their Advisor, but she didn't care.

Azahr shot a disturbed look at his daughter, who had rudely burst into the hall. "*Princess Amilana,*" his voice rang out. "Were you not aware of *this* meeting? I am sure we informed you about it this time."

"I am sorry, father. What I have to ask cannot wait. This is important."

"What is it?"

Amilana looked around the room and noticed the angry sneers she was receiving from a few of the council members. "Maybe you should dismiss everyone."

"I will do nothing of the sort. Just tell me what it is before I lose my patience."

"Well...it's about the...signal. From—"

King Azahr waved his hand at her. He knew word would eventually get out and he would hear from her sooner or later. He gestured for the Jmugean Council to leave the room. "We will discuss this matter at a later time," he told his Advisor.

The Advisor, an elderly man, nodded and left the room, looking down his nose at Princess Amilana. She ignored him and waited until they left, before speaking again.

"Father. I heard word of a distress signal. From Omordion. Is this true?"

King Azahr and Queen Serai glanced at each other. A brief, silent exchange passed between them before either of them spoke.

"Yes," Azahr confirmed. "It is true."

"When? When was it sent? Why was I not notified?"

"It is none of your concern."

"None of my *concern?*" Amilana approached their thrones. "I was appointed Jmugea's Ambassador. Anything involving another planet *is* my concern. I need the details of the signal right now!"

King Azahr sighed. "We have already decided the course of action to take in regards to the signal. We will not be lending our assistance. Remove it from your mind and focus on other important things. Like the function being held for—"

"Don't try to change the subject, father. I am twenty-two years old. Your old tricks do not work with me."

Azahr stood up. "How dare you speak to me in such a way? We will *not* be coming to the aid of a planet we know nothing about. Do I make myself clear? I suggest you turn around and forget we ever had this conversation *right* now."

Amilana turned to her mother, who only shrugged and gestured for her to leave. Looking back at her father, she gave an exasperated sigh. "It's wrong, father, and you know it. The last time we rejected a distress signal, an entire planet, and the innocent lives on it, was destroyed."

"That was over three hundred years ago, Amilana."

"The Dokamis—our people—were killed. Our ancestors stood by and did nothing. We cannot ignore this signal. We just can't."

"Yes we can. The Dokamis on Dokar *were* killed. Let us not forget. We have no idea who sent the signal. Furthermore, we have no intention of finding out who it is and risking our lives in the process. We have survived. Let us keep it that way."

Amilana turned away from her parents. She could say no more. She knew she could not convince her father to change his mind. Taking one last look back at them, she stormed out of the hall, almost crashing into her sister once again.

"You were listening."

"Yes," Drissana said. "I heard everything." She followed Amilana all the way back to her chambers on the third floor of the castle. When Amilana shut the double doors behind her, she let out an exasperated sigh.

"Ami, do you think it might be...?" Her sister looked disturbed and frightened.

Amilana gave another frustrated sigh. "I don't know Drissana. I just don't know." She sat down on the green armchair closest to her four-poster bed and buried her face in her hands.

"Well...what are you going to do?"

"There's nothing I *can* do. What the king said is true. We have no way of knowing who contacted us from Omordion. It could be a trap. We are unable to take that risk."

Drissana sat down next to Amilana, feeling just as depressed as her sister was. And uncomfortable. The dress she wore was much too tight and she longed to change as soon as possible. She also could not possibly meet with her professor *now*. Usually, Amilana would argue that Drissana did not want to go to her lessons, but she would deny it, of course. It is not as if she did not want to go. This time was different. This situation was much more important than her studies.

A soft knock came at the door.

"You may enter," Amilana said angrily.

The double doors to her chamber flew open and Queen Serai came rushing in. She quickly, but silently, shut the doors behind her. Shocked, the two princesses stood up to greet their mother.

"Mother!" Drissana ran up to her.

"Shhh," Serai told her youngest daughter. "Amilana. I must speak with you." Frantically, she gestured for the two girls to move to the far side of the room, away from the doors. Her eyes were big and she was rubbing her hands together in a nervous way, perhaps trying to calm herself. "Do you honestly believe we should help whoever sent the signal?" she said in a barely audible whisper.

Amilana frowned at her mother. "Yes," she said firmly. "I think we *should*."

"There are some details about the signal you should know." Queen Serai stopped to listen as someone walked by the chamber. She waited until the footsteps went away and turned back to her daughters. "I could get into a lot of trouble for this."

"Tell me, mother. Before someone comes. When was the signal sent?"

"About fifteen days ago."

"That *long?*" Amilana was furious. She then searched her brain. She remembered that day...fifteen days ago. "That day–the day I felt like something was wrong–you said it was my imagination. It was when the distress signal came through. Wasn't it?"

"Shhh. Yes."

"Why didn't you tell me, mother? Why did you wait so long?"

"When the king suggested keeping it quiet, I thought he had made the best decision. You must understand, I could not go against his wishes. I did not want to worry you for no apparent reason...so I... helped you forget."

Amilana's jaw dropped open. "Mother, how could you use your powers against me?"

"What?" Drissana said, more confused than ever.

Serai sighed deeply and placed a hand on Amilana's shoulder to pacify her. "You have to understand. I knew, because of the gift you possess, you would stop at nothing to find out what was going on. I had to help you forget. For your sake, dear." When Amilana nodded, she released her shoulder and brought her arm back down to her side. "But when you came to the throne room today, I knew you were right. We have to do something about this." Serai looked back and forth between her daughters. "Are you prepared to hear what I have to say?"

"Yes, mother," they said in unison.

"Okay. A message came along with the distress signal."

"A message?" Drissana said, her voice escalating into almost a shout.

"Shhhh!" both Serai and Amilana said at the same time.

Amilana cursed her sister under her breath. "What did the message say mother?" she asked.

"It said...*Dokami*."

Amilana gasped. She took a step back, trying hard to catch her breath. "Are you positive, mother?"

"Never have I been more positive in my life."

"Do you know what this means?"

"Yes, I do."

"And father chose to reject it?" Drissana said.

"He thought it was best."

Amilana took a deep breath and let it out slowly. "So there are Dokamis on Omordion. There are members of our clan *living* on Omordion." She heard it, but it would not register properly in her head. It was something she could never even fathom. "This means they didn't die on Dokar. They *survived*. By now, there could be hundreds of thousands, if not millions..."

"I believe so," Serai said. "Our ancestors forbade us to mention their possible existence. They did not want us risking our lives to save them and bringing them back here."

"That's awful," Drissana whispered. "Why?"

The queen did not respond.

Amilana knew not to press the issue. Her mother could only tell them so much. "They need our help, mother," she said and groaned. "But there is nothing we can do now. It's probably too late."

"There *is* something you can do, my daughter." Serai took her by her hand. "The signal is still active. It is resonating from the device they used to send it. I have been tracking it. I will give you the tracker so you can find out who sent it."

Amilana took a step forward. "You mean…you want me to *go* there? To Omordion?"

"Absolutely. Today. If possible. Time is of the essence, my child."

"You *are* serious then."

"I have already arranged for your departure. You have a couple of hours to prepare. The communicator you will need to locate the signal will be on the spaceship I chartered for you. I know of a good excuse to tell the king in regards to your absence." Serai grabbed Amilana's hand and looked deep into her eyes. "Do not linger there, Amilana. Find out the reason for the distress signal and return to me at once. I must go now before he wonders where I am." She hugged her daughter. "Good luck, my dear." She then hurriedly left the room, leaving her two stunned daughters staring at the closed door in shock.

After a few moments, Amilana grabbed a black, leather bag from her armoire and began packing some clothes, ignoring her sister's desperate eyes. She knew what the sixteen-year-old was going to say before it even left her mouth.

"Can I go with you?" Drissana said after a few minutes.

Amilana shook her head. "No. Things could get dangerous."

"Exactly why I should go. You may need my help."

"I'll be okay. Besides, mother will be worried about you."

Drissana laughed. "When has she ever worried about me? She knows I can take care of myself. She didn't exactly tell me I couldn't go, you know. She might even expect me to go. Besides, I would feel more worried for whatever enemy we may have on Omordion."

Amilana stopped and looked at Drissana. She knew her sister was right. She needed someone to watch her back. "Okay, Drissana. But mark my words. If things get too dangerous, I want you *out* of there."

"Of course," Drissana said. As she made her way out of Amilana's room, she smiled. "They don't know what's coming."

PART FOUR
SOUTHERN UDNARUK

CHAPTER 32

"You were right to call us," Major Garunburj said.

The group of six: Atakos, Fajha, Cristaden, Zimi, Zadeia, and Prince Aillios, nodded in agreement. They had no choice but to contact the Western Army in Udnaruk to pick them up from Saiyut. In the end, it made sense. As long as war still raged against the East, the Western Army still required their help, and would happily agree to assist them. Once the enemy was no longer a problem, they would address the corruption of the Western Army. Until then, they still had a great advantage over them.

The Dokami Council also informed Major Garunburj, by letter of course, that Prince Aillios, or Lio, was a member of the Dokami clan. That he was sent to aid in the fight against the East, due to Hamilda's absence. Once again, they stressed the importance of Aillios keeping his origin a secret, even if someone suspected he was from the East and might be an escaped slave. This, Aillios gladly accepted, making sure not to speak near Major Garunburj or his soldiers, so they would not hear his Mituwan accent.

The five members of Omordion's Hope and Prince Aillios sat comfortably in a large, passenger airship and they were even offered to sleep until they reached Udnaruk, which they quickly refused, unable to imagine closing their eyes among potential threats. They could not help but to look back and forth between Major Garunburj and the fourteen soldiers he had brought along for 'added security'. The major told them they did the right thing by calling on the Western Army for help. They had been worried when the teenagers had run away, they did not know where to begin looking for them, and they were elated when they received their message.

"Furthermore," Major Garunburj said, "we received a message a while back from the Dokami Council, informing us of the illegal operations of General Komuh." Six pairs of eyebrows rose at the mention of the corrupt general's name. "You need not worry," Garunburj said, taking their bewildered expressions as fear. "We arrested Komuh a couple of weeks ago. We found him in the Suthack Desert, where the Dokami Council said he would be. We also released your principal, R. K. Rohjees, from prison so he could resume his role of overseeing your school. General Komuh is being detained in our army base in Southern Udnaruk. He will no longer be of any danger to you."

Zadeia and Zimi rolled their eyes. Having grown up in the army base in Southern Udnaruk, they knew what the prisons were like for army officials. It was more like an indoor recreational facility where detainees played games all day and were free to move about the grounds daily without any harassment from the other soldiers. It was more like a summer camp they were unable to leave. For all they knew, General Komuh was having an insanely good time when he wasn't in his prison cell.

"So just sit back and relax," Garunburj said.

Prince Aillios put his head back against his seat. His horse, Thashmar, came to mind then. He had sadly given the horse away to the Dokami Council's groundskeeper. He figured Thashmar would be happier away from the battlefield and Brulok's minions. He would be safe on the grounds of the museum, with the groundskeeper, who was lonely most of the time and needed a friend. Aillios was going to miss Thashmar, for all they had been through together since the day he was given to him to aid him in his mission to follow his father and his escape from Effit.

"We are over Pontotoma right now," Garunburj said. "We will reach Udnaruk in a few hours."

Atakos eagerly looked out the window closest to him, but was disappointed to see only dark clouds below them. *Must be raining*, he thought and immediately began to feel homesick. He dreamt of going home, becoming oblivious to the destruction of the rest of the world, and aiding in the care of his ill mother. It was a false dream; a dream he had so often lost himself in. If the East won the war, their freedom, as they knew it, would come to a dreadful end. His family and friends, along with millions of others, would be subjected to slavery and could very well die in the hands of the tyrannical kings of the East.

Atakos silently prayed they would be able to stop them and not let that happen.

As the Western Army airship began its swift descend through the clouds, the twins knew they were home. The tall trees of Udnaruk reached up towards them, while the flat ground revealed ordinary life in their home country. Tiny huts dotted the landscape and fires burned in the middle of each village community. It was quaint, with no mansions or mountains in sight, like Saiyut had. The leaves were changing with the cooler climate, turning bright orange, yellow, and red, and falling from their branches onto the forest floor. Udnaruk was charming. The four people in the airship, who were experiencing Udnaruk for the first time, were so captivated by it; they had no words to describe the natural beauty of untouched magnificence before their eyes.

Then they saw the rocky cliffs, bordered by pine trees. At first, it seemed like a line had been drawn between them, as if the earth had cracked during an earthquake. However, the closer they got, the more the group could see the deep chasms between the cliffs. Chasms filled with raging, white water. They even spotted the occasional waterfall among the sea of splendid colors.

"Beautiful..." Cristaden breathed.

"Agreed," Zadeia said. "I love it." Even if war was not coming to Southern Udnaruk, and they were wrong about the dreams, she was going home and would see her parents again soon. Normally, she would not see them again until the following summer, which was always so sad for her. Zadeia leaned forward and peered out of the window with eyes filled with tears at the sight of the forest below. Hamilda lost her husband, Captain Jogesh Shing, within those very forests, fighting against the soldiers of Feim. Hamilda's devastation over his death had sparked her rage, causing her to become possessed with evil. During the fight with Evil Hamilda, Zadeia thought she would never live to see home again. Now she was there.

Home.

Zimi, on the other hand, felt a pang of anxiety as they came closer and closer to their final destination. All he could think of was the disappointed look on his father's face when they arrived at the army base. A couple of weeks prior, he and Zadeia were unable to speak to him when they contacted their parents at the Sheidem City Army Headquarters. He had been on a special mission to track down the Feim soldiers, who were attacking Udnaruk's southeastern villages. He and his platoon were ambushed and he was lucky to be one of the few to escape. When Zimi saw his father again, he knew what he would be thinking. That his son was an idiot for running away from school and running away from the one thing his father trusted and treated with the utmost regard. The Western Army. The ones who swore to protect them when Hamilda was thought to have been kidnapped. A shudder went through Zimi. He was not looking forward to it at all.

The knot in Zimi's stomach tightened as the Udnarukan Army base came into full view. Very different from the Sheidem City army base, it was like a small city in its own right. Surrounded by tall fences, the army base incorporated the use of many buildings, such as army headquarters, training facilities, and a cafeteria for army use, along with hundreds of residential homes for the soldiers and their families. As they hovered over the ground, preparing to land, Zimi's already upset stomach did a full turn, making him moan in silent pain.

A hand touched Zimi's shoulder, interrupting his thoughts. He turned to see Cristaden looking concerned. *Just wonderful*, he thought. Cristaden probably heard all his anxiety issues. She must have known the obvious truth. He was deathly afraid of his father. "I'm fine," Zimi said, with a reassuring smile. Cristaden smiled back and told him it was time to disembark. Zimi sighed. *Here goes nothing.*

No one on the ground seemed to take notice of the airship, or who might have been on board. As the group of six made their way through the throngs of people, who had sought refuge at the army base during the Feim invasion a few months prior, they noticed a sense of calm. The displaced people drifted about their lives, oblivious to what could possibly lay ahead. Children were running around with their blue and white uniforms on, having just come from school, and adults carried out their daily activities with dignity. They felt safe, surrounded by trained professionals who would protect them with their lives. The Dokami Council might have been mistaken about Prince Aillios' dream. There did not seem to be any danger surrounding Southern Udnaruk at all. Even Cristaden did not sense anything unusual.

Prince Aillios, or Lio, tried hard not to visibly react whenever someone looked directly at him. He had to keep reminding himself that the people in the West had no idea who he was or how 'the cruel Prince from the East' looked like. It occurred to him that his friends were hidden in plain sight as well, with only certain members of the Western Army knowing who they actually were. Udnaruk was culturally diverse, with traders from the North, escapees from Feim and other Eastern countries, and people just looking for a change of life, so the fact that they were all from different countries did not bring any unwanted attention to them.

Prince Aillios found himself relaxing a little, but his newfound sense of security was regrettably cut too short. He saw a familiar face, within the crowd of refugees, which made him draw in a breath and hold it. Then the person was gone. He tried to look around the crowds of people, but could not find it again. Did he just imagine it?

"What's wrong Lio?" Cristaden said, mindful of his nickname. "What did you see?" She looked confused, as if she could not understand his reaction to the face in his mind.

For a moment, Aillios did not respond because he could not even *comprehend* what he saw. Was is someone he knew? Someone from Mituwa? His heart started to beat faster. He wanted so much to duck into the nearest home and hide. It had to be his own imagination. But, what if it wasn't? "I...I, uh—"

"My darlings!"

Prince Aillios was interrupted by an explosion of emotion from a woman, who had pushed her way through the crowd, and greeted Zadeia and Zimi with opened arms. She had their almond shaped, brown eyes and tan complexion. Her hair was midnight black, tied together in a long, thick braid. She wore a black, military-like, formfitting suit and a pair of black boots. It was not the type of outfit you would see on military personnel, but it was made from the same material.

"Mummie!" Zadeia cried out, bursting into tears as she flung her arms around her mother. Zimi came in for a hug as well, but awkwardly, as if he expected his mother to pull away from him, which she did not. In fact, she seemed on the verge of tears.

After what seemed like a long time, the twins' mother finally stepped back, gave them a once over and told them how worried she had been about them since they left Lochenby. Even though she was happy to see them, for a brief moment they noticed a flash in her eyes, showing how upset she truly was. Prince Aillios instantly understood why Zimi had seemed so awkward.

The twins apologized and, in whispers so no one around them could hear, explained their ordeal to her. Their mother listened in stunned silence, looking back and forth between them and the other members of Omordion's Hope, her eyes widening with every twist and turn to their story. When they were finished, she expressed how grateful she was that they were still alive and beamed with joy when her children introduced her to the rest of the group.

"This is our mother," Zadeia said. "Shala Emyu." Shala shook everyone's hands, cordially greeting them.

"It's nice to meet you," Atakos said.

"Likewise," Shala said.

"Where's father?" Zadeia asked when everyone began to walk again.

"He is at Army Headquarters," Shala said. "He will be joining us for dinner."

Zimi kept quiet and tried not to show how scared he was.

"Did you miss us?" Zadeia asked.

"Of course we've missed you… but we do have someone with us now. Someone who has kept us…" Shala dropped her voice to a whisper. "…a little *busy*." She stopped and looked around. "Now where did the child go this time? She is always running off." She stopped walking and looked around. "Kireina!" she cried.

A young girl, wearing a white shirt and a navy blue skirt with brown sandals, appeared beside Shala from within the busy crowd. She shyly kept her eyes down and did not look up when she said "Hello," in a small voice.

"Oh!" Shala said, jumping slightly in surprise. "There you are."

Prince Aillios was taken aback by her. This was the face he saw in the crowd, causing him distress. Clearly, this girl was from his very own country—Mituwa. She had the same features as his people. Like his, her hair was black and curly, unlike the people of Udnaruk with their straight, thick, black hair. She must have been one of the many slaves who escaped his father's cruelty. If it was true, if she was an escaped slave from Mituwa, surely she would recognize him.

Shala was speaking again. "Your father rescued Kireina after the first attack in the northeastern villages. She was the only one left alive in her entire village. She believes there are others, still alive, being held captive on the other side of Rostumik Pass, in Feim." Sadly, Shala looked the girl over. "Including her mother. Her body was never recovered."

"That's terrible," Zadeia said to Kireina. She then extended her hand for the girl to shake. "It's nice to have you with us. I am Zadeia. This is my brother Zimi and my friends, Atakos, Cristaden, Fajha, and Lio."

"I am so glad to meet you," Kireina said and looked up with sad eyes.

Prince Aillios felt like falling over.

Her eyes. Piercing green, *Mituwan* eyes. There was no doubt in his mind anymore of where she came from.

Prince Aillios felt a hand on his arm, looked up, and made eye contact with Cristaden. She obviously knew what he was thinking. If this girl recognized him, and his cover was blown, not only would the Western Army have a field day with him, but the displaced people there would be more than happy to torture him for all they've been through—just for the fun of it.

"Kireina," Cristaden said, turning back to the girl. "Have you lived in Udnaruk all your life?" A simple, but important question.

In a small voice, Kireina answered. "Yes," she said. "I was born here."

"How old are you?"

"I am in my fourteenth year."

Relief flooded through Prince Aillios. This girl was alone and, even if her parents were there, they would not recognize him either. He was eight years old fourteen years ago. At the time, he had barely left the castle. He let out a small chuckle and cleared his throat when everyone turned to look at him. Cristaden smiled, knowing the relief he was feeling.

"Come," Shala said. "I would like for all of you to join us for dinner. We will then find a place for you to rest in our home, of course."

"Thank you," Atakos said and his friends thanked Shala as well. Atakos was interested to see how the twins lived on the Udnarukan Army base, when they were far away from Lochenby, during the hot, summer months of vacation.

CHAPTER 33

Colnaha's eardrums were throbbing with every shrill cry. It did not take him long to figure out why the siren in his airship was going off. He had run out of fuel. He realized he did not know where exactly on Omordion he was. All he saw were forests of trees and tall mountains in the distance. His airship was rocking back and forth, the engine sputtering, about to shut down at any moment. Colnaha had to think fast. He needed to land—and quickly. If only his airship would hold until he found a clearing big enough to land it. At this rate though, landing it safely did not seem possible.

Colnaha brought the airship down from the sky, closer to the treetops in case he had to jump out before he lost complete control of it. This proved to be a bad move as the airship dropped even further on its own, hitting tree branches along its way to certain destruction. Colnaha panicked. After trying desperately to pull the airship back up, he let out a scream when the ship hit a large tree branch with a loud smashing sound, leaving vein-like cracks on his windshield.

Now would be a good time to jump, Colnaha thought. He released the steering wheel and clumsily shuffled towards the door, trying hard to remain standing, but finding it extremely difficult. The orb suddenly came to mind, but he tripped as the airship hit a tree and shifted violently to the right.

Forget the orb, he thought, *I have to leave it.*
No, you must not leave without it, the voice in his head said.
I must abandon this ship. Now! Before it is too late.

You are not *leaving without it.*
"I am going to die," Colnaha said aloud. "I do not want to die."
Get the orb.
"No!"
Get the orb. Before it is too late!
"Arrrg!" With a grunt, Colnaha dove towards the bag, which he had tucked safely under one of the passenger seats. Holding the bag tight against his chest, Colnaha braced himself as the airship hit tree after tree, literally falling apart with each impact. Meanwhile, he was being thrown around like a rag doll, all over the airship floor.

This can't be happening, Colnaha thought. He could feel a small trickle of blood sliding down his face from having smacked his head hard a few times. Ignoring the pain, he tried to stand up, but felt woozy, out of focus. He must have received some sort of concussion when he hit his head.

One thing was clear though.

Colnaha might die because of the cursed orb.

With one final smash, the airship hit the ground hard and Colnaha was thrown sideways. He took his last breath, it seemed, when his head hit the door and everything went black.

Colnaha opened his eyes.

The first thing he noticed was a severe, throbbing pain on the left side of his head and, slowly, the pain he felt all over his body began to register. He was curled up in a ball, the bag with the orb held tightly against his chest, in the corner of the now wrecked airship.

"Ohhhh," Colnaha moaned, attempting to stand up. He carefully moved his arms and legs, making sure he did not have any broken bones. Although bruised and bleeding, he was relieved. No bones had been broken. A dizzy spell overtook him all of a sudden, most likely the result of hitting his head so many times, so he had to stop trying to move and rest. He tried to see through his distorted vision at the damage the airship had sustained.

How am I still alive? Colnaha thought, after looking around.

After he wiped blood off his brow with a shaky hand, Colnaha tried to stand up again. His vision was beginning to clear so he finally realized the airship was resting on its side. The doorway he had tried to use to exit the airship, before it crashed, was now underneath him.

Glancing around, he saw everything he brought onto the ship, when he left Osmatu, had been thrown around. Sacks and jars of food, if not broken or shattered everywhere, were now blocking the entrance to the back door. The other side of the ship, which was now the ceiling, had been ripped clean off, and smoke billowed from the engine beyond the completely broken windshield. For a few moments, Colnaha looked up to watch the clouds rolling by in the sky above him before he attempted to stand again. This time he was successful.

Colnaha slowly moved towards the control panel, all the while feeling dizzy and grimacing in pain with every small jerk of his muscles. He decided it was best to throw the bag with the orb out through the broken windshield panel so he would not have to hold it anymore, knowing the orb was indestructible anyways. With his now free hands, he painfully pulled himself up and out of the broken windshield, being careful not to cut himself with the sharp, protruding glass still hanging on the edges. One of them ripped his shirt as he slid to the ground, but he did not care. He just wanted to be free of the wrecked airship.

After hitting the ground, it took Colnaha a few minutes to get back up again and to get his bearings. When he finally did look around, his breath caught in his throat and he held it for a moment before releasing it. "What is this place?" he said when he carefully stood up, trying hard to ignore the pain in his legs.

It was nothing like he had ever seen before.

Colnaha took several steps towards a giant crater in the ground, mere feet from where his airship had crash-landed. Surveying the area, he noticed the trees in the forest surrounding him were dead. In fact, it seemed like the whole area was entirely lacking of life. Nothing green as far as the eye could see. No little animals scurrying about and no birds chirping in the trees.

Everything was dead.

Colnaha looked around the extensive crater in the middle of the dead forest. A tall, tower-like structure stood in the middle of it, rugged and jutting out of the ground, as if it was a small mountain in its own right. Dead tree branches covered it, reaching out, resembling skeleton-like fingers. Letting his eyes scale the body of the scary looking structure, Colnaha shuddered when he spotted a dark opening about halfway up. He immediately decided he was not going in there and planted himself on the ground.

What am I going to do now? Colnaha thought, sighing. His airship was destroyed, he had no idea where he was, and, obviously, he was nowhere near any sign of life. In fact, it was unclear to him why he had decided to leave Saiyut in the first place. Colnaha brought his hand up to his throbbing temple and looked up at the sky. It hurt his head even more just trying to think about what made him leave. Sure, he was upset. Nonetheless, he had no reason to—

Colnaha jumped up at the sight of lightning illuminating the sky overhead and the inevitable, earsplitting crash of thunder following shortly afterwards. Just seconds before, the sky had been clear, without a cloud in sight. Now dark clouds were rolling in, threatening to release buckets of rain at any moment. Baffled, Colnaha grabbed the bag with the orb in it and, ignoring the pain in his legs again, quickly limped back to his airship, thinking it might be a good place to seek shelter. Before reaching it though, lightning hit the airship, knocking him off his feet. Seconds later, the rain started, pelting his body so hard, he found it difficult to stand up for even a brief moment without cowering.

Thinking his day could not get any worse, Colnaha glanced at the only place he could seek shelter. The tall, mountain-like structure in the middle of the giant crater. If he could just manage to climb up without being struck by lightning, it would be a miracle. Colnaha placed the bag over his shoulder and half-ran, half-limped to the edge of the crater. He jumped down about four feet to the ground, and grimaced as a shot of pain flew up his right leg. After taking a deep breath, he ignored the pain and skittered the rest of the way to the structure. A lightning bolt struck a tree in the dead forest nearby, causing him to jump with fear and move along even faster.

When Colnaha reached the base of the structure, he took a deep breath before climbing it. At any moment, he could be struck by lightning and he would cease to exist. No one would know where to find him. Especially all the way there, wherever he was, in a desolate place such as it was.

Shaking his head after wiping water from his eyes, Colnaha reached for the first branch and pulled himself up. He steadily climbed the freakish structure, all the while continuing to pray over and over again that he would not get struck by lightning. He breathed a sigh of relief once he hoisted himself into the opening he saw from the ground. A knot formed in his throat when something frightening and unexpected happened.

All of a sudden, everything *stopped*.

Turning around, Colnaha was shocked to see that the torrential rain, the terrifying storm he had just fought through to survive, was *gone*. In fact, it seemed as if it had never happened. The ground was dry. Bone dry. His clothes, his hair, his shoes were dry.

But that wasn't all.

Colnaha wondered if he had finally lost his mind when he noticed something else, which made him gasp and his breath come out in rapid successions.

His airship.

Was *intact*.

Colnaha peered at it from where he stood, trying to make sense of what he was seeing. The airship, the same one he had been in a short while before, wrecked and hit by lightning, looked as if he had landed it perfectly in the clearing by the crater. Looking down at his own body, Colnaha realized he was no longer in pain and it seemed as if he had never been injured in the first place. His shirt, which had ripped as he exited the wreck, was no longer torn. "No," he said under his breath. "Am I dreaming? Am I dead?"

A noise, deep within the cave, made Colnaha turn around in fear. He had not noticed it before. A light was shining from the end of a tunnel. Was it possible someone could actually be living there? Colnaha hesitated for a moment and wondered if he should find out what was in the cave or go back to the ship. His curiosity took over as he took a few steps into the tunnel.

"Hello?" Colnaha shouted. Although he was scared of what might answer him back, he felt like he needed to know what or who it was to satisfy his curiosity. Receiving no response back, Colnaha slowly inched towards the light. The closer he got to it, the more he noticed how stuffy the tunnel was becoming. Then came the horrible stench. It was such a putrid, nasty smell, he had to lift his shirt up over his nose and mouth to keep from vomiting. He pressed on through the tunnel though, interested to know what he would find when he reached the end.

When Colnaha stopped in front of what seemed to be an entrance to a chamber of some sort, he began to breathe a little easier. The quality of the air had improved and the putrid smell had dissipated. He lowered his shirt as he entered the chamber and slowly took in what he was seeing. Surprisingly, it appeared to be a throne room, similar to those found in castles. A long, faded, red-gray carpet stretched out to the other end of the room and old-fashioned, lit candles hung on the walls, providing the only illumination. It only took Colnaha a few moments to realize he was not alone in the strange chamber.

There was indeed a throne.

And someone was sitting on it.

Colnaha, still as curious as ever—even more so now—inched closer so he could get a better look. It was an old man with a long gray beard, dressed in a faded black robe. He seemed to be in a deep sleep or dead, but Colnaha felt drawn to him, as if he needed to be close to him for some reason. He inched his way closer and closer, until he was only mere feet away. Now he could see him even better. The old man was covered in dust, as if he had not moved from his position in a long time, years even. He was ancient. So old, Colnaha could not even place how old he was. Definitely much older than his grandfather, Olshem.

Colnaha took a couple of steps forward and grinded to a halt when the old man slowly opened his eyes and lifted his head. His gray eyes regarded Colnaha for a moment, looking him up and down with what seemed like inherent distaste. He shifted in his chair, causing spirals of dust to swirl in the air around him, and grunted. "The orb," he simply said.

In a trance, Colnaha reached for the bag he had slung over his shoulder and placed it on the ground. He opened it, intent on taking the black orb, with waves of green light undulating all over it, out, but stopped when the old man quickly put his hand out. "No," he said. He gestured for Colnaha to give him the bag, which he so willingly did, stepping forward to place the bag in the old man's hands. "Excellent. You may sit."

Colnaha did what he was told, leisurely sitting down on the ground by the old man's feet, a small smile playing on his lips. He felt a sudden sense of belonging, as if he was where he should be. As if everything he had ever done his entire life had lead him to this man. Colnaha allowed his eyes to wander around the chamber until it fell on a flame from one of the candles on the wall. He watched the flame flicker back and forth for a long time. He could not tear his eyes away from it no matter how hard he tried.

What a lovely flame it was.
A truly, lovely flame.

Brulok sat back in his throne, the bag with the orb resting on his lap. *Everything was going as planned*, he thought. He only needed to do one last thing to finish what he started. Closing his eyes and sinking back into complete meditation, Brulok astral projected himself back to the camp the Eastern Army had set up in Feim. He found himself standing inside the large tent intended for him. Menyilh, his most loyal and trusted servant jumped up from his place at the corner of the tent when he saw him.

"Master," Menyilh said with a smile. "You were gone for so long, I thought you would never return."

"I am not staying," Brulok said. "And I will not be returning. I need you to write a letter for me."

Menyilh looked disheartened as he scrambled to find a piece of parchment paper, a pen, and a bottle of ink. "Addressed to whom, my lord?"

"That foolish, incompetent man, who calls himself a *king*."

Menyilh chuckled softly to himself and eagerly began writing the letter under Brulok's dictation, addressing it to Tholenod, gleefully omitting the king's title to show him who was really in charge.

CHAPTER 34

The house given to the Emyu family by the Western Army was a single floor house, attached to other homes belonging to military personnel. According to the twins, their father, Lieutenant Emyu, respected and loved the army so much, he collected art depicting battle scenes, had lots of army memorabilia, and displayed his trophies, certificates, and awards everywhere around the house for his comrades to view when they stopped by.

Upon entering the Emyu home, Atakos, Cristaden, Fajha, and Prince Aillios could see exactly what they were talking about. The man was in love with the Western Army. The main part of the twin's home was an open floor plan, with the living room, dining room, and kitchen in one large, open space. It was beautifully decorated and they could see the memorabilia, paintings, and awards hanging along the walls, on the mantelpiece over the living room fireplace, and on a tall bookshelf by the couch. Zimi and Zadeia's bedrooms were to the right, by the living room, and their parents' bedroom was by the kitchen.

The twins also mentioned how Lt. Emyu set up military styled training devices in the basement to train while he was off-duty. He never took a break, they said. Not for one second. And he did not allow them to rest during their time off, but encouraged them to train as well. Shala was no exception. She would train diligently with her husband even though she was no longer in the military. It was the way the Emyu household was run and their parents preferred it that way.

"Please have a seat," Shala said, gesturing for them to sit down at the long dining room table. "Kireina, I know you have eaten already, but you are welcomed to sit with us."

Kireina shook her head. "I have an assignment I have to finish with the research group," she said. "There's not much left to do so I will return once it is complete."

"That's fine, dear."

After Kireina said goodbye and left, Shala sighed to herself and whispered softly, "Poor child," before going to the kitchen stove. To the rest of her company, she said, "When I heard you were coming, I started cooking because I was sure you would be famished after your trip."

Famished was an understatement, Fajha thought. He felt so hungry, he thought his stomach was going to devour itself at any moment. When they all sat down, he tried everything in his power not to get up and help Shala pass out the food.

Just then, Lieutenant Emyu walked in. Dressed in the Western Army black uniform and hat; he had reddish-brown features and brown eyes, much like his wife and children. He walked with his back straight and shoulders back, as if he was still marching with his fellow soldiers.

Prince Aillios quickly looked down at the plate of food Shala had placed in front of him, and refused to make eye contact with the lieutenant for fear that he would recognize him, even though he was sure he would not. Zimi wasn't doing so well either. Along with Zadeia, he stood up to greet his father, saluting him with his eyes to the floor. Zadeia seemed happier to see her father than her brother was. She was grinning from ear to ear and bouncing slightly as she saluted him. Following the twins' actions, Atakos, Fajha and Cristaden stood up and saluted Lt. Emyu. Prince Aillios reluctantly did the same, but kept his eyes lowered.

"It is a pleasure to have you here," Lt. Emyu said. "Welcome to my home." He took the seat at the head of the table and invited everyone to sit down. Shala planted a kiss on his cheek as she put a plate of food down in front of him and he looked up at her and smiled, breaking the momentum of his entire stern, military facade. His greeting and smile actually made Prince Aillios relax a little. He did not seem so bad after all.

"Major Garunburj mentioned he was picking you up on his way from Sheidem Island," Lt. Emyu said, looking around at everyone sitting at the table. He stared hard at Prince Aillios for a brief moment, causing the hairs to stand up at the back of his neck, and then he focused his eyes on Zimi, who did not return his gaze. "Can I ask you how you ended up in Saiyut and not under the protection of the Western Army in Sheidem City?"

Zimi looked at his father and tried to speak, but ended up stumbling over his words. "Well–uh–um–so–Ha–milda–uh–was kidnapped."

"I understand that. Go on."

Zadeia piped in to save her brother. "We set out to save her because we felt like General Komuh was following the wrong leads. We also thought he was holding us prisoner instead of trying to keep us safe. It's...difficult to explain."

"I see," Lt. Emyu said, while nodding his head. "General Komuh gave the army a bad name by his actions. I am grateful he was brought to justice for what he did." He turned to Zimi again. "What became of your teacher? *How* did you end up in Saiyut?"

"Well–we–um–so–Ha–milda–uh," Zimi said, stammering once again. It was apparent his father intimidated him.

The others thought it was sad to watch their friend of many years act so different, so unlike his usual spunky, obnoxious self. When Zimi stammered again, they came to his rescue. Each one of them took turns recanting the story that took them from Lochenby to the Dokami Council in Saiyut, even throwing in that the Council had sent 'Lio' to go with them to offer his services. They described their dreams to him, omitting the parts about Prince Aillios' younger self being the one who warned them about the battle coming to Udnaruk.

At the end of their explanation, Lt. Emyu looked at each of them with terrible concern.

"The monsters you fought," Lt. Emyu said. "They belong to a man-wizard–named Brulok, you say?"

"Yes," Zadeia said.

"You were told by a...fairy...that Brulok has teamed up with King Tholenod to help him with the war?"

"...yes," Atakos said, trying hard not to look at Prince Aillios for confirmation. "Tholenod sought his help when he realized he was losing the war. Our dreams strongly indicate that they will be coming here."

"But why here of all places?"

"We're not sure," Fajha said. "We don't even know if they'll actually come."

"Perhaps the Rostumik Pass is the closest point connecting Eastern and Western Omordion, without an ocean in between?" Shala suggested. "If they were to launch an attack, why *not* here?"

Lt. Emyu quickly stood up. "Our borders have already suffered unspeakable destruction from Feim. When they came here, they destroyed three villages, killing so many innocent people without hesitation, and annihilated my entire platoon. I was lucky to get out alive with Kireina. What those horrific soldiers from Feim then did to your teacher's husband, Jogesh…I cannot describe. They are the epitome of evil. I can't even look at the colors black and red without thinking of them and their monstrosity.

Since your dreams and visions have proven to become true many times, I cannot take any chances. I will discuss this with the major. It's better to be prepared than to be caught unaware." Lt. Emyu turned to leave and almost crashed into Kireina, who had walked into the house just as he was talking about the Feim soldiers. "Please, excuse me," he said.

Kireina nodded, but everyone could see she seemed devastated. She looked at Shala with fear in her green eyes. "They're coming back?" she asked, her voice trembling.

Shala walked over to her and put her arms around her shoulders. "We're not sure yet, dear," she said. "It's just a precaution."

Kireina then burst into tears. "I wish my mother was here. I wish she could be rescued."

"I know," Shala said, wrapping her arms around Kireina. "Hush now and stop your crying. Your mother will be alright."

The six onlookers from the table glanced at each other in sadness. They could not imagine being in the situation Kireina was in. She lost her mother and an entire village in one day. It must be horrible for her to believe her mother was still alive and being held captive somewhere, possibly being tortured while in captivity, and not being able to do anything to save her. They knew what Shala said about her mother being okay was a false statement. For all they knew, Kireina's mother may have already been killed in Feim. The teen may never know what became of her.

Suddenly, a thought dawned on Prince Aillios. It was as if all the years of not being able to help his people came flooding back to him all at once. Trying his best to speak softly so his accent would not be so strong, he spoke for the first time since leaving Saiyut. "Ah...Kireina, is it?" he said.

"Yes," Kireina said in a barely audible whisper. She stepped away from Shala and wiped her eyes to get a better look at who was speaking to her.

"You believe your mother is still alive?"

"I do."

"Has the army attempted to find her?"

Kireina was about to speak when she was cut off by Shala. "The Feim soldiers came here via the Rostumik Pass," she said. "The river beyond the Cliffs of Thegahn. It is dangerous on the other side of the Pass. Even if you were to get across and into Feim, there's no way of knowing what waits for you there or where the enemy has taken the captives." She was obviously trying hard to defend the Western Army for not taking any initiatives in rescuing the captives.

"Understandable," Prince Aillios said. "They've already lost so many men." To Kireina, he stood up and bowed his head. "Even if I have to put my life in danger, I will do what I can to rescue your mother."

Kireina stared back at him, her eyes widening. "Do you mean what you say?"

"Yes."

"I second that," Atakos said, standing up as well. "There doesn't seem to be anything bad happening around here. It would be good to get some exercise."

Fajha laughed. "Exercise! Ha ha haaaaa..." But he did not look amused. Just when they were done recuperating from being in eminent danger, there goes Atakos, throwing them into something even more dangerous.

"Come on Fajha," Atakos said. "We could use your location ability to find the captives."

"Sounds like a great idea," Zadeia said.

"With your help," Prince Aillios said, "we could sneak in and out without them even realizing we were there."

"Yes," Cristaden said. "It would help—"

"Location ability?" Kireina said with a frown.

The group froze.

How could they be so careless?

"He makes an excellent tracker," Prince Aillios quickly said.

Kireina still looked puzzled, but she pulled something out of her pocket and walked over to Fajha, holding the object out for him to see. "This was painted long ago," she said, tears welling up in her eyes again. "It is all I have been able to retrieve from my village. The Feim soldiers burnt down my home and everything in it. Except this. Are you sure you will be able to track her? It has been a few months."

Resigned, Fajha took the small painting of Kireina's mother from her extended hand and stared at it for a moment. The woman on the painting looked very similar to Kireina. She had curly, black hair, gray eyes and appeared to be in her late forties. He nodded. "I will try my best."

"Great," Atakos said. "It would be best if the three of us go and the rest of you hang back. It's easier to spot more of us than only a few."

"Sounds like a plan," Prince Aillios said, while the others agreed.

Shala looked distressed. "You don't know what those soldiers are capable of," she said. "It would be a treacherous mission."

"Yes," Kireina said, her voice quivering with fright. "I've *seen* what they can do. Please...just...don't let them catch you."

"We won't," Prince Aillios said. "We will be back here before you know it."

CHAPTER 35

The boat rocked from side to side. In the cool, damp night, Atakos, Fajha, and Prince Aillios silently paddled through the choppy water of Rostumik Pass. The light of the full moon illuminated the cliffs, and the pine trees on top of them, on either side and they could barely see the rocks jutting out from the shoreline, threatening to obstruct their journey. Their nerves were on edge with the anticipation of being attacked by the enemy at any moment.

Fajha felt a sudden chill. He glanced up at the forest on top of the cliffs and shivered. "Do you feel that?" he said. He glanced at Atakos, who was looking around as well.

"Yes," Atakos said.

"Feel what?" Prince Aillios said.

"Like we're being watched," Fajha said. "I feel it on both sides of the cliffs."

"So do I," Atakos said.

"Do you think it is the soldiers from Feim?" Prince Aillios said in a whisper. "Do you think they are watching us?"

"It would make sense if we were being attacked right now. They probably wouldn't have allowed us to get this far."

Prince Aillios grunted. "If only that were true. You don't know the East like I do."

"I see a light," Fajha said, interrupting their thoughts.

Atakos and Prince Aillios looked up ahead and spotted it too. A tiny light in the darkness ahead of them. It appeared to be a light from a lantern, but they could not tell if it was on land or on a boat.

"It is best we slow down and move closer to the cliffs up ahead," Prince Aillios said. If soldiers from Feim were watching them, the risk of being hit with an arrow was greater if they remained in the light of the moon. They would have a better chance of survival if they were shielded in complete darkness.

Moving away from the middle of the river, they paddled as close as they could to the cliffs without crashing on any rocks jutting out from its base. Here, the light from the moon was lost in the trees, which aided in shrouding them in darkness, but also presented a challenge. Often they would get stuck in between a pile of rocks they did not see coming and had to go in reverse to pull free of it.

As they steadily came closer to the light, more lights appeared in the distance and they began to hear voices. Many voices. Voices of men, shouting and barking orders up and down the coast. It was clear the entire Feim Army was there, resting along the shores of Rostumik Pass, so close to Udnaruk, it was sickening.

"Why are they gathered here?" Fajha said. They half expected to run into a few villages before reaching the Feim Army base.

"I'm not sure..." Atakos' heart was in his throat. What *were* they doing there? The closer they got, the tighter his throat felt.

Prince Aillios' pulse was racing. Something was wrong. Something was definitely wrong. The shouting—the barking of orders—sounded so *familiar* to him.

He suddenly gasped when he realized why.

As they rounded a bend in the river and stopped paddling, what they feared the most became a harsh reality.

When they saw the ships, they knew.

When they saw the fires, they knew.

The catapults.

The sheer masses of soldiers.

It was not just the Feim Army gathered there.

Prince Aillios knew why everything sounded so familiar to him. "My father. He's *here*."

"You can't be serious," Atakos said. Unfortunately, he knew it was true, due to the masses of soldiers camping out on the shore. There had to be thousands of them as far as the light from their camps permitted them to see. Their dreams *were* warnings. The entire Eastern side was planning a major battle. To attack Udnaruk in this way, without warning, was not war.

It was a planned *massacre*.

"It is not just my father's army and Feim," Prince Aillios said in an angry whisper. "It's every army in the East. I see the colors of Srepas and Effit as well. They are *all* here."

"They must be planning on taking out each country in the West one at a time," Fajha said, in shock. "If Udnaruk does not prepare for this, they just might succeed."

"We must go back and warn them," Atakos said.

"What about the girl's mother?" Prince Aillios asked.

Atakos turned to Prince Aillios with raised eyebrows. "Are you *insane*? Are you seeing the same thing I am seeing? You do not expect to just waltz into something of this magnitude. Find one person. Free her. And then just walk right out of there without being seen—"

"I fully intend to carry out the promise I made to the girl."

"You're not making a lot of sense right now."

"She is expecting us to return with her mother. If I can help her, I will try."

"Do you realize what you're saying?"

Prince Aillios looked Atakos right in the eyes. "Of course I do. Yes." He did not expect him to understand. He wasn't doing it just for Kireina's mother. He had made a promise to do whatever he could to save his people, but for a long time he had felt like a failure. If he could just do this one thing, for one Mituwan soul, he felt like he could redeem himself and his promise. He would not let another Mituwan down again. It was something he *had* to do.

Atakos shook his head. "It's suicide."

"If we do it right, it won't be."

"You're crazy." Atakos glanced at the sight ahead of them. He knew he would not feel right giving up on finding Kireina's mother either. He sighed heavily. "Fajha, can you locate her mother?"

"Are you nuts?" Fajha said in a whisper. "We're actually doing this?!"

"Faj—"

"Okay, okay. I'll do it." Fajha removed the small painting from his pocket and closed his eyes. "I doubt this will work, it is just a painting. And I doubt she's still alive."

"We have to try," Prince Aillios said.

"Shhh!" Fajha said with one eye open. "I need as much quiet as possible." He closed his eyes again, attempting to drown out the sounds coming from the shore, and directed his attention to finding Kireina's mother. After what seemed like a half an hour, he opened his eyes and smiled. "You won't believe this."

"Let's have it," Prince Aillios said impatiently.

"See that hill? I think there's a village back there, but I'm not sure. That's where we'll find her."

"Good work." Atakos said.

"Now listen carefully," Prince Aillios said. "Our next move will be tricky."

Fajha grunted. *Tricky?* he thought. *More like fatal.*

Within the next hour, Atakos, Fajha, and Prince Aillios had tied the boat around a dead tree stump, near a group of boulders. They silently swam to one of the smaller, empty ships and quietly slipped onboard. Like shadows in the night, they scurried below deck, where they found what they were looking for. Blood-red and black Feim uniforms. They were ghastly, with monstrous masks made to look like beasts to cover their faces. When they were ready, the three casually climbed up to the deck and off the ship. It was the most nerve-racking thing Atakos and Fajha had ever done, but Prince Aillios was a graduate in hiding in plain sight. He sauntered along as if he belonged there, confidently sticking out his chest and pulling his shoulders back, prompting the two boys to do the same. Aillios effortlessly imitated the way the Feim soldiers moved without a hitch.

When orders were barked at them to fetch more wood for the fires, Prince Aillios snapped to attention and showed his allegiance. Atakos and Fajha did the same, but could not believe their luck. To fetch more wood for the fires meant they had free range to go wherever they pleased to find it. Their plan was working out better than they ever imagined. After agreeing to find the wood, they entered a forest of dead trees and headed straight for the hill leading to Kireina's mother, hoping no one would notice they were suspiciously going to fetch wood far away from the campsite.

"How many guards do you see?" Atakos said. He could not see over the heads of Prince Aillios and Fajha. The three were crouched in the dense brush near the occupied village, trying to figure out what their next move would be.

"There's about ten of them," Prince Aillios said. "All from Effit. Maybe more. I can't see that well."

"Why are Effit soldiers keeping an eye on Feim captives?" Fajha asked.

"Maybe the Feim soldiers are busy."

"Fajha, can you sense where she is now that we're closer?" Atakos asked.

Fajha thought for a moment and slowly pointed to a rundown shack just thirty yards away from them. "She's in there."

"Okay," Prince Aillios said. "Are we ready?"

"Do we have to do it this way?" Atakos asked.

"We have these uniforms for a reason." Prince Aillios stood up, put his mask back on, and waited for the other two to do the same. "Follow my lead," he said.

The soldiers in the village noticed them as soon as they stepped into the clearing. One Effitian soldier steadily walked over to them and removed his green mask.

"Any word about the battle?" the soldier asked. "Are we moving out?"

"No," Prince Aillios said in a gruff voice. "Not yet."

The soldier frowned. "Then what business do you have here?"

Aillios could not understand why it seemed strange for a Feim soldier to be walking around on *Feim* land. He decided not to point that out to the Effit soldier, because he did not know the real reason why, and came up with a different tactic. "King Tholenod ordered us to fetch him a woman…for his…amusement."

The soldier laughed. He motioned for two more soldiers to join them. "That idiot king is requesting a woman to join him!"

The other two laughed–hard. One of them took his mask off and wiped at his eyes. "I'm surprised he did not want a friend for the old wizard. He runs him like a dog."

Prince Aillios cringed at the mention of the old wizard's name and looked back at the two teenagers. *Brulok was there*. Most likely, he knew they were there as well. Aillios had not even considered that notion. He hadn't even noticed the oddity of the dead trees they had to travel past to get the village. Thinking back, he recalled seeing them. Just like the forest surrounding Brulok's mountain in Effit. Still, if the wizard knew they were there, why wasn't he coming after them? This could get bad. They had to play their cards right, or they were not going to make it out of there alive.

Prince Aillios, Fajha, and Atakos laughed heartily at the soldier's comment. The three kindly excused themselves after the Effit soldiers granted them their permission. They made their way to the closest shack and opened the straw door. The first thing they noticed was the smell. It reeked of filth, with a small hint of decaying flesh. The walls were caked with mud and dirt and so were the people inside. Twenty or so of them crowded the room wearing rags. So completely covered in filth, it was difficult to see how they looked like. The three imposters felt bad for them and wished they could set them all free. They knew deep inside it was a senseless notion. They would never be able to take every single person out of there alive, without giving away who they were. They would have to return for them, if they could possibly win the battle yet to come.

While studying their faces, Prince Aillios immediately recognized the Mituwan woman sitting in the corner. The only one there with matted black, curly hair and eyes reflecting gray in the light. "This one," he said, pointing to Kireina's mother. As he advanced towards her, she started screaming and tried to move away from him. "Calm down," Aillios said, but he knew it was no use. As far as she knew, they were monstrous Feim soldiers with scary masks on. The very people who destroyed her village. "Atakos! Fajha! Grab her!" The three disguised soldiers leapt at her, grabbed her hands and feet, and carried her out of the shack.

One of the Effit soldiers laughed. "You picked a wily one. She is a tough girl. She would give that idiot king a good fight. Ho ho!"

Another one removed a club from his belt and came up to them, offering to knock her out.

"N-no!" Atakos cried out.

"That won't be necessary," Prince Aillios said. They were attempting to leave the clearing with the woman but, since she was fighting and they did not wish to do harm to her, it was proving more difficult than they anticipated with every step.

The Effit soldier raised his eyebrows and took a step back. He watched silently as the three supposedly ruthless soldiers of Feim struggled to keep a slave woman from escaping their clutches. While trying not to hurt her. He looked back at the other two soldiers, who frowned back at him. Before the three Feim soldiers could explain themselves, one of the Effit soldiers took a step forward.

"*Fou mein, alled parma dougeios?*" he said and raised his eyebrows.

Atakos looked at Fajha and he shook his head slightly. It was not a language he knew.

They were being tested.

Prince Aillios cleared his throat. He knew some of the Feim language and got the gist of what the soldier was asking. 'My brother, would you like a drink?' Strange. If they did not answer, they were in trouble. If they did answer, and it was wrong, they were in trouble. He felt the tension rise in the air. To answer 'yes' was most likely wrong. To answer 'no' would probably be wrong too. It was a question, which needed to be answered a certain way. He did not know what way it was. The three Effit soldiers stared back at them with sharp eyes and their hands slowly balled into fists. The hair on the back of Prince Aillios' neck stood up.

They were already in trouble.

Prince Aillios smiled underneath his mask and came up with the only thing he could think of in such a short time. "*Nehenma,*" he said. 'No thank you'.

The soldiers did not say anything at first. They stood staring at the three Feim soldiers. Their struggling captive stopped fighting and froze. She looked back and forth between the three Feim soldiers, confusion written all over her face. She could tell the wrong answer had been given. And if so, who were the Feim soldiers attempting to take her away?

"Imposters!" one soldier cried. The other soldiers in the village drew out their weapons and came in fast to attack from all directions.

Atakos and Fajha pushed them away with their minds, clearing a path for the four of them to head straight into the forest. The Effit soldiers were in shock, unable to understand what just happened to them. Nevertheless, the deceivers' surprise attack made them even more furious. While several of them angrily ran into the forest after them, the warning bells began to ring.

Within seconds, every soldier within a three-mile radius knew they were there.

CHAPTER 36

King Tholenod jumped at the sound of bells ringing. His heart leapt in his chest. He could hear soldiers screaming "Intruders!" as they ran to and fro, gathering their weapons. He rushed out of his despairingly small tent and grabbed the first soldier he could find. The man was from Effit, decked out in a forest green uniform, and actually appeared *frightened*.

"What is it? What has happened?"

"I am n-not sure, sire. It seems like we are being infiltrated, s-sire."

"*Infiltrated?*" Tholenod scoffed at the idea. Impossible. The West was not smart enough to figure out…. or where they? He looked over at the banks of the river and saw no foreign ships or soldiers, nor did he see any attack being launched whatsoever. All he could see was the massive Eastern Army running haphazardly around the banks of Rostumik Pass, throwing on their armor and gathering their weapons. "What is this *nonsense?*"

Tholenod marched towards the largest tent in the camp, made especially for Brulok. He did not even realize the wizard's demon horse was not there, nor did he notice the tent was dark, until he flung the curtain aside and stepped inside. He stood staring at an unoccupied tent.

For days, this was Brulok's hiding place. He never ventured out to speak with the armies gathered there. He left the tedious task to Tholenod, saying he would only lend a hand when needed.

Brulok was needed now.

And he was *gone*.

Tholenod was confused. Had he finally left the tent to venture out among the slew of soldiers? Somewhere, deep in his confused brain, he knew it was not the case. When he noticed something white on the small table by the bed, gleaming in the light emanating from outside, his fears were confirmed.

Brulok left a letter.

With hands beginning to shake with anger, Tholenod lifted the white sheet of paper off the table. After reading it, he felt a rage boiling up inside him, getting stronger with every passing second he stood there, clutching the letter in his hand. A small noise made the king quickly turn around. Crouching in the corner of the tent was Menyilh. *Menyilh*. The assistant who had been so loyal to him for decades. Menyilh stood up and sneered at him, the ends of his mouth curling upwards into an evil grin.

"He has gone," Menyilh said. He unexpectedly burst into a strange bout of laughter as he raised his hand to point at Tholenod. "You did everything as you were told. And he thanks you. For a job *well* done."

Screaming violently, Tholenod started throwing things around and destroying anything he could find in the tent. Menyilh's eyes opened wide with fear. He then tried to escape, bolting through the curtain, and running out into the throngs of soldiers preparing to attack whoever infiltrated their camp. Within minutes, Menyilh was dead, stabbed, and burning with the tent, which Tholenod had set on fire. None of the soldiers around him understood why he felt the need to kill his assistant. They figured the little man was there at the wrong place and the wrong time.

As dark clouds quickly rolled in and blanketed the night sky, covering the light of the moon, Tholenod felt a violent rage overtake him like a steady, growing fire, engulfing his entire body. He stood there, blinded with hate. So much so, he did not even notice the mysterious fog creeping in. Wiping the blood off his fingers with a dirty rag, he swore he would kill anything lying in the path of his army.

Beginning that very night.

"Who are you?" Kireina's mother frantically asked. Her eyes darted back and forth between the three masked Feim soldiers, pulling her through the dead forest. "What do you want with me?"

Prince Aillios' heart jumped in his chest. Her voice reminded him so much of his people. Such a distant memory of how things used to be when he was younger. Daring to look back at the group of soldiers chasing them, he tried his best to reassure her. "No time to explain. You must trust us!"

"What have we done?" Fajha said, panicking. "How are we going to get out of here? How? Go back through the Rostumik Pass? They'll follow us. The people in Udnaruk will be in danger!"

"They are already in danger," Prince Aillios said, pointing out the obvious.

"We'll figure it out, Fajha," Atakos said. However, as he was saying those words, he knew they were in for the biggest fight of their lives. About twenty soldiers were chasing them now and catching up. Ahead of them, he saw the torches. Soldiers running about, gathering their weapons, preparing to kill whomsoever infiltrated their camp at any cost. Those who were prepared had their weapons drawn, ready to attack at any moment. Thousands of soldiers stood in the path between them and their only way out. The boat.

The group of four broke through the dark forest into the clearing. They stopped dead in their tracks. Ahead of them, thousands of soldiers stood waiting for them and, behind them, the soldiers from the village were stepping out of the forest, eyes full of rage.

They were surrounded.

Gathering into a tight circle, with their backs facing Kireina's mother, the three friends braced themselves for the fight they were not going to win.

"Oh, look what we've gotten ourselves into," Fajha said, and grumbled. "Should we just let them have it?"

"Do you know any other way we can do this?" Prince Aillios said.

"We're not ready for this," Atakos said, his voice shaking. "We need our friends and an entire *army* to fight this kind of battle."

"Well. It looks like we have no choice," Fajha said. "Unless you want to be taken prisoner…"

"Or die," Atakos said. "Which one's worse?"

"Prisoner," Kireina's mother said, her voice quivering. Her face was pale and her head was darting back and forth, staring wide-eyed at the soldiers surrounding them. She was terrified.

"Then we will fight to the death," Prince Aillios said.

A violent scream erupted over the shouts of the soldiers, and a large tent in the distance burst into flame.

The masses of troops around them suffered a brief moment of confusion. They wondered if they were being attacked from behind and should be watching their backs as well.

No one had enough time to react when a fierce wind rapidly blew in and dark clouds covered the night sky and the moon, rolling with thunder. A thick fog quickly came up from the river and blanketed the entire clearing in less than three seconds.

"What the…?" Atakos said under his breath. The fog was strange, almost magical, as it wove its way between the soldiers and blinded them to the point where no one could see even a foot in front of them. Atakos could hear the frightened shouts from the soldiers, but he could no longer see them. He was about to devise a new plan when a vision in white appeared directly in front of them.

Cristaden.

"Hurry," she said in a barely audible whisper. "A path has been made for you. Hold hands and run with me. We must go quickly before the fog clears!"

Without any hesitation, the group of four formed a line, holding each other's hands, and allowed Cristaden to pull them through the fog.

Besides being blinded by the fog and their fires snuffed out by the wind, the soldiers on either side of them were even more confused when they were shoved aside by an unseen force.

Feet splashed on water and the five escapees felt it rise up to their knees as they ran forward.

"Careful," Cristaden said. "The boat is right here."

Each of them eased onto the small boat, feeling their way around so as not to bump into each other.

"Row," they heard Zadeia say and the boat lurched away from shore.

"Whew!" Fajha said. "I have never been so happy to see you guys!"

"Zimi?" Atakos said. "You here too?" He knew, from their trainings with the Dokami Council, that the fog encircling them could only be administered by both of the twins.

"Yup."

"Good," Prince Aillios said. "Very good."

A small voice broke through the fog. "Is anyone going to tell me what's going on?" Kireina's mother asked. "Who are you people? Why did you take me? What is going on here??"

Cristaden reached over and took the woman's hand into her own, instantly soothing her. "We came to rescue you. It was a long shot but we took a chance to find you. For your daughter's sake."

She gasped. "Kireina? She's alive?"

"Yes. She's waiting for you at the army base in Udnaruk."

The woman started crying and chanting praises.

Cristaden backed off and let the woman weep. She leaned over to Atakos who was sitting next to her. "We had a bad feeling so we came after you."

"Thank you," Atakos. "You saved us."

"Yeah," Fajha said. "Thanks."

"No problem." Cristaden glanced at Kireina's mother and then looked back her friends. "I can't believe you guys didn't tell her."

"We had no ti—" Atakos was interrupted by a roar coming from the Feim shoreline. It was a terrifying roar, sounding like it came from an angry monster.

The hair on the back of Prince Aillios' neck stood up. "It's the king," he said. He would recognize his father's war cry anywhere. It meant King Tholenod was planning to do something irrational, which usually involved a great loss of life. "We have to warn the Western Army. The battle is coming to us sooner than we think."

CHAPTER 37

"Please, have some more," Shala Emyu said to Kireina's mother, whose name was Ilahne. She was putting more rice and beans on Ilahne's plate after she finished eating.

Ilahne laughed. "I don't think I can eat anymore," she said. "I feel like I've been eating non-stop since last night!" She looked much happier and full of life after a few good meals and a nice hot bath. Her hair, which had been matted with mud and dirt the previous night, was now curly black, and her golden skin tone matched that of Kireina's. She looked over at her daughter and sighed, still not believing she had survived the brutal attack, which killed most of the people from their village. She tried not to think of the past couple of months, when she thought her daughter had been discovered and, since she was not taken to the place where Feim held the prisoners, was most likely dead. She tried not to think of how she cried relentlessly for days, feeling hopeless and wishing she could die too.

Kireina leaned over and gave her mother a hug before resting her head on her shoulder. She never thought she would ever see her alive again. When her new friends came back with Ilahne, she was sure her heart would explode in her chest. What a feeling. They did it. They actually found her and brought her back without getting themselves killed in the process. She gazed at each and every one of them, sitting around the long, wooden table, and smiled. She knew there was something incredibly special about them. Moreover, she was beyond delighted they had come to Udnaruk.

The sound of propellers could be heard outside and Atakos jumped up to see who it might be this time. He unzipped the flap of the large, brown tent they were stationed in, and stepped outside. During the night and into most of the day, the army had set up a camp close to the Cliffs of Thegahn and the Rostumik Pass. Major Garunburj called for most of the Western Army to deploy to Udnaruk immediately after Atakos gave him the warning that the entire Eastern Army was headed their way. Airships, carrying soldiers from all parts of Western Omordion, were arriving on a constant basis. Atakos was excited to see the airships from his country, Pontotoma, finally arriving and dropping off their soldiers. They were all there now. Soldiers from Laspitu, Sheidem Island, Saiyut, Pontotoma, and Udnaruk. Garunburj said there were twenty thousand of them altogether, who could lend a hand with the fight against the East, without removing all of them from the protection of the other Western borders. Although it seemed like a small number, Garunburj stated they had an advantage. Being at the head of the Cliffs, they would be able to attack the incoming armies coming down Rostumik Pass on three sides instead of one.

At that moment, an Udnarukan soldier ran up to their tent and saluted Atakos. Not sure what to do, Atakos tried to imitate the same salute but felt awkward doing so. Ever since Major Garunburj announced to the soldiers that he and his four friends were going to be key players in the upcoming battle, the soldiers had begun treating them like high officials. Definitely not how they were used to being treated at all. Well, except Fajha. He was a seasoned veteran.

"Major Garunburj requests that you and your friends meet with him in his tent," the soldier said. "Immediately."

"Okay," Atakos said, frowning. After the soldier saluted him again and turned on his heels to run away, he went back inside. "The major needs to speak with us."

"Now?" Fajha said, putting down his fork.

"Yes," Atakos said. Prince Aillios looked up at him expectantly but he shook his head. It was only him and his other four friends who had been requested to go. He knew it felt strange for the prince to be excluded from battle strategy discussions but it was too much of a risk for him to show the major how much he knew. They were bound to figure out he was not who he said he was.

After the five teens left the tent, Prince Aillios glanced around at the remaining three people there: Kireina, Ilahne, and Shala. He cleared his throat, attempting to hide how disappointed he was. "Pretty soon you will need to leave this area," he said, wiping his mouth with his napkin. "Things will start getting dangerous if you remain here."

Kireina frowned and sat back in her chair, folding her arms across her chest. "This isn't fair," she said. "I want to stay and fight."

"Kireina!" Ilahne said in shock.

"But mother. You were there when those soldiers from Feim destroyed our villages. You saw them kill our friends. They are still holding some of them hostage. I want to fight. I want to fight for *them*."

"Dear," Shala said, reaching over to touch Kireina's shoulder. "Going into battle is not a joke, sweetheart. It is *serious*. When you are on the battlefield and the enemy is coming at you with fire in their eyes, they could care less if you are fourteen years old or forty. They will cut you down before you even have time to *blink*. They have trained for hours *every day* to kill anything standing in their way. You *will* be killed."

Kireina looked bewildered for a moment. Her eyebrows then drew together in a frown and she pouted. "They won't kill me. I can fight."

Shala shook her head slowly, while Ilahne just stared at her daughter, her mouth opened slightly in shock. Prince Aillios watched the three of them with amusement. He tried to picture Kireina on the battlefield, the petite individual of fourteen she was, attempting to wield a sword against great beasts of soldiers coming down on her, without any training or powers to defend herself. It was enough to make him burst out laughing, unable to hold it all in.

"What is so funny, *Lio*?" Kireina said.

"Have you ever been faced with something so horrifying as battle in your life?" Aillios said, laughing. "Do you even know how to hold a sword?"

"Yes. I do."

Ilahne waved a finger at her daughter. "You've never even *seen* a swo—"

"Prove it," Aillios said, challenging the fourteen-year-old.

"Now wait just one sec—," Ilahne started.

"Give me a sword," Kireina said, her nostrils flaring.

Aillios stood up, grabbed two swords from the corner of the tent, and handed one to Kireina, who had stood up as well. Ilahne appeared stricken, so Aillios tried his best to reassure her. "Don't worry," he said, flashing her a toothy grin. "I won't let her kill me."

As Prince Aillios walked out into the early afternoon sunshine with Kireina, a large group of soldiers, in rows of three, marched by them, reminding him of the times he had prepared for battle with the other soldiers of Mituwa. Unfortunately, it reminded him of his people back home, now without someone there to fight for them. He hoped they knew that, even though he was not there, he was still fighting for them and their freedom.

"Ready?" Kireina said, interrupting Aillios' thoughts.

"Lift up your sword."

Kireina lifted the heavy sword and held it tightly with both hands. Her body was rigid and tense, with her shoulders coming up practically to her ears and her knees squeezed together, creating an awkward stance. Her eyebrows came together in anger and she pursed her lips as she intensely locked eyes with Aillios, ready to fight.

Aillios shook his head. "No," he said. "The first thing you have to do is relax. Loosen up those arms! Drop those shoulders! You cannot possibly swing a sword correctly being so tense. Your feet should be shoulder width apart, not together. You need to have balance so you will not fall over."

Kireina tried to do what she was told but ended up in an even more awkward stance, her legs too far apart, and her hands holding the sword too low. She now looked more confused than upset as she tried to imitate Aillios to no avail.

Aillios sighed and put his sword down, leaning it against the tent. He stepped up to Kireina and physically moved her body so she stood correctly, the same way his father had assisted him when he was a young boy. He remembered being exactly like Kireina, determined to learn how to fight, and excited to be training to lend a hand to a greater cause. Except Kireina's determination to fight was justified. The battles he had fought in were not.

"Okay," Prince Aillios said, picking up his sword again. "That's it. Now, take a deep breath in and slowly release it. Try to relax."

Kireina allowed her tense shoulders to relax and she slowly let out the breath she was holding. "Now what?" she said anxiously.

"You must maintain a level of complete control. Do not lose your focus. Now. When I come at you with my sword, try to sidestep my advance." He showed her by quickly sliding to the right and then to the left.

"Does it matter which side?"

"No."

Kireina nodded and Aillios came at her with his sword drawn, but she was too slow. Aillios had his sword against her neck before she had a chance to move.

"That's not right," Kireina said. "You didn't even give me the opportunity to move."

"In the battlefield, *no one* will give you a chance to move. You must be quick. It could mean the difference between life and death."

Kireina groaned as Aillios stepped back to try again. This time, when he came towards her, she doubted herself while sliding to the left and ended up changing her mind and sliding to the right at the last second.

With the tip of his sword less than an inch away from Kireina's abdomen, Aillios sighed. "What was that about?"

"I–I'm not sure. I thought it would be better this way."

"You can't do that when you're being attacked by someone who wants to kill you."

"Fine," Kireina said, clearly showing how frustrated she was. "Let's try again."

"No, I want to see how you do attacking me. Remember to focus and do not hesitate. Be sure of your attack or your opponent will go for the kill. Do not underestimate your opponent."

"Right."

Kireina came at Aillios the way he had come at her, but, before she knew what was happening, she was lying on her back on the ground, with his sword pointed at her throat. "Ow!" she shouted.

"Like I said. Do not underestimate—"

"Let's just try it again," Kireina said, standing up with a growl.

"Oh–kay," Aillios said. He waited for her to attack him and he quickly slid to the left, tripped her with his right foot so she fell backwards, and pointed the sword at her throat again before she even realized she hit the ground.

"Don't say it," Kireina said, avoiding his eyes.

"You're not ready. If you were out in the battlefield right now, you would have died about four times today. Unfortunately, you only have one of those lives to spare."

Kireina looked up at the sky and watched as another army airship flew by, tears gathering in her eyes. Aillios felt sorry for her. He knew she wanted to avenge her mother's captivity and her murdered friends but she had to face reality. She would die so easily in battle. Turning around to go back into the tent, Aillios hesitated when he noticed Ilahne had been standing by the entrance, watching them. She smiled at him and mouthed the words 'thank you' as he walked towards her. Aillios nodded but felt uncomfortable about the way she was staring at him. He silently hoped she wasn't comparing him to the people back in Mituwa. All he needed right now was to be arrested and unable to lend a hand to the fight against his father.

Instead of going back in the tent, Aillios decided to keep walking to find the teens. At least they would not have to worry about Kireina getting killed out in the battlefield anymore. Now, all they had to worry about was the rest of Western Omordion.

CHAPTER 38

Atakos saw Prince Aillios approaching them as they headed back to their tent and waved him over. After speaking with Major Garunburj, the reality of being thrown into a real battle, and the logistics of it, had finally hit them.

"What is happening?" Prince Aillios asked, while walking with them. He could tell they were worried.

"Nothing," Zimi said. "Except we've just been made generals of the entire Western Army."

"Are you serious?"

"Ya."

"Serious as we'll ever be," Fajha said.

"You do realize we've been training for this for the past ten years, don't you?" Cristaden said to Zimi and Fajha. "I mean, look around us. This is our destiny. Why we were chosen in the first place."

Zadeia wrung her fingers together as they walked and looked around at the soldiers running around, informing the civilians to move out and head back to the army base, while they began their preparations for battle. "Right," she said. "But we weren't supposed to be commanding an army until we turned eighteen. We still had three more years."

"But now you don't," Prince Aillios said, beginning to understand their fear. For him, it was just another battle. "I suggest you forget the timeframe set in place for you ten years ago. That no longer exists. You must think about the battle and what we have to do to be victorious."

"I agree," Atakos said. Although he was worried he may never see his parents again, he knew he had to try his best to help the Western Army win. He wanted the Eastern slaves to be free and could not imagine the people of the West being forced into slavery, including his family and his friend's families as well. It was unfathomable.

"I will help you prepare," Prince Aillios said.

"Thank you," Atakos said with a sigh.

"Good," Fajha said. "We will have to go over the strategies the major has suggested with you."

"Yes," Prince Aillios said. "Please do so now."

The five teens stopped walking and told Prince Aillios everything Major Garunburj had informed them. They described how they were going to be divided into three sectors; the largest group would meet the Eastern Army directly at the head of the Cliffs, and two, smaller factions will be on either sides of the Rostumik Pass, one in the Northern Forest and one in the Southern Forest. Major Garunburj, Lieutenant Emyu, and Fajha would command the large group of about ten thousand soldiers at the head of the Cliffs, Zadeia and Zimi would command the group of about five thousand soldiers in the Southern Forest, and Atakos and Cristaden would command another group of five thousand soldiers in the Northern Forest.

"That is not a bad strategy," Prince Aillios said. "We can work with that. Let us go back to the tent and strategize how you are going to handle different things that could happen out there. This is going to be a tough fight."

The teens agreed as they walked back to the tent. Upon reaching it, they informed Shala, Ilahne, and Kireina that the army was asking the civilians to move out as soon as possible.

"Now?" Kireina asked. She had been lying on one of the cots when they came in and she now sat up with a look of pure dismay written across her face. She looked at her mother expectantly as if to ask her if she could stay.

"No," Ilahne said sternly. Apparently, the embarrassment Kireina had faced with Prince Aillios meant nothing to the girl.

Shala reached into one of her bags and removed what appeared to be black armor. She handed it to Zadeia. "I brought along armor for you and your friends to wear but… I wanted to be sure to give you mine."

Zadeia looked down at her mother's armor in awe. She could not believe she was giving it to her. "But mother, I—"

"I wore it when I was your age. When I was in the army. I never did get a chance to fight in a real battle since the war began after I gave birth to you and your brother. Nevertheless, when the two of you were chosen for this mission, I made sure I saved it. For you."

Zadeia studied it for a moment, turning it over in her hands. It had the Udnarukan crest on the black leather breastplate, a dark red flower, lined in shining gold. It reminded her of the times their father would put on his uniform and she would stare at the crest at the back of his hat until he had disappeared from view. "Thank you, mother," she said, with tears in her eyes.

Shala returned to her bag, pulled out another suit of armor, and walked over to Zimi. "This was your father's, Zimi. He wore it when he was just a little bit older than you. I kept it, so you would be able to wear one of his as well."

Zimi looked apprehensive before taking the armor from her, as if he did not deserve to wear it. "Th–thanks," he said.

Shala pushed it into his hands and came close enough to look deep into his eyes. "Your father *is* proud of you." Zimi started to shake his head, but she grabbed his shoulders. "He's proud of *both* of you. And I am too." She pulled Zadeia in to embrace both of them as tears collected in her eyes.

"It's okay, mother," Zimi said, hugging her back. "We'll be okay."

"Promise me?"

"Yes," Zadeia said, between sniffles. "We promise."

"It's time for everyone to move out," Atakos said. He did not want to seem insensitive, but he had taken a glance outside and saw the civilians already starting to walk back towards the army base, being escorted by several soldiers. The other soldiers were already starting to head to the Cliffs of Thegahn.

The Emyu's broke their embrace and Shala took out the other suits of armor she had brought for Atakos, Fajha, Cristaden, and Prince Aillios. They thanked her and watched as she, Ilahne, and Kireina grabbed their belongings.

"Thank you again," Ilahne said to all of them. "Thank you for rescuing me and for bringing me back to my daughter safe and sound."

"Yes," Kireina said, her green eyes looking back and forth between all of them. She made eye contact with Prince Aillios, who nodded and smiled at her. Kireina seemed disappointed she was leaving when she looked down at the ground after smiling back at him. Aillios hoped she had come to her senses and given up on the idea of fighting in the battle.

"Let's go," Shala said to Kireina and Ilahne as she walked out of the tent, looking back only once to get a good look at her twins before departing. "I will see you soon, my dears," she said.

After saying their goodbyes, the five teens turned to Prince Aillios. "We will change into our armor first," he said, "and go over the strategies before heading out. Quickly. We are running out of time."

Northern Forest
Campsite
Cliffs of Thegahn
Rostumik Pass
Southern Forest

CHAPTER 39

Atakos was standing at the cliff's edge, by the Northern Forest overlooking Rostumik Pass, lost in his thoughts. It was still black as night outside; the morning sun had not yet risen. Throughout the night, the army had been gathering at the head of the Cliffs of Thegahn, to await any sign of the battle yet to come, and to prepare to fight. Atakos took a moment to think about his ill mother. He wished he had been given a chance to speak to her before heading off to war. Unfortunately, there had not been enough time. Although he did not show it on the outside, he admitted to himself that, deep down inside, he was scared.

Everything was happening so fast.

Along with Prince Aillios' assumption that his father was going to strike soon, when Fajha had taken some time to meditate after they reviewed their battle strategies, he had woken up in a fit. He was so shaken up, he had tears in his eyes. Fajha took his time to describe his vision to everyone. He had seen death and destruction everywhere in Udnaruk as a blood-red sun rose in the sky. It felt so real, it was like he was there, experiencing it all. He could smell the burnt embers of wood and the scent of death and burnt flesh hung in the air. He remembered feeling sick to his stomach, trying to turn away and leave, only to turn and see the dead bodies of everyone he knew, piled on top of each other. He saw himself among the dead. Fajha said he tried to scream but no sound came out. When he awoke, he was positive, before the next sunset, they would have already lost the battle.

Atakos removed the communication device from his pocket and examined it. The silver object still had a little power left so he was able to turn it on. He suddenly wished they could reach out to Jmugea again, but the only person who knew how to send a direct message was Colnaha. Fajha only knew how to pinpoint the planet they needed, that was all. Atakos sighed, put the device back into his pocket, and zipped it so it would be safe during battle. They tried once. There was nothing more they could do.

"Atakos?"

Atakos looked back and saw Cristaden, walking towards him. She seemed to glow more and more in the darkness as the sun began to rise in the horizon, that she almost illuminated the forest around her. She had tied her long blonde hair together into a long braid and wore the signature Udnarukan war garments given to her by Shala. The breastplate was thick, black, leather armor with metal underneath for added protection. The leather was tight around her waist and came out as a skirt hanging over a black, leather bodysuit. Quite the contrast to her pale skin, hair, and light, blue eyes. Atakos' gear was pretty much the same except for the skirt, the leather came down with front and back flaps hanging over the black bodysuit.

"You are worried," Cristaden said, stopping a few feet away from him.

Atakos turned to study the tide crashing on the rocks of Rostumik Pass, at the base of the cliffs. "What do you suppose Fajha's vision meant?"

Images of their dead bodies floated into Cristaden's mind. It made her stomach turn but she fought the uneasy feeling, knowing it was just a vision. "I think visions, especially Fajha's, do reflect what the future *can* be. By having this vision and speaking of it, he has already altered it, giving us the warning to expect the worst. We would not know what we were truly up against if it was not for his vision. Without it, there would have been an extreme loss of life, perhaps including our own. Now we can avoid it." Cristaden realized her explanation to Atakos *did* make sense. For many reasons. The future *could* be altered. Therefore, the vision *she* had could possibly be altered as well. If only Reyshi had not told her to keep it to herself and she could tell Atakos. If only, for one moment, she could pretend she never had the vision. Believe it would never come true.

"I suppose you're right," Atakos said, turning to look at Cristaden with a smile.

Cristaden took a few steps forward and gently touched his face, catching him by surprise. Not knowing what to do, Atakos hesitated before bringing his arms up around her shoulders and pulling her even closer still. Cristaden allowed the embrace to happen. The heat and energy, transferred between them, was enough to make her knees weak. Atakos felt it too and hugged her tighter. Her glow seemed to illuminate both of them and, for a brief moment, it felt like they were floating in air. All the sounds in the forest, even the loud sounds of the Western soldiers, making their way to the edge of the Cliffs, became nonexistent. It felt like they were the only two people left in the world.

Atakos bent down to kiss her.

Cristaden wanted so much to forget her vision. She wanted so much to break free of it. However, the distant memory of the first time they kissed made her take a step back, breaking their connection. She did not want to see the vision again, even if it was something in the future, which could possibly be altered. It was the hardest thing she ever had to do.

"What's wrong?" Atakos asked, disappointment flooding his eyes.

"We should be getting into position."

"I thought we were."

Cristaden looked up at Atakos with a startled look but before she could say anything, they were interrupted by the sound of a horn. Major Garunburj was calling another meeting.

"We should go," Atakos said quickly, as if suddenly waking up from a deep spell. "It sounds urgent."

Cristaden nodded. Unbeknownst to Atakos, she was relieved they were interrupted, so she would not have to experience the horrible vision all over again.

When the last of the Western soldiers had gathered, the sky was turning a dark shade of purple with the promise of the rising sun. Twenty thousand soldiers stood along the Cliffs of Thegahn, overlooking the banks of Rostumik Pass. Some were new recruits, fresh out of training, antsy with the anticipation of defending the Western lands. The veterans, who had fought many battles in their lifetime, and who were called back to assist, were ready to fight to the death for Omordion. Yet a silent fear was going around that the evil, unruly Eastern side would overpower the Western Army. The Eastern Army had always proven to be ruthless and cunning, having no regard for human life whatsoever.

Cutting down whomsoever stood in their way, without a single flinch. Until now, the Western Army had been the more powerful one, pushing the Eastern side off their shores and back to where they came from, time and time again. However, from what Omordion's Hope, Prince Aillios, and Kireina's mother had witnessed, this time was much different. The four giants of the East had come together for the first time. Srepas, Mituwa, Effit, and Feim. They outnumbered the Western Army three to one it seemed. Separately, those four nations were just menaces, like annoying flies, swatted away as soon as they attacked. Together…? The Western Army was nervous about the outcome of a battle with all of them at once.

With the attendance of all of the soldiers sent to Udnaruk to fight, Major Garunburj briefed them about their secret weapon. The five members of the Dokami Clan and their extraordinary powers. Of course, rumors had spread among the army, since their fight with General Komuh in the Suthack Desert, so the soldiers were not surprised. Some doubted the teens' powers could do much to help the battle. Others scoffed at the idea that they actually had real powers at all. Nevertheless, Atakos, Fajha, Zimi, Zadeia, and Cristaden were made generals of the entire Western Army. Whenever orders were given by them, every soldier was instructed to obey. Prince Aillios fell in line with the other soldiers but remained close to the teens. Until the battle commenced, he felt it was his duty to continue to instruct them on battle strategies as much as he could and waited for his opportunity to speak with them in private again.

"Okay, you two—" Garunburj said, pointing at Zimi and Zadeia.

A loud horn sounded, interrupting him.

It seemed like everyone, soldiers and the members of Omordion's Hope alike, held their breath and looked to the pine trees, where the sound was coming from.

"What is it?" someone shouted among the multitude of soldiers.

One of the lookouts, perched high in a pine tree, lowered his horn, and pointed with a shaky finger. "Look!" he cried.

The morning sun was still rising slowly and the horizon was a brilliant shade of purple and orange. Unfortunately, it was still too dark to see anything in the distance.

Atakos' eyes darted back and forth over the horizon. He glanced at his friends, who frowned and shrugged. No one could see anything.

A few minutes later, they saw it. Everyone else saw it too. Little black specks, dotting the horizon, coming closer each passing second. At first, they thought them to be arrows but some of them were wavering, dropping low and coming up high.

"What the…?" Zimi said under his breath.

Major Garunburj shouted a command for the soldiers to raise their shields and hold their ground. He wasn't sure what the black dots were either.

The objects, flying in the distance, were coming in fast.

"Can anyone get a read on what they are?" Prince Aillios whispered. The teens did not have an answer for him. They just did not know.

Major Garunburj's voice rang out over the soldiers. "These are not arrows," he shouted. "Prepare for an attack!"

The soldiers, in the front with the bows, bent down on one knee and pulled out their first arrow. As the objects came even closer, they prepared their arrows for flight. By accident, one new recruit released his arrow too soon. It soared through the sky, straight for the flying objects.

"No!" Cristaden shouted. Her hands flew up above her head and she destroyed the arrow in mid-air, shattering it into several pieces. "Don't shoot! Please! Do *not* shoot!"

Before anyone could think about what just happened, dozens of birds, from the forest nearby, burst out of their resting places in the pine trees. With deafening shrieks and wings flapping all around them, they dove at the soldiers, causing them to duck, while flying haphazardly towards the heart of Udnaruk, and away from Rostumik Pass. They could now see that the objects flying towards them were screeching as well and joined the other birds, trying to get as far away from the battlefield as possible.

They were birds.

Hundreds of them.

They flew so close to the ground, some of them crashed right into the soldiers' shields. Some soldiers had to fight the birds attempting to peck at their heads.

When the throngs of birds had finally passed them with one final squawk, everyone stood up. The fear among the soldiers was evident. They knew whatever just happened was not a normal occurrence.

Atakos noticed Cristaden was still on her hands and knees, her head bowed and staring hard at the ground. With the aid of Zadeia, they helped her to her feet. There were tears in her eyes, which she tried to wipe away, but found it was no use because she started crying fitfully.

"What's wrong?" Zadeia said, while the rest of her friends crowded around her.

It took Cristaden some time to speak. She just could not get words to come out. Every sound came out as a sob.

"Take deep breaths," Fajha said. "Try to see if that helps."

Cristaden did as he suggested and was able to calm down enough to speak. "I felt their fear," she said, tears still streaming down her face. "They were trying to escape…*death*. There's something truly evil coming." She turned to Atakos. "It scared them. And it scares me too."

Atakos looked around at his friends and Prince Aillios. They knew Brulok was possibly coming to fight them as well. This might have been their confirmation that indeed he was.

Another horn sounded.

"I see the ships!" the soldier in the tree shouted.

They had no time to react to the news that Brulok and King Tholenod was coming. No time for Prince Aillios to go over battle strategies with the teens one last time.

The battle was commencing.

CHAPTER 40

That morning began like any other day. Frolemin awoke just as the sun was beginning to peak over the hills by the castle in Mituwa. She yawned and stretched her aching muscles, thinking of all the chores she had to begin.

Suddenly, she paused.

Today was not going to be just like any normal day. Today was the day to end all days, and it might possibly be her last. It made her stomach twist in pain just thinking about it. For now, she knew she had to rise and begin the day as if nothing was wrong, as if nothing terrible was about to happen.

Frolemin glanced around the small room and watched the servants sleeping for a few minutes before getting up. They were up for most of the night, going over their plan repeatedly so there would be no mistakes and the minimal loss of life. At this point, failure was not an option. The plan had to work.

Frolemin slowly got out of bed and made her way to the washbasin by the door. After splashing water on her face and combing her hair back into a bun, she chuckled, thinking of how unnecessary it was for her make herself look halfway decent that day.

Trisalan lifted her head when she heard Frolemin chuckle and sighed. "I wish morning did not have to come so soon," she said.

Frolemin glanced back at the young handmaiden and grunted. "It had to come eventually, Trisalan. Get everyone up. The time has arrived."

"Yes, Frolemin."

Frolemin walked out of the room, slowly closing the door behind her, as if the slightest sound would alert the soldiers to their plan, and made her way to the kitchen. The cook, a short, round man, was already up with two young kitchen slaves bustling around, preparing the morning meal for the guards. She could see his hands were shaking as he separated the bread dough into smaller pieces to place into a large wood-fired oven. The young boys, who were gathering the plates and chopping the fruits, most likely did not know what was going on. When the time came, they would be taken to a safe place, where they would not be a part of the imminent chaos. When asked, they would answer truthfully that they did not know of a plan to revolt if anything were to go wrong.

Frolemin's stomach flip-flopped with renewed pain as she watched them and she let out a despairing sigh. The cook took one look at her and nodded once and she nodded in response.

Things must go on as planned.

There was no turning back now.

Frolemin walked to a corner closet and took out a mop and a bucket. She filled the bucket with water in the sink and, once it was full, lugged it out into the hall and began her daily ritual of mopping the floors, all the while keeping her eyes lowered to the floor so no one would notice how scared she was. And she was scared. Terrified something could go horribly wrong. Terrified the guards knew about their plan already and were just waiting for them to execute it. Terrified King Tholenod and the strange old man, named Brulok, would return to the castle, changing their plans to attack the West at the last minute.

Anything could go wrong.

At the same time, Frolemin wished everything *would* go as planned. She wished they would all be free. It seemed impossible such a thing could come true, but anything was possible if they at least tried.

She was sure of it.

CHAPTER 41

"How do you do it, Shala?"

Shala turned to Ilahne. "How do I do what?" she said. They were just about at the end of their long walk to the army vehicles, waiting to take the civilians back to the Udnarukan Army Base.

"How are you able to watch your husband and children, heading off into battle?" Ilahne said. "I hate to say it, Shala, but they are all you have."

Shala smiled and lowered her eyes. "It's definitely not easy," she said, staring at the dead leaves on the ground. "The only thing I have left is faith. Faith that they will be okay. Faith that they will come back to me safely." She looked back up at Ilahne. "It was a risk I was willing to take when I married my husband. It was a risk I took ten years ago, when our children were chosen to carry out the mission to defeat the East. I knew what it entailed. Over the years, I had to force myself to be brave and expect what might be coming. At this time, I have to rely on my faith more than ever. Because I still haven't accepted something bad will happen to them."

Ilahne nodded her head slowly, taking in everything Shala had said. "You are an amazingly brave woman, Shala. Braver than you think."

"Thank you," Shala said and smiled at her. She looked up ahead when she heard a voice ring out over the crowd. It was the army soldier leading them towards the vehicles. "We are just about there," she said to Ilahne. "The vehicles are just behind the small hill up ahead."

"That's wonderful." Ilahne was so happy to be done with their two-hour walk. Her feet were so tired. "Kireina, dear, we are almost there."

When she did not get an immediate response, she quickly stopped and turned around.

Kireina was not behind them.

"What's wrong?" Shala said, stopping to turn around as well.

"Kireina," Ilahne called out, her eyes searching the crowd behind them. When she did not get a response back, she started to panic. "She's gone!"

Shala gasped and searched the crowd with Ilahne, hoping to find the fourteen-year-old and praying her mother was mistaken. When they did not see any sign of Kireina, they knew it was true.

She was gone.

Ilahne started panicking. "Where is she? She was walking behind us the whole—"

"My bag," Shala suddenly said. "She has my bag."

"Yes," Ilahne said impatiently. Her daughter was missing and Shala was worried about a bag? "You let her carry it for you." She paused when she noticed the way Shala's eyes practically bulged out of her head, her skin paling with each breath she took. "Shala. What was in the bag?"

"Well…I had given the armor to the children, but I kept my sword, which I was going to give to Zadeia. I thought it wasn't as good as the swords the army would give her. I had another uniform in there as well. I brought it in case the one I gave Zadeia did not fit. When Kireina asked me if I would like her to hold my bag, it never crossed my mind what was in it."

Ilahne's hands flew to her mouth and she stifled a little scream. "Sh-she went back. To fight. Shala, she went back to fight." She was trying hard not to hyperventilate.

Shala's shoulders dropped. "It appears to be so, my friend."

"I must go after her. I have to try and stop her before it is too late."

"Okay, let's go find her."

"No. I cannot let you do that."

"Ilahne, I am coming *with* you."

Ilahne put her hand out to stop Shala. "No. You must go to the base. Your husband and children need someone to come back to should anything happen to one of them on the battlefield."

"But I can help you find her."

"They need you to *stay safe*, Shala. I will go. I will try and stop her before she gets there."

Shala slowly nodded and hugged her friend. Ilahne thanked her, returning her embrace before running back in the direction they came. Ignoring the pain in her back and feet as she ran, she prayed the whole time she would run into Kireina before she made it back to the camp. She prayed it was not too late to stop her.

CHAPTER 42

'Although we live in a world of despair, our actions may not define who we are. You should not have to take blame for someone else's faults. What matters most is what is in your heart. You know who and what you are. What you are is good. Do not dwell in the past. It cannot be avenged. Look ahead to a better beginning. Fight for what is right. But I must warn you, you may be defeated. Do not despair...'

The words of Asmis, the spirit of the witch who died in a stream in Mituwa, came back to Prince Aillios. It was easy to blame himself. To feel as if something more could have been done in the past to prevent everything happening presently. He could have fought harder against his father. In all actuality, he was a coward all those years. Fighting alongside his father in battles he knew were unjust. Yet he kept going, killing men who were only fighting for their freedom.

Prince Aillios often repeated Asmis' words in his mind so he would not forget what she said. He especially needed to repeat those words now as he, along with the soldiers of the Western Army and the teenagers he had grown close to, watched as ship after ship, with thousands of ruthless soldiers upon them, steadily approach the Cliffs of Thegahn. They were all in position now; Atakos and Cristaden, leading the soldiers in the Northern Forest, Zimi and Zadeia, leading the soldiers in the Southern Forest, and he, Fajha, Major Garunburj, and the twins' father, Lieutenant Emyu, leading the ten thousand soldiers in the middle of it all, at the head of the Cliffs of Thegahn. *Look ahead to a better beginning and fight for what is right*, Prince Aillios thought. He pulled the black hood of his uniform over his head so he would not be recognized by the Eastern soldiers, and made sure his double sword waist belt was tightly fastened. He then mentally prepared himself for the battle.

"Catapults!" a lookout shouted from the trees.

In the distance, huge stones were set on fire and launched from catapults on enemy ships. They sailed through the air, heading straight for the cliffs and the awaiting army.

"Incoming!" Major Garunburj shouted.

As the soldiers prepared to dodge the fireballs as they approached, something strange happened. They began to explode in mid-air, as if hit by an invisible shield. The soldiers watched in amazement as some of the fireballs turned back around towards the enemy ships, knocking over their masts and setting some of them on fire. They could see Eastern soldiers lowering lifeboats and others jumping right off the burning ships and swimming towards the cliffs.

The sudden turn of events did not deter the enemy. Many more fireballs were released from the ships left unscathed by fire. Fajha prepared himself to protect the area once again as the fireballs ripped through the sky. He knew he only needed to worry about the ones directed at the head of the Cliffs and had to trust that his friends were taking care of the ones thrown in the direction of the Northern and Southern Forests. Still, being by himself proved more difficult than he thought possible. He caused several balls of fire to explode but misjudged their distance and ran out of time to blow up the rest of them. Before he knew it, a few stray fireballs were closing in on them and he found he could only explode two of them in time. The worst part of it was, after seeing the strange display in front of them, the soldiers were not prepared to dodge the last fireball.

"Watch out!" Fajha shouted but it was too late. The fireball hit several soldiers as it crashed, severely wounding some of them. Fajha stood frozen in shock. Another slip up could mean certain death. Their lives were in *his* hands.

"Don't lose focus!" Prince Aillios shouted by his side.

"We got more coming!" Major Garunburj shouted.

Fajha had to snap back into focus. Before, he was floating on air with the euphoria of being in a real battle. Now, the situation became all too *real* to him. This was not like the practices they had with Hamilda. This was not like fighting the monsters on Sheidem Island and Paimonu. Many innocent lives were at stake here. Many *human* lives.

"Don't think about it!" Fajha heard Prince Aillios shout after he blew up several fireballs from a distance. "Concentrate!"

"Brace yourselves!" he heard Major Garunburj shout to the soldiers around them as the fireballs came closer.

Not wanting to make the same mistake again, Fajha quickly exploded several more fireballs and used his energy to push some away, back towards the water and the ships. A few fireballs he missed careened towards the ground but, this time, soldiers in their path dove out of their way. Fajha was grateful no one had gotten hurt again because of him.

Glancing in the directions of the forests before the next wave of fireballs came, Fajha realized the twins were having trouble pushing the fireballs away on the Southern side with their wind power. There were several pine trees on fire and he could see a few soldiers running away from the forest, fearful for their lives.

Definitely not a good sign, Fajha thought.

After he caused several more fireballs to explode in midair, Fajha silently prayed the twins would make it out alive.

Zimi and Zadeia glanced at the soldiers who were retreating to the head of the Cliffs, clearly not believing their lives were safe in their hands. "Let them go," Zimi told his sister. To the remaining hundreds of soldiers behind them, he shouted, "Stand your ground!" as the next wave of fireballs came their way. The soldiers looked worried but braced themselves for the attack.

Using their wind power, the twins pushed some of the fireballs back at the enemy ships. Some of them turned to ice and dropped to the river below, while others hit the ships, setting them on fire. Unfortunately, the twins missed a couple of fireballs once again.

"Duck!" Zadeia screamed as the fireballs hit the pine trees above their heads and came crashing down. That was when she noticed the spreading forest fire, raging out of control—the real reason the soldiers were running away. "We need water," she told Zimi and pointed to the rapidly spreading fire.

"Right," Zimi said.

The twins reached out towards the river and pulled at the water. Bringing it up over their heads, they shouted for the soldiers to move and dumped the water on the trees. They had no time to take even a single breath before the next wave of fireballs descended upon them. After pushing some of them away, they dove to the ground when a stray fireball sailed over their heads and struck the trees above them, sending embers and debris everywhere, injuring everyone close, including the twins.

Zadeia looked down at her bleeding arm where a sharp piece of wood had struck her. She carefully pulled it out and then rolled up her sleeve to put some pressure on the wound to stop the bleeding. Zimi helped her stand up and Zadeia could see burn marks on his face and hands from the embers that had rained down on them. Without examining herself, she knew she was not burnt anywhere because of her fire ability, which prevented fires from doing any damage to her.

"Look," Zimi said, pointing across the way at the Northern Forest where Cristaden and Atakos were trying their best to keep their side clear. Unfortunately, a few of their trees were now on fire as well. "We need to do something. We have to put out these fires."

"Rain," Zadeia said, grimacing slightly in pain.

"Exactly."

Zadeia looked up at the sky and wished for rain. At first, she thought it would not work unless she was sad, but the combination of fear she felt regarding the outcome of the battle, her hurt arm, and the probability of seeing people being killed must have been enough emotions to get the storm started. In mere seconds, dark clouds began to collect in the sky.

Zimi smiled. "You're doing it!" he said. "I'll try my best to cover you." He froze some fireballs and then tried to push as many back as he could towards the ships with his wind power. Both he and Zadeia had to duck again as a few fireballs sailed pass their heads and struck the ground close by. By now, the soldiers behind them had backed up far enough to avoid being hit by the fireballs they missed.

Zimi was embarrassed that the soldiers did not trust them, but he could not blame them. He urged Zadeia to continue bringing on the storm when he noticed her hesitation. Zadeia nodded. She wanted to help him push the fireballs back but she had an important job to do.

Even darker clouds rolled in, blocking out the sun, and the distant sound of rolling thunder indicated a lightning storm was approaching fast. It happened so quickly that many—Eastern and Western soldiers alike—glanced up at the sky in wonder. Even the catapults stopped firing at the cliffs for a short time.

The storm began with a few steady drops of water, raining down on the heads of all fighting in the battle. Within a few seconds, the steady drizzle turned into a heavy downpour. The rain put out the forest fires and the fires used to light the stones. Even though visibility suddenly became difficult, the rain did not discourage the enemy, who began to launch the catapults again regardless of the strange turn of events and without the use of fire.

As Zadeia and Zimi struggled to push away the stones thrown their way, lightning pierced the sky, giving Zimi a bright idea. "Use the water against the ships," he told his sister. "I have a plan."

Immediately, Zadeia reached out and pushed her energy against the water, which resulted in wave after wave crashing against the ships, becoming bigger and bigger with each thrust. The ships rocked back and forth as the river became increasingly angry. Zimi stretched his arms towards the sky and waited for the next lightning to strike. Almost as if in slow motion, he watched as it blazed across the sky. He was able to grab a hold of it with his ability and aim it in the direction he wanted it to go. The lightning hit the closest ship and electricity quickly spread across it, transferring to another ship when it crashed against it in the narrow river way. This transfer of electricity continued as the ships crashed into each other left and right. Catapults were collapsing and the ships began to sink into the treacherous water. Thousands of men were seen lowering lifeboats or jumping into the water to avoid being electrocuted or burnt alive and a steady cheer could be heard across the Cliffs of Thegahn. The catapults were no more. The ships had been destroyed.

With the excitement from what was happening, Zadeia could no longer keep the storm going so, against her will, the sky abruptly cleared. A steady stream of sunlight poured out from behind the disappearing clouds, bringing light to the darkened battlefield. They could now see hundreds of tiny boats headed their way. The enemy was fast approaching the cliffs. Before Zimi and Zadeia could discuss their next course of action, Zadeia noticed a few large boats, further downstream, approaching the Cliffs closer to the Rostumik Ocean than the Pass. Something was familiar about the colors on the boats. Red and black… red and black…why did those colors alarm her?

All of a sudden, Zadeia shouted, "No!"

"What is it?" Zimi said.

"Zimi. Do you remember when father told us about the soldiers who attacked the villages? You know? The ones who killed Jogesh? How brutal and savage they were?"

"Yes?"

"Look over there," she said, pointing towards the Rostumik Ocean. "Can you see them?"

It took a moment for Zimi to see what Zadeia was referring to, but when he did see the large boats, a sudden chill went down his back. Those ruthless Feim soldiers, who destroyed three villages and killed countless people, were sneaking up on land, heading straight towards Cristaden and Atakos, who were most likely focused on the small boats quickly approaching the cliffs.

"We have to warn them," Zadeia said, beginning to panic.

"It will be too late," Zimi said. "And you heard what the major said. We have to stay at our posts. No matter what."

Zadeia nodded her head slowly. He was right. They had to stay there and fight. She hoped their friends would make it out alive and looked over at the head of the Cliffs, noticing the archers standing ready. Zadeia followed suit and yelled for their archers to come forward. Looking back down at the vast number of approaching soldiers, she could not help wondering if any of them would make it out alive.

"Archers!" Cristaden shouted. "Ready...Fire!"

Hundreds of arrows shot through the air. Some found their mark, while others hit the boats or plunged straight into the water. The Eastern soldiers decided it was a good time to paddle faster or jump off the boats and swim towards shore.

"Fire!" Atakos shouted.

The archers did as they were told, raining arrows down the steep slope at the soldiers closer to shore. There were so many of them—thousands even–so determined, with fire in their eyes, shielding themselves from the arrows, and climbing up the side of the cliff, ready to annihilate anyone in their way.

Atakos and Cristaden used their powers to throw back the closest soldiers. They watched as around twenty of them flew up in the air and careened backwards, hitting the water or the boats with incredible force. Their friends, Zimi, Zadeia, and Fajha, must have noticed what they did because they followed their lead, throwing back as many soldiers as they could with energy and wind on their side, while the archers continued to send their arrows sailing over the cliffs, so the enemy would meet their fate before climbing up. They suddenly saw small fireballs being thrown from across the way. They knew instantly that Zadeia was doing it, throwing them at the soldiers, attempting to set some of them on fire.

After pushing back several more soldiers, Cristaden began to notice her loss of strength. When the soldiers she used her energy against flew back only a few feet, she glanced worriedly at Atakos.

He *had* noticed. "Fall back," he told her, as he pushed some soldiers back down to the water. The archers released their arrows again but the soldiers below were finding ways to avoid being hit by them.

Then the unthinkable happened. Hundreds of soldiers came up from beneath the water, swords drawn, throwing aside the empty boats and dead bodies floating around. Atakos recognized them immediately as Effit soldiers because of their forest green uniforms. They must have been using the overturned boats as shields and swam underneath them. A steady war cry escaped their throats as they lunged for the rocks all at once and began climbing over them with incredible speed.

With hearts thumping, Cristaden and Atakos yelled for the archers to fire their arrows at the incoming soldiers. Their effort was not enough. The soldiers were climbing the cliffs too fast. The two teenagers tried pushing some away but, with their diminishing strength, only several fell back, hitting the rocks as they plummeted back towards the water.

"Prepare to fight!" Atakos shouted and the soldiers behind them yanked out their swords.

All of a sudden, Cristaden grabbed his arm. She was looking over the heads of the soldiers beside her and through the trees. "Atakos," she said in a shaky voice. She had sensed something.

Something *awful*.

Atakos peered over Cristaden's head. At first, all he saw was the black and red colors through the trees. Then he saw the soldiers. He recognized their colors from when he went to Feim to rescue Ilahne with Fajha and Prince Aillios. He recalled how Lt. Emyu had described the way they destroyed three Udnarukan villages and killed Jogesh.

Soldiers from *Feim*.

Thousands of Feim soldiers marched towards them through the forest. A man, whose uniform did not resemble theirs, was leading them. He held a threatening black sword, with what appeared to be large claws near the hilt, and his armor was silver. Atakos and Cristaden recognized him right away because he resembled someone they knew, but much older. He had the same facial features and even marched the same way as his son.

It was King Tholenod.

The ruthless tyrant of Mituwa.

The man who started it all.

And he was leading the monstrous Feim Army straight to them.

CHAPTER 43

It happened so quickly, they did not have any time to come up with an effective strategy. With the thousands of soldiers coming up from the river and King Tholenod launching a surprise attack at the same time, Atakos and Cristaden pulled out their swords, along with the five thousand soldiers who stood with them.

The time had come to fight.

Atakos immediately took off, shouting for half of the soldiers to attack the Feim soldiers with him, leaving the rest to come forward and fight the soldiers climbing up from the river with Cristaden. King Tholenod saw them headed his way so he yelled for the Feim soldiers to attack. They started running forward with their swords drawn, belting a loud war cry at the top of their lungs.

Atakos' heart was pounding. He was no war hero. He had never even fought in a war before. He never had to kill other humans to save his own life and the lives of so many innocent people. However, seeing the horrendous faces of the same soldiers who took out three villages, killing and torturing hundreds of people, and the same ones who were responsible for Jogesh's death, Atakos could not help but feel anger. The anger boiled up inside him as he ran, to the point where he became enraged, giving him the adrenaline he did not have but needed in order to fight. When his sword clashed with the swords of the enemy, he did not hesitate to use the power of explosion against the foul soldiers. He placed his hand directly on them and watched as fragments of bone, muscle, and blood burst out of their chests as they flew back, hitting other soldiers and trees behind them. Atakos immediately wielded his sword against another Feim soldier, who came up behind him, and repeated his actions, exploding the evil soldier's chest. The soldier flew back, hollering in pain, and slammed against a few soldiers who pushed him away and came at Atakos with fire in their eyes. Atakos evaded the attack, moving quickly around them with his speed ability, temporarily confusing them. He rapidly hit each of them with his explosion power before they even had a chance to figure out where he was. Without wasting any time, Atakos turned around and slashed his sword across the shoulder of another soldier, before another one turned and tried to take a swing at him. Atakos avoided the sword by ducking and then shattered the soldier's kneecaps. As the soldier let out a horrific cry, Atakos drove his sword into his heart.

While he was fighting several more soldiers, Atakos could not help but wonder where King Tholenod went. It would have been his pleasure to cause the heart of the evil tyrant to explode, but he seemed to have virtually disappeared, since he ordered his soldiers to attack. Nevertheless, Atakos kept on fighting. When a fellow comrade was brutally killed, Atakos angrily slashed his sword across his opponent's knees and caused his chest to explode on his way down to the forest floor. He was determined to win the fight, to honor the lives of those they were losing in battle, no matter what it took.

Suddenly, everything changed.

Feim soldiers, coming up from the cliffs overlooking the river, charged through Atakos' line of defense. Monstrous and ruthless, they killed every soldier who came in their path. One of those Feim soldiers came at Atakos. His face was nothing the fifteen-year-old had ever seen on a human being before. Distorted and demonic, the Feim soldier seemed to come from the stuff of nightmares. He was not even wearing a mask! Atakos tried to use his abilities against him, but the soldier caught him off guard by sidestepping him and punching him on the side of his head. The force was so strong, Atakos felt as if his eardrums had burst and, for an instant, he felt as if he would pass out from the blow. He fought the feeling and pushed the soldier back with his power, causing him to explode as he flew back.

Suddenly, someone grabbed a hold of Atakos' ankles. An extremely injured Feim Soldier was holding on tightly to him as he lay on the wet, pine needle-ridden forest floor, smiling up at him with blood soaked teeth. Atakos quickly used his ability on the arms of the cunning soldier and watched as they split open, causing the soldier to release his ankles as he hollered in pain. While the soldier on the ground distracted him, Atakos did not see a great beast of a man, coming out from behind a tree with a sword pointed right at Atakos. Atakos tried to move out of the way, but was too slow to react. The sword went through his shoulder and the beastly man then yanked it out to strike Atakos again.

"No!" Atakos shouted with rage before blowing up the demonic soldier. Breathing heavily and pressing the wound on his shoulder to stop the blood flow, he quickly observed the scene around him. *No, he thought. This can't be happening.* He watched as the Western Army soldiers, the ones he was supposed to be leading, were being taken down, one by one, at a rapid pace around him. All he saw was red and black between the trees. Red and black *everywhere*. They were positively surrounded and things appeared to be falling apart very quickly.

"Fall back!" Atakos shouted. He started running through the soldiers, dodging blows and pushing enemy soldiers out of his way with his ability. "FALL BACK!"

The Western Army soldiers heard his shout and tried falling back to retreat to the cliffs where Cristaden was, but the Feim soldiers were not letting them go so easily. They were relentless with their attacks and chased down the fleeing Western soldiers, intent on killing every single one of them. Atakos tried his best to push them back as he ran, but his momentary burst of energy was quickly failing him. Moreover, it seemed like endless streams of soldiers were climbing over the cliffs to attack them. Atakos tried pushing some back into the water but he barely managed to throw back three of them. With the pain in his shoulder, it was difficult to use his power efficiently. He thought of Cristaden and decided to find her as quickly as possible. If anything bad had happened to her, he would never forgive himself for leaving her side.

The sounds of swords clashing and soldiers shouting and yelling were deafening to Atakos' ears. He couldn't bear to see his fellow comrades being killed right before his eyes. Yelling again for his soldiers to fall back, Atakos glanced behind his shoulder so he could further evaluate their dire situation.

There was too many of them now.

Atakos knew they were all as good as dead.

"Kireina!" Ilahne screamed.

Kireina looked up when Ilahne burst into the tent they once occupied. She was trying to adjust the armor she had just put on, but stopped and stared back at her mother as if she was the last person she expected to see.

"What do you think you're doing?!" Ilahne shouted.

"I am going to fight," Kireina said without emotion.

Ilahne came towards her with fear in her eyes. "Haven't you been listening to anything we've said? You *can't* fight. I forbid it! We need to get out of here. Now. While we still can. We're much too close to the battlefield for comfort." When Kireina did not make a move to leave, she lunged at her and grabbed her arm. "We have to go. *Now.*"

"Mother," Kireina said, pulling her arm out of Ilahne's grip. "No." She grabbed the sword she had taken from Shala's bag. "I survived the attack on our village for a *reason*. I know now what that reason was. I am meant to fight for Omordion's freedom. I can't expect you to understand. So please let me go fulfill my des—"

Both Kireina and Ilahne paused when several fruits suddenly rolled off the table and hit the ground. Just then, they noticed the ground beneath them had begun to shake. Before they could think it was an earthquake, shouts were heard outside, along with the steady clanging of swords.

The pair hurriedly ran outside to see what was happening and were shocked to see the battle headed straight for the campground. The sheer force of the enemy was pushing the Western Army back towards them.

"What…?" Ilahne said under her breath. She could not believe her eyes. They were *losing*.

Kireina quickly kissed Ilahne on the cheek and gave her a tight embrace. "Goodbye, mother. I must go find them. They need my help. Please go. Before it's too late!"

Before Ilahne could grab her and prevent her from going to fight, Kireina had already run away from her. Ilahne screamed for her to come back, but Kireina ignored her, running towards the retreating army as fast as she could.

"No!" Ilahne screamed. "No. Come back!" As Kireina kept running, refusing to turn around, she knew she had to make a quick decision. Knowing she was in danger if she stayed where she was, knowing it was too late to get out of harm's way, knowing her daughter would most likely be killed on the battlefield, Ilahne ran back into the tent and grabbed the first sword she saw, leaning up against the wall. When she grabbed the hilt of the sword, she was reminded of a moment in time—a long time ago—when she had done the same thing to save the life of the baby entrusted to her care. Ilahne had vowed she would never pick up a sword again for the rest of her life.

At that moment, she made the decision to fight to save Kireina again.

Even if she died trying.

Fajha yanked his sword out of the chest of a Srepan soldier he had just killed and quickly spun around to push several soldiers over the cliffs and back into the river, hoping they would hit sharp rocks on their way down. He jumped over a slippery wet, large rock and thrust his sword towards a soldier, who was about to kill one of his comrades, but missed him. An angry shout escaped the soldier's mouth as he turned to plunge his sword into Fajha's side. Fajha used his power to knock the sword out of his hand and pushed him down to the wet ground.

"I don't think so," Fajha said before opening his hand over the soldier's chest and causing it to explode. Pushing away a few more soldiers with his power, Fajha quickly looked around for Lt. Emyu and Major Garunburj. He saw both of them running to aid the soldiers retreating from the Southern Forest. Fajha then looked around for Prince Aillios. The prince was not too far from him, doing his best to fight as many men coming up over the cliffs as he could with two swords. Fajha ran over to him, lifted several soldiers up in the air, and tossed them back into the water.

"Thanks," Aillios said, wiping his brow. He jerked his head towards the Northern Forest. "Do you see what's happening over there?"

Fajha quickly looked towards the north. No, he had *not* noticed. What he saw shocked him beyond belief.

No one was guarding the cliffs.

Thousands of soldiers were steadily climbing over them and taking out the entire northern division.

Fajha gasped. "Atakos and Cristaden!"

"Let's go," Prince Aillios said.

Trying to get to the Northern Forest proved to be anything but easy. With Eastern soldiers climbing over the cliffs and attacking whomsoever came in reach, Prince Aillios and Fajha had to keep fighting their way through, while trying not to trip over bodies lying all over the ground. Halfway there, they began to realize they were pushing against their own men. The soldiers from the Northern Forest were retreating towards the head of the Cliffs.

The Western Army had lost the Northern Forest.

Fajha's heart sank when his horrific vision came to mind He was terrified to think something bad might have happened to his friends. The image of their dead bodies, lying crumpled on the forest floor, flashed in his mind, causing the tiny hairs to stand up at the back of his neck and his hands to ball up in fists. He shook his head, trying not to see the image again, and continued to move through the crowd of retreating and fighting soldiers. The way the battle was going, he wasn't even sure Zimi and Zadeia were okay. "Do you see them?" Fajha yelled over the noise of clashing swords and shouting.

"There!" Prince Aillios shouted.

It was hard not to miss Cristaden's white-blonde hair as her and Atakos fought against the power of the Feim soldiers, while trying to retreat at the same time. Fajha was happy to see they were still alive and silently wished the same for the twins.

"We have to move!" Zimi shouted, grabbing his sister's hand. Eastern soldiers were overpowering the forest surrounding them. They needed to retreat to open land if they were going to have any chance at winning.

"Fall back!" Zadeia shouted. "To the head of the Cliffs!"

Those soldiers, who heard her cry, moved with them, attempting to fight and retreat at the same time. Zimi and Zadeia used their diminished wind power as they moved, knocking enemy soldiers off their feet or throwing them against each other. Their efforts helped the Western soldiers break free of the circle of death they were caught in and advance towards open land.

"You've got to be kidding me," Zimi said when they reached the end of the forest and broke free of the line of trees. He did not have to explain what he saw, because Zadeia clearly saw it too. The Eastern soldiers were still climbing over the cliffs at an alarming rate. When there had been thousands of Western soldiers there to prevent them from coming up before, they were all gone. No one was there to stop them. By the look of it, most of the soldiers, who were protecting the head of the Cliffs, were dead and the enemy soldiers were running over their dead bodies towards the retreating army, withdrawing to the campsite.

"Zimi," Zadeia said. She let go of her brother's hand. "Father."

Zimi cringed. "I'm sure he's fine."

"But he could be lying somewhere—"

"Zadeia. We knew going into this that we could all die. If something happened to him, he would want us to keep fighting to save our people." He looked up at the sky as gray clouds started rolling in again. "Better gain control of your emotions. The rain will make it more difficult for us to fight."

"I know…" Zadeia tried to think of something else as they ran, but could not direct her focus away from the possibility that their father could be one of the bodies they were trying hard not to trip on. Glancing down at the faces of the Western soldiers from time to time, to see if one of them was her father, Zadeia lost her footing and tripped, falling flat on her face.

Zimi stopped dead in his tracks when he heard her scream. Turning around, he saw Zadeia trying to pick herself up from the ground, but he could see she was hurt. The Srepan soldiers who were chasing them were catching up. Fast. "Zadeia!" Zimi cried, running back to his sister. An enemy soldier spotted her and came at her with his sword held tightly in his hand, looking as though killing her would be his greatest achievement. *No*, Zimi thought. *I won't let you!* He reached his hand out, intent on sending a blast of ice at the soldier, but his power took an unexpected turn. Instead of ice, his power drew from the impending rainstorm and sent a bolt of lightning at the soldier straight from Zimi's hand. The soldier flew back and slammed into the other soldiers behind him.

"What…?" Zimi looked down at the hand the lightning came out of as he helped his sister up with his other hand. He was in so much shock, he did not hear Zadeia shout his name. The clashing of swords brought him back to reality and he realized the Western soldiers stopped retreating to come to their aid.

"Zimi," Zadeia said. "We have to g—"

"Look out!" Zimi shouted when an Effit soldier came up behind Zadeia. Zimi pushed her out of the way and blasted the enemy with a powerful bolt of lightning. It was so strong, it shook the ground beneath them and some Eastern soldiers ran back towards the forest in fear.

"Whoa," Zadeia breathed. Since she was distracted, the sky instantly cleared up and pockets of sunshine cascaded over the battlefield.

Zimi grabbed her arm. "Run!" he shouted when he noticed countless Effit soldiers climbing over the cliff and running towards them.

Atakos and Cristaden fought back against the brutal force of the Feim soldiers as best as they could, while retreating to the head of the Cliffs, away from the overrun forest. Even though Cristaden had been able to heal Atakos' shoulder, the two were exhausted, their reflexes not as quick as they were at the beginning of the battle. They continuously had to watch each other's backs when the enemy got too close for comfort.

Atakos looked towards the head of the Cliffs and saw Fajha and Prince Aillios fighting their way through the masses of soldiers to get to them.

"There!" Atakos said, pointing so Cristaden would see them too.

Cristaden nodded and headed towards Fajha and Prince Aillios with Atakos following close behind her. She had never been so happy to see some familiar faces before in her life. It was like a bright light, shining among the darkness all around them. She could tell Fajha was excited too. He was shouting something inaudible and pointing…no, it wasn't happiness written all over Fajha's face at all. It was fear. In addition, as he and Prince Aillios came closer, she could tell the prince appeared stricken as well. "Wha—" Cristaden began to say, but was interrupted when she heard a voice shout:

"Noooo!"

Atakos cried out as blood started dripping from his mouth. Confusion swept all over his face and he shakily looked down. It took Cristaden only a second to realize what had happened. A sword had pierced Atakos' abdomen from behind.

Cristaden screamed and reached out to catch Atakos before he sank to the ground. Fajha was full of anger when he reached them, shouting curses at the soldier who so cowardly attacked Atakos from behind. He ran forward and lunged at him, intent on blowing him up before he had a chance to yank the sword out of Atakos' back. Suddenly, someone shoved him aside, sending him crashing to the ground next to his wounded friend. The malicious soldier behind Atakos took the opportunity he was given to wrenched his sword out of the teenager, barely flinching when Atakos hollered in horrifying pain.

"Sorry, Fajha," Prince Aillios said, feeling bad for shoving the teen aside. "He's *mine*." He then glared at King Tholenod. "Father."

Tholenod sneered back at him with dark eyes. "Aillios," he said. "I see you are still alive. Fighting for the wrong side, of course. However did you manage to get *here?*"

Prince Aillios glanced down at Atakos and was relieved to see Cristaden healing him and Fajha up and keeping the enemy away from them. Quickly looking around, he noticed the Western soldiers had them surrounded as well, trying to protect them from being attacked as much as possible. He looked back at his father with fire in his eyes. "Does it matter? I am finally fighting for the *right* side. Your reign ends here, when your blood is spilt on *Western* soil."

King Tholenod growled defiantly and came at his son, his face red with anger. Prince Aillios never knew this moment would ever come. Even when Brulok claimed he would bring on the death of his father, he did not believe it. Yet there they were, just weeks later, thousands of miles away, fighting each other to the death.

Only one of them could win.

Prince Aillios was determined to live, to see his people freed at last. Even if it meant having his own father's blood on his sword.

CHAPTER 44

Not much was documented about the planet known as Omordion. Back on Jmugea, history lessons only described it as a distant planet, which closely resembled their own, given the distance from their sun and its ability to sustain life. The only thing the Jmugeans knew was that, during the interplanetary wars, centuries ago, a considerable number of people from Dokar, before the Dokamis migrated there, travelled to Omordion in an effort to save their lives before their planet was demolished, never to be heard from again. Although Dokar was not destroyed until the Dokami clan left, no one originally from Dokar ever returned. Omordion, the Jmugean history books said, was a safe haven. For some odd reason, powerful planets like Dre-Ahd and Jmugea never sought to concur it, leaving it to thrive freely on its own accord for thousands of years.

This worried Princess Amilana. Without any interplanetary rules or regulations to abide by, what would they find when they reached their destination? She glanced at Drissana, who was busy observing the approaching planet from the co-pilot seat, and sighed heavily.

"Don't worry about it," Drissana said.

"Easy for you to say," Amilana said and looked back at Omordion. "We're not exactly sure what we're going to find when we get down there. This is another *planet* we're talking about." She surveyed Omordion again, observing the large, blue bodies of water and the green land spread around it. She sighed again. "I was a fool to let you come."

"Why? You need someone to be your backup in case you need help. Besides, how could I pass up an opportunity to visit Omordion?

You think you're a fool, but I would have been an even bigger fool *not* to come."

Amilana looked at her sister again and rolled her eyes. Drissana's logic never made much sense to her. Their lives could be in imminent danger but, to her, it was the best sightseeing tour of her life.

Amilana picked up the spaceship's communicator and observed the tiny, blinking light, indicating where the communicator, which was utilized to contact them, was located. She guided the spaceship in the direction they needed to go, while entering Omordion's air space.

As they flew, the sisters could not help noticing how beautiful the lands of Omordion were. Among the many rivers and lakes, tall mountains and hills dotted the landscape, providing a glorious and, oftentimes, majestic scene. Everything seemed so peaceful, it was hard to believe members of the Dokami clan were under enough duress to have to reach out to Jmugea, of all places, for help. It almost seemed unnecessary. Amilana was expecting to see a planet in ruin, at the brink of being destroyed. However, it did not seem like that was the case at all.

Until, of course, Amilana was hit with a horrible feeling. A feeling so dreadful, she almost lost control of the spaceship.

"Ahh!" Drissana cried out, trying her best to hold onto her seat as the spaceship righted itself. "What was that about?" She turned to look at Amilana, who was gripping the control stick so hard, her hand was turning white. "What's wrong?"

"You don't feel it?" Amilana said.

"Feel what?"

"Terror. Fear. There's so much of it! It's so *heavy*..."

"Where do you think it's coming from?"

"All over! It's everywhere."

"Well, I don't see anything bad happening down there."

"Whatever is happening cannot be seen from this high." Amilana lifted the communicator again and saw they were quickly approaching their target. She looked back up to see if she could see anything worth notating in the direction they were headed. "We would have to land soon..." Allowing her voice the trail off, Amilana sucked in her breath and held it.

Drissana rose slightly from her chair to get a better look at what Amilana saw. "What the...?" she whispered.

Coming from a peaceful planet, such as Jmugea, and never witnessing war as it had been centuries before they were born, the two princesses were speechless as they observed what could only be fire, raging out of control. Smoke was filling the sky ahead of them, threatening to take away their visibility. It did not take long for Amilana to figure out what was going on. "They're at war."

"Are you sure?"

"They have to be. This feeling I have. It's absolutely dreadful. People are dying down there as we speak. I've never felt this way before, Drissi. So much *death*." Amilana shuddered.

"Is this where we're headed?" Drissana asked.

Amilana glanced down, but knew, before even looking at the communicator, that this was the reason Jmugea was contacted. "Yes. It is." She looked back up and maneuvered their ship a little way away from the battle so it would not get caught up in the smoke from the fires. She tried to see what was happening on the ground, but it proved difficult because they were too high. "Are you ready?"

"Ready to rescue some of our brethren?" Drissana said with a big smile. "Of course. Are you going to land this thing?"

Amilana pushed the hover button and waited for the ship to adjust its position before letting go of the control stick. "It's best we leave this here. If our ship is destroyed, we would be stuck on this planet forever, with no way back."

"Makes sense." Drissana unbuckled her seatbelt and reached for the door handle beside her, but Amilana grabbed her arm.

"Wait," Amilana said.

"Oh, what now?"

Amilana looked Drissana straight in the eyes. "We are going down there, sister. Now, we do not know what we will find when we do. Do not, and I repeat, do not do *anything* without my permission." When she felt Drissana was about to protest, she cut her off. "Do we have an understanding?"

"Okay," Drissana said with a sigh. "But if we're going to stop this war, can we at least go down there in…style?"

"What?"

"Can we make a grand entrance?"

"We shouldn't be alerting anyone to our presence until we find out what's happening down there."

"But people are dying. *Our* people. You said so yourself. We have to stop whatever is going on one way or another. Why not put an end to it with a bang?"

"That's so juvenile."
"Please?"
"No."
"*Pleeeaaase???*"
Amilana rolled her eyes. "Fine. But don't do anything until I say so."
Drissana giggled with glee and, on Amilana's count, the two sisters pushed their doors open against the high winds, and jumped from the spaceship without any further hesitation.

CHAPTER 45

Twins Zimi and Zadeia took off running again, after fighting back against a dozen Srepan soldiers, changing their direction to head towards the campsite. If they were going to find their friends, the campground would be the best place to start. It was the only landmark near the battlefield the others would retreat to if they were in danger. From what they could see, they were *all* in terrible danger.

The last person the twins expected to see, though, was *Kireina*.

The fourteen-year-old was wearing Shala's war gear, which was loose around her small frame. She held a sword tightly in her hand, running towards the battle with sheer determination written all over her face. What was worse, coming from the direction of the camp, the twins could see someone chasing after her.

Ilahne.

Zimi pointed to the direction Kireina was headed. "Let's go," he said. "We can intercept her there. We have to stop her!"

"Is she nuts?!" Zadeia shouted. "As if her poor mother hasn't been through *enough*." She quickly created fireballs and tossed them at the soldiers chasing them. Some avoided being hit by them, while a couple of them burst into flame.

Zimi used his wind power to aid the Western soldiers ahead of them by knocking down several Srepan soldiers who were fighting them, clearing a path for him and Zadeia to run through without having to stop and fight. For a moment, they lost sight of Kireina, but, when both of them cleared a path in front of them, they spotted her not too far away.

She had just entered the battle, intent on killing a few Eastern soldiers. In fact, she thrust her sword into the back of one who was busy fighting a Western soldier. The soldier put his arms up as he felt the sword drive into his back and the Western soldier took the opportunity to decapitate him. Right in front of her eyes.

Zimi and Zadeia continued to run towards Kireina when she started screaming and dropped her sword. When Zadeia shouted her name, Kireina looked up but did not appear to recognize her. After looking around frantically, she blindly sprinted through the ongoing battle, towards the Northern Forest and the Feim soldiers who were driving the Western soldiers back.

"No!" Zadeia shouted. "Kireina! Stop!"

"Kireina!" the twins heard Ilahne scream. She was attempting to avoid the battle raging around her in an effort to reach her daughter.

"I got her," Zadeia said.

Zimi nodded and took off after Kireina, using his wind power to clear a path on either side of the terrified girl as he ran to catch up to her.

Zadeia flung a fireball at an Effit soldier who was coming at Ilahne, setting him on fire, along with the soldier he crashed into next to him. Ilahne looked surprised, shocked even, as her daughter had been. Her faced lit up when she saw Zadeia running towards her. There were tears in her eyes and she seemed on the brink of exhaustion.

The woman has been through so much in captivity, Zadeia thought. *Now she has to deal with* this. "Come with me," she said to Ilahne and grabbed her arm. She began to drag her in the direction of the campsite, pushing a couple of soldiers, who had been charging at them, away with her wind power.

Ilahne suddenly jerked her arm away. "No," she said, tears now rolling down her cheeks. "I have to find my daughter."

"You're going to get *killed*. It's too danger—"

"I won't go back without her," she said sternly. "Even if I have to carry her back with me. Even if I have to *die* with her. You cannot ask me to leave. I *won't* go back."

Zadeia quickly glanced around. The Western soldiers were still retreating towards the campsite, while trying to fight off the Eastern soldiers. At the rate they were going, the camp would not be safe for long. "Okay," she said. "Follow me. But *stay close.*"

Prince Aillios was not afraid. This was the moment he had feared for a long time. But his fear was no more. Watching his father plunge his sword into the back of his fifteen-year-old friend brought him back to all of the times he had cut down anyone who stood in his way, uncaring of whether it was man, woman, or child. For an instant, Prince Aillios was brought back to the riverbank separating Mituwa from Effit, when his father had slashed a teenager's face with his whip, cutting it open because the boy failed to get the ship ready in time. For an instant, he was brought back to the cave on the side of the mountain, within the dead forest in Effit, when his father's voice rang out in the hall, ordering the death of his only son.

King Tholenod lunged at Prince Aillios, who immediately brought both of his swords up to block the attack. The king angrily swung his sword along his side but the prince blocked that move as well. The two men came at each other with fire in their eyes, intent on finishing what began many years ago. In clashes of steel against steel, they swung left, right, right, and then left, blocking each other's attacks. It was apparent the training Aillios had received from his father growing up was preventing either one of them from getting the upper hand. Even though Aillios had surpassed his father in combat, Tholenod knew his moves well.

Too well.

To break the monotony, Prince Aillios bent low as he blocked Tholenod with one sword, and sliced his leg with the other. The king hollered in pain, raised his sword above his head, and brought it down towards Aillios' head. Aillios fell back on the pine needle-ridden ground and rolled to the side to avoid the sword's blade. Thrusting his leg up, he kicked Tholenod hard in the chest, sending him stumbling backwards, allowing enough time to stand up again.

King Tholenod regained his balance, trying hard to ignore the pain in his leg and the blood beginning to seep through his pant leg. Aillios brought his swords back and lunged at Tholenod with a loud cry. Tholenod spun around to avoid him and stepped forward with his right foot, holding his sword horizontally and swung his arm across, cutting Aillios across his cheek. When Aillios dropped one of his swords and brought his hand up to his face, Tholenod suddenly came close to him, attempting to cut off his head, but Aillios blocked him with the sword he had left in his free hand. The two became locked in a strange, wild embrace, pushing against each other, neither one wanting to budge first for fear the other will take full advantage of the situation. When their eyes met, Prince Aillios realized he did not recognize the man he once called father. It seemed as if a demon had taken over his soul. The look in his eyes was downright frightening. Aillios' heart beat faster in his chest. *This has to end*, he thought. *This has to end* now.

What happened next would completely change the outcome of the Eastern and Western battle, forever.

Suddenly, a loud booming sound resonated across the sky. The sound was so loud, it shook the ground, causing every beating heart on the battlefield to skip a beat or two. The powerful boom inadvertently caused everyone, Western and Eastern soldier alike, to stop fighting and lower their weapons as they looked up at the sky. It was nothing they had ever seen before. A great ball of fire, possibly a meteor, headed straight for them but in slow motion, creating another loud, piercing sound, shaking the cores of everyone on the battlefield. The soldiers, who had been standing around awestruck, started backing away from where they thought the massive fireball would land, not wanting to be scorched or blown up by it when it did. Some ran away, knowing the impact could wipe out everyone in the vicinity and perhaps beyond. Even Prince Aillios and King Tholenod slowly backed away from each other, lowering their arms and their weapons. The fireball in the sky appeared to be more threatening—much more severe than the battle they were fighting.

Fajha readjusted the glasses on his face, as if what he was witnessing must have been caused by their crookedness.

Atakos made eye contact with Cristaden as she helped him up off the ground. "Do you think we're all going to die?" he absentmindedly asked her, as if she knew the answer to his question.

Cristaden defiantly shook her head. "I don't think so," she said. "But we should brace ourselves, nonetheless."

"Yeah," Fajha said. "Prepare for anything." He looked at Atakos and confirmed his growing suspicions. "This is *no* meteor," he said.

Atakos nodded and quickly glanced around. Astonishingly, he spotted Zimi coming towards them and a smile spread across his face. *He's alive!* he thought. His smile, however was short lived when he noticed Zimi was slowly walking behind a stunned Kireina of all people, dressed in full battle gear. *What is Kireina doing on the battlefield?* he thought. Suddenly, he became fearful. *And where is Zadeia?* Zimi must have seen the look on his face because he gestured with his head, indicating that Zadeia was behind them. Atakos could see her now, steadily making her way through the crowd of shocked soldiers with Ilahne in tow, a look of confusion written all over her face. Ilahne rushed over to Kireina, flung her arms around her, and then burst into tears. It did not seem like Kireina noticed that Ilahne was the one hugging her. She continued to look up at the fireball, mesmerized just like everyone else. Atakos made eye contact with the twins and they nodded. *Expect the worst*, he wanted to say to them. He knew, however they would be ready for anything.

It was not long before they could feel the intense heat radiating off the fireball as it came closer to the ground. The five friends came together and did, in fact, brace themselves, or more so, each other. So many thoughts rushed through their minds. What if the fireball crashed and killed them all? What if they were living the last few moments of their lives? What would become of Omordion? Would everyone die as well? Including their families?

"Shouldn't we do something about this?" Zimi said, beginning to panic. "Like push it back? Blow it up while it's still far from the ground? If we all work together we could—"

"It's not a meteor," Fajha said.

"He's right," Cristaden said. "I *feel* something..."

Everyone turned to look at her.

"Feel what?" Atakos said.

Cristaden held her breath and concentrated hard on the fireball. Yes, there it was. She felt it again. "*Life.*"

"You can't be serious?" Zadeia said.

"Life?" Fajha said. "Inside it?"

"Yes."

"That seems...impossible," Atakos said.

"I know it seems strange but I feel it. It's *alive*."

All five pairs of eyes turned to the fireball with growing curiosity. As it bizarrely came in for a swift but *steady* landing, those on the ground had to bend low to keep from falling over when a powerful wind erupted from it, blowing dirt and rocks in all of their faces. As everyone stood up, they saw something they were definitely not expecting to see.

Cristaden's odd proposition, that life existed inside the fireball, had been confirmed.

Two females stood before them where the once raging fireball had landed. One appeared to be in her early twenties and the other was younger, sixteen or seventeen at the most. They were a remarkable sight. Wearing fitted brown, leather attire with knee-high strapped, brown leather boots, the girls were tall and beautiful. The older one had jet black, wavy hair and dark eyes, while the younger one had fiery, red hair and golden eyes. Both seemed intimidating, looking down at the throngs of soldiers on the battlefield as if they were the lowest creatures they had ever encountered.

Atakos glanced at Cristaden and she slowly shook her head. "It's strange. I can't get a read on who they are or where they're from. I know one thing for sure. They are definitely not from here."

"What do you mean?" Zadeia whispered. "Here as in…Udnaruk?"

"Here as in…Omordion."

Cristaden only confirmed what Atakos had been thinking. "They're from Jmugea," she said.

"No way," Zimi said.

"I think so."

The older one, with the black hair, stepped forward. "Who is responsible for this war?" she said, glaring at everyone. Her accent sounded very much like that of the Dokami Council, accept it was heavier. Her dark eyes suddenly fell upon the members of Omordion's Hope, who stood out like sore thumbs among the sea of warriors, the only ones who did not back up when the fireball came down from the sky. When she received no response from them, she asked her question again, this time slowly, unsure if they even spoke her language.

"Answer the question!" the younger one suddenly shouted. She impatiently stepped forward to stand next to the older one. Glaring at everyone standing around them, she demanded for the instigator to step forward. "Do it. If you are not a *coward*."

All of a sudden, a voice boomed from behind the five teenagers. "I AM NO COWARD!" King Tholenod shouted and ran forward, shoving everyone out of his way, his sword held high in a menacing way, ready to attack the two females.

The older one glanced at the younger one with fear in her eyes. "Drissana!" she quickly said, while reaching out to try and stop her. "NO!"

Nevertheless, it seemed like whatever she was trying to stop from happening was irreversible. With a slight squint of Drissana's eyes, King Tholenod abruptly dropped his sword. His body bent at an abnormal angle so fast, everyone in close proximity could hear his bones *breaking*. As he fell to the ground, the five teenagers turned to look at the two females in shock. They had never seen that sort of power before. The older one dropped her arms to her side and shook her head as if she regretted bringing the other one along.

"Stop!" a voice rang out in the crowd. Prince Aillios ran forward, glaring at the two visitors. Looking down at his mangled father on the ground, Prince Aillios felt absolute horror. Although he knew his father would have had to perish, in order to put an end to the war, the way his body bent in odd angles was frightening, not something he ever wanted to see.

Little did he know, everything Prince Aillios thought he knew about his life was about to change.

CHAPTER 46

Prince Aillios knelt beside King Tholenod's broken body. Tholenod was staring up at him in shock. He then tried to move, but his back was bent at an extremely odd angle, so he could not. He tried to speak but blood dribbled from his open mouth. He tried to cough to clear his throat, but it only made the pain in his back feel even more unbearable. No one near Tholenod could understand how he was still *alive*.

Prince Aillios' heart dropped to his stomach. As much hatred as he felt for his father, knowing full well he had persecuted and taken the lives of so many innocent people, it still pained him to see him in the condition he was in.

He was dying.

A slow, excruciating death.

Prince Aillios looked up at the five teenagers. They were in shock. No one moved. It was as if the world around him had frozen in time, with only his father's irregular breathing to indicate how real the situation was. He never thought it would pain him to see his father in so much pain. Yes, he should die. But he was still his father, the man who raised him, and the only parent he had left. To see him like that disturbed Aillios. He was so disturbed, he reached down and grabbed his father's hand. Tholenod looked scared, frightened that his life was ending. His eyes searched Aillios' face, as if he wanted to say a million things, but did not know where or how to begin.

Prince Aillios' voice came out in barely a whisper. "Cristaden…?" he said and then looked up at her.

Cristaden glanced at the others. The evil tyrant from the East was finally about to be defeated. The war, which took the lives of so many in over a decade, would be over with the death of their malicious king. This was what they wanted. This was what their mission was all about. To defeat King Tholenod and the cruel alliance he had formed. To end slavery in the East. To stop the war.

Atakos shook his head.

Cristaden knew what he was thinking. The war had to end. Therefore, she had two choices to make on her own. It was either take Tholenod's life or save it. She knew what her decision would be when she looked at the hurt in Prince Aillios' eyes. Ignoring Atakos' seemingly better judgment, Cristaden took a step forward.

"No," King Tholenod said, finally able to speak after he spit out some blood. "Do not help me. Do not take pity on me."

Cristaden reluctantly took a step back.

"Father," Prince Aillios said, pleading with him.

"No. I have done so much…wrong in my life. I do not deserve to be saved. I am responsible for *countless* deaths…all those…innocent lives…"

"We can help you."

Tholenod grabbed his son's arm with the one hand he could still move. "I have to tell you something my son. Hear me speak! Before it's too late."

"Yes, father."

"Aillios. You may not believe me. I never (cough) I never meant to cause any *harm*." His eyes filled with more tears and they trickled down his face.

"I understand father. You did it to save the monarchy."

"No!" Tholenod coughed again, attempting to clear his throat, but moaned in pain instead. "You do not—understand—that man—that evil man!"

"Who? What evil man?"

Tholenod searched his son's face. "*Brulok.* He possessed everyone. He possessed *me!* My assistant—Menyilh—Brulok—he admitted everything. He said Menyilh—that miserable wretch—was one of his *minions.* You *have* to believe me!"

"What do you mean, father?" Aillios was confused. "How could he—"

"He wrote me a letter. Brulok did. He said he had sent Menyilh. Years ago. To make the world suffer. Starting with me. Menyilh enticed me to enslave our people. He told me the West was abundant with wealth and we had *nothing*. I allowed myself to be–sucked into his *madness*. I was weak. You have to believe me. When I succumbed to Menyilh's plan, Brulok possessed me–he possessed my army. He possessed the leaders of the West and their armies as well. We all wanted so much power! Ultimately, we would have destroyed each other. That was what he wanted. We would have completed what Brulok himself did not want to–*dirty* his hands doing."

"He possessed everyone? How is that possible?"

"His evil deeds even affected *you*, Aillios. When you were a small boy. You don't even remember what happened…I am so sorry, son. Brulok is the epitome of pure *evil*. Anything he wants, he can and will do. He sees things. He sees what is going on all over the world. He sent me on a mission to kill any threat coming *his* way. He even viewed those… teenagers as a threat and tried to kill them many times…but failed."

"You said he possessed everyone," Zadeia said. "Could it be possible…?"

Fajha gasped. "My grandfather," he said.

"General Komuh," Zimi whispered.

"Our teacher," Atakos said. "Hamilda."

"Most likely all under his control," Tholenod said, verifying everyone's suspicions. "Can't you see? He sat on his throne–in the dead forest in Effit–for hundreds of years–devising a plan to destroy all the living creatures of this planet. Starting with the people who would most likely be able to destroy him."

"I don't believe it," Prince Aillios whispered.

"You *must* believe me, son. He used me as his pawn. He used all of us–pitting us against each other–and he will use you too. If you let him. Be careful. Do not trust anyone! I lost everything… *everything*." He was crying now, trying hard not to choke on his own blood.

Drissana shrunk back to stand next to Amilana. She had only done what came naturally to her. She had eliminated a threat, which was what she was taught to do. However, before now, she had never actually faced a real threat. Not on Jmugea. That was Amilana's job. She suddenly wished she had listened to her sister and stayed home.

"Drissi," Amilana whispered, sensing her disparity. "He started this war."

"But you told me to stop. And I–I did not listen."

"You did what you felt was right."

Drissana was not sure what was right anymore. It seemed the man she attacked was not the real problem after all. She looked at her sister with fear in her eyes. "He was not the reason the distress call was sent to Jmugea."

"I understand that now," Amilana said, her eyes darkening. "It was this...Brulok person."

"How could I be so stupid?"

"You stopped the *war*, Drissi."

"I am sure you felt as if you did not have a choice," Prince Aillios said, overhearing their conversation. He turned to Drissana. "Do not put any blame on yourself."

"Aillios—" Tholenod started to say but was suddenly interrupted by a woman's voice, coming from behind Aillios.

"Prince Aillios? It *is* you."

The hair on the back of Aillios' neck stood up. He did not dare look back to see who had said it. By now, everyone knew he was the son of the treacherous King Tholenod. Whoever it was, this person finally realized who he was, and most likely knew all the heinous things he had done. An escaped slave? An Eastern soldier? Whoever it was, he mentally prepared himself to be judged by her.

A shadow fell over the dying man when the person took a few steps forward to stand next to Aillios. Tholenod lifted his eyes to see who blocked out the sun. He took one sharp breath in and then another, gasping for air. "Ilahne," he croaked, tears welling up in his eyes once again.

Prince Aillios turned to look up at the woman in shock. How did his father know her? His eyebrows came together in a frown as he watched the strange exchange between the two, as if they were long-lost friends, reunited after an extremely long time.

"Ilahne—you—you are alive!" Tholenod said, trying desperately to sit up but failing to do so. "Where...?"

Ilahne had tears in her eyes. "Please do not try to get up, my lord." She placed her hand on his shoulder in an effort to persuade him to stay still.

Prince Aillios' frown deepened. *My lord?* he wondered. He knew Ilahne was from Mituwa but how did Tholenod know her? *An old servant maybe?*

Ilahne spoke softly to Tholenod, her voice cracking with every word. "I was in Chrulm Village when we were attacked some time ago. The Feim soldiers—they kidnapped me along with some of the other villagers and brought us across the Rostumik Pass, to Feim. They intended to make slaves out of us. I was rescued…"

"The mission—to rescue a captive in Feim—was to save…*you?*"

"Yes."

"I am so…sorry, Ilahne." Tholenod squeezed his eyes shut and tears escaped his eyes once again, the damage he had done weighing heavily on his heart. All of a sudden, his eyes flew open. "What became of the child?"

Ilahne smiled and nodded as if to say he had no need to worry. "Her name, sir, is Kireina. She narrowly escaped the attack by hiding in a safe place when they came. I had promised to keep her safe. And I fulfilled my promise."

"I didn't know—I didn't think—"

"Do not blame yourself, my lord. You did not know we were here."

"I wish I could see her. Just once. Before—"

"Of course, my lord." Wiping fresh tears from her eyes, Ilahne called Kireina over.

Tholenod tried to sit up again. "She's here?"

"Yes."

Kireina was just as confused as Prince Aillios was. She sauntered over to stand next to him, all the while looking back and forth between her mother and the evil tyrant the entire world despised so much. So many thoughts raced through her mind. Why would he want to meet her? She did not know him and she did not *wish* to get to know him at all. No matter how many more minutes he had to live. Furthermore, why *was* he still alive? By the way he looked, it was clear he should have been dead a long time ago. She wished he would just die already and stop his nonsense.

"She has grown so much," Tholenod said. "Has it—has it been that long?"

"Yes, my lord. Fourteen years…"

"…fourteen—?"

"Can someone tell me what's going on here?" Prince Aillios asked, interrupting them.

"I would like to know, as well," Kireina said, folding her arms across her chest. "Honestly, mother. You can't possibly be *friends* with this barbaric man."

"She makes the same face Aillios does when he's upset." Tholenod said, chuckling softly between coughing spasms.

Prince Aillios and Kireina looked at each other, more confused than ever. Aillios had noticed the similarities in their features before, but had ignored them. Now they looked at each other in a different light. Could it be possible?

"Yes," Ilahne said, as if answering their questions. "Kireina is King Tholenod and my sister, Meriahne's, daughter. Your sister, Aillios."

CHAPTER 47

Fate.

Prince Aillios never quite believed in it until he left Mituwa. The belief that there were no coincidences, that a greater power affected all happening in the world, did not seem real to him. However, standing where he was, thousands of miles away from home, fighting a battle against his own father, finding out he had rescued his aunt from certain death in Feim, discovering Kireina, the girl who had wanted to fight in the battle so bad, she had ended up by his side on the battlefield, was his actual *sister*. If all those occurrences were not the effects of fate, he did not know what was.

"I don't believe it," Kireina said, turning to Ilahne. "You're not my mother...? He is my father...?" She then turned to Prince Aillios. "Aillios???"

Aillios could not believe it either. "Yes," he said. "That is my real name. I am the son of King Tholenod. And you are...my sister..."

King Tholenod fell into another fit of coughing spells as blood suddenly poured out of his mouth. Ilahne looked sadly down at him. She pitied him. She knew who he was before he had succumbed to the evil brought upon him by Menyilh. She felt the need to explain what happened, why his children were separated, so they would understand. So they would forgive him before he died. "One day, when he had slipped out of the evilness caused by Menyilh for a short time, he had asked me to take the two of you, along with your mother, away. The day you were born, Kireina. While we were preparing to leave, Menyilh heard of it and the evil descended upon your father like a dark cloud once again. Tholenod forbade us to go, accusing us of deceiving him and being traitors. In his fit of rage, he…killed Meriahne and locked Aillios in his room. I had no choice but to run away with Kireina, the only one I could save at the time. I regret the day I left you, Aillios," she said, turning to look at her nephew with tears building in her eyes. "Every day. I am so sorry."

"Why don't I remember any of what you are telling me?" Prince Aillios asked her. He was so confused.

"I'm not sure. It might have been so traumatizing you probably… blocked it out."

Aillios shook his head and squeezed his eyes shut before looking back down at his dying father. At one point in time, he would have never believed his father was capable of killing his own wife, the mother of his children. He remembered the crazy look in his eyes though, the day he ordered the death of his only son. It must have been the same that day. *When he killed Meriahne.* He must have been blinded by evil. Yet there they were, fourteen years later, watching the evil, which had taken over Tholenod for so long, finally slip away like a strand of hair caught in a breeze. Aillios always remembered a time when his father was a good man. It would explain why he was so easily influenced by him when it came time to fight his own people during the rebellion. He remembered the man his father used to be and he held on to it, no matter how evil he became, until he had enough and started fighting to save his people.

King Tholenod gurgled and his eyes rolled back in his head.

"Father!" Aillios cried out, tears filling his eyes. He never knew it would hurt so badly when his father took his last breath. He had set out to stop him from hurting anyone else. In the end, it was he who was hurting most of all.

Someone suddenly knelt down beside him. It was Kireina, appearing sorrowful, her green eyes surveying the face of the dying man. "I always wondered who my father was. My mother—I mean—yes, my mother—only told me he had died in a war when I was born. I guess, in a way, his spirit did die…a long time ago."

Aillios smiled at her and nodded. He felt the same way.

Suddenly, Tholenod's body started jerking violently. Aillios and Kireina quickly stood up and took a few steps back. The five teens rushed over to stand next to them as Tholenod's body continued to jerk back and forth. It lifted off the ground and slammed back down several times.

"What's happening?" Kireina shouted.

Prince Aillios wanted to reach out to him, to grab a hold of him, to keep his body from suffering any further damage. "I don't know!" he cried. He looked up at the two females from Jmugea in anger. They shook their heads. It wasn't them.

"Something's wrong," Cristaden said. "King Tholenod is no longer in the land of the living. He has passed on. Whatever is causing this is trying to—*get out*."

"Get out?"

Cristaden did not get the opportunity to explain any further because Tholenod's body stopped moving as fast as the violent spasms had begun. A gurgling sound started in his throat and a foul smelling, green vapor slowly slid out of his mouth. With a loud, hissing sound, it wormed its way up into the air and dissipated slowly into the atmosphere, leaving Tholenod's body lying on the ground, an empty shell, devoid of life.

"What—?" Prince Aillios began to say, but was interrupted when the eyes of every single soldier, Eastern and Western alike, rolled back in their heads and they collapsed, leaving a massive field of bodies lying on the ground with only Prince Aillios, Kireina, Ilahne, the five members of Omordion's Hope, and the two Jmugean princesses, still standing.

CHAPTER 48

The phenomenon sweeping throughout the battlefield in Southern Udnaruk was not the only one of its kind. All over Omordion, leaders of the East, the West, and their soldiers were dropping like flies in a seemingly uncontrollable state of unconsciousness. Even in the army base in Southern Udnaruk, General Komuh was lying on the floor of his prison cell, his eyes staring blankly up at the ceiling.

In Mituwa, Frolemin had just informed all the house slaves that the time was upon them to fight and to take back what was theirs. They were to start with the guards, who had sat around the long, dining room table in the main hall, waiting to fill their stomachs with food the poor slaves in the fields had worked hard—sometimes to death—for. Each person had his or her weapon concealed among the folds of their uniforms and the slave children were nowhere in sight, hidden away in a safe place with Trisalan, in case the plan failed. The castle slaves picked up the trays of food and nodded at each other, prepared to die, if necessary, for their freedom. The long walk down the hallway to the grand hall was the longest walk in Frolemin's entire life.

This was it, she thought. *No turning back now.*

When Frolemin, who had been King Tholenod's handmaiden all her life, pushed opened the double doors of the grand hall, she stopped dead in her tracks.

"Keep going," someone behind her said, in a barely audible whisper.

But Frolemin could not move. She was baffled, unsure if what she was seeing was real or some horrific illusion.

The guards, who had been sitting around the table, were either slumped over in their chair, had their heads down on the table, or had fallen over, lying flat on the floor. The cook pushed past Frolemin, gasped when he saw what happened, and dropped the tray of bread he was holding. Murmurs erupted all around as the procession filed into the hall one by one, taking in the strange scene.

"What has happened here?" Frolemin said, with a shaky voice.

No one had an answer for her.

No one could explain what they were seeing.

Suddenly, they heard someone coming down the hall towards them in a hurry. It was Omlit, the teenaged stable boy who had helped Prince Aillios escape the castle with Thashmar. He appeared frightened while he ran, trying hard, it seemed, not to alert the guards in the hall, but needing to say something extremely important to the other servants. When he entered the hall and approached Frolemin, she asked him to take a deep breath before speaking.

"What has happened, Omlit?" she said.

The teenager took a few deep breaths to steady his breathing. He then looked around the grand hall and paused, in total shock.

"What is it, Omlit?" Frolemin asked, beginning to lose her patience. She was still trying to wrap her head around what happened to the guards in the hall herself.

"The soldiers—in the fields—they all fell—the overseers—all of them." He looked around again. "Did you...?"

"No. We found them like this. You say this has happened outside as well?"

"Yes."

Frolemin looked around at the servants surrounding her. Could the soldiers have been poisoned? No. No one had access to poisons of that magnitude. Walking forward, she bent down to feel for a pulse on the nearest guard, lying on the floor. She then carefully lowered her head and listened for a heartbeat. "Get some rope," she suddenly told a few of the slaves. To the others, she demanded they retrieve as many axes as possible. The guards were still alive, so she knew they had to act quickly in case they were to wake up unexpectedly. When the slaves returned, Frolemin ordered the ones with the axes to go out into the fields and break the chains linking the slaves together. The ropes would be used to tie the soldiers up. "Hurry!" she yelled. "We don't have much time!"

Frolemin did not understand what had happened but she was not about to take any chances by waiting to find out what will happen when they woke up.

For the people left standing on the battlefield, the right words could not form at first. For a moment, they stood around, quiet, waiting for the same thing to happen to them. But nothing transpired.

Prince Aillios reached down to check King Tholenod and confirmed his passing. He then took his sword and laid it on his chest, putting his hands around the hilt as a sign of respect.

Atakos glanced around the battlefield. "What is going on here?" he asked his friends. He looked at the two Jmugeans, but they seemed just as confused as the rest of them were. It was as if they had all walked into some simultaneous dream sequence. All of the soldiers lay on the ground either unconscious or dead, Atakos could not tell which.

"They're still alive," Cristaden said, answering his thoughts.

"How is this even possible?" Fajha said.

Kireina stepped closer to Ilahne, who put her arm around her in an awkward embrace. "I'm scared," she whispered.

"So am I," Ilahne said.

Zadeia turned to the two Jmugeans standing nearby. "May I ask your names?" She glanced around the battlefield. "And did you…?"

The older of the two stepped forward. "We are not the ones responsible for this," she said, staring hard at Zadeia with her dark eyes. "My name is Princess Amilana and this," she gestured to Drissana, "is my sister, Drissana. My parents are King Azahr and Queen Serai, rulers of Jmugea. A distress signal was sent to us a few weeks ago and we came to answer the call." Amilana bent down and removed a small device from the inside of her knee-high boot. It was silver and compact, but her audience could see it resembled the communicator they had, except a small, bright, red light was blinking fast on its surface. "This is our communicator. It told us the exact coordinates to find this place."

"You *are* from Jmugea," Fajha said, confirming what they already knew. "But you…speak our language?"

"Yes," Amilana said. "We have spoken this language since we existed on Jmugea. It's very odd that we speak the same language when we are so far away…" She looked back and forth at the five teenagers. "Do you know who sent the signal?"

"We did," Atakos said, removing their communicator from his pocket to show them.

"You..." She looked back and forth between the five teenagers and Prince Aillios. "Are all of you...descendants of the long lost Dokami civilization?"

The teens exchanged glances with each other. *Long lost Dokami civilization?*

"I guess you could call us that," Zimi said with a shrug.

"It is true then." Amilana turned to Drissana with amusement written all over her face. Her sister stared back at her, a tiny smile playing on her lips. For a moment, it seemed like they were explorers, who had just unearthed a five-hundred-year-old tomb. Amilana turned back to the teens and cleared her throat. "What are your names?"

"My name is Atakos," Atakos said and gestured to each of his friends. "This is Cristaden, Fajha, and twins Zimi and Zadeia."

"It is nice to meet you," Amilana said as she approached them and shook all of their hands. Drissana did the same, perhaps a little more apprehensive than her sister was. "And what of these ones?" she asked, glancing at Ilahne and Kireina before staring hard at Prince Aillios. "The son of that—" She stopped herself from continuing, her face softening, remembering he had just lost his father by her sister's hand.

Prince Aillios shook his head and stood up. "We are not of Dokami blood. They are the only ones here who are."

"What is...Dokami?" Kireina asked. Ilahne looked just as confused as they looked back and forth between the five teenagers and the two strangers from the sky.

"We will explain it to you," Atakos said. "When we are given the opportunity—"

"Oh!" Zadeia shouted, realizing Prince Aillios' statement, that they were the only ones of Dokami blood on the battlefield, was far from the truth. Who knew *how many* Dokami descendants were among the Western soldiers, lying on the ground all around them? One thing she knew though, her father was of Dokami descent, most likely lying among the living or the dead.

"What's wrong, Zadeia?" Atakos said.

"Fajha," Zadeia said, grabbing Fajha so hard, he thought she would take his arm off. "Can you locate him? I mean—can you locate our father? Lieutenant Emyu?"

Fajha's eyes opened wide. He remembered fighting alongside Lieutenant Emyu for a short time, but when the masses of soldiers climbed over the cliffs, they had to split up. He never saw him again after that. "Oh—of course," he stammered, looking back and forth between a teary-eyed Zadeia and Zimi, who's eyes had opened wide with the realization that his father might have perished during the battle.

Fajha reluctantly closed his eyes, terrified of what he might discover. As soon as he brought his focus on locating Lt. Emyu, he immediately found him. "There!" Fajha shouted, pointing in the direction of the Southern Forest. "We must hurry, though. His signal is fading."

"What is that supposed to mean?" Zimi said as the group took off running in the direction of the forest, with Amilana and Drissana trailing close behind them. "Why is it fading?"

Fajha frowned, hopping over a body in his path to avoid tripping over it. "I think it means he's dying," he said.

"What?" Zimi frightfully said before he could stop himself from showing any emotion. Whatever negative feelings he had towards his father instantly became irrelevant. The fact that his only father was dying was enough to break down the wall he had built up most of his life. Deep down inside, he knew his father cared about him even if he rarely showed it. He just hoped they were not too late, that Cristaden could heal him, and he would be okay.

When the determined group reached the area Fajha felt Lt. Emyu's presence, they stopped to look around. It was difficult to see the faces of each soldier lying on the ground so they had to examine each one closely. The two princesses did not know who they were looking for so they stood off to the side, surveying the area and observing the search with curiosity.

"Found him!" Kireina shouted.

Everyone rushed over to where Kireina was bent over Lt. Emyu's body. They could see his skin paling and a large gash seeping blood down his arm, along with an ugly wound on his leg. It might have been possible that, despite his injuries, he had continued to fight, because he was still holding on tightly to his sword. Cristaden quickly knelt down beside him and administered her healing power over his wounds. White, bright light shot out from her hands, surprising Kireina and Ilahne. They could not believe what they were seeing. Within seconds, Lt. Emyu's wounds had closed and color rushed back to his face. Cristaden also took a moment to heal Zadeia's cut arm and any other wounds her friends received during the battle.

Amilana and Drissana exchanged glances with one another. Only a few Dokami were known to have the ultimate gift of healing. Back on Jmugea, they only knew of one person in their entire kingdom who could heal anything. They called him Tasonar, The Healer. When someone fell ill, or was severely wounded, they would visit him and his apprentices. He would examine them and fall into deep meditation. Within days, or sometimes within moments, the person would be healed. His ability to heal was a much more complicated process. The two princesses had never seen *any* healer administer the act of healing a wound the way Cristaden so easily did.

"Lieutenant Emyu," Cristaden said, gently shaking the fallen soldier's arm, after she realized he was still not waking up.

"Father?" Zimi said.

Just like the other soldiers on the field, Lieutenant Emyu neither moved, nor opened his eyes.

"What's wrong with them?" Zadeia asked, tears forming in her eyes.

Cristaden examined him again, but did not see any other wounds or feel any trauma to his head. She could not find anything preventing him from waking up. In fact, there was really nothing to indicate why the other soldiers were not waking up either. "I'm not sure—" she said.

"You cannot wake him!" a voice boomed from the direction of the Southern Forest, interrupting Cristaden.

Everyone slowly stood up and turned towards the forest, eyes wide with shock. Amilana frowned deeply and balled her fists, preparing for a fight. Drissana only stared, unwilling to make the mistake of eliminating a threat without asking questions again.

What they saw seemed so unreal, most of them sucked in their breath and held it for a moment in awe. Walking out of the forest was a large group of people. They carried bows and arrows and were dressed in, what could only be described as, *leaves*. Headdresses, clothing, and sandals made of green, brown, orange, and red leaves. All of them had brown hair and eyes. They appeared to be frightened, staring wide-eyed at the battlefield before them. Furthermore, they *glowed*. There were many women walking among them and few men. One of the men, the one who had spoken, seemed to be their leader, because he was walking several steps in front of the crowd.

"They have all fallen," the leader spoke again. His voice was incredibly deep, which matched his incredible height. He appeared to be around the same age as Prince Aillios, but walked with a tall, wooden staff as if he was an old traveler. "The curse plaguing them for many years has finally abandoned their bodies, leaving only an empty shell behind." He stopped several feet away from them. "Any moment now, their lost souls will find their homes again and they will awaken."

"Who are you?" Cristaden said.

"We are your distant cousins, Cristaden," the man said with a smile. "The woodland fairies of Udnaruk. We are able to come here now to speak with you because, after five hundred years, Brulok has withdrawn and has taken his monsters with him. He is gone."

CHAPTER 49

"What do you mean 'he is gone'?" Cristaden said.

"The presence of his creatures have simply disappeared," the leader of the woodland fairies, said. "This is why we are able to walk out of the forest unharmed and stand here today for the first time. In centuries."

Amilana spoke, taking a few steps towards the woodland fairies. "Who is this Brulok?" she glanced at Aillios. "Your father mentioned him before he died." She looked back at the woodland fairies. "Why have you been in hiding?"

"My name is Aoak," the leader said. "Hundreds of years ago, my people resided in this part of Oeua, much like the Udnarukans do now. When a group of human settlers came, they brought with them a monster, by the name of Brulok. At first, he did not appear to be a threat."

"Brulok showed my father a map," Aillios said. "Oeua was written on that map. So it is true then. That was the original name of Omordion."

"Yes. It was. When Brulok brought forth the beasts from under the ground, we were ill prepared to deal with such an attack. My people fought long and hard, but to no avail. Those creatures were the most brutal we had ever seen. Even with our magical powers, we were unable to defend ourselves against them."

Magical powers? Amilana frowned at her sister, who returned the same frown. *These people, who were not of Dokami origin, could stand there and claim to have powers?* This was the first she had heard of such a thing.

Aoak continued, ignoring the exchange between the two sisters. "For the survivors of the first attack, we developed a shield to keep us hidden from anyone who could sense us, even the fairies in other parts of Oeua. I had to do what I could to save the woodland creatures, even if it meant losing contact with everything we loved and held dear. Our fairy families, and all of the magical creatures we knew, thought we had all perished. It was selfish of us, I know. However, at the time, it seemed like the best thing to do. Especially when wave after wave of attacks kept coming, destroying the planet and everything on it. After some time, it seemed like Brulok had grown tired and ceased his attacks. Nevertheless, he knew we were still out there. So he left his minions everywhere to kill us if we were to come out of hiding."

"How did you know I am half-fairy?" Cristaden said.

Amilana looked back and forth between Cristaden and Aoak. *So she is half of their species*, she thought. *Could this be where her power to heal comes from?*

"When we felt like the minions had gone, we carefully brought our shields down. As soon as we did, Queen Lhainna of Sheidem Forest, your mother, felt our presence and immediately reached out to us. It was a shock, for both of us, that there were more of us out there. And we are not the only ones either. There are pockets of fairies hiding all over Omordion. From what I gather, we fairies were not the only survivors. Fairies from all over are reporting flitnies, ceanaves, and chlysems who are still alive, just hiding all of these years behind cloaking spells and shields."

"I knew it!" Atakos said. "The ceanaves saved us from drowning in the Hejdian Sea weeks ago."

"Yes," Cristaden said. "And a chlysem came out of nowhere to help us escape the Western Army in the Suthack Desert. Afterwards, it just…disappeared."

Aoak nodded. "They came out of hiding to help you," he said, looking at all of them. "You—all of you—are incredibly special."

The five members of Omordion's Hope looked at each other and smiled. The rest of their company only frowned, not knowing what flitnies, ceanaves, or chlysems were. It was especially daunting to Kireina and Ilahne, who had just realized fairies were real and their friends were of the Dokami race—whatever that was.

Amilana and Drissana were just soaking in the information. They couldn't wait to go back to Jmugea to tell their mother all about Omordion, or Oeua, as the fairy mentioned.

"When we went to Feim," Fajha said. "We felt like we were being watched. Was that you?"

"Yes," Aoak said.

"Brulok has been gone since then?"

"That was when we began to let down our defenses, yes."

"This is unbelievable," Cristaden said. "Why, after all these years, has Brulok chosen to pull his minions now—?"

A moan escaped the lips of a waking Lieutenant Emyu, bringing everyone's attention to him. He slowly opened his eyes and shook his head from side to side, attempting to sit up.

"Father!" Zadeia cried. She and Zimi bent down to help him. The rest of their company glanced around the battlefield and saw soldiers waking up all around them.

"They're coming back," Cristaden said. She turned back to the woodland fairies. "You were ri—"

They were gone.

"Where did they go?" Atakos said.

"I–I don't know," Cristaden said. It was as if they had vanished, but she knew they must have turned to fairy size and quickly flew away when the soldiers began to open their eyes. In fact, she thought she saw small lights dart around the trees in the forest. "I'm kind of sad to see them go."

"So am I," Fajha said. "I can't believe there are more magical creatures left on this planet. There's so much we may never know about Omordion."

"Yes," Amilana said, rubbing her chin. "This planet is interesting indeed." She looked at her sister, who could only nod her head in agreement.

Prince Aillios shook his head. "You have no idea."

Lt. Emyu seemed more coherent now, finally noticing the thousands of soldiers around him waking up, just as he was. "What is going on here?" he wearily said, bringing his hand to his head.

"I think," Zadeia said, while looking around, "the battle is over."

"How?"

Zadeia lifted her eyebrows and looked at her friends. "We'll explain later."

Major Garunburj groggily walked up to them, holding his arm, wounded during the battle. "I am assuming you five had something to do with this?" he said in his booming voice.

"No, sir," Atakos said. "We're just as confused as everyone else."

Lt. Emyu looked around at every soldier on the battlefield. He shook his head and grunted. "I know what's going on here, major. Let me ask you a question."

"What is it, lieutenant?" Major Garunburj said.

"In order for the West to be successful and resourceful, do you believe we need to make the Eastern slaves our own?"

Major Garunburj frowned deeply. "Is this meant to be a joke lieutenant?" he said so loud, everyone standing nearby stopped to look at him. "You know all men should be free to live their lives as they see fit. That is the Western philosophy. And it has always been. Were you just born yesterday?"

"No, sir."

"Good. Stop talking nonsense. The war is over. The Eastern slaves should be freed." The major then stormed away, barking orders for his soldiers to send for the airships and to take their deceased to the campsite. It seemed he no longer viewed the Eastern soldiers as a threat. In fact, he ignored them as he gave his orders. The soldiers from the East seemed confused, most of them shaking their heads to try to clear it.

Lt. Emyu smiled. "Whatever happened to us was the best thing that has happened in a long time."

"The curse," Zimi said, "which perpetrated all of the leaders of the world, and their armies for so many years, has been lifted."

"You don't have to tell me, son," Emyu said, turning to look at Zimi with a smile—the first smile he had given him in a long time. "The major can't feel it and he won't understand, even if I tried to explain it to him. But *I* can feel it. Maybe it's because of our heritage. I don't know."

Zimi smiled back, realizing for the first time that his father had been under some kind of spell for so many years, which was why he had grown to be scared of him. He did not feel so intimidated anymore.

"So," Fajha said. "What happens now?"

Lt. Emyu straightened his back, finally feeling like he could stand on his own. "The airships will come to take the armies back to their homelands and we will be sending an envoy to bring back the captives from Feim. What became of the Mituwan king?"

"My father," Prince Aillios said, "has perished."

Lt. Emyu looked amazed. "You…are the son of King Tholenod?"

"Yes…I *was* his son. And Kireina, the girl you saved so valiantly, was his daughter. My sister."

Lt. Emyu was surprised but did not appear too shocked. "I knew there was something special about her. She was not from Western Omordion. I knew that much." He then paused before smiling at Aillios. "Thank you. For helping us."

"You are most welcome."

"So this makes you the new king of Mituwa."

Prince Aillios froze. The thought never occurred to him. He was the new ruler of Mituwa and, technically, the head king of Eastern Omordion. Looking around, he realized the entire Eastern Army was technically under his control. But what should he do with them? "Do you think the Western Army would lend us some airships to take us back to the East?"

"I don't see why they wouldn't. They might have to make several trips, but I am sure they can handle it. I will talk to Major Garunburj."

"Thank you," Aillios said and watched as Lt. Emyu walked away to talk to the major. He then turned to Kireina and Ilahne. "Would you like to stay in Udnaruk or return with me, to our castle in Mituwa?"

Ilahne thought for a moment. They did not have a home to return to and, as long as the war was over, Mituwa would be at peace again. It would also be nice to return home for the first time in fourteen years. "We will gladly come with you, Aillios."

"Yes," Kireina said with a big smile. She was finally going to a place she felt could give her a sense of belonging. Her real home. To travel to the East would be the biggest adventure of her life.

"You have to mind your manners from now on, Kireina," Ilahne said, smiling. "You're a princess now."

Aillios laughed. "As long as she's good, she can be whatever princess she would like to be."

"Thanks, brother," Kireina said with a wink.

Aillios turned to the teenagers he was sent to fight alongside with, the ones who had accepted him, despite everything they knew about his past. "This is goodbye, it seems," he said.

"Yes," Atakos said sadly. He reached out to shake Aillios' hand. "Thank you. For everything you have done for us. We will forever be grateful and indebted to you."

"No need," Aillios said, shaking Atakos' hand. "You have all done so much more than I could have ever done in my entire lifetime. Anything you need, please do not hesitate to come find me."

"Thanks, we will."

Fajha, Cristaden, Zimi, and Zadeia thanked Aillios and shook his hand as well. It was a sad moment for them, to part from the rebellious prince they had grown to trust and depend on. Aillios had become a part of Omordion's Hope just as much as they were. To see him leave was heartbreaking.

"I will miss you," Aillios said. "All of you."

"We'll miss you too," Zadeia said.

Aillios smiled and then nodded at Amilana and Drissana before walking away with Lt. Emyu and Major Garunburj. Amilana returned his nod and watched as he walked away. She knew he would never forget who caused the death of his father. There was nothing they could do to take the horrible image away from him.

Drissana tore her eyes away from Aillios and nudged her sister. "Shouldn't we be leaving? Their major threat—Brulok—is gone. Seems like they no longer need our help."

Amilana shook her head. "Little sister, since we are here, I would like to learn more about this planet and the history of the long lost Dokami civilization before returning to Jmugea. I want to know how they managed to escape Dokar and what they have been doing since they came here."

"Oh?"

Fajha cleared his throat and approached the two sisters. "We can help you fill in the blanks," he said. "I know exactly where you should go to satisfy your curiosity. We'll take you there."

PART FIVE
ISRE, SAIYUT

CHAPTER 50

It was like seeing the Saiyutan Museum of Cultural History for the first time all over again. Well, it was the first time for Princess Amilana and her sister Drissana. For the others, they still could not get over how beautiful it was. It would have made a perfect castle had it not been converted into a museum long ago. The intricately designed statues of ancient war heroes bordering its entrance and the brightly colored fountain gave it a look of sheer magnificence.

When the Saiyutan airship landed on the grounds of the museum, the five teens and the two princesses disembarked. The pilot saluted Fajha as he stepped off the ship. "Master Fajha," he said quickly. "We will wait here until further instructions."

"Thank you," Fajha said, embarrassed the pilot called him 'Master' in front of his friends.

As they were walking away from the airship, Zimi burst into laughter. "Would you like me to tie your shoes, Master? How about a cup of tea? Master."

Fajha shot him an ungrateful look and was about to respond when Amilana nudged him. "No," she said. "Ignore his jealous tendencies. I got that a lot too when I was growing up. I grew up hating when people called me 'princess' or 'your highness'."

"Hey," Zimi said. "I am *not* jealous."

"Yes, you are," Zadeia said laughing.

Fajha could only shake his head as they approached the back door of the museum. The man who greeted them the first time they came was not there but the door was left slightly ajar. A sure sign the Dokami Council was expecting them.

"You say these people are your *leaders* in a way?" Amilana said as they entered the back hall and proceeded to climb their way up the stairs to the third floor.

"Yes," Atakos said. "I mean—it's hard to explain. They have been around for an exceptionally long time."

"Hm," Drissana said, glancing at her sister. She wasn't so sure what he meant by an exceptionally long time but, if the history of the lost Dokami clan was at their fingertips there, it was worth meeting the members of the Dokami Council.

When the group reached the third floor landing, they noticed all the lights were lit. They walked down the length of the hallway and took a right turn at the end. They then opened a door at the end of the next hall, which opened up into another hallway.

"How do you people not get lost here?" Drissana said.

"We were instructed to use our senses when we came here for the first time," Fajha said. "After that, it was sort of easy."

"Right here," Cristaden said, opening one of the doors on their left, which opened up into yet another hallway.

At the end of the hallway was a flight of stairs, leading up to where they needed to go. The grand meeting hall of the Dokami Council, which resembled a large ballroom. Upon entering, they could see the Dokami Council waiting for them there and not in their meeting room. All five of them were wearing their long, ivory robes and looking as graceful as ever.

"Welcome," Lady Feir, or Reyshi, said, greeting them with her hands out as her way to invite them in. Her fiery red hair flowed down her back and her green eyes sparkled. To the two princesses, she greeted them and introduced herself.

Princess Amilana confidently stepped forward with her sister and the five teens followed close behind. "It is nice to meet you," she said, sticking her hand out to shake Reyshi's hand. "My name is Princess Amilana. My sister, Drissana, and I," she glanced at her sister, "come from the planet Jmugea."

Reyshi slowly shook her hand and introduced the other members of the Dokami Council, one by one, explaining what their names meant before turning back to look at the two girls. "You bear the name of our first princess, Meela. A-*meela*-na. Did you know that?"

"No," Amilana said with a frown. "My name has been passed down from my grandmother and her grandmother before her, who bore the same name."

"That is interesting."

"How so?"

Reyshi nodded her head slowly. "Yes. It is time you and your people came to know the truth." She stepped away from Amilana and greeted the five members of Omordion's Hope as if they were her children returning from a long trip.

"I am so happy you have survived the battle," she said to each of them after giving them a tight embrace. "When you first came here, you lacked the confidence you needed to fight a war so early in your mission. However, you have grown. And you have succeeded. I am so proud of all of you."

Amilana cleared her throat. "I do not mean to interrupt," she said loudly so everyone could hear. When she got their attention, she lowered her voice. "What *truth*?"

Reyshi's smile faded as she looked from Amilana to the other members of the Dokami Council. They nodded as if giving her permission to speak. However, before she could open her mouth, the door to the meeting room opened.

Everyone became silent and all eyes turned to the doorway. The five teens were astonished that someone else was there, other than the Dokami Council. All others were forbidden to be in their presence. They were even more shocked when they realized who it was. The light gray eyes, the long, flowing blonde hair, the way light seemed to radiate all around her long, white dress.

It was Queen Lhainna.

Cristaden sucked in her breath and held it, as if she were seeing her for the first time. "Mother?" she whispered.

"Yes, my darling," Lhainna said, her voice resonating throughout the hall. She steadily approached Cristaden and halted when she came within a few of feet of her. "It was not my intention for you to find out the way you did. I wanted you to live a normal life, free from the clutches of the forest and Brulok's minions. I wanted you to be *safe*."

"Mother." Cristaden's eyes filled with tears when she remembered Kheiron, her father, who had reluctantly separated from his one true love to save her life. She knew how hard it must have been for Lhainna to say goodbye to both of them and to lose the man she loved so dearly.

"I am so sorry, Kira," Lhainna said. "So sorry, my daughter."

The two embraced, the light emanating from Lhainna seemingly wrapping itself around them. When mother and daughter stepped away from each other, Cristaden wiped her eyes and asked the question on everyone's minds. "Why have you come?"

Lhainna glanced over at Reyshi. "Have you said anything about the…?"

Reyshi shook her head slowly. "No, not yet," she said. "I think it's best to show them." To the five teens and the two princesses, she smiled. "Please. Follow me."

As everyone turned to leave, Queen Lhainna pulled Cristaden to the side to speak with her in private. "Reyshi told me of your vision," she said sadly when everyone had left the room.

"She did?" Cristaden said. Even though she was surprised Reyshi had told Lhainna what she had revealed to her in private, she was somewhat relieved. At least she could get another opinion on what to do about it.

"Yes, she did. She told me…because I had the same vision as well."

"What?" Cristaden searched Queen Lhainna's face, looking for any signs she might not be telling the truth, her heart hammering in her chest.

"The day we met in Sheidem Forest. When I tried to say something of importance to Atakos, but could not remember. Do you recall that moment?"

"Y–yes."

"I remembered what I was trying to say," Lhainna said and sorrowfully looked down. "This is the real reason why I came here to see the Dokami Council."

Cristaden's hands flew up to her mouth. She wasn't lying. "Please tell me this isn't happening."

"Unfortunately, it is." Lhainna grabbed a hold of Cristaden's hands and pulled them away from her face. "Kira, I must ask you to do something you probably will not like or understand. The Dokami Council asked me to instruct you on what you should do. Will you accept what must be done?"

Cristaden nodded, even though she knew Lhainna was right. She was not going to like it.

"Please walk with me to find the others and I will tell you what you must do along the way."

It was a silent walk down seven flights of stairs to what seemed like the basement of the museum. The four teenagers, Princess Amilana, and Drissana followed the Dokami Council all the way down without saying a word, eager to find out what they were about to be shown. Amilana was rubbing her hands together in nervousness. She had a feeling she was not going to like what the Dokami Council had to show them.

After opening a door in the basement and descending down yet another, but smaller flight of stairs, the group approached two large, wooden doors. Reyshi waved her hands in front of the doors and they creaked and rattled as they slid open. "Watch your step," she advised.

The group carefully followed Reyshi down three steps and into a large chamber with a very high ceiling. When Reyshi waved her hands again, this time lighting the many torches lining the walls, the confused group behind her took in what looked like to be an extensive mural decorating the walls from the floor all the way up to the ceiling. At first, it was difficult to make out exactly what they were looking at. The mural was mostly a shiny bronze color with green and brown beautifully carved lines all over it. Tiny black words etched into the wall, branching off from the beautiful lines, as if they were branches from a tree. A single, spiral staircase stood against the far wall and it seemed to be the only thing in the room allowing anyone access to the words written up high and close to the ceiling.

"A family tree..." Zadeia said under her breath.

Cristaden and Queen Lhainna came in to the chamber then and took in what everyone was seeing as well.

"Yes," Drae said. "You are right, Zadeia." He took a few steps forward to stand next to Reyshi. "This is a family tree. *Our* family tree." He looked directly at the two princesses and nodded. "The family tree of the 'lost Dokami civilization' as you so graciously call us."

Amilana's heart went up to her throat. Forget that he just read what she was thinking, even though she was a master at blocking her thoughts from all Dokami mind readers. He was looking at her and her sister in a strange way. As if he was dreading what was about to happen as much as they were. Amilana could not help but wonder who the members of the Dokami Council truly were. She knew one thing though.

They were strong.

Exceptionally strong.

Unexpectedly, Drissana grabbed Amilana's hand and squeezed it. She gave her a small smile to let her know everything was going to be okay. Drissana, who was so much younger than she was, appeared to be the braver one at that moment, when she felt like crumbling. It was enough to give her strength. Amilana cleared her throat. "This is impressive," she said. "But—"

Lady Arren, the one with the long, white hair and light, blue eyes, spoke with her wispy voice, interrupting Amilana. "It is important for you to know the reason why we have brought you here." With a slight wave of her hand, she invited everyone to follow her to the spiral staircase against the far wall.

To the five members of Omordion's Hope, it was more than they could bear. An actual family tree. The Dokami Council, and all of the Wise Men, must have kept careful track of every single Dokami born over the past centuries. There were thousands of names, etched along every corner of the bronze tree, beautifully embedded into the walls.

"I wonder if they actually do have everyone on these walls," Fajha said.

"Do you think they have my name?" Zimi said, looking around eagerly with his mouth hanging open.

Atakos frowned and hit Zimi's arm with the back of his hand. "Considering we're standing *in* Council headquarters...even being able to *look* at this tree firsthand? No, I don't think they knew you existed."

Zadeia erupted in giggles and looked at Cristaden. Her friend appeared stone faced, barely looking at the thousands of names on the wall, just looking straight ahead. "What's wrong, Cristaden?" Zadeia asked her.

Cristaden seemed to snap out of her trance and blinked once at her friend. "N-nothing," she said and smiled reassuringly. She glanced back at her mother when Zadeia had turned away and the queen could only shake her head. This was not going to be easy.

Lady Arren started to climb the spiral staircase with everyone, except the other members of the Dokami Council, who hung back. As they climbed, they could see a difference along the wall next to them. Unlike the green and brown branches they were getting used to seeing, they saw the only different colored branch in the room. It seemed as if it was its own tree, with many different branches stemming off it, all the same color and shining brightly. It was *gold*.

"Why is this branch so different than the others?" Fajha said.

Lady Arren smiled slightly as she made her way up to the platform resting at the top of the stairs. "Allow me to bring your attention to the names etched here and you shall see why." She waited for everyone to climb up to the platform before she pointed to the wall. At the highest point of the golden branch, the five teens and the two princesses could see two smaller branches, stemming from the main golden branch, intertwined together in the shape of a heart. It was no surprise whose names they saw at the ends of the two branches.

"Soli," Lady Arren said, "and Rueslon. The first queen and king of the Dokami clan." To the two princesses, she smiled. "I am sure you know their history."

Amilana took a few steps closer to the wall. "Yes," she said. "Dokami children are taught the tragic story as soon as they could talk. They are also taught that all of the founding members of the Dokami clan perished, along with Soli, on that fateful day. Only a select few in my kingdom know the truth."

"Yes," Lady Arren said. "I am living proof of that truth." She gestured to everyone standing around them. "We are all living proof." Turning back to the wall, she pointed to several names near the golden branch but marked with brown and green branches. "Here we have Reyshi, who you've been introduced to as Lady Feir." Ignoring the startled gasps from the princesses, Lady Arren pointed to Drae's name. "Lord Watten." Moving along the wall, she pointed to two more names, Amzin and Ollige. "Lord Lovanthe and Lord Eavthon." Finally, she pointed at another name. "Nariele. That's me."

"How is that even possible?" Amilana said. "That would make you…five hundred years old!"

"Yes," Nariele said. "We are. The first ones born from Jmugean and Shaergan parents. We have the power to live long lives. This was one of the Dokami gifts we were born with. Dokamis born after us never possessed the same gift." She lowered her eyes. "We had to learn this the hard way."

"Why do you think that was?"

Nariele looked up at Amilana. "We never understood it. Of course, no one existed to teach us the ancient Dokami ways. We only had visions of our past lives. Dreams. Even they did not explain what we needed to know."

Amilana and the others looked thoughtful as their eyes glided over the many names etched on the walls. Nariele instructed them to follow the names, etched along the golden branch, making their way back down the spiral staircase. Meela, the daughter born to Soli and Rueslon, had three children with a son born to Ollige, or Lord Eavthon. Those children had children of their own and so on and so forth, until the full, golden branch stopped expanding and thinned out drastically, back to only one line.

"Why didn't all those people have children?" Atakos said.

"The Dokar war," Nariele said. "Most of the families were almost completely annihilated by the Dre-Ahds before the Dokami left Dokar for Omordion. Only one branch of the royal line survived." She pointed to a name, which stood out among the rest, because he was the only one who had children and continued the golden line. "Tre-akelomin Gre-ashyu."

"Whoa," Zimi said. "He was a direct descendant of Soli and Rueslon. I never considered the Kings and Queens of the past were put in place because of their bloodline. I thought they were elected…in some strange way."

Nariele nodded. "Per Tre-akelomin's request, the monarchy was eradicated. We had always kept the records of births, unbeknownst to the general population on Dokar and even the Dokamis here on Omordion. This was all classified information."

"So the royal line," Zadeia said. "It still exists today?"

Amilana cringed when Nariele nodded as they stepped off the staircase and turned around. The other four members of the Dokami Council and Queen Lhainna were standing by the wall next to the end of the golden branch with grave expressions on their faces.

"Yes," Nariele said. "At one point we feared it would end. Some Dokami descendants chose not to have children because of the inability or the fear of teaching them the laws of restraining their powers at such a young age. It was a daunting task many people chose not to endure. However, the bloodline carried on. A single branch of it still exists today." She gestured for them to have a closer look.

Nothing could have prepared them for what they saw. A sense of sudden dread overtook Amilana and she took a step back in shock. Tears sprung up in Zadeia's eyes and her knees buckled so Zimi had to grab her arm to hold her up. Fajha and Atakos stood dumbfounded, not believing what they saw. Cristaden chose not to approach the wall at all. She hung back because she knew the truth. She had known for some time.

Queen Lhainna spoke, breaking the awkward silence in the room. "It was what I was trying to say. Weeks ago. When I had the vision in the forest." She ran her hands along the engraved name at the end of the golden branch.

"Atakos Croit. You are the true king of Jmugea."

CHAPTER 51

The glorious rushing water, the trees, and the snow-capped mountains surrounding Nikul River would captivate anyone peering down at Nikul Pass—a pass which separated Feim and Effit from Mituwa—from the air. King Aillios had never experienced Eastern Omordion the way he was experiencing it now. The lush forests. The rolling green hills. The tall mountains. These countries were meant to be enjoyed by its people. He was ashamed he was the son of the king who took their enjoyment away from them.

All that was about to change.

Aillios glanced at Ilahne and Kireina, who were looking out of the windows by their seats across from him. Kireina seemed in awe of the scenery, having never seen any other lands besides Udnaruk in her entire life, and Ilahne was busy explaining the names of the different mountains and rivers they flew over. She also told tales of all the fun things she used to do as a child growing up in Mituwa and the games her and her sister used to play. Aillios was fascinated and saddened at the same time by the stories. He was given the opportunity to see his mother's life through someone else's eyes for the first time. Someone who had been the closest to her. Ilahne joked about Meriahne's beauty and headstrong attitude, which did well for her when the prince, at the time, was looking for a bride. Tholenod was enthralled by her and took many years to woo her before she finally agreed to marry him.

"Oh, and what a wedding it was!" Ilahne said, boasting. "The castle was beautifully decorated. There were flowers everywhere, white flowers to be exact. Meriahne's favorite. I had never seen anything more beautiful in my entire life. And they were in love. So much in love." Her face fell and she turned towards the window to stare out of it again. It was too late. Aillios saw the tears in her eyes before she had turned away. Although the thought of his mother saddened him, he was happy to hear that, at one point, she was happy with his father. That, had Menyilh not entered into his father's life, things would have been different for them. He knew now his father had loved his mother and tried to save his family from the evil that corrupted him, but could not in the end.

Aillios was about to comfort Ilahne, but one of the Udnarukan pilots stepped away from the cockpit to announce that they were approaching the castle. Moans erupted all around as the Mituwan soldiers, in the airship with them, awoke from their deep slumbers. They were exhausted from the battle, from having a curse lifted from their possessed minds, and from being knocked unconscious for a long period of time. Aillios glanced out of the window closest to him and saw soldiers, from other Udnarukan airships, disembarking on the grass near the castle as their ship landed. What he did not see were the slaves working the fields and even the thick, black smoke from the furnaces. The same furnaces, which never stopped working day and night for so many years.

They were *off*.

Fearing something bad happened to his people while he was not there to protect them, Aillios quickly stood up just as the airship touched the ground, but he suddenly realized he could not just run off. There were two people on the ship he could not ignore. There were also countless soldiers he was responsible for now. He had to remind them he was their new king. "Ilahne," Aillios said with a quick nod. "Kireina. Welcome back home."

Kireina appeared apprehensive and scared when she stood up and followed Ilahne off the ship and onto Mituwan soil, not at all like the determined, stubborn teenager, who sought to fight in a battle to have revenge for the people she loved and lost. Stepping out onto the rolling green grass seemed to be rather difficult for her as she carefully took tiny, quick steps, while shifting her eyes about, to keep up with Ilahne who had immediately took off towards the castle.

Aillios shifted his gaze away from his aunt and sister and barked orders for the Mituwan soldiers to exit the ships faster. "Line up men!"

311

he shouted. He watched the soldiers quickly line up, almost as if they were fearful of his wrath. It felt good to be the one in power but only because, for the first time in his life, he was finally in the best position to help his people the way he saw fit.

No one was there to stop him.

Aillios paced back and forth, waiting for the Udnarukan airships to leave, giving them quick nods and a wave to signify his appreciation for their help.

When the ships had left, Aillios finally stopped pacing and cleared his throat. "For as long as I can remember," he said, "our people have been enslaved. Their blood and tears were what kept the digging machines in the mines going and what has enabled us to be prosperous and eat well every day. For so many years, they worked hard, breaking their backs against their will, at times dying in horrible and agonizing pain, only to be dumped in the marshes with countless others when they died. No graves to mark their final resting place and no rituals to help them pass on to the next life. We can't bring back the dead, but we must do what has to be done to honor their memory the best way we can." Aillios looked around at the faces of the soldiers who stood before him. "We will work to correct the injustice brought upon our people by my father and the evil that plagued him."

Remembering the battles he fought, which made him responsible for the deaths of so many men, Aillios lowered his eyes as an upsurge of dread overtook him. "We must work hard to correct *all* of our mistakes." Again, he was brought back to that awful place. When he thought the commoners, who were justly rebelling, were responsible for his mother's death. They were innocent and he killed them one after another on the battlefield with pure hatred in his heart. Aillios felt himself slipping into sadness, as he so often did. The dead witch, Asmis', pale face came to mind then, her brown hair floating around her as if submersed in water, and the words she had spoken to him, came back. He must never forget her words. He *was* good. Nothing could ever change that.

Aillios clasped his hands behind his back and took a few steps towards the soldiers standing to the right of him. "The slaves will have to be freed. Every last one of them. That will be your task. You men will also be in charge of rebuilding the villages, devastated during the takeover. I will appoint delegates from each village who will take a group of you back to resurrect their homes. This will be an incredibly long and arduous process, but it will be a worthwhile one. Take care to do the best you can for our people, for we owe them so much more than we can give."

To the soldiers on his left, Aillios' jaw tightened. The job he was about to bestow on them would most likely be the worst job he could ever request of anyone. "The marshes…" he said. He took a deep breath before continuing. "The marshes are to be drained. They should then be filled with earth so the people, who have lost their lives, would have a proper place to rest. We will perform rituals to help them move on to their next lives and declare the land there to be sacred ground. A memorial will be erected in their memory and a field of flowers will be planted there and tended to each passing year, so their final resting placing would be a beautiful one. This will be a reminder that what has happened in the East was the worst atrocity to Omordions everywhere and will never be replicated. Our people, their children, and their children's children will be safe from now on."

A sudden gasp made Aillios quickly turn around. Frolemin was standing several feet behind him with Ilahne and Kireina seemingly holding her up as if she was about to faint at any moment. Her hands were over her mouth and tears were rolling down her cheeks.

"You are *alive*," Frolemin said after slowly dropping her hands. "Ilahne. Kireina. What they said was true. Tholenod is no more. You are our new king. I never thought I would see the day."

Aillios nodded at Frolemin with a sad smile. "Yes," he said. "It is true."

"I am so sorry, Aillios–*King* Aillios. About your father. About the secrets withheld from you so long ago. I–I was forbidden to tell you the truth about your mother. Those of us who were there at the time were sworn to secrecy."

Aillios could only shrug. "There was nothing you could do but obey him. We have all made many mistakes. I should be the one to apologize to our people. The only thing to be done now is to fix our mistakes and learn from them." When the head maid nodded in agreement, Aillios decided to ask the question nagging at him since he stepped foot on Mituwan soil. "Frolemin. I noticed the sky is clear–I mean–the fires from the furnaces, they are no longer burning. What has happened?"

"It is a rather simple explanation, sire," Frolemin said. She turned towards the castle and waved her arms in the air.

At first, Aillios was confused when he heard the shouts. The shouts turned into cheers when, out of every corner of the castle, across the grass, and even over the hill behind the soldiers, came thousands of people. Dirty and malnourished, they ran. With sunken eyes and old wounds, they ran. They ran through the soldiers, at times pushing past them to get as close as possible to their new king, shouting praises, while laughing and crying. Aillios was overwhelmed with joy and sadness when he saw them. How wonderful it was to see their happy and smiling faces, but how sad it was to see how the years of torture and slavery had turned them into mere wisps of human beings.

"Frolemin!" Aillios said, shouting over the cheers and the celebration going on around him. "They are all free! How?"

Frolemin quickly explained to him how they had planned to take over the castle, while the army was away. She described how their plan was hindered when the guards and overseers fell unconscious. This allowed them to free the slaves and carry on without lifting a hand in battle for their freedom.

Aillios laughed. "The same thing happened on the battlefield in Udnaruk. All of the soldiers passed out at the same time."

Frolemin searched his eyes. "All of them? But why?"

Aillios lowered his voice, so the people around them would not hear him. "They were possessed by evil, Frolemin. Even my father. Possessed by the worst kind of evil. When my father died, they were released from their dreadful prison. The demons that plagued them have left their bodies."

"*Demons?*" Frolemin said under her breath in shock.

"Yes. They are now free. Just like our people."

"This is unbelievable."

"Believe it." Aillios raised his eyebrows. "What happened to the guards and overseers after they…?"

"Well…we tied them up and tossed them into the dungeons."

Aillios laughed again. "They must be extremely confused. I order their release. Have them wait for me in the throne room. Also, send a messenger to all of the kings of the East. They must report here at once. I have much to discuss with them."

"Will do, sire," Frolemin said with a smile. After she disappeared through the crowd with Ilahne and Kireina in tow, an old couple approached Aillios with tears in their eyes.

"Over a decade ago," the woman said, "we lost our only son during the takeover of our village." She reached out and grabbed Aillios' hand. "We will never forget the day he was killed while trying to escape to the forest, King Aillios."

Aillios held fast to her hand and felt tears stinging his eyes. "I am so sorry for all you have lost." He could barely get the words out.

The woman smiled. "Today, I am happy we are both still alive to see this moment. When we are free to go back to our village and live out the rest of our lives in peace."

"Yes," her husband said with a broad smile. "Thank you."

"I had vowed to save everyone," Aillios said. "It was my duty."

"Yes," the man said before looking thoughtful. He appeared as if he was struggling with whether or not he should say something.

"What is it?" Aillios asked, releasing the old woman's hand.

The man looked up at him and frowned. "There's something you should see—right away—in the mines. It is *important*, my lord. Do you have some time to spare? Will you come with me?"

Aillios searched his eyes and found himself frowning as well. *Something in the mines?* he thought. *What could possibly be so important?* He was almost afraid to know what it was. "Why yes... Of course."

"Please. Follow me."

King Aillios had never visited the mines before. He was never allowed to step foot anywhere near them. His father always told him it was no place for the son of a king to venture to because it was a scary and dangerous place. Aillios always asked him why the slaves were allowed to work in the mines if it was so dangerous. His father, in pure Tholenod fashion, would say only animals could enter because they belonged there. In the depths of the deep, dark caves.

As he climbed onto the lift the slaves had used to descend down a large hole in the earth, Aillios could not help wondering how anyone could work for days on end in such a dark and oppressive place. The only light there was came from the lantern the old man, whose name was Chalun, was holding.

"My wife and I have worked down here every day since the day of the takeover," Chalun said. "I will not miss this place when we go back to our village."

Aillios could only nod slowly while looking around. What could he say? What a horrible way to live. Tied to chains...beaten if you stepped out of line or was not fast enough. Starved. Aillios squeezed his eyes shut and opened them again in an attempt to get the images out of his head.

"Here we are," Chalun said. He stopped the lift and opened the gate so they could step into a wide tunnel dug into the rock.

Aillios cautiously followed Chalun down the large tunnel. "Were you ordered to dig here?" he asked.

Chalun laughed. "No. We were sent down here during the first days after our capture. When the soldiers saw what was down here, we were ordered to leave immediately and this tunnel has been off limits ever since. No one was allowed to come back here or even speak of what we saw. If we even uttered a word of it, it was death."

"Death? Why so *extreme?*"

"Well," Chalun said, looking back at him. "If you knew what was down here, and you didn't want anyone to know because it could throw off the whole reason behind declaring war against the West, you would do what you could to keep it a secret."

"Oh." Aillios' heart skipped a beat as they kept walking. He was anxious to find out what secret was so worth keeping, that people would be killed because of it.

"Stay right here," Chalun said as they reached the entrance of what appeared to be an extensively large chamber, due to the way his voice echoed. It was so pitch black, Aillios was finding it hard to adjust his eyes to see what was in it. He, instead, did what he was told and waited while Chalun entered the dark room. He still could not see much of anything beyond the small area of light emanating from Chalun's lantern, but he could see that dusty, yellowed tiles covered the floor. It appeared at one point the room might have been intricately decorated.

But why?

A sound next to Aillios made him look to his left. He was on his guard, as if he was about to be attacked. Nothing there. He shivered slightly when a cool breeze touched his skin and turned around to look behind him. Seeing nothing down the dark tunnel, he turned back to the room Chalun had entered and paused.

Someone or *something* was standing beside him.

He could feel it now.

"Wha—"

A cool hand touched his hand, grazing it, and it took everything he had not to run away, screaming.

Still *nothing* there. At least, nothing he could see.

Aillios.

He heard the all too familiar voice in his head. It brought him back to the night he followed his father on his journey and had fallen asleep. The dream he had. That was where he had heard that voice before.
Aillios.
It sounded so far away but close at the same time.
"Asmis?" he said cautiously, in a low voice in case he was hallucinating. Out of nowhere, he felt it. A kiss placed on his cheek from a pair of soft lips. He closed his eyes, feeling her presence and trying to imagine her standing there, next to him. Her long, flowing brown hair and her beautiful, pale face. He was not afraid anymore. She had helped him. Now she was there. She was with him again.
She began to speak to him, her words steadily weaving through his mind like a cool breeze on a warm day.

> *It is time, Aillios. It is time for me to leave. I could not leave without saying goodbye one last time. You did good, Aillios. Your ancestors would have been so proud.*

"No," Aillios said. He tried to reach out to her, to grab a hold of her, but all he felt was empty air.

> *I cannot stay. My time is up. The fairies...they no longer need my help. Brulok is gone. I need not protect them any longer. Fairy spirits do not have a place on Omordion now. Your time has finally come. Good luck, my sweet, sweet prince. My king.*

Before Aillios could say anything else, Asmis was gone. Just like that. He no longer felt her by his side. "Goodbye," he whispered, not expecting a response. "Thank you." A thought crossed his mind. *Asmis was a fairy*, he thought. *A fairy spirit, she said.* It definitely explained a lot—her ability to give him a disguise, a face no one would recognize, her power to awaken the spirit of a boy he long forgotten, his younger self—but he still had so many questions. How was she persecuted by his people if she died at a time when Brulok's minions were roaming about, looking for magical creatures to kill? *She must have been bold enough to wear a magical cloak as Kapimia had worn when she came to find him, shielding herself from Brulok but living among humans.* It was the only explanation he could come up with.

"Did you say something, sire?" Chalun said from inside the dark room, interrupting his thoughts.

"N–no," Aillios said, wiping at his eyes before Chalun could see his tears. "Carry on."

"Sure. I am just looking for…oh, here it is." Chalun flipped a switch. An actual *light* switch. The entire chamber was instantly illuminated with lights from every corner of the room.

Aillios slowly stepped inside and looked around, shocked beyond belief, his final encounter with Asmis abruptly forgotten. "What—?" he gasped. "What is this?"

"Take a good look around, my king. This is our *past*."

Looking around the room, Aillios felt like he had stepped into a holding chamber from Western Omordion. Aillios had never seen so many airships, lined up against each wall. Beautifully designed airships, with layers upon layers of dust, which had settled on them over the years, untouched for a very long time. "How long do you suppose these have been down here, Chalun?"

"I am not sure," Chalun said. "But I have an idea…My grandfather used to tell me stories when I was a little boy. Stories of airships, flying across the Mituwan sky and the different, technological things they were able to do at the time. Things they were not allowed to do anymore. Motor vehicles–replaced with horses. Even the lights–replaced with lanterns and candles. I would laugh at his stories. I thought he was crazy. A crazy old man who had dreams of what he would like our *future* to look like. Until I stepped into this room, I never believed what he told me was true."

"Who could have done this?"

"Your great-grandfather. The late King Tholenod's grandfather." When Aillios turned to look at him in shock, Chalun pointed to a door closest to the light switch. "Do you want to know something else? There are many more rooms. Just like this one. With vehicles. Electrical equipment. Whatever you can dream of. It's down here."

"This is *unreal*."

"It's as real as you and me."

King Aillios could not believe what he was seeing and hearing. His great-grandfather, perhaps a hundred years ago, had ordered the removal of all technologically advanced machinery from the people of the East. By what means would he have felt the need to do something like that?

Who would not want to keep moving forward? Who would want to take away everything that could help them, while the people on the other side of the world had life so much easier?

"I am such a fool," Aillios said under his breath.

"Excuse me, sire?" Chalun said, lifting his eyebrows.

Aillios did not respond. When he was with Omordion's Hope, they spoke of airships and spaceships from many hundreds of years ago, bringing people to different planets. *All the time.* Even the first humans to land on Omordion came in a spaceship. The technology was there. It had *always* been there. The people of the East were either too blind or too brainwashed to see it. But, who would go to the extent of brainwashing millions of people, leading them to believe the West was so much more technologically advanced than they were? Leading them to believe they needed to declare war in order to gain access to the resources of the Western world?

Only one answer came to mind.

Brulok.

Aillios felt like hyperventilating but tried to keep it together for Chalun's sake. Brulok set his plan in motion to destroy the humans hundreds of years ago, beginning—not with Tholenod—but with his great-grandfather. By creating a situation where the people of Omordion would eventually kill each other *for* him. Without him having to lift a finger. And his father, King Tholenod, was the final piece to his puzzle. Aillios shuddered at the thought. Well, the evil man was gone now. His plan was foiled. They need not worry about him any longer. The people of Omordion, even the magical creatures, were free to live their lives the way they should have been living it hundreds of years ago.

"Chalun," Aillios said, his blue eyes shining.

"Yes, sire?"

"We will gather every soldier available. We must get all of these things above ground and distribute them to the villages. Immediately. I will speak with the other kings of the East. It would not surprise me if they have caves and mines full of these things in their countries as well. We will bring the East back to its former glory."

King Aillios felt more determined than ever to correct the mistakes of his father and their ancestors before him.

Our time has finally come, he thought with a smile. *We will live as we were meant to live. For the rest of our days.*

CHAPTER 52

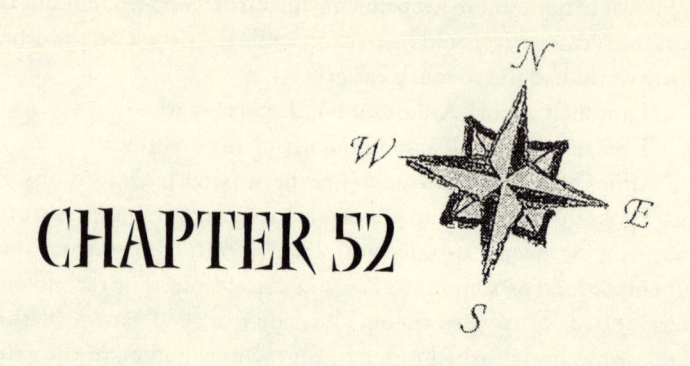

"Atakos," Reyshi said. "You are the true king of Jmugea. You have a duty—"

"This is crazy," Atakos said in frustration. "I can't be the king of Jmugea. What do you expect me to do? Go to Jmugea and demand the throne? Do you know what you're saying?"

Reyshi nodded as if she knew he was going to react that way. "Atakos, this is your destiny."

"You can't be *serious*?"

"Yes. We are."

Atakos turned to look at his friends, who were still standing around in shock. "This is unbelievable." To leave all he knew? He glanced at Cristaden, who was hanging back, and made eye contact with her. She seemed so sad, as if she had known all along what was about to happen. Thinking back to the time they had kissed, and the way she reacted, he was almost positive she had figured it out. This was her vision. Turning back to the Dokami Council, Atakos shook his head. "I refuse to go. Never. And besides, what about Amilana, Drissana, and their family? You can't possibly expect them to step down. What about the people of Jmugea? They will not accept me as their king."

"If I might say something," Amilana said. Her eyes were sad and Drissana had her hand over her mouth, and she was looking down at the floor with tears falling from her eyes. "Before I was sent on this voyage, I was ordered to ignore the rumors of the distress signal sent from this planet. I knew of the one sent to Jmugea, when the Dokamis were on Dokar, and how, it too, was unfortunately rejected. I could not understand why we were ordered to reject the signals. The Dokamis here on Omordion—you—all of you are our *brethren*. I demanded to know why, but was not given a reason. I was only told to forget I even heard about it.

Then our mother came to us. She asked me to answer the call. I saw the guilt in her eyes. I knew she was keeping something from me, something she was too scared to address. She knew she had to do what was right. She knew we would find the true king of Jmugea here and my parents would have to renounce the throne. This was the reason the Dokamis on Jmugea did not answer the signals sent three hundred years ago and why they refused to answer it now." Amilana looked deep into Atakos' eyes. "You must come back with us. You must accept the throne. It is your birthright."

"Why doesn't Reyshi—or Drae—go?" Fajha said. "They have as much right to the throne as Atakos does."

Reyshi shook her head. "We—Drae and I—are not heirs to the throne. The royal bloodline started with Soli and Rueslon and extended to Meela and *her* children. Our job was to look after her heirs and keep the bloodline going strong. You, Atakos, are a direct descendant of our Queen Mother, Soli. No one else has the right to claim the throne but you. Because of your training—the abilities you possess—your mother, a direct heir as well, cannot rule as you can. You will make a great king, Atakos. Our place is here, making sure the Dokamis on Omordion have direction and continue to strive as a clan."

"No." Atakos turned to look at his friends. He looked at Cristaden. "No, I can't leave all of the people I love." Turning back to the Council and Amilana, Atakos shook his head. "My mother. She's sick. She has an incurable illness. I am not sure how long she has to live. I can't leave her now. You can't ask me to leave her."

It was Drissana's turn to talk. The tears, falling from her eyes were gone, wiped away during her sister's speech. She too wanted to do what was right. "Your parents are welcomed to join you, Atakos. Our master healer on Jmugea—Tasonar—can cure her illness indefinitely."

"What? Your...healer?"

"Yes. When Dokamis fall ill, simple medicines cannot cure them. Our healers have spent centuries developing a proven method to heal Dokami illnesses. She will be well taken care of. She will survive if she goes back with us to Jmugea."

Atakos thought long and hard before responding. "What about our mission? What about Brulok?"

"He's gone," Queen Lhainna said. "As you know, he has withdrawn, along with all of his minions. Most likely for good this time. And the leaders of the Eastern and the Western armies no longer pose a threat to the Dokami clan."

"So your mission," Lord Watten, or Amzin, said, "has been dissolved."

The hairs on the back of Atakos' neck stood on end as everyone grew silent. He knew what they were all thinking. He had no reason to stay on Omordion any longer. There were no more excuses he could give. He was Jmugea's rightful king, the heir to their throne. Nothing he could do or say could change that fact.

Reyshi walked over to him and took his hand. "You will make a great king," she said again, giving his hand a tight squeeze. The other members of the Council nodded in agreement.

Atakos turned to his friends. Zadeia had tears in her eyes, but smiled back at him as if to tell him it was the right thing for him to do. Zimi and Fajha nodded in agreement.

"You can't pass this up Atakos," Fajha said.

"How often will you get an offer to be a king of an entire planet?" Zimi said. "I mean—wasn't that what Tholenod died trying to do? You don't have to die fighting for it, you know. It's *yours*." Zadeia shoved an elbow into his side and he yelped.

Atakos glanced at Amilana and Drissana, shook his head at his insensitive friend, and turned to Cristaden again. Curiously, her eyes were locked with Queen Lhainna's, who was staring back at her. For a brief moment, they stood this way before Cristaden nodded. She looked at the floor before raising her eyes to make eye contact with Atakos. She seemed determined all of a sudden, taking a few steps towards Atakos, as if she had something important to say.

"What's going on?" Atakos said.

"I will be leaving now," Cristaden said. "To join my mother and the rest of my fairy family in Sheidem Forest. I have decided to stay with them. Permanently."

Atakos took a step towards her. "Why?"

"I have—I *want* to." Cristaden quickly glanced at her mother and then smiled back at him. "I have a lot of catching up to do on the fairy side. It would be nice to learn all about them and be taught in their ways."

Atakos' shoulders dropped. *She can't be serious*, he thought. It was as if Cristaden was brushing aside all they had been through. Even how they *felt* about each other. "Please. Don't do this."

Cristaden smiled. "You will make a wonderful king, Atakos. It is your destiny."

"But what about—?"

"This is bigger than anything you will ever accomplish in your entire life. It's bigger than...us." Cristaden gestured to the entire group, but Atakos knew what she meant.

She meant the two of them.

Atakos' eyes searched Cristaden's, looking for any sign she was lying, that she did not mean what she was saying. However, when she smiled at him again, he knew she *was* serious. Unfortunately, he could not mask the stabbing pain he felt in his heart by returning her smile. Going to Jmugea meant that he would never see Cristaden or any of his best friends ever again. It would be goodbye. And Cristaden–all of them–were *okay* with it.

"Goodbye, Atakos," Cristaden said quickly, confirming his thoughts. She turned to her other friends and told them goodbye as well. Without hesitation, she walked out of the room with Queen Lhainna and never, not even once, looked back.

Zadeia burst into tears so Zimi put his arm around her, pulling her away so he could talk to her privately. Fajha had his arms across his chest, looking defeated. And Atakos...Atakos felt like he had been stabbed in the heart with so many daggers all at once. He was to leave his friends and Omordion to become king of Jmugea, a whole other *planet*, Cristaden was happy to walk away from him forever, his whole life was about to change, and no one could or cared to do anything about it.

This was it.

This was farewell.

"Okay," Atakos said, turning back to look at the Dokami Council. "I'll go."

CHAPTER 53

Atakos placed the last of his belongings in his blue travel bag and fastened the clasps holding it together. He glanced around his room one last time. Within months, he was told, his house, the house he grew up in, would be sold, and the furniture most likely given away. It was a sad thought among the sea of unhappiness he felt for leaving Omordion and his friends. He had vowed he would return one day, but now he was not so sure it was possible. Amilana told him her father rarely left Jmugea because his place was there, ruling the planet, and nowhere else.

Atakos sighed and lifted his bag off his bed, trying his best to hold it together. *Do not breakdown*, he thought. *It never did anyone any good to cry. Well…except Zadeia.* He had to show his strength on the outside even if he did not feel it on the inside. He was a king. The true King of Jmugea. This was his fate—no—his destiny. No matter which way he looked at it, it was the right thing to do. As he walked out of his room, Atakos looked up at his parents, who were waiting by the front door for him with their bags by their feet. His tall father was holding his mother up to keep her from falling over. Atakos' hair was very similar to hers—light brown coils—and her hazel eyes were also the same. She was so weak and fragile from the sickness; she seemed on the verge of collapsing at any moment and much shorter than Atakos was, when she had always been his current height. It hurt him so much to see her that way. When she saw Atakos come in, she smiled slightly and he returned her smile, knowing she would get the healing she needed from Tasonar, and she would be well again.

"Are you ready to go?" Atakos' father asked.

"Ready as I'll ever be," Atakos said with a shrug. "I'll help you with the bags."

"Thank you, son."

When his father opened the back door, Atakos used his power to transport all of the bags to the porch. He stepped outside with his parents and his mouth opened slightly in surprise. Amilana had brought her spaceship down from the sky and landed it in their backyard. It was nothing like he had ever seen before. Black and sleek, it was so shiny, the sun's rays reflected off it like a beam of light, meant to blind anyone who crossed its path without proceeding with caution. Amilana was waiting next to the ship along with Drissana and, surprisingly, Fajha, Zimi, and Zadeia. Unfortunately, it did not take long for Atakos to realize Cristaden was not there.

"Whoa!" Atakos shouted, dropping his bag. The two Jmugean sisters did not hesitate to rush to the porch to help his parents board the spaceship with their belongings. Atakos thanked them and bounded off the porch as his friends ran over to him. "What are you guys doing here?" he cried.

"Ha," Zimi said, punching him on the arm. "We came to see you off, you idiot."

"Yeah," Fajha said. "You think we would let you leave without saying goodbye?"

"But how did you *get* here?" Atakos said.

"Fajha got one of his pilots to pick us up," Zadeia said. "His airship is just up the road."

"Have you heard from…?"

Zadeia knew who he was referring to and instantly appeared disheartened. "No. I haven't heard from her since she returned to Sheidem Forest with Queen Lhainna." She had tears in her eyes when she said it. Although they were all the best of friends, she was the closest one to Cristaden, having practically grown up in the same room as her for most of their lives. Life, without her, would never be the same.

Atakos glanced around quickly in an attempt to hide how hurt he was that Cristaden did not come to say goodbye. "That's too bad," he said. He looked back and saw Amilana and Drissana putting the bags in the spaceship after helping his parents board. He turned back to his friends and suddenly lost it. "I'm so glad you're here," he said, his voice cracking.

Atakos' friends came in and surrounded him with a tight embrace. This was it. Omordion's Hope was no more. For ten years, they had been the closest of friends. From the moment they were introduced to Lochenby at the age of five, they were inseparable. They learned together, played together, ate together, and even comforted each other when they missed their families. For ten years, Hamilda had taught them everything she knew and became a second mother to all of them. When she went missing, they stopped at nothing to rescue her, coming together as a team to defeat all the odds stacked against them. They fought alongside each other in battle, the final battle they would ever fight together. Atakos realized suddenly he would never get a chance to say goodbye to Hamilda. When the four friends pulled apart, they had tears in their eyes, which they quickly wiped away.

"So where are you all going from here?" Atakos said.

Fajha cleared his throat. "After bringing these guys back to Udnaruk, I will be returning to Lochenby."

Atakos was shocked. "Lochenby? Why?"

"Well, there isn't much for me to do in Saiyut. Being the grandson of the emperor doesn't help either. A private tutor has to come in and teach me—because of my status. In Lochenby, I can be free to attend school, make friends, and be my own person."

"Makes sense, I guess," Atakos said. He turned to the twins. "How about you two?"

Zimi cleared his throat, imitating Fajha, which prompted an immediate eye roll from his friend. "Zadeia and I will finish our schooling in Udnaruk," he said. "The Udnarukan Army would like us to take over as their generals when we are of age, so we will be training with them along the way. We will also be helping with the rebuilding of the villages destroyed during the attacks from Feim."

"That's great," Atakos said with a smile.

"Yes," Zadeia said, looking down at the ground. It was not what they wanted, but they were given no choice. There was absolutely no reason to return to a private boarding school such as Lochenby. Especially since their mission was complete.

Atakos' father walked up to the four friends. "It's time to go, son," he said sadly.

"Y—yes," Atakos said, trying hard to keep tears from filling his eyes again. "Well. This…is farewell, I guess."

"Not farewell," Zadeia said with a smile. "Until we meet again."

"Sure…" Atakos politely returned the smile and turned away from them, walking to the ship with his father. Zadeia's statement was never going to come true, but he did not want to shatter her hope to reunite, so he didn't say anything. Even if he knew the truth, he did not want to kill their dreams of reuniting one day.

It wasn't until they were high in the sky, breaking free of Omordion airspace to head to Jmugea, that Atakos finally had an emotional breakdown. He could not be consoled. Not by his father. Not by his mother. Not by the two princesses who had effectively come to take him away.

This *was* goodbye.

Goodbye to Omordion and all he had ever known his entire life.

Forever.

EPILOGUE

It was turning out to be another glorious day. The sun was shining brightly in the sky and the weather was unseasonably hot for the typically warm weather of the Pensiki Islands, off the coast of Saiyut. It was the perfect day to go to the beach, splash in the water, and stare out at the gorgeous Saimino Ocean.

So peaceful.

"Mummy! Look what I made!"

Hamilda Shing looked down at her three-year-old son, who had just dumped out his bucket of wet sand to form an amazing volcano. He had Jogesh's facial features and resembled him completely, down to his black, curly hair and olive complexion. They even shared the same name. The only things he inherited from Hamilda were her green eyes, which sparkled when he looked up at her, so proud of his new accomplishment.

"Very good, Jo," Hamilda said with a big smile. "Now, let's see if we can build a city around this wonderful volcano."

"Okay," he said, quickly filling his bucket with sand again with his mind, as he so often did without thinking. He quickly looked up at Hamilda when he realized what he had done, worried he was in big trouble for using his powers out in the open. Hamilda only laughed and shook her head. He was not in trouble as long as no one was around to witness it.

Little Jogesh's determination reminded Hamilda of her former students and how they were when they had been around the same age. It had been four years since the traumatic events, which nearly took the lives of her students, her life, and the life of the child growing inside her. Nearly four years since her husband, Jogesh, had perished in battle. She tried not to think about it, but when she did, when she tried to recall everything that occurred, there was always some black holes she could not fill. As if her brain had blocked them out completely. She remembered being in the cave, remembered *part* of the fight with her students—not all of it—and most of what came afterwards in the spirit realm, but she did not remember how she got to Paimonu or what made her turn so *evil*. For a couple of years afterwards, Hamilda had feared she would regress to being the monster she had become again. She had lost most of the people she loved dearly. Her parents, Jogesh, Bontihm... It was enough to send her over the edge on countless occasions. She recalled the time she had run into her students outside the Medicinal Goods shop in Saiyut and how she had run away from them to keep them from getting hurt again. It was the hardest thing she had ever had to do.

Eventually, Hamilda sought help from the Pensiki natives, learning to redirect the anger she still felt towards more positive things, especially the care of her child. Without the villagers, Hamilda would not have healed at all and might have sunk back into permanent despair. Even after four years, Hamilda did not feel like she was completely healed. She constantly worried her son would be exposed to her pain. Looking at him now, she knew he had no idea what she was going through mentally, and she preferred to keep it that way. He was not to know any of it as long as she lived.

Hamilda often wondered what became of her beloved students since she last saw them. She had heard from the villagers that the war had ended not too long after she had suffered her ordeal. There were strange rumors about a meteor, which came down from the sky and ended the battle, but no one truly knew or understood what actually happened. All they knew was the evil King Tholenod was dead, the war was over, and the Eastern slaves were free to live their lives the way they should. For years, Hamilda taught her students to fight the Eastern Army when the time was right. Since the battle ended, they had no need to fight any longer. She missed them all the time and hoped one day they would meet again.

"Yes," Hamilda told her son. "Place it here...that's right...good." She smiled at the little huts and people Jogesh was creating around the volcano. He had such an incredible imagination and loved to be creative with everything he did. His favorite time of day was when she read fairy tales to him before it was time to go to sleep. Tales of adventures, mythical creatures, and magic fascinated him and he would always ask a million questions before she had a chance to put the book down.

Hamilda ruffled Jogesh's curly hair and smiled at him when he looked back up at her. She then heard a sound behind her, which caused her to turn around. It sounded like wind, whipping through leaves in a forest of trees. After glancing around, she realized nothing could have caused the sound. Looking further along the beach, she saw empty huts the natives had built under several palm trees, whose leaves were not even swaying. *There's no wind*, Hamilda thought to herself. *Strange.* She turned back to look at the growing city Jogesh was building. He obviously did not hear anything. He was busy humming a little tune to himself while working diligently on his fifth hut.

That was when Hamilda heard the sound again.

"What—?" she said as she turned around but–again–nothing there. Her eyes searched the horizon, trying to find what could have caused the sound she heard so distinctly. "I'm going crazy," she whispered.

"What did you say, mummy?" Jogesh asked.

"I thought I heard—" Hamilda started to say as she turned back to look at him. Only it wasn't little Jogesh she saw when she turned back around. The entire beach was gone. Even the sun was nowhere to be seen. Hamilda slowly stood up, her body shaking with fear. The sky was completely black. No moon. No stars. All around her, it seemed like a super volcano had erupted. Pockets of lava spewed violently here and there. The air reeked of sulfur and...*death*. Looking around, all Hamilda saw was devastation. Bodies lying everywhere, either burnt or covered in blood. Fires burning every structure still left standing. In fact, Hamilda realized, the sound she had heard was not the wind blowing through a forest of trees at all, it was the raging fires. *Everything* was burning.

Tears formed in Hamilda's eyes. *How could this happen?*

Then she saw *him*. It was as if she was reliving what happened to her parents in the forest, when she was seven years old, all over again. Hamilda saw the man in the robe, pointing to whoever was still alive, whoever was trying to run to save their lives, shouting inaudible words of anger. Just like what happened to her parents, the beasts came out of nowhere. Horrifying beasts. They chased the fleeing survivors, caught them with their teeth, pinning them down to the ground and eating them.

Alive.

Hamilda began to cry. "No," she moaned. "No, no, no…"

It seemed like one of the beasts had heard her. All of a sudden, it turned on its heels and ran straight for her, huffing and puffing like a bull with red eyes and razor sharp teeth.

Hamilda started screaming and squeezed her eyes shut.

She screamed and screamed and screamed.

"Mummy! Mummy! What's wrong, mummy? *Please.* What's wrong?"

Hamilda opened her eyes and saw little Jogesh standing over her with tears in his eyes, trying to get her to snap out of whatever horrifying state she was in. Wearily sitting up, Hamilda realized she had been in a fetal position, hugging her knees and crying–right on top of her son's now destroyed volcano city.

"Oh," she said. "I am so *sorry.*" Her hands were shaking and she could not stop the tears from falling.

"What's wrong, mummy?" Jogesh asked her again.

Hamilda glanced in the direction of Saiyut. After wiping her tears, she quickly stood up and grabbed hold of Jogesh's little hand. "We have to go."

"Where are we going?"

"We have to warn them."

"Warn who? About what?"

Hamilda stopped and looked down into Jogesh's tearful green eyes. She could not shelter him any longer. No need for that now. He has to know everything. *Everyone* has to know what was coming.

"The end of the world."

Stay Tuned for the Final Installment
of the Omordion Trilogy:
RETURN TO OEUA

GLOSSARY

Characters (by order of appearance):

Omerik ~ (ooh-MER-ick) Shaergan man who migrated to Jmugea after Shaerga was destroyed
Ghosh Hres ~ (Gosh-hress) leader of the Jmugean Council
Jreslan ~ (Dres-LEN) Soli's mother
Soli ~ (SO-lee) girl born from Jreslan and her Shaergan husband; the first Dokami on Jmugea
Fremi ~ (FRE-mee) Jreslan's neighbor who gives birth to the second Dokami—Rueslon
Rueslon ~ (rooz-lawn) second Dokami born on Jmugea and Soli's best friend
Reyshi Maephit ~ (ray-shee may-fit) one of many Dokami children born after Soli and Rueslon
Fhoten ~ (FOE-tin) sixteen-year-old boy who has a crush on Soli
Drae ~ (DRAY) Rueslon's brother
Nariele ~ (NA-ree-ELL) one of many Dokami children born after Soli and Rueslon
Princess Meela ~ (MEE-la) daughter of Soli and Rueslon
Mayor Jubi ~ (JOO-bee) Mayor of Enshatmu City on Jmugea
Amzin ~ (AM-zin) one of many Dokami children born after Soli and Rueslon
Ollige ~ (Oh-leege) one of many Dokami children born after Soli and Rueslon
Faslin ~ (Faz-len) teenaged Dokami girl on Jmugea

Braechal Yu-omi ~ (BRA-cal yoo-OH-mee) king of the Dokami Clan on Dokar during the Jmugean war

Gemnon Gre-ashyu ~ (GEM-non gray-AASH-yoo) king of the Dokami Clan on Dokar during the fatal Dre-Ahd war

Tre-akelomin Gre-ashyu ~ (Tray-AH-ke-lo-men gray-AASH-yoo) inherited the Dokami throne after the death of his father Gemnon

Dokami Clan ~ (do-KA-mee) secret race of people who blended in with the inhabitants of Western Omordion for three hundred years

Atakos Croit ~ (A-ta-kos Croyt) fifteen-year-old member of Omordion's Hope, born in Pontotoma with the power to lift heavy objects

Hamilda Shing ~ (Ha-mill-da) teacher of Omordion's Hope

Cristaden Feriau ~ (Kris-STADE-en Fe-ree-ah-o) fifteen-year-old member of Omordion's Hope, born in Laspitu with the ability to heal, half-fairy

Zadeia Emyu ~ (Za-day-A Em-yoo) fifteen-year-old member of Omordion's Hope, born as a twin in Udnaruk with the power to manipulate wind, water, and fire

Zimi Emyu ~ (Zim-ee Em-yoo) fifteen-year-old member of Omordion's Hope, born as a twin in Udnaruk with the power to manipulate wind, water, and lightning

Fajha Bayaht ~ (Fa-ja Bay-YAHT) fifteen-year-old member of Omordion's Hope, born in Saiyut with the power to move objects; the 'brains' of the group, he is excellent with geography, knows several different languages, and learns how to 'locate' people from afar

Brulok ~ (BROO-lock) evil man who attempted to destroy Omordion's magical creatures five hundred years ago but disappeared, leaving his minions to finish the job for him

King Tholenod ~ (Thaw-lin-odd) tyrant of Mituwa who forms an alliance with Brulok to defeat the Western Army

Queen Lhainna ~ (LIE-na) the fairy queen of Sheidem Forest

General Komuh ~ (Ko-mo) general of the Sheidem City branch of the Western Army

Kheiron ~ (Kay-ron) Queen Lhainna's lover, father to twins Keirak and Kira

Kira ~ (Kee-ra) Queen Lhainna's daughter, Keirak's twin sister

Keirak ~ (Kay-rack) Queen Lhainna's youngest daughter, Kira's twin sister

Colnaha ~ (COLE-na-ha) Dokami born runaway from Osmatu, Maldaha's son

Prince Aillios ~ (I-lee-os) King Tholenod's son
Menyilh ~ (Men-yeel) King Tholenod's straggly assistant
Kapimia ~ (Ka-PI-mee-a) Queen Lhainna's eldest daughter
Dokami Council ~ (do-KA-mee) secret council who watches over the Dokami Clan of Omordion
Thashmar ~ (THASH-mar) Prince Aillios' horse
Princess Amilana ~ (ah-mee-LAA-na) twenty-two-year-old princess of Jmugea, Drissana's older sister
Lenasi ~ (lin-NA-see) twelve-year-old Jmugean villager
Jadien ~ (jay-dee-an) ten-year-old Jmugean villager
Ayairi ~ (I-YA-ree) seven-year-old Jmugean
Bontihm Fhakaemeli ~ (Bon-tim Fa-KAI-me-lee) the late Wise Man of the Dokami clan
Tasonar ~ (ta-SONE-ar) Jmugea's Master healer
Princess Drissana ~ (dre-SA-na) sixteen-year-old princess of Jmugea, Amilana's younger sister
Jmugean Council ~ (jim-OO-gee-an) group who gives council to the royal family of Jmugea
King Azahr ~ (a-ZARR) King of Jmugea
Queen Serai ~ (Sir-I) Queen of Jmugea
Lady Feir ~ (fair) member of the Dokami Council
Lord Lovanthe ~ (Love-Anth) member of the Dokami Council
Lord Watten ~ (WAH-tin) member of the Dokami Council
Lord Eavthon ~ (AVE-ton) member of the Dokami Council
Lady Arren ~ (AR-rin) member of the Dokami Council
Maldaha ~ (Mall-DA-ha) leader of the Tackeni village in Osmatu, Colnaha's father
Olshem ~ (Ole-SHEM) Maldaha's father, Colnaha's grandfather
Emperor Vermu ~ (Ver-moo) emperor of the Western country of Saiyut and Fajha's grandfather
Rehahn ~ (Ray-HAAN) Princess Amilana's best friend
King Haudmont ~ (Hod-mont) king of Srepas
King Gomu ~ (Go-moo) king of Effit
King Basanpanul ~ (Bah-SAN-pahn-ool) king of Feim
Frolemin ~ (Fraw-li-min) King Tholenod's handmaid
Trisalan ~ (tri-SA-len) Prince Aillios' former handmaiden
Asmis ~ (AZ-miss) a witch who was executed by drowning in Mituwa
R. K. Rohjees ~ (Row-jeez) principal at Lochenby Boarding School

Major Garunburj ~ (Gar-UN-Berj) major of the Southern Udnaruk branch of the Western Army
Jogesh Shing ~ (Jo-GESH) Hamilda's late husband
Lio ~ (Lee-oh) Prince Aillios' nickname suggested to him by the Dokami Council
Shala Emyu ~ (Sha-LA) Zimi and Zadeia's mother
Lieutenant Emyu ~ (Em-yoo) Zimi and Zadeia's father
Kireina ~ (Kee-RAY-na) fourteen-year-old girl rescued from the destroyed Rostihme Village whose mother was taken captive
Ilahne ~ (EE-laan) Kireina's mother
Meriahne ~ (Meh-ree-AAN) Prince Aillios' mother
Omlit ~ (Ohm-lit) stable boy in Mituwa
Aoak ~ (a-oh-AK) leader of the woodland fairies
Chalun ~ (CHA-loon) slave in Mituwa

Places:

Shaerga ~ (SHER-ga) a devastated planet, destroyed during the interstellar wars
Jmugea ~ (jim-OO-gee-a) planet where the Dokami clan were originally from
Eynta Province ~ (AIN-ta) major province on Jmugea
Dre-Ahd ~ planet who sought to conquer most of the known planets
Enshatmu City ~ (IN-shat-moo) city at the heart of Eynta Province
Dokar ~ (doh-KAR) planet the Dokami Clan moved to after leaving Jmugea
Omordion ~ (oh-MOR-dee-an)
Lochenby ~ (Lock-en-bee) a boarding school on Sheidem Island
Paimonu ~ (PI-mo-noo) island near Sheidem
Sheidem Island ~ (SHAY-dim) an island south of Laspitu where Lochenby is located
Sremati Volcano ~ (Shri-MA-tee) volcano on Paimonu
Suthack Desert ~ (soo-TAHK) desert between Osmatu and the Hejdian Sea
Mituwa ~ (MI-too-wa) a country in Eastern Omordion where King Tholenod rules
Osmatu ~ (oz-MA-too) rocky terrain after Sheidem Forest and before the Suthack Desert
Saiyut ~ (Say-yoot) a country west of Pontotoma
Isre ~ (Eez-ray) capital city of Saiyut
Saimino Ocean ~ (sigh-min-oh) ocean which lies between Sheidem Island and Saiyut
Saiyutan Museum of Cultural History ~ (say-YOO-tun) museum where the Dokami Council reside
Kingdom of Eynta ~ (AIN-ta) new name for Eynta Province
Ghoshie ~ (Go-shee) an island the Jmugeans were forced to live on after the original Dokami left for Dokar, named after Ghosh Hres
Pensiki Islands ~ (Pen-SEE-kee) islands off the coast of Northern Saiyut
Pontotoma ~ (pon-toe-toe-ma) country south of Sheidem in Western Omordion where Atakos is from

Rostumik Pass ~ (rust-oom-ick) waterway between Udnaruk and Feim
Cliffs of Thegahn ~ (thee-GEN) cliffs overlooking Rostumik Pass
Southern Udnaruk ~ (OOD-na-rook) southernmost country of Western Omordion where Zimi and Zadeia are from
Feim ~ (fame) southernmost country of Eastern Omordion
Effit ~ (EFF-it) country below Mituwa and east of Feim
Laspitu ~ (lahs-PEE-too) northernmost country of Western Omordion where Cristaden is from
Srepas ~ (SHREE-pahs) northernmost country in Eastern Omordion
Thackenbur ~ (ta-kin-BER) Island where Maldaha lived before he moved his family to Osmatu
Rostihme Village ~ (RUS-teem) village in Southern Udnaruk where Kireina is from that was attacked by Feim soldiers in the middle of the night, killing hundreds while taking some people captive
Chrulm Village ~ (shrull-m) village in Udnaruk
Stream of Asmis ~ (Az-miss) beautiful stream Tholenod follows heading towards the Nikul River, named after the witch Asmis who was executed by drowning
Nikul River ~ (NI-cool) river that separates Mituwa, Feim, and Effit from each other
Oeua ~ (oh-E-oo-a) Omordion's original and ancient name

Magical Creatures:

Flitnies ~ (flit-nees) small people who tended to the land and performed magic; lived on Omordion hundreds of years ago
Chlysems ~ (kli-zems) large blue birds with multicolored wings that breathed fire; lived on Omordion hundreds of years ago
Ceanaves ~ (See-An-naves) strong sea creatures who resembled humans but had tinted green skin and fins on scales, eyes the color of the sea, and pink, blue, green, or purple hair; lived on Omordion hundreds of years ago

Beasts of Prey:

Oblots ~ (OB-lots) minion of Brulok, bear-like large beasts with red beady eyes and razor sharp teeth and claws
Desert Karsas ~ (Kar-sus) Brulok's minions who resemble an oversized, oddly shaped lizard; as tall as a grown man with scaly flesh, short arms and a long tail
Unknown creature in Paimonu ~ Brulok's minions who closely resembled humans but have green and black, sometimes red and black scales all over their body, with abnormally long arms and legs
Unknown creature in Isre Square ~ one of Brulok's minions who comes in a dream: very large, dragon-like creature

Language Translations

Mituwa:

Gral fi hadomna. ~ They are coming.

Feim:

Fou mein, alled parma dougeios ~ My brother, would you like a drink?
Nehemna. ~ No thanks.

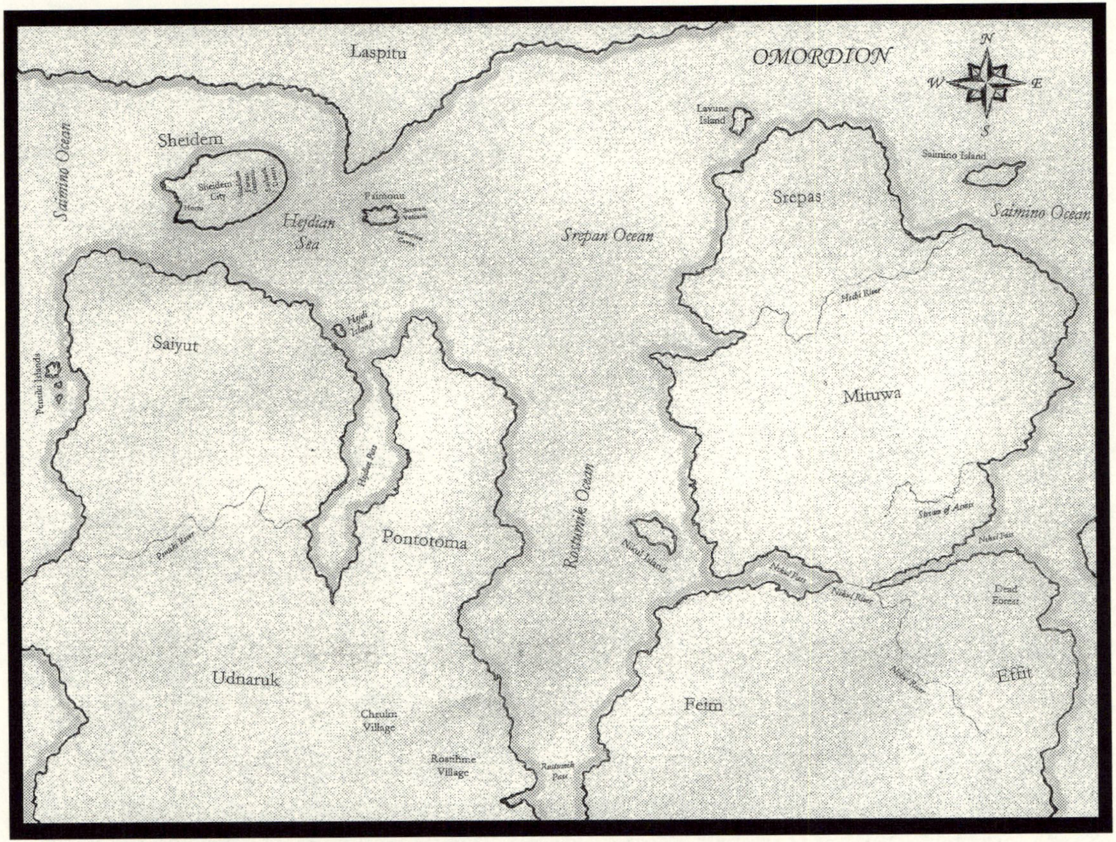

OMORDION
N
W
E
S
Laspitu
Sheidem
Sheidem City
Saimino Ocean
Hejdian Sea
Srepan Ocean
Lavune Island
Saimino Island
Saimino Ocean
Srepas
Hedji River
Saiyut
Hejdi Island
Mituwa
Pontotoma
Rostumik Ocean
Nikul Island
Stream of Ateas
Nikul Pass
Nikul River
Dead Forest
Udnaruk
Chulm Village
Rostihme Village
Feim
Efft

Printed in the United States
By Bookmasters